"A beautiful, crumbling mansion ... a charming but enigmatic viscount; ghosts; rumors; and a lady with of dark secrets, lies, twists, and well-executed turns . . . As if that weren't enough, add rich atmosphere and an American-heiress heroine determined to settle her own future. Kennedy has crafted a delicious, romantic gothic mystery that will keep readers guessing even as they're feverishly turning the final pages."

—Megan Chance, author of *A Splendid Ruin*

"I was riveted by Paulette Kennedy's *Parting the Veil*, a dazzling debut that hearkens to the best of the classic gothic tradition but with a sensibility that will appeal to modern readers. Kennedy writes with compassion, attention to detail, and the confident prose of a seasoned writer. Deliciously eerie, passionate, and suspenseful, this book is an emotional roller coaster that kept me turning its pages long into the night."

—Jo Kaplan, author of *It Will Just Be Us*

"If you love a gothic tale full of twists and turns and things that go bump in the night, Paulette Kennedy's *Parting the Veil* is a not-to-be-missed treat. This debut is the perfect book to curl up with on a stormy night, but don't expect to put it down easily. And don't forget the Earl Grey and biscuits."

—Barbara Davis, bestselling author of *The Last of the Moon Girls*

"An American heiress with a scandalous past meets a mysterious British lord in this swoon-worthy gothic thriller. *Parting the Veil* takes familiar plot elements—a ruined mansion, family secrets—and gives them a sexy, modern twist. This stunning debut from Paulette Kennedy kept me guessing until the very end!"

—Elizabeth Blackwell, author of *Red Mistress* and *On a Cold Dark Sea*

PARTING
the
VEIL

PARTING

the

VEIL

a novel

Paulette Kennedy

LAKE UNION
PUBLISHING

Text copyright © 2021 by Paulette Kennedy
All rights reserved.

Published by Lake Union Publishing, Seattle

www.apub.com

Amazon, the Amazon logo, and Lake Union Publishing are trademarks of Amazon.com, Inc., or its affiliates.

ISBN-13: 9781542032117
ISBN-10: 1542032113

Cover design by Faceout Studio, Amanda Hudson

Printed in the United States of America

For Della . . . who started it all.

CHAPTER 1

Port of Southampton
June 1899

England was freedom. For Eliza, there was a certain kind of irony in that.

A sharp blast of steam announced the SS *Evangelina*'s arrival, coal smoke billowing from its twin stacks. Eliza steadied herself against the railing, her pulse fast behind her ears. On the other side of a gangway, a new life awaited. A life free of black dresses and scandal, where no one would see the spinster in the crepe-shrouded house on Metairie Road. Here, they'd only see a woman poised between twenty and thirty, with coppery blond hair and blue eyes set in a foxlike face. Best of all, there wouldn't be a whisper of shame to endure. Not a raised eyebrow or single narrowed glance across a ballroom.

At least, that's what she hoped.

The ship found its berth, coming up so snugly abreast a sleek ocean liner that Eliza could have tossed a ball over its railing. She repinned her hat and joined the uneven queue jostling toward the lower deck.

"Liza! There you are. You're always running off." It was Lydia, her skirts beaten back by the wind as she pushed through the crowd.

"Goodness. This weather is a bit cool for summer, isn't it? I hope we've brought the right sort of clothes."

Eliza looked up at the heavy, lowering clouds. It *was* beastly cold—colder than she'd ever thought summer could be—but she would grow used to it.

A life written by her own hand was worth a thousand cold summer days.

"*Allons-y, cher.* Getting off this boat and away from the water will warm us." Eliza grasped Lydia's sleeve and led her through the jumble of passengers onto a wharf bristling with cranes as high as church steeples. In the distance, a locomotive whistle pierced the briny air.

"Where do we find the trains?" Lydia asked.

"I'm not sure." Eliza stood on tiptoe to see over the throng of people. Many seemed to be tourists, given their wan and sickly faces, but across the way, she spied a burly stevedore loading barrels onto a wagon. "He looks like a local fellow. Perhaps he can help. I'll puzzle out the trains if you'll go to customs to fetch our trunks."

"All right," Lydia said. "But don't go running off again, and don't be too friendly with strange men. It makes you seem louche."

Eliza shooed Lydia on her way and went toward the stevedore, using her parasol to steady her wobbly steps. He offered a gap-toothed grin and doffed his cap. "Good day, love."

"I'm so sorry to interrupt your work. But you wouldn't happen to know where I'd find the train for Cheltenbridge, would you?"

"Cheltenbridge, eh? Idn't much there. Most Americans are on their way to London." He scratched beneath his close-cropped hair and replaced his cap. "There's no direct line, miss. The four o'clock from Winchester is the next train, and you'll need to ride to West Moors to make the connection."

She blew a puff of air through her lips. Complicated railway schedules made her head hurt. "That business sounds a bit confusing for a newcomer. Perhaps we'd better hire a carriage."

"Right, then. You'll see hansoms at the end of the pier. Welcome to 'ampshire at any rate, love."

Eliza thanked him, then strode toward the carnivalesque pavilion, where a gold-and-white carousel spun with a raucous tune. She purchased a tin of cigarettes from a roving vendor and perched on a nearby crate to wait for Lydia. As she smoked, she took in a marionette show across the pier, the puppets beating one another with sticks beneath a red-and-white-striped canopy. After a few minutes of the queer puppet-beating, Lydia came along with a porter in tow, their freshly stamped trunks on a hand truck.

Just as the stevedore had said, the edge of the boardwalk was lined with hansom cabs hitched to sturdy ponies. A bowlegged driver climbed down from a rickety trap and limped toward them. "Where to, then?" he asked.

"Fourteen Hammond Lane, Cheltenbridge." Eliza pulled a creased envelope from her pocket and squinted at the return address. "At least, I think." She offered the letter to the driver for a look, and he nodded.

"That'll be extra, of course." His rheumy gaze rested on the jade cameo pinned to the lapel of her traveling suit. "Anythin' outside S'oton proper is extra. Twelve shillings."

Merde. How much was twelve shillings? "I'm afraid I only have American money."

"It'll do. Three dollars on arrival."

Lydia's brown eyes narrowed. "Three dollars?"

"Fine. Two dollars. Firm."

"How about one?"

The driver sneered. Eliza nudged her sister's hand. "Lyddie, two dollars is an honest day's wages and he likely won't have another fare. You're being petty."

Lydia shook her chestnut curls and opened the door to the cab. "I may be petty, but you're far too easy with our money."

Giving a resigned sigh, Eliza settled next to Lydia on the worn leather seat, brittle tufts of horsehair poking through the upholstery. The driver loaded their trunks, climbed up to his bench, and cracked his whip. With a lurch, they trotted away from the pier and the bellowing steamship that had carried them far from New Orleans and everything familiar.

⚜

Once on their way, Lydia dropped into a deep, snoring sleep beside Eliza. As they reached the outskirts of a forest thick with birches, Eliza reopened the letter that had set her on her journey. It was dated March 6, 1899, the spidery writing barely legible on the ink-spotted page.

> *Dearest Elizabeth,*
> *If you have received this letter, it will mean I have departed this life for the next.*
>
> *You may not remember who I am, as you were very young when we met. Your maman was quite dear to me, having watched her grow up on St. Martin. As I am a widow without issue, it is my wish that my estate fall to you upon my death. You will have the full terms of the bequest from my solicitor, who will meet with you upon your arrival to Hampshire.*
>
> *Sherbourne House was once grand, and I have hopes you'll care for it well. After your troubles, you may find a new beginning will be just the thing to restore your spirit. It is my dearest hope that you find happiness here with a family of your own. It warms my heart to think of the laughter of children in these halls.*
> *With fondness,*
> *Tante Theo*
> *Baroness Sherbourne*

"We're nearly there, ladies."

The driver's brusque voice startled Eliza from her reading, quiet as he'd been for most of their journey. She folded the letter and tucked it away. "How much further?" she asked.

"Only a few more miles. We'll turn onto the lane after the village."

The afternoon swiftly fell to evening as they rolled through Cheltenbridge, passing a collection of whitewashed shops nestled around a square. Vendors offered their wares on tables along the curb, boasting silk cravats in bright colors and trilbies stacked in neat rows. The village women milled about on their errands, wearing simple calicos and wide-brimmed hats. It was altogether languorous and quaint compared with the bustle of Canal Street. The air was fresher here, cleaner—unspoiled by the fetid miasma of disease and mold.

After they crossed over the arched bridge the town had been named for, the road became an earthen lane rutted by wagon wheels. They went through the turning, the cab creaking and groaning with the effort. There was a sudden break in the trees, revealing the eaves and mansard roof of a large mansion.

"Now there's a blasted wreck of a place," the driver snarled. He spat out the side of his mouth. Eliza's stomach rolled. "Me mum worked there as a girl. Said it was haunted and the walls crawled around the edges of your eyes. Still . . . shame to let a fine house like that go."

Eliza leaned forward, perking up. "Did you say it was haunted?"

"That's right. Me mum weren't prone to no fancy."

Whether there were spirits about the place or not, he was right concerning the letting go; the gardens around the house were a rampant tangle of rosebushes and Italian cypress swaying behind a gate adorned with twining ebony serpents. The unkempt gardens obscured most of the mansion's façade, but the roofline was lovely, punctuated by a row of arched transom windows. It was the sort of house meant to sit in one's imagination and take up residence. Eliza looked up at its high oriel window and wondered who lived inside.

They bounced on for a bit, until a squat gatehouse with a copper roof appeared to their left. The words *Sherbourne House* were pressed into its cornerstone, along with the address and its date of construction: 1759. The gates were padlocked, their spiked ironwork forbidding and cold.

Eliza nudged Lydia. She jerked awake with a snort. "We're here. The solicitor said a groundskeeper would be about to open the gates, but I don't see anyone."

"Is there a bell?" Lydia craned her neck. "It certainly seems desolate, doesn't it?"

"You should see the neighboring estate—according to our driver, we'll be living next to a haunted house. It looks like something from a penny dreadful."

The driver cleared his throat and spat again. "I needs to be getting back to my wife and a warm dinner, good ladies. But for another dollar, I can stay put with ye 'til someone shows up. There's been reports of a highwayman around these parts."

"That's quite all right, sir," Eliza said. "You've already been more than accommodating." She dug through her chatelaine bag, pawing past peanut hulls and meal cards until she produced two silver dollars and a few bits of change for good measure. She pushed them through the hinged opening at the top of the hansom, and the driver released the door to the cab. He unloaded their luggage with an abundance of sighing before turning his rig to trot away with nary a glance behind him.

Eliza peered over the ivy-tangled gate. "Hello?" she called, cupping her hands around her mouth. They waited for an answering call and were met with silence. No light shone through the purple dusk, and no sound stirred beyond the chirruping of toads. The air had grown dank and sodden, threatening rain. Eliza rubbed her arms to fight the chill. For a moment, a wave of helplessness washed over her, but there was no time for that now. Not after months of planning. Not when everything she'd hoped for was within reach.

"What should we do?" Lydia banged the lock against the gate in frustration.

"I'm not sure," Eliza said, "but I've a fierce need to relieve myself. That carriage ride was a bit long for my bladder."

"Can't you wait until we're inside?"

"Why? There's no one here." Eliza pushed behind the thick branches of a yew bordering the gates and gathered her skirts to squat. Suddenly, there was a scurrying, and a sharp face with beetle-dark eyes emerged from the shadows. Eliza leapt to her feet. Her cheeks burned with embarrassment.

"You Miss Elizabeth Sullivan?" the man asked, squinting at her through the gate's fretwork.

Eliza ran a hand over her rumpled skirts and came out. "I am. And this is my sister, Lydia."

"I be Giles Mason. Groundskeeper."

Lydia shifted from side to side, wearing her impatience like most women wore perfume. "Can we please come in, sir? It's so cold."

"Right, then." Mason fiddled with the padlock, then cranked a pulley wheel. The gate swung free with a metallic groan. "House idn't rightly comfortable—housekeeper quit after Lady Sherbourne died. You'd probably rather a hot toddy and a room at the pub."

"We'll endure the discomfort, Mr. Mason," Eliza said. "It's been a tiring day."

He gave a terse nod and disappeared into the gatehouse. A moment later, he produced a hand-drawn wagon and loaded their trunks with surprising vigor, then motioned for them to follow along the gravel drive.

At first glance, Sherbourne House was statelier than Eliza had imagined. Made of yellow limestone, it sat upon a small plateau in the Georgian style, flanked by a formal garden. An oak tree stood in front of the terrace, as ancient and gnarled as the trees in Louisiana, lacking only a raiment of Spanish moss. Mason left their trunks on the terrace and led them beneath the portico. He pulled a ring of keys from his pocket and worked the lock. The door swung open, scraping an arc on the dusty marble floor.

Eliza blinked as they crossed the threshold, her vision adjusting to the liminal light. She pulled off her gloves and spun in a circle, taking in the high coffered ceiling and paneled walls. Woven tapestries hung along the foyer, depicting naval battles and pastoral scenes.

"I'll fetch some candles," Mason said. "There's gas, but I'd not chance it until you have an inspector come out. House been boarded up like this one the next town over blew to high heaven when the new tenants moved in. Rats chewed through the lines."

"Comforting thought," Lydia murmured after he'd gone. "Can you imagine?"

Eliza's shoulders sagged. "I'm fairly certain that won't happen to us."

A few moments later, a flickering came from the rear of the house, and Mason reemerged with a multitiered candelabra. The flames cast ghoulish shadows beneath his eyes. "I gathered as many candles as I could find and left them in the kitchen. I'll fetch a boilermaker tomorrow, first thing. Bedchambers are upstairs. Chamber pots under the beds." He raised an eyebrow at Eliza and smiled, showing a row of crooked, gray teeth. "No need to do your business on the verge again, miss."

Eliza returned his smile and took the candelabra, the tallow rancid in her nostrils. "Thank you, Mr. Mason."

"Right. I'll be in the carriage house should you need anything."

The old man trudged off, leaving Lydia and Eliza at the foot of an L-shaped staircase. They went up, finding a narrow hallway at the top lined with closed doors, a tattered runner snaking over the wooden floor. Eliza opened the first door they came to. The scent of stale ashes wafted out as they entered. A small four-poster bed stood in the corner of the room, its velvet canopy shrouded in a fine layer of dust. The carpet was worn through in places, the mirror above the dressing table foxed with black spots. Eliza's white face floated like a specter within. The entire room held a sad, gothic fustiness.

"Shall we sleep in the same room tonight?" Eliza set the candelabra on the bedside table. Light jumped across the ceiling, throwing their shadows large upon the wall.

"Yes. I'm not wandering through the rest of this house alone." Lydia turned down the bed. Dust bounced from the quilted counterpane, drawing a ragged cough from Eliza. "This place could do with a good airing out."

They freshened up as best they could, then helped each other undress down to their chemises. Eliza nestled beside Lydia under the musty sheets. "I do hope Tante Theo didn't die in this bed."

"Wouldn't that be a thing, to find her ghost staring at us in the middle of the night?" Lydia tied a silk scarf over her loosened curls, blew out the candles, and flopped back onto the mattress. "Tomorrow, we'll burn a little sage to freshen things."

"Tomorrow, cher." Eliza wadded the lumpy pillows beneath her head and closed her eyes. Sleep crawled up and found her quickly, sitting heavily on her chest.

♦

Eliza flew awake, paralyzed, her heart racing like a wild thing. *Not again.* A scream threatened at the back of her throat. Black, watery shadows loomed in the corners. Eliza closed her eyes and opened them again, grounding her senses in the here and now. She traced the pleats on the canopy with her eyes and counted: *One, two, three.* Slowly, her pulse steadied. *Four, five, six.* The feeling returned to her fingers. She gripped the edge of the mattress until they ached. *Seven, eight, nine, ten.* Her head ceased its crazed spinning. She could breathe.

The dream had been too real this time. Too much like a memory. She could still feel the sharp, choking sting of water and the weight of her dress dragging her to the bottom of the pond, no matter how hard she fought for the surface. But she wasn't drowning. She was safe in England. *Home.*

Moonlight streamed through the drapes and limned the room with silver, creating a chiaroscuro painting out of otherwise normal objects. In the distance, thunder crackled a warning. The wind picked up, tearing through the eaves with a wicked howl. A shutter came loose and began thumping against the house, steady as a carpenter's hammer. Eliza pushed the covers aside, careful not to wake Lydia, and crossed to the casement.

The moon cut a clean, gray path on the ground, broken only by the shadows of scudding clouds. She swung open the sash. Frigid air slammed her full in the face. As she leaned out to pull the wayward shutter to the sill, a familiar sound met her ears. She strained to listen. Hoofbeats.

Suddenly, a horse and rider burst through the trees bordering the ruined mansion she'd seen from the road. They tore across the heath at a full gallop, the horseman's caped coat flaring out behind him. He sat well in his saddle—riding high in his stirrups as he made a clean jump over a low stone wall and returned to a run. The horse was big and rawboned, perhaps a warmblood or a Friesian. Impressive animal. Bred for kings and war.

A fierce gust of wind hissed through the trees. The shutter tore free from Eliza's hand and slammed into the side of the house with a crack as loud as a pistol shot. The rider slowed, pivoting in his saddle. From this distance, she could only make out the moonlit oval of his face, but his eyes seemed to meet hers for a long moment. She gasped and took a step backward, the hem of her gown luffing over the sill.

Clouds raced to cover the moon. Sharp droplets spat at the windowpanes as the earthy scent of rain dampened the air. The rider turned and urged his horse back to speed. They were soon gone, disappearing into the birchwood forest. Eliza pulled the drapes closed against the storm, her imagination uncoiling.

CHAPTER 2

The next morning bloomed bright and sunny—a marked departure from the day before. Something smelled wonderful. Was it bacon? Eliza wiped the sleep from her eyes and sat up. Her long curls fell around her shoulders, tangled from her fitful night. Lydia was gone, her chemise lying across the foot of the bed.

Eliza went to the window and parted the curtains. The scene out-of-doors held far less mystique than it had by moonlight—daytime revealing the true state of the distant manor. From her vantage point, she saw the house was shaped vaguely like the letter H, with a glass-topped conservatory nestled like a jewel box in the hollow between wings. While the north-facing wing seemed to be in livable condition, the roof was collapsed at the rear elevation, its scorched attic rafters bared to the sky. So, there had been a fire. A recent one, by the look of it.

Eliza let the curtains fall back into place, her curiosity further stoked. An ewer of clean water stood on the washstand. Lydia must have brought it up earlier. She washed her face and hands in the basin, braided her hair into a knotted plait, and went downstairs.

She was greeted by the sight of Lydia panfrying eggs in the simple, delft-blue kitchen, her curls tied back with a scrap of lace. Thick slices of bacon sat on the sideboard, alongside a crusty baguette. Lydia scooped the eggs from the cast-iron skillet and handed a plate to Eliza. "I wondered when you'd be getting up."

"You found food? And coal for the cookstove?"

"We have chickens out back—three fat little hens and a rooster. Mr. Mason brought us the rest of the groceries and filled the coal scuttle."

"Oh, that was generous." Eliza piled food onto her plate, then followed Lydia to the trestle table in the corner, where a porcelain teapot steamed. She shook out a napkin and hungrily tucked into her eggs. "We'll go to market later and get everything else we need. I'd have been up earlier to help cook if the storm hadn't woken me last night."

"Storm?" Lydia shook her head, curls bouncing. "I don't recall any storm."

"It was quite the banger. I'm surprised you slept through it."

"Having your dreams again?"

"No, this wasn't a dream, I'm sure of it." Eliza took a sip of tea, the tang of Earl Grey sharp on her tongue. "There was a rider across the way—coming from the ruined mansion next door. He saw me standing at the window."

Lydia shrugged her shoulders and stirred milk into her tea. "You always liked to ride Hercules at night. Oh . . . that reminds me, we've a trap and horse in the stables. A handsome little Arab. I walked the property with Mr. Mason this morning. I met a few of the tenants. Things aren't nearly as dire as I thought they'd be."

Eliza pushed back a sudden twinge of jealousy. Lydia was four years younger—twenty-one to Eliza's twenty-five—but no one would know it from the way she acted. She was ever taking charge.

There came a shrill whirring from the far wall. A clock with a peaked top, carved like a Swiss chalet, chimed eight times. A grotesque little red-eyed bird emerged, its beak on a hinge. It finally gave up its tired cuckooing and disappeared with a snap.

"That clock has got to go," Lydia said.

"Well. I quite like it," Eliza said with a crisp nod. "It can stay."

❦

They were beating rugs on the portico after a long morning of house-cleaning when a young courier wobbled up the drive on a cycle. He dismounted, tipped his cap to Lydia, and turned to Eliza. The sunlight caught a strand of his sandy hair, turning it to pale gold. Eliza startled and took a step back.

It isn't him, Liza. Not every fair-haired boy you meet is him.

"Are you Miss Sullivan?"

"I am." Eliza clutched her apron to still the sudden tremor in her hands.

"I've brought a note from Miss Polly Whitby. She's your neighbor." The boy passed her a sealed envelope addressed with a feminine hand.

"How kind. Does she live in the big house next to us?" Eliza motioned in the direction of the fire-scarred manor.

The boy gave a nervous laugh. "No, miss. That's the old Havenwood place. Miss Whitby lives on the other side of you. She's the admiral's daughter. If it wouldn't be too much trouble, she's requested your answer while I wait."

Eliza opened the envelope as Lydia peered over her shoulder. Inside, there was an invitation to afternoon tea and a pressed violet. It tumbled onto the flagstone pavement and the boy bent to retrieve it, handing it to Eliza with a shy smile.

"Thank you very much. What was your name, young sir?"

"I'm Nigel Phelps, miss. I'm always round the lane."

"Please tell Miss Whitby we'd be delighted, Nigel."

"I surely will." He replaced his cap and climbed onto his cycle, wobbling back through the gates.

"Our first proper English tea, Lyddie," Eliza said. "What shall we bring our hostess?"

Lydia's mouth twisted. "Perhaps you should go alone. My name wasn't on the envelope."

"She likely doesn't know about you, cher."

"I suppose you're right. Let's finish these rugs, then we'll go freshen up."

❦

Polly Whitby was every bit the perfect English rose. That was Eliza's first thought upon seeing her neighbor's bright blue eyes and ash-blond hair. She ushered them into a parlor replete with tufted velvet divans and salmon-pink curtains that matched the rather overblown dress she was wearing. Eliza presented the bouquet of peonies she'd gathered from the garden and took a seat across from their hostess while Lydia stood off to the side, arms crossed over her waist.

"Miss Whitby, this is Lydia. She's my sister."

Polly offered Lydia a prim smile. "Please, Miss Sullivan, have a seat. Bandini will be in with our tea in only a moment."

"It's Miss Tourant, not Sullivan." Lydia swept her lilac-hued skirts to the side and perched next to Eliza, as if she were a terrified bird about to take flight. "Eliza is only my half sister."

"I see." Polly looked from Lydia to Eliza, quietly assessing.

Eliza wondered how long it would be before the inevitable questions began. *Have you the same father? Or mother?* The comparisons would come next—often politely silent, but still made—eyes darting from her own pale, freckled skin and copper-blond curls to Lydia's luminous olive complexion and coiled brown ringlets.

Polly's demure scrutiny was interrupted at that moment by a maid in a brilliant fuchsia sari. She was bearing a tray stacked with dainty cakes, fragrant steaming tea, and a silver service. Polly poured and passed an enameled teacup to Eliza. "You'll want lots of milk and sugar in this." She dropped two lumps into Eliza's cup, following it with a generous splash of milk, then did the same for Lydia. "Now stir."

After a few turns with a spoon, the saffron-colored liquid melted into a lovely shade of gold. Eliza raised the cup to her lips and was rewarded with an exquisite, spicy sweetness. Her eyebrows lifted. "This is delightfully uncommon."

"Magical, isn't it? Bandini makes the very best chai. I grew up in Calcutta, you know. When my father was raised to admiral, he sent me home to manage the estate. We're all tied to the navy here, every last one of us. They even weave sailcloth for the fleet in the village." Polly took a breath, crossing her legs and sitting back against her chair. "My friend Sarah Nelson will be joining us shortly. I hope you don't mind. We've all been a bit curious about you. We were most surprised when Lady Sherbourne didn't will her estate to the church. She must have cared a great deal for you."

"That's the funny thing—I didn't know my aunt at all. She and my mother were close, but I was barely four when I met her. I only remember a tall woman in a very large hat. It was a shock to find I'd been granted her estate. I'm meeting with her solicitor to go over the details of the will tomorrow."

"Well. Sherbourne House is a fine home, and should you need a housekeeper, a butler, or any other staff, I should be pleased to provide references for you."

"Thank you, but I think we'll manage on our own. Lydia and I were raised on a farm. We're used to housekeeping."

Polly's cheeks colored. "Perhaps you might change your mind. These country homes require constant upkeep. They tend to decline rapidly without the proper care. The damp weather, you know. You'll at least need a cook. The Wards' cook just trained a new girl and they're sending her out. She's Irish, but she's a hard worker and doesn't blather on too much about her popery."

Lydia covered the dainty crucifix at her throat with quick fingers.

"Our father was Irish," Eliza said, the corners of her mouth curling. "From Kildare."

"Well." Polly cleared her throat.

"Regarding houses in disrepair, who lives in the house at the crossroads?" Eliza asked, eager to change the subject. "The Second Empire with the metal gates?"

Polly shifted in her chair and looked down. "They're an old Hampshire family. It's a tragic story, really."

"Was there a fire? It looks it."

"There was. Three winters ago. Thomas Winfield—he was the fourth Viscount Havenwood—died in the fire as well as his son Gabriel," Polly said. "His eldest son, Malcolm, is the only remaining person living there. He's inherited the title."

So it had been Malcolm out riding the night before. "And was there a mother? A viscountess?"

"Yes, but no one knows what happened to her." Polly's eyes widened as she relaxed into a gossiping tone. "She disappeared afterwards. They dredged the river, searched the forest, but she's never turned up. She'd gone quite mad, you see. She hadn't been out in society for some time before the fire."

"How terrible it is to lose your entire family." Eliza blinked twice. "It's difficult to carry on after something like that." She swallowed more of the tea to chase the sudden taste of metal from her tongue and concentrated on the dizzying wallpaper.

"They've always been an odd family—scandalous, even. There's talk of murder. That he might have even killed his mother. We really don't associate with him." Polly gave a tight smile. "I'd advise you do the same."

The doorbell rang, and a young woman with plump, pretty features and dressed in mannish clothes was let into the room. Polly stood to receive her kisses. "Sarah, these are our new neighbors: Miss Eliza Sullivan and her sister, Miss Lydia Tourant. I was just telling them about Lord Havenwood and the fire."

"Polly!" Sarah scolded. "Bringing out all the mad cats straightaway, are we? You'll terrify them!" She turned to Lydia and Eliza, sweeping her hat from her head with a gallant flourish. "Hello. I'm Sarah Nelson. Our Polly's a raging gossip. Pay her no mind. Malcolm's a bit strange, that's all."

"Pleasure." Eliza offered her hand. "I found the conversation invigorating. I want to learn everything about Hampshire I can. It's delightful to finally be here."

Sarah gave Eliza's fingers a squeeze and turned to greet Lydia. "Our first Americans in Cheltenbridge! They're like perfect dolls, aren't they, Polly?"

Polly inclined her head, her eyes narrowing. "Quite."

"If you're all settled in at Sherbourne House, you should come to our ball. Grandmama is inviting all the local gentry."

"Sarah's grandmother is Countess Gregory," Polly explained. "She holds a country ball to ring in each summer solstice."

Sarah gave a conspiratorial grin and wrinkled her nose. "It's a *matchmaking* ball."

Eliza's back stiffened. "Oh, I'm not looking for a husband." She gripped the arm of the chair, counting the rounded upholstery tacks beneath her fingers. She was wary of this sort of conversation—the same one she'd had every year since her eighteenth birthday, in parlors just like this one an ocean away.

"Surely you and your sister are of marriageable age and status?" Polly prodded.

"Yes, but . . ."

"Well," Sarah interrupted, "*I'm* wed this past spring, but my husband dislikes social functions. They give him dyspepsia. I'd rather like to see the two of you there. I'd imagine you cut fine figures on a dance floor."

"Do they *have* coming-out balls where you're from?" Polly asked.

"Of course, Miss Whitby," Lydia said, her tone measured.

Polly sniffed. "Yet, neither of you have married?"

Eliza sighed. *Mon Dieu*, this one wasn't giving up. "Obviously not."

"But who controls your inheritance and your allowance?"

"We do," Eliza and Lydia answered in unison.

Sarah clapped her hands and perched on the arm of a nearby chair. "Independent women. How admirable!"

"Still," said Eliza, "it would be lovely to have the occasion to dress up. It's been too long since we danced. If your grandmother is receptive to two more guests on her list, we'd be honored, Mrs. Nelson."

"It's settled! I'll send a carriage to your door at nine o'clock next Tuesday night!"

CHAPTER 3

Eliza inspected the brass shingle above the tatty, wooden door, ARTHUR BRAINERD, SOLICITOR, then grasped the lion-head door knocker and rapped three times. There was a muted shuffling on the other side, followed by the low barking of a dog.

"Settle, settle, Monty!" a gruff voice muttered. The door swung wide, and a well-dressed gentleman of advanced years peered out at her, squinting his watery blue eyes as he clutched the collar of a monstrous wolfhound.

Eliza stepped back.

"Never mind Monty, love. He won't bite. He's all legs and tail but no teeth."

The dog whined and looked up at her through his fringe of coarse gray hair. Eliza put out her hand. He sniffed her glove, his great tail whisking from side to side.

"You're Miss Sullivan, I presume?"

"Yes, sir. Lady Sherbourne's grandniece." She scratched Monty behind the ears. His tongue lolled from his mouth as encouragement.

"Right, right. Have a seat in the parlor and I'll have Myrtle bring a spot of tea while I fetch the documents."

Eliza crossed over the threshold into the dim light of a squarish room. It was lined floor-to-ceiling with messy stacks of gold-embossed books, their spines a confusing array of letters and numbers. A desk stood in the corner, its legs ending in gryphon's claws, the top laden with sheaves of paper and a typewriter. Eliza removed her gloves and sat in the high-backed chair facing the desk. Monty circled the floor at her feet three times, then lay down, resting his hoary head against her shin.

Mr. Brainerd came in, muttering to himself and carrying a green leather portfolio. A woman with eyes like raisins and gray-streaked brown hair done up in a topknot followed him. She set a tea service down on the spindly Italian-style table next to Eliza, then gave a peck to Mr. Brainerd's cheek as he wedged himself behind the desk.

"Thank you, Myrtle," he said, patting her red-knuckled hand. She nodded at Eliza, then disappeared, sliding the pocket door shut behind her. "I take it your passage was satisfactory?" He produced a pair of demilune magnifiers from his pocket and perched them on the end of his bulbous nose.

"It was, although I'm not much suited to sea travel. I don't care for water. I'm only now recovering from being tossed about."

"I'm a creature of the land myself, I daresay." He gave a dry chuckle and held a sheet of parchment up to the feeble light. "Ah. Here are the deed to Sherbourne House and the clauses set forth in Lady Sherbourne's will."

Eliza took the documents from him and scanned them. The deed was simple, describing the dimensions of the house as well as a surveyor's appraisal of the land. She shuffled the deed behind the next document and read. Everything was standard until she came to the final clause. She put her hand to her mouth, pressing her lips against her teeth. "I'm so sorry, but would you mind explaining this clause, sir?" Eliza converted the Roman numerals in her head. "Number nineteen?" Eliza handed the will back to the solicitor.

His eyebrows quivered for a moment. "Very specific, that one. It says . . ."

"I do know what it says, Mr. Brainerd, but what does it *mean*?"

"Right, right. It's a small thing, really. Lady Sherbourne's fiduciary accounts and the tenants' leases will only be released upon occasion of your marriage, which must occur within three months of your arrival, else your claim to the estate shall be rendered null and void. It's a rather sizable amount. Shall I convert the numbers for you?"

Eliza pushed two fingers to her temple. Monty whined in sympathy. "No, that's quite all right." She understood the amounts well enough. She'd be a millionaire by American standards. *If* she married. And to think two days ago England had represented freedom! Her daydreams of living out her days as a moneyed spinster were dissolving as fast as spun sugar on her tongue.

It wasn't that Eliza was opposed to love. She *had* loved. Twice. First there was Giselle—the buxom daughter of one of Maman's church friends, who came each Tuesday afternoon to teach Eliza the harp. The lessons were eagerly anticipated but gradually grew shorter, the music replaced by whispered secrets and stolen kisses behind the potted palms, until finally the harp no longer sounded from the front parlor at all. *We needn't have Giselle any longer,* Maman had said with a tone of finality. *You've grown quite proficient at the harp. So proficient you never play.*

A frenzy of wealthy suitors came courting soon after, but in her heartbreak, Eliza had snubbed every Creole planter her parents offered up, each one just as boring as the last. There was no man who could provide the easy companionship she'd had with Giselle.

Until Jacob—her father's new groom. He was a quiet young man with a lisp and gray-green eyes, sensitive and kindhearted, who came to her aid one day after she fell from her horse into a stand of stinging nettle and read to her from Keats to keep her from clawing at her welted skin. She'd kissed him once on impulse, and he'd returned her ardor. They'd enjoyed weeks of bliss, until the day Maman discovered their secret trysting. Eliza put a hand to her cheek, remembering her mother's stinging slap and the fierce set of her fine, French jaw as she pulled Eliza from Jacob's bed. *Putain! Tumbling with a common groom. Who will want you now?*

After Jacob left Anaquitas Farm, no more fine Creole suitors came to call, and Eliza had shut herself away like a fallen saint awaiting martyrdom.

"I can see by your expression you're upset," Mr. Brainerd said, pulling her sharply from her thoughts. "Please understand, Miss Sullivan, your aunt only wanted to ensure the continued upkeep of her loyal tenants and her household in the event of her death. Lady Sherbourne was afraid, with your being American, that you'd come over, sell the house, collect the money, and then leave. And single women *do* tend to struggle with managing property on their own. It's highly irregular. A lovely young woman such as yourself will have no issue attracting suitors. Find a husband and Sherbourne House and the fortune attached to it shall be yours in perpetuity."

"I understand. But won't my property default to my husband if I marry? Isn't that the law?"

The old man shuffled the papers on his desk. "Yes, well. That *was* the old doctrine of coverture. It's still that way in America, I believe, but this is where you are fortunate to be in England. Due to the Women's Property Act, the title to Sherbourne House will have your name listed alongside your future husband's."

"And yet, if I decided to lease the property or sell it, I'd need his permission to do so. Unless I become a widow like my aunt, of course." Eliza gave a sharp laugh. "It seems falling into widowhood is the only way a woman is guaranteed her full rights."

"Gracious. That's a rather dire way of looking at things." Mr. Brainerd coughed, a rattle at the back of his throat. "There are several bachelors of quality here in Hampshire. Why, the Earl of Eastleigh is looking for a wife, even. You could end up a countess. That wouldn't be so terrible, would it?"

Eliza's curiosity pushed through the wall of her frustration. "And what of my neighbor? Lord Havenwood? Isn't he a bachelor as well?"

Mr. Brainerd's face collapsed. "Oh. That one. He's certainly single, but I'd not . . . well. Let's just say there are much better prospects for you."

Eliza gave an exasperated sigh, her shoulders slumping. "I was hoping to start again. To build a business here. I wasn't keen to marry, at least not right away. Only three months to find a husband! Bit of a rush, isn't it?"

"Well, Lady Sherbourne *was* an eccentric, but I'm certain she had her reasons for the clause." Mr. Brainerd stood, extending his hand. Monty padded to his master, his tail beating a constant rhythm. "Your aunt was very clear about the matter, but you do have choices, my dear. You could always go back to America if you find the terms do not suit. The estate will revert to the Crown, of course. Shame to let that happen."

Eliza shook her head. No. Going back to New Orleans was not an option. There was nothing for her there but painful memories, old suitors, and shame. Eliza pulled on her gloves and followed the solicitor and his dog to the door, her brows pulled together in irritation.

"Chin up, darling," Mr. Brainerd said, taking her hand. "Being married is no curse. My Myrtle and I have enjoyed well over thirty years together. With your charms, you'll have the pick of the litter here in Hampshire, to be sure."

CHAPTER 4

"Lyddie, I'm worried." Eliza patted her upswept hair in the mirror as Lydia tightened her corset.

"Whatever for? You know that's my job."

"Do you suppose the men of Hampshire have heard the extent of Theodora's fortune? Polly seems quite the gossip."

"They'd only know about the estate, wouldn't they?" Lydia cast an eye toward the worn furniture in Eliza's room. "It's apparent your aunt lived *well* below her means."

"Yes, but we aren't poor yet. Even without her bequest." Eliza's hand hovered over the necklace resting against her clavicle—three pear-shaped diamonds surrounded by pearls. It had been her mother's wedding gift from her father—a sparkling remnant of a time when money had been of little concern.

"They'll find out about the money eventually, won't they, Liza? The right man would marry you even if you were penniless."

"That's just the thing. With all the other rich Americans coming over to snatch up the bachelors in recent years, we won't make fast friends with the local girls. They'll see us as dollar princesses."

"Sarah seems genuine. At least she seemed to be at tea."

"Sarah's already married. We're no rivals for her." Eliza huffed as Lydia tightened the final laces of the longline formal corset she hadn't had occasion to wear in years—a corset that was now two sizes too small for her burgeoning waist. Too much cream in her coffee and too little care to how her clothes fit. "Can you pull it tighter, sister? I've gained a few pounds." Lydia placed her knee against Eliza's back and tugged, drawing her waist in sharply and making the rounded tops of her pale bosom swell.

"I'm not so sure about Polly, though." Lydia frowned. "Did you see the way she looked at me when she found out I went by a different surname? She nearly gave herself a headache trying to puzzle it out."

"If people asking questions bothers you, I don't see why you don't take Papa's name. He was your father too, and people wouldn't know the difference."

Lydia shook her head, the emeralds in her ears twinkling. "I don't expect you'll understand. The world looks different through your eyes. Just because I was raised for white doesn't mean I am. And if I gave up my name, it would be like turning my back on Mimi Lisette's memory and my own maman, wherever she is."

Lydia had never known her maman—Justine, Mimi Lisette's only daughter. They'd come to Anaquitas Farm to work after the long and bloody war, when Papa was more concerned with patching cannonball holes on the roof than finding a high-society wife. But marry he did— and a French Creole wife at that, with flaming red hair and the temper to match it. Helene DeSaulnier's dowry came with the kind of money that turned the small but prosperous farm into a booming plantation. No one seemed to mind that Eliza had arrived four months sooner than the wedding date said she should have.

But even though Maman was ever swanning in the background of Eliza's life, soft-voiced Mimi had been the one to soothe Eliza to sleep after her nightmares, while her own mother slept on, unaware of her childish fears. On the days Eliza was supposed to be sitting at her lessons under her surly French tutor, learning to be *une fille de la noblesse*, she would escape to the kitchens instead, where Mimi shared a special kind of magic—one wrought of spices and measurements, patience and time.

Together, she and Lydia learned to spin sugar into sticky sweet pralines at Christmastime and took turns tending the gumbo pot as Mimi told them old Haitian stories in her lilting patois.

As for Justine, Eliza's memories were as elusive as shifting light. She only remembered a young woman with balletic, long-limbed grace who moved across polished floors on gliding feet. When Eliza asked about Lydia's mother, one afternoon in springtime when Lydia had stormed off in a fit of pique over Eliza's new Easter dress, Mimi's eyes had grown hard. *Justine fell in a bad way with a white preacher. That man wanted her, but he didn't want no child. After Lydia was born, my Justine run off. I never seen her since.* At this, Mimi's eyes spilled over, her dark brown irises clouding to black. Eliza learned not to ask about Justine again, because when Mimi cried, her tears brought sadness into the whole house.

But the truth had come years later, crashing like a rogue wave from behind. She would never forget the betrayal she felt as she sat next to Lydia in the attorney's stifling office, her parents three days cold in the tomb. *To my natural firstborn daughter, Elizabeth Marie-Claire Sullivan, I bequeath my land and property. And to my natural-born, undocumented daughter, Lydia Anne Tourant, I bequeath . . .*

She hadn't heard the rest of the will. She'd only heard Lydia's sobbing.

The feckless preacher had been a lie to protect the reputation of the man—the *father*—Eliza had thought she'd known. The man who taught her how to read a green horse and gave her a roan stallion on her tenth birthday. The gentleman farmer who had walked with her over spring pastures and knelt in his fine clothes to show her the subtle differences between the sprouting alfalfa and fescue. A man built like a bulwark, with a ready laugh and a dimple in his chin, known for his work ethic and how well he treated his servants.

But her noble papa had been an invention, his honor forever altered by a single line of script. The man who had scorned others for taking improper liberties with their servants had been a hypocrite. While he'd been willing enough to provide for the child he'd gotten with Justine, he hadn't had the decency to acknowledge Lydia as his trueborn daughter until death absolved him of facing his shame. Eliza was wrestling with it still. But at least they had one another. With Lydia, she'd never be alone in the world.

Eliza emerged from her broken memories with a shake of her head. As she fastened her pearl earrings, she caught and held Lydia's gaze in the mirror. "You know, cher, I've grown fond of things the way they are. You and I, living a free life, without men telling us what to do. Between Theo's will, and now this ball—I'm feeling backed into a corner." She thought of Mr. Brainerd's hound curling at her feet. "I think I'd rather have a dog than a husband. Their hearts are much more steadfast."

Lydia laughed and shrugged into her dress—a burgundy Worth concoction shot through with gilt beads. It was her best color, meant to set the amber freckles in her eyes aflame. "Yes, but if you want to remain in England and construct this fantastic new life you've imagined, you'll need to do as your aunt wished. We won't have enough money to last forever, even with the sale of the farm—not the way you like to spend it," Lydia chided. "Besides, being married wouldn't be such a bad thing. *I'd* like to marry as soon as I find someone suitable. People are already starting to give me queer looks."

Eliza gave a rueful snort. "Yes, sister. I know those looks well."

"I was thinking of our old suitors the other day. Do you remember Eustace?"

"Poor Eustace. He tried his best at winning you, didn't he?"

"He was hopeless. My toes are only now recovering from being stomped upon. I found out his poor wife is on her fifth child in as many years!" Lydia turned and lifted the cascade of ringlets from her graceful neck. "Do me up, would you?"

Eliza grew pensive again as she fastened Lydia's buttons. "I didn't care for any of the men in New Orleans. Except for Jacob. He wrote to me from Cuba. Twice. I never told you."

"Oh?"

"He asked me to marry him."

Lydia gave a sharp frown over her shoulder. "And did you answer him?"

"I did . . ."

"You turned him down, didn't you?"

"Only because he deserved better, Lyddie." Better than a stupid girl who hadn't stood up for their love in the face of her mother's rage. Better than a girl who had hidden herself in a dark house, full of shame at her own recklessness. Eliza struggled with Lydia's final button, which stubbornly refused to be threaded through its loop. "He married a girl—a nurse—he met at the army hospital. Her name was Yolanda, I think."

"Well, you can't blame him for marrying someone else. You were being foolish. I don't . . ." Lydia sighed. A crease etched between her brows. "There will be someone that catches your eye again, Liza. Someone who will make you just as happy as Jacob did. But you *must* give things a chance."

"Yes, but three months is hardly enough time to be choosy . . . to even get to know someone. And what if no one fancies me? I am getting old, after all."

"You may be old, but I've not seen a truly pretty girl since we've set foot in this town. I've a feeling your odds are quite good."

"You are horrid!" Eliza said, laughing despite herself. "My eyes are much kinder than yours, cher." She stepped into her layered, frothy petticoats, then into the gown of cornflower-blue silk. The dress had been made in Paris and cost more than most men made in a year, but it exaggerated her curves in a decidedly becoming fashion. Society balls were such a game—the fine clothing and dancing, the artful flirting. Tiring. All of it. Eliza checked her reflection in the mirror and pulled on her gloves, then gave a swift kiss to her sister's cheek. "I suppose if I *must* marry, I'd hope to find a husband who respects my dreams as well as his own—and one who'll cover me with passionate kisses, too."

"Careful with that," Lydia teased. "You may end up like poor Eustace's wife."

❦

Lydia and Eliza stood on the terrace of the rambling Tudor mansion before them, waiting to be let inside. A glittering queue wound through the fragrant courtyard—a sea of unfamiliar faces wearing nodding feathers and silk top hats. It was a temperate night, but Eliza was growing dizzier and more flushed by the moment.

"Are you all right?" Lydia asked.

"Yes, only a bit overheated. My corset is bothering me."

"It wouldn't be so tight if you stopped eating so many sweets."

The line advanced as footmen led the guests through the gabled doors. A maid took their cloaks and smoothed out their skirts before handing their calling cards to a haughty butler, who raised an eyebrow at Eliza before ushering them into the receiving room. An escort came forward and took her elbow, leading her over the threshold of a half-timbered drawing room blazing with electric chandeliers.

"Miss Elizabeth Sullivan, grandniece of the late Lady Sherbourne. From America," the butler announced in a booming voice.

Eliza snapped her fan shut, took a deep breath, and stepped forward. Everyone seemed to stop what they were doing at once. Monocles were raised, men coughed, and women whispered to one another. Her heart fluttered like an insect trapped in a jar.

Remember to smile, you look so unpleasant when you do not. Her mother's voice was a ghost in her head, harsh and cutting as the posture board she'd fashioned to the back of Eliza's chair, knife points ready to dig into her shoulder blades if she slouched. *Mon Dieu, cher! Keep your blessed back straight.*

Liveried servants stood at attention all along the red-and-gold-carpeted floor, presenting trays of champagne. A quartet played atmospheric music at just the right volume to accompany conversation. Gardenias spilled from vases set upon plinths of marble, perfuming the air. The bouquet of colorful ball gowns streaming through the room was a decadent sight.

Eliza thanked her escort and made her way toward Polly Whitby, who was chattering away with a stunning woman dressed in violet shantung, her dark hair braided into a high crown over her valentine of a face. They turned as one. "Miss Sullivan." Polly's gaze raked over Eliza's gown, pausing on the circlet of diamonds around her neck. "My, but you do show up well."

Eliza inclined her head. "Miss Whitby. You look lovely yourself." And she did, although Polly's mauve concoction, with its exaggerated *ballon* sleeves and ruffled bodice, was decidedly four seasons outdated.

The dark-haired woman tilted her pointed chin to Eliza and offered her hand. "Una Moseley. Pleasure. Our men will be agog. Americans rarely come to Cheltenbridge."

"Miss Moseley, you are too kind. But I assure you, American or not, I'm nothing extraordinary."

Una's brown eyes narrowed, though the crisply etched line of her pink mouth never wavered from a smile. "Indeed."

Lydia was introduced and joined them, her escort placing a saucer of champagne in her gloved hand as he took his leave. Eliza noted the slight tremor as Lydia lifted her glass to her lips. She wrapped a comforting arm around her sister's waist. Large gatherings among strangers always rattled Lydia.

"So, there's two of you. Polly, you didn't tell me *that*." Una smirked, studying Lydia. "And this one's even more exotic. What hope will the humble maidens of Hampshire have now?" Any pretense of friendliness had gone. There was nothing but icy disdain in Una's voice. Eliza's arm tightened protectively around her sister.

"Miss Sullivan! Miss Tourant!" It was Sarah, bustling up in penny-bright silk to save the treacherous conversation. "Getting acquainted,

I see." Her gaze lingered on Eliza's hoisted bosom as she took her hand in greeting. "My goodness. Your gown certainly flatters your . . . eyes. I just knew you and your sister would get all the attention tonight! People are positively abuzz. Let's introduce you to Grandmama. She's been anxious to meet you both. Come along now, let's show you off." Sarah crooked her arm through Eliza's elbow, her grasp firm as she pulled her away from Una. "A pit viper in silk, that one," she whispered. "Do be careful what you say around her. Both of them, rather. Polly has a gentle heart, but she can be swept away by envy and forget herself."

They trailed to the end of the long room, the eyes of the mingling guests falling on them as they passed. In a recessed alcove, an elderly woman with gaunt features sat upon a carpeted dais, surrounded by small dogs that resembled miniature prancing lions. She was dressed in full mourning, a dark crepe bonnet shadowing her wrinkled face, though her eyes were lively and keen, and they lit up when she saw Sarah. "Ah, granddaughter. Look at your gown. So exquisite. I see you took my advice and finally saw my seamstress."

Sarah gave a tight smile and dropped a curtsy. "Grandmama. You're sharp as ever. This is Elizabeth Sullivan and her sister, Lydia Tourant, from New Orleans. Remember, I told you all about them. Eliza has inherited Lady Sherbourne's estate."

"Oh, yes." Countess Gregory assessed Eliza and Lydia, an inscrutable expression playing over her face. "Lovely. Your gowns are from Worth?"

"Yes, my lady. We are honored to make your acquaintance." Eliza gave the deep curtsy she'd been taught at cotillion, her knees nearly folding to the floor.

Lady Gregory erupted in a gale of high-pitched laughter. The tiny dogs echoed with shrill barks. "Easy, child. Save your court curtsy for the queen. I'm not *that* important." The dowager shifted in her seat, leaning forward. "Bertie loves girls like you—saucy, decadent Americans with your new money." The dogs growled. "Oh, I know. I shouldn't call him Bertie. He's going to be our king soon, God save us." She sighed and sat back. One of the dogs hiked its leg and pissed on the countess's hem. Eliza bit her lip to stifle her grin.

"Eliza's mother was French," Sarah said. "Descended from Eleanor of Aquitaine."

"I know all about Theodora's French relatives and their supposed aristocratic ties, Sarah. It's not at all unique or special." Lady Gregory's lips hardened into a line across her face as she turned to address Eliza. "You have a fine country house now, Miss Sullivan, and you and your *Creole* sister may very well marry noble husbands as your kind seek to do, but I'm sorry. You'll never be one of us."

Eliza's shoulders stiffened and her smile faded. She glanced at Lydia. Her eyes glistened at their corners, her round cheeks flushing as burgundy as her ball gown.

"Grandmama!" Sarah admonished. "You promised."

Lady Gregory batted her fan. "Child, at my age, I'll speak my mind. These American chits are ever crossing the pond to snatch up our bachelors. And the scandals they bring!"

"My lady," Eliza said, her ears burning, "with all due respect, I did not come to Hampshire to seek a husband, but to collect my fortune. I am a businesswoman, not a debutante."

Lady Gregory gave a condescending smile. "Ah, an entrepreneur. Agriculture? Mining?"

"Horses, ma'am. Fast ones."

Lady Gregory laughed sharply. "Appropriate."

"Ma'am." Eliza bit the inside of her cheek and backed away. "I'm honored to have made your acquaintance."

Once they were out of earshot, Lydia grasped Eliza's hand. "I had no idea a member of polite society could be so rude."

"I'm stupefied," Eliza whispered. "The way she looked at us! Like we were common slatterns."

"We don't belong here, Liza. I want to go home."

Sarah caught up to them, white-faced and breathless. "Goodness. I'm so very sorry. My grandmother is old guard, and with that comes a hefty dose of prejudice. It's atrocious. I promise, I do not feel the way she does. Please, darlings, let's make merry. Your evening is not lost. You'll find the other ladies most agreeable."

While Eliza had her doubts, Sarah's garrulous manner couldn't help but put her at ease. She showed them to the refreshment room, babbling the whole way, where they had a light supper of kippers and cheese at the buffet. Even Lydia's mood improved after two tumblers of champagne punch. A bugle sounded, and Sarah and Polly led the way to the ballroom, where the orchestras were warming up on opposite ends of the room. Two lines began to form in the middle of the dance floor—on one side the ladies, on the other, the men.

"Come, let's have a turn!" said Sarah, grasping Eliza's hand and pulling her into the quadrille. As the men and women circled one another, there were very few faces that stood out to Eliza. Still, she met her would-be suitors, young and old alike, with courtesy as they sped through the steps of the dance. They were making their final pass through the room when she glimpsed a man standing at the top of the staircase. He was strikingly tall, dressed in well-cut white tie with a glimmering emerald peeking out from the folds of his lapel. He met her gaze and smiled. Eliza's stomach did a somersault.

"There's Viscount Havenwood," Sarah whispered as they passed each other down the line. "Malcolm."

She lost the dance as she followed Lord Havenwood with her eyes, standing up on tiptoes to see over the throng of revelers. Too late, she realized she hadn't taken a breath for some time. Black fringes clouded her vision and a distant ringing sang in her ears. As it had been threatening all evening, heat and ice enveloped her at the same time, the floor tilted at a mad angle, and all the air went out of the room. When she came to, the acrid smell of ammonia in her nostrils, she was lying on a divan in a narrow hallway. Her mouth felt as if someone had stuffed it full of mattress ticking.

Lydia was there, swabbing at her face with a cool cloth while a man with a blond moustache and spectacles leaned over her. "Ah. She's coming around. Hello, Miss Sullivan. I'm Dr. Fawcett—Clarence—the one what caught you. I'm only in medical school, but I can fetch Dr. Gilmore in a moment to have a proper look at you. I don't believe he saw you faint."

"No, no. I'm fine, really. I am." Eliza pushed up onto her elbows, her head swimming. "I've only laced my corset tighter than I should have."

"Are you quite sure you're all right?" Clarence asked, blinking. His spectacles made his gray eyes owlish and comically large for his face. "You may faint again if you exert yourself."

"I'll be careful, Doctor. I promise."

"Right." The doctor turned to Lydia, his mouth twitching beneath his moustache. "After your sister is recovered, I should like a place on your dance card, Miss Tourant, if you'd do me the honor."

Lydia beamed. "Of course! I'd be delighted."

He nodded. "Very good, very good. Do take your time getting up, Miss Sullivan. Have some water instead of champagne. And for goodness' sake, don't lace your corsets so tightly. Women's fashions can be such a danger in their frivolity."

Lydia helped Eliza loosen her stays in the washroom, going on about Dr. Fawcett's chivalry and strong arms as they made their way back to the outskirts of the ballroom. Thanks to Sarah, their dance cards were soon filled, and Eliza was kept busy turning waltzes in the arms of eligible men from all over the countryside. As for the mysterious Lord Havenwood, he'd disappeared as quickly as he'd arrived, much to Eliza's disappointment.

The orchestra struck up a boisterous polka, her least favorite dance. She thanked her partner and excused herself from the dance floor. As she made her way through the swirling skirts and feathered headdresses toward the refreshment room and its gloriously heaving dessert table, someone suddenly grasped her elbow—too firmly—and spun her around. She found herself face-to-cravat with a man. She lifted her eyes to a finely sculpted chin, a sandy flop of wavy hair, and a pair of sapphire-blue eyes. He was certainly a fine specimen of masculine charm, although a bit too bold in his advances for her tastes. As if sensing her discomfort, he released her elbow and gave a lopsided grin. "Miss Sullivan. Beg pardon. I was only coming to claim my spot on your dance card." He bowed stiffly. "Charles Lancashire, sixth Earl of Eastleigh."

Ah, the bachelor earl Mr. Brainerd had mentioned. Eliza quirked an eyebrow. "I don't recollect seeing your request on my card, Lord Eastleigh."

"Perhaps Lady Gregory didn't deign to tell you." He extended his hand. "We arranged it during your fainting spell. Shall we? The polka *is* my best dance."

She truly doubted that Lady Gregory would suddenly turn so solicitous, but who was she to spurn an earl? Especially with the clock ticking on a fortune that she might very well lose if she remained too reticent. With a resigned sigh, Eliza allowed herself to be led back to the dance floor. She soon regretted it.

Lord Eastleigh put her through the paces of the dance so quickly, and lifted her off her feet so many times, that breathing, much less conversation, proved nearly impossible. Infernally hot and hemmed in by strange faces, Eliza felt the need for air, or else she would faint again, just as Dr. Fawcett had warned. With a hasty apology, she broke away from Lord Eastleigh and rushed to the French doors lining the ballroom, relieved to see they led to an exterior balcony.

Alone and thankful for the quiet, she rested against the stone railing. The soft strains of a Brahms waltz floated through the closed doors. Eliza counted its steady three-four rhythm to control her breathing. Once her head had ceased its frantic spinning, she lifted her eyes and gazed out over the formal, manicured landscape below. A fog had begun to settle in the low places, the wild spikes of evergreens punctuating the mists beyond the gardens. It was lovely and cool, as far removed from the overcrowded ballroom as she could get at the moment.

"I saw you swoon. I do hope Fawcett was attentive to your needs. Our young doctor always seems to be at hand when the most attractive ladies need catching."

Eliza startled at the deep voice and turned from the railing, her heartbeat quickening. It was the viscount—Lord Havenwood. He strode into the yellow swatch of light filtering from the ballroom, tucking a long-stemmed smoking pipe into his waistcoat. He joined her at the balustrade, the earthy musk of saddle leather accompanying him. Up close, his features were lean and fine-boned, with high cheekbones and a well-cut jawline, surrounded by an abundance of curling, dark hair. He offered a smile, which thinned out his lips and gave him a wolfish demeanor. "You look frightened. Have I said something to alarm you?"

"Not at all, Lord Havenwood. I only thought I was alone."

"As did I," he said, his voice lifting. "I do hope I'm not a disappointment."

"Quite the contrary." She pulled in a deep breath and turned to face him, her hip pressing against the railing. "I was just taking in the view. We don't have landscapes like this where I'm from."

"New Orleans, isn't that right?"

"Yes. I suppose you've already heard all sorts of things about me."

"I daresay your arrival has been the favored talk of Cheltenbridge." He gave another teasing smile. "And if I may, Miss Sullivan, it appears I've been the subject of some prior conversation as well—we've yet to be formally introduced, though you've greeted me by name as if we had been."

"You've caught me off my manners. I fear my nerves have gotten the better of me tonight." She laughed, too brightly. "Sarah Nelson told me who you were when you came in."

"It's all right. I'm used to being talked about and your lack of guile is charming. I'd imagine it's quite tedious to be the shining new fish in a muddy, small pond."

"Yes, more than I expected. I'm not used to this kind of attention."

"Indeed. We're rather fond of American girls at the moment," he said. "You're so fresh, witty, and, well—rich. We've been conquered by our own beautiful traitors, it seems."

"I'm not so sure about the traitorous part, my lord," Eliza said coyly. "A certain river battle with cannons made it quite clear Louisiana would never become your colony."

"I suppose you're right." He lifted a brow. "Should we be enemies, then?"

"As we're neighbors, I'd rather not be." There was a heavy pause as the boldness of her words lingered between them. Eliza felt those marvelous eyes falling over her again—first on her hands, then on the pulsing hollow of her throat.

"I saw you on the night you arrived, you know."

"Oh?"

"At your window, before the storm. I'd heard a sound like a pistol shot and looked over my shoulder. The wind was blowing your night-gown about. I couldn't help but notice."

The sly innuendo in his voice met its mark. A flushing heat climbed from Eliza's bosom to her neck. Unbidden attraction danced within her anxiety—a swell of carnal tension that frightened as well as thrilled her. She suddenly wished she had a cigarette—anything to distract herself from the florid green of his eyes. He'd captured her attention as surely as if she'd been caught in a snare. "I . . . I saw you as well," she stammered. "You sit handsomely on your horse, Lord Havenwood."

"I do enjoy night rides. They bring me out of the dank air of Havenwood Manor. Do you ride, Miss Sullivan?"

"I grew up on a farm with stables. Thoroughbreds. I've been in the saddle since I was a girl."

"Perhaps we'll ride, then. When I come to call."

Eliza's mind swirled as she grasped for a response. Mon Dieu, where was her head? She closed her eyes and reopened them. "Yes, I'd . . ."

But her words had gone unheard. Where he'd been but a moment before, there were now only shadows.

CHAPTER 5

The front parlor of Sherbourne House resembled a fragrant conservatory, with vases sprouting from every surface. Lady Gregory's solstice ball had brought the kind of attention neither Eliza nor Lydia knew how to address, with cards arriving in a near-constant stream. They pored over each one as soon as it was delivered, but none bore the name Eliza was hoping to see.

Lydia wove her way through the flowers, exclaiming over the blushing folds of a damask rose or the perky face of a violet, while Eliza watched from the window seat, anxious to see if another messenger was coming up the path.

"These flowers came from Dr. Fawcett." Lydia tipped her nose into the petals of a white rose and inhaled. "I have never smelled such a divine fragrance. You simply must experience this!"

Eliza sneezed. "I shall take your word for it."

"Lord Eastleigh is coming to tea today. Do you remember him? He led you in that marvelous polka."

"Oh, yes. The most eligible bachelor in Hampshire. How could I forget? I nearly fainted again after dancing with him. I had to go out and take the air." Eliza gave up her vigil by the window and joined her sister, taking the shears Lydia offered and clipping the stem of a peony.

"That's where you disappeared to. I wondered. I was left alone with Miss Moseley. She didn't have anything pleasant to say about anyone. I'd the feeling she was vexed by our presence."

"I'd agree. Sarah warned me about her. She's certainly pretty. She should have little cause to feel threatened by us, though I'd warrant many of the ladies felt the same as she—they were only too polite to say so." A sheepish grin pulled at Eliza's mouth. "We did steal a lot of the attention, didn't we?"

"It was grand! I don't think I've ever had a dance card so full."

Eliza bit her lip and threaded the peony's verdant stem between a cluster of gladiolus in a crystal vase. "I met Viscount Havenwood. On the balcony."

"Oh? Did Sarah introduce you?"

"No, we were alone."

Lydia's eyes widened. "Liza! Did anyone see you?"

"No, cher—we were only outside for a few moments, but he was more charming than I expected—and wickedly attractive in an eccentric sort of way."

Lydia gave her a stern look. "Of course you'd fall for the scandalous one. You read far too many novels." She snipped the stems off a cluster of pinks and pushed them into a drinking glass. "Well, I've yet to see flowers or a card from him."

"The day isn't over yet. He did say he'd call." Eliza thought of the way Lord Havenwood had looked at her during their brief conversation and wondered if she'd imagined his interest.

"At any rate," Lydia said, "Lord Eastleigh will be here in less than an hour, and we'll be entertaining Mr. Dix and Sir Tate later this afternoon. Our social calendar is filling."

"It's a good thing we've gotten the gaslights working and the parlor shipshape. I'd like to take the silver out and polish it before asking anyone to dinner. It needs doing." Eliza's eyes flitted to the dusty gilded cherubs above the mantelpiece and the grate that needed a fresh coat of blackening. "I've a feeling something will always need doing in a house like this. Perhaps we should consider hiring help after all."

After helping Lydia arrange a few more of the bouquets throughout the room, Eliza excused herself to freshen up. As she slipped into her lilac tea gown trimmed with Valenciennes lace, she cast a look toward Havenwood Manor. Gray clouds hung low over its chimneys and the arched windows seemed darkly pensive, the shadows long under its eaves. It gave the structure an air of almost human melancholy. Eliza shook her head at her silliness. It was foolish to imagine a house could have feelings.

The tinkling doorbell rang, announcing Lord Eastleigh's arrival. She blew out an annoyed breath, put on her best debutante smile, and went down the stairs.

❦

"My father said to me, 'Charles, that chap has a foul temper and arms the size of an oak tree. Best to move on like a gentleman.' Alas, letting other people win isn't my strong suit."

Lord Eastleigh, impeccably dressed for the day in gray serge, was proving himself to be a blowhard and a braggart. Though the breeze on the open veranda was cool with the promise of rain and brought with it the fresh scent of summer roses, Eliza's mood was growing hotter by the minute. If there was one thing she couldn't abide in a man, it was abject arrogance, no matter how charming he might otherwise be.

"I rolled up my sleeves, handed my coat to my man, and engaged in a bout of fisticuffs right there at the betting counter," he continued. "Do you know I was undefeated as a boxer during my turn in the Royal Fusiliers? That chap soon found out why." Charles laughed. "I knocked him dead out with a single left hook to the chin."

Lydia batted her lashes over her teacup. "Lord Eastleigh, now that we've heard all about your exploits, perhaps you'd care to ask my sister about her own?"

Charles turned to Eliza, dabbing at his mouth with a napkin, delicate as any woman. "Yes, Miss Sullivan—please, do tell us about your latest square up."

"I hardly engage in fistfights, my lord. I tend to lean more toward the interest of business. Our family owned Thoroughbred stables in Louisiana. I was in charge of keeping our studbook and overseeing the breeding program."

"Is that so?" Charles asked. "I didn't take you for the horsey sort."

Eliza didn't know if *the horsey sort* was meant to be compliment or criticism. "My father came to America from Ireland as a young man, with nothing more than his knowledge of horses. He started out mucking stables for the plantation owners in Kentucky and got a good break, as they say. He became determined to create demand all over the world for the very best bloodlines. Our breeding stock has produced champion horseflesh as far away as India and even here, in England. I believe one of our derivatives won your Ascot Diamond Jubilee last week, making several of your compatriots quite wealthy—perhaps even that fellow you knocked out."

The earl looked at her, slack-jawed. "I had no idea . . ." He shook his head. "Should a woman really be versed in equine husbandry? It's all a bit coarse, don't you think?"

"My lord, women where I'm from learn to be savvy about agriculture at a young age—our mothers survived a war in which many of the menfolk died, after all. But I promise you, I do all the usual things as well. I embroider, I play the harp, I pour tea." She topped off his cup. "As a daughter of the old Creole aristocracy, my mother was quite eager to teach us those sorts of things."

Charles nodded, looking relieved.

"Our father, on the other hand, was keen to teach us how to survive in a man's world." Eliza fixed the earl with her gaze and gave a sweet smile. "Why, it's only natural for a stallion to cover a broodmare in estrus, if that's what you're considering coarse. I've never been fazed by it. I only see the vast amounts of money to be made."

Charles wrenched his mouth as if he had a sudden bout of indigestion and coughed into his napkin. Eliza went on. "In fact, I was hoping to begin a new enterprise right here, in Hampshire. The local gentry could benefit a great deal from my knowledge of horses."

"Right," Charles said. "But, if you were to *marry*—say an earl, or even a baronet—you'd inherit a large estate with as many grooms and servants as you'd see fit to employ. Your days would be spent in leisure, not at work. You'd need not lift a finger but to play your harp or embroider at your loom."

"You've forgotten about the work of bearing children, my lord. Wouldn't a countess be required to do that as part of her marriage contract?"

The red-faced earl was spared having to answer by Nigel, who appeared through the gates, his bicycle wobbling up the gravel drive. Eliza rose to greet him, her pulse quickening in anticipation. He parked his cycle against the hitching post and climbed the steps to present the envelope in his hand. "For you, Miss Sullivan."

The envelope was heavy, the weight of its paper demonstrating an eye for luxury. She turned it over, and a thrill went through her at the sight of the insignia on the wax seal—two serpents twining around a myrtle tree. The same crest adorned the gates of Havenwood Manor. Gates she'd visited on more than one occasion since her arrival, her fingertips skimming over the raised metal scales of its serpents as she peered through the bars to catch a glimpse of whatever mysteries lay beyond.

As Eliza turned back to the veranda, Lord Eastleigh stood, his blue eyes flickering with unease as she tucked the envelope inside the lace folds of her gown. "Are you well, Miss Sullivan? Your color has gone quite high. Feverish, even."

"Yes, my lord. Only, if you'd please excuse me for just a moment. This letter brings a matter of urgent import I must attend to."

"What is it?" Lydia asked, concern creasing her brow as she rose. "Bad news or good?"

"I'll explain later." With a hurried curtsy to their guest, Eliza went into the perfumed foyer, shutting the door behind her. She broke the seal with trembling fingers. Inside was an engraved card bearing a coat of arms and a message written in a decisive, bold stroke.

> *Malcolm Winfield*
> *5th Viscount Havenwood*

> *My dear Miss Sullivan,*
> *I should very much like to call on you this Saturday eve-*
> *ning if your calendar is not full. Even if it is, I should*
> *still like to whisk you away from your other suitors. It is*
> *most advisable to choose a worthy mount. Apollo likes to*
> *let loose at a run, as do I. Shall we?*
> *Regards,*
> *Malcolm Winfield,*
> *Lord Havenwood*

She pressed the cool paper against her heated face, smiling so hard that her cheeks ached. He'd made good on his word. His interest had been no vague imagining, and here was the proof. Aglow with infatuation, she took a few breaths to compose herself, then went out.

Lord Eastleigh stood. "I see from your smile your letter brought good news."

"Indeed, sir. It did."

"Oh," he said, lifting her hand, "it seems you've injured yourself." Sure enough, a slow trickle of blood ran between her thumb and fore-finger and dripped onto the pavers. "One must be careful opening let-ters, Miss Sullivan," Lord Eastleigh chided. "Some of them can cut like knives."

⟪✦⟫

After the teapot had been drained for the day and their final caller departed with hat in hands, Eliza sat at her desk to compose her response to Lord Havenwood. She sought the right words, studying the plaster ceiling and its latticework frieze. When she finally put her pen to paper, she grasped the barrel too tightly, snapping the nib within the first few strokes of her writing. She crumpled the ink-splattered paper into a ball, attached another nib, and, after dipping it into the inkwell, began again.

> *Lord Havenwood,*
> *I would very much enjoy entertaining you Saturday eve-ning. Come after dinner, at eight o'clock. I'll pack a picnic and we shall ride to the meadow to watch the sun go down.*
> *Fond regards,*
> *Miss Elizabeth Sullivan*

Eliza sat back, her rickety chair shrieking its displeasure. Did she sound too easy, too presumptuous? She wished courtship weren't such a game. He interested her far more than any of the others, but she mustn't seem entirely wanton, either. How quickly her mood had changed—from recalcitrant spinster to nervous maid—all because of a pair of wicked green eyes and a clever turn of phrase. She crumpled the letter in her hand and started yet again.

Lord Havenwood,
I would be pleased to ride out with you on Saturday
evening. Come after eight o'clock.
   Regards,
   Miss Elizabeth Sullivan

There. Simple, polite, and succinct. Before she could talk herself out of sending it, she sealed the envelope and addressed it. With a sigh, she flexed her fingers around the bandage she'd applied to her paper cut and turned to the pile of calling cards on her desk, trying to recall the faces belonging to the names. There was a sharp knock at her door. Without looking up, Eliza muttered a hasty "Come in."

Lydia padded in on stocking feet and sat on the foot of Eliza's bed. "Look at all your cards! Is there anyone else you'd like to invite for tea?"

"Only Lord Havenwood. I've just written my response."

"I do wish you'd consider entertaining others, even for propriety's sake," Lydia said. "I'm having two of the gentlemen I danced with over tomorrow—one of them is a barrister and the other a navy lieutenant. Isn't it funny how the British say *lieutenant*?" She giggled and stretched her arms overhead with a voluptuous yawn. "Lord Eastleigh is intriguing, isn't he? He's completely smitten with you. I've invited him to dinner Saturday evening. I learned today while you were inside that he has three estates and may soon acquire another!"

"That's all very well, and while he may be rich, his arrogance is off-putting. He also strikes me as something of a playboy. He's every bit of thirty, yet unmarried. We'd be ill suited, I'd warrant. He sparks nothing in me but anxiety and irritation."

"I'll admit, he's a bit brash for my tastes, but perhaps you should give things a chance. What did you think of Mr. Dix and Sir Tate? I found both to be polite and steady."

"And boring." Eliza flopped down on the lumpy mattress next to Lydia, kicking her slippers off. "Mr. Dix is so soft-spoken I could barely hear him, and Sir Tate is but two moons from the morgue. Besides, you're one to talk. All I've heard since this courtship business began is Dr. Fawcett this, Dr. Fawcett that." Eliza rolled onto her back, gazing up at the faded velvet canopy. "I'm afraid no one else has intrigued me in the way of Lord Havenwood. I was surprised how intensely I was drawn to him—it was positively magnetic, Lyddie. Like I'd been hit with a galvanic charge!"

Lydia frowned. "You're being impulsive. For someone who was so contrary to courtship and marriage just a day or so ago, you've gotten yourself nearly betrothed to him. Don't the rumors bother you? Polly told me more. It's all scandalous. Every last thing."

"I really don't care to know what she said. She's a gossip and I'd rather hear the story from Lord Havenwood himself before I make any judgments." Eliza turned onto her side and linked her fingers with Lydia's. "I'm learning to trust my gut, sister. I feel he's only misunderstood and perhaps a bit lonely. There's something maudlin in his eyes—it makes me want to learn more about him. And that house! It's really something, isn't it?"

"Something haunted and falling down! Remember—a bit of a rivalry between suitors would do no harm. I've a feeling Lord Eastleigh won't be easily persuaded from courting you. You'd do well to consider his attentions, if only to annoy Polly Whitby." A slow smile spread across Lydia's lips. "I hear she's struck on him."

Eliza laughed and sat up. "Now that *would* be entertaining. He's certainly pretty to look at, and I *am* on a tight schedule. Have him round for dinner if you'd like on Saturday, but I'll be riding out with Lord Havenwood afterward."

"By yourself?"

"We only have one horse."

"Which we *could* attach to the gig."

"Lydia, I'll be fine. I have two sharpened hatpins and I'd wager my right hook is meaner than Lord Eastleigh's left."

CHAPTER 6

Despite Lydia's many attempts at turning the conversation, Lord Eastleigh's favorite subject at dinner proved to be the same as it had been at tea—himself. His stories of manly prowess were tempered only by his demands for wine. One decanter was drained well before the bouillabaisse went cold, and while the earl was rather more florid in complexion than he had been on arrival, he was demonstrating he could drink any man, or woman, under a table.

As for Eliza, her eyes were fixed on her hard-won cuckoo clock in the hallway. They'd served dinner an hour early to avoid a confrontation between suitors, but the time of her outing with Lord Havenwood was drawing perilously near. Time to get things moving.

After they finished the final course, Eliza rose, her wineglass held high for a toast. "To you, Lord Eastleigh, for illumining us with your wit and irrepressible . . . confidence." Eliza smiled tightly, tapping the toe of her slipper on the rug. "Now, shall I see you to your carriage?"

Charles gulped down the last of his wine, setting the goblet hard on the table. "Indeed, Miss Sullivan. There's a matter I'd like to discuss with you in private." He gave an obliging nod to Lydia and offered his arm to Eliza. As they went outside, he turned and took her hand. "Some concerning things have come to light, and I feel I must be frank with you, for your own benefit."

"Oh?"

"I hear I may not be your only suitor." He paused, fixing her with his cool gaze. "I've heard Havenwood means to sink his talons in."

"Why, I've only met Lord Havenwood once, at Lady Gregory's ball. We've barely spoken ten words to one another."

"He's a dangerous man. Ask around. You needn't hear it only from me."

Eliza measured the guarded anger in his words and the tension in his long-fingered grasp. He was jealous. *Letting other people win isn't my strong suit.*

So. She'd become a prize. A conquest.

Eliza jerked her hand from his, heat running through her veins. "My temperament dictates I make up my own mind about people, Lord Eastleigh. As I do not know the man well, I shall refrain from thinking ill of him until he demonstrates reason to regard him poorly."

"That's all very admirable, but you should know the scandal has its basis in fact—that fire was no accident, and his mother's disappearance holds suspicion of murder. She knew certain things about her son— things he'd never want revealed. There's a darkness in him you'd do well to regard with caution."

"And what would Lord Havenwood have to say about *you*, sir?"

Charles's smile faded. "Your cheek does not suit a lady, Miss Sullivan. I've business to attend to in London, but I'll be around to call upon my return. Do *not* entertain other suitors. Mark me—I will be your strongest ally here in Hampshire. One you'd do well to indulge if you'd see your successes manifest." He lifted the brim of his hat, then turned on his heel to go to his coach-and-four.

Eliza exhaled, hugging her pelisse around her shoulders. As soon as he'd gotten far enough down the drive that she could no longer see the white plumes of his horses, she turned to go inside.

Lydia was standing on the terrace steps. "I heard everything. Was he threatening you?"

"I'm not sure, but it seemed that way." Eliza hurried through the doors and took the stairs to her room two at a time. She kicked off her shoes as she struggled out of her dinner gown, sending a button skittering across the worn carpet. "He sets my nerves on edge. And how on earth did he know Lord Havenwood was calling on me?"

"It certainly wasn't me! If I had to venture a guess, I'd say it was a certain blond-haired, blue-eyed gossip," Lydia said, shaking her head. "If she has designs on Lord Eastleigh, she'd have reason to let him know you've been entertaining other suitors, wouldn't she?"

"Our business will get around much too quickly in this little village, I'm afraid." Eliza stepped out of her petticoats and into a pair of dark-green riding trousers, styled so they looked like a voluminous skirt. Next came a high-necked shirtwaist and a cropped velvet jacket with frog closures.

The bell rang downstairs, echoing through the house.

"He's here," Lydia said. "I'll see him in. You really should have me chaperone, especially after all that. It'll breed more gossip if you go out alone on a ramble with him. Think of your reputation! And what if he's as bad as they say he is?"

"Don't worry, sister. My reputation has been muddied before, and as for protection, I can handle myself." Eliza pulled two wickedly sharp hatpins from her dressing table drawer and pinned her riding hat at a jaunty angle. "I'm not a scared little girl."

"All right. But don't go too far, and if you're late coming home, I'll send out a search party. I do mean that. With lanterns and guns and great barking dogs."

A hiccup of laughter burst from Eliza's lips. "And you say *I'm* dramatic."

Lydia swept from the room, muttering to herself. Within a few moments, Eliza heard Lord Havenwood's voice floating up from the foyer. She shook off her nerves and walked decisively to the stairs, her riding crop in hand.

As she turned the corner on the balustrade, she saw him. His back was to her—his shoulders broad, the rest of him lean. He was kitted out in well-worn but once-fine riding gear, with leather boots up to his thighs, trimmed with silver spurs. When he heard her step, he turned, his lips widening into a vulpine grin. Eliza's stomach and heart lurched at once, as if she'd ridden too fast down a hill. As she drew near, she noticed the ring of amber rimming his viridian irises like fire, flaring as they took her in.

Eyes of amber and of green, a courageous heart and a noble mien. Eliza thought of the silly childhood love spell she had cast to the wind so many years ago—in the days when she still believed in magic, true love, and the fantastical.

"Miss Sullivan, how eagerly I've awaited this evening." Malcolm offered his hand as she descended the stairs.

When they touched, the same powerful kick of attraction she'd felt the night they met soared through her. "Lord Havenwood. I'm ever as pleased."

They went out, and Eliza was grateful for the coolness of the evening air on her flaming cheeks. Two horses stood tethered to the hitching posts in front of the house—one as massive and dark as fresh coal and the other as pale and fine-boned as a goat.

"This is Apollo," Malcolm said, leading her to his horse. "He looks like the devil but he's gentle as a lamb."

"He's a Friesian, isn't he?"

"Yes. How astute of you."

"If there's one thing I know, my lord, it's horses." She stroked the arching line of Apollo's neck and he whickered at her softly, then bent his head to snuff her other hand.

"He thinks you might have a carrot," Malcolm said, laughing. "I've got him a bit spoiled."

"Just like my Hercules. Only with him, it was sugar cubes."

"You'll surely conquer him if you ever offer him sugar, and I may jolly well find myself without a horse. Shall we?"

"Of course." Eliza went to Star, Theo's little Arab gelding. At her gentle touch on his flank, he raised his pale head and looked at her with wary eyes. Eliza stepped into the stirrups, then swung her leg over Star's back. She took her time settling into her saddle under Malcolm's gaze. "Still think me a lady?" she asked, arching a brow at him.

He mounted Apollo and winked at her. "I think you're every bit my match."

"We'll see." She returned his wink and nudged Star with the heel of her boots. He was off, his white tail arching into the air as she urged him on with her crop, rising up in her stirrups and racing down the long driveway. Mr. Mason jumped to attention, cranking the gate open just in time.

Apollo's heavy stride pounded the earth behind her as they galloped into the shaded expanse of the birchwood forest. At times, the big horse's breath was hot upon her neck as Malcolm began to gain ground—but unlike Star, his horse was meant for long journeys pulling artillery carts and carrying warriors in armor, not for speed. After running on a bit with the lead, Eliza let off her crop, content she'd proved her prowess.

As they came out onto the meadow's wind-ruffled grass, Malcolm overtook her. He galloped on for a bit, then slowed Apollo to a high-stepping trot at the bottom of a low hillock, its edges touched with orange light from the fading sun. He dismounted as she brought Star up next to him. "You let me win," he teased.

"Perhaps, but I've never had so much fun letting someone win, my lord. I've been longing to go on a proper ride ever since I arrived. Thank you for taking me out of that musty parlor and its endless cups of tea." Eliza pitched forward to dismount. As she'd hoped, Malcolm grasped her by the waist as she swung her leg over the saddle, easing her gently down, just as Jacob had always done after her riding lessons.

"Are our proper English courtship rituals boring you already?" Malcolm asked, his hands lingering on her hips.

"Yes," she said, tapping his shoulder playfully with her riding crop. "And I'm quite ready to be done with any kind of boredom."

His lips quirked up in a smile. "We'll not have any, then."

"We're already leagues ahead." Eliza reached into the pannier buckled to Star's saddle and brought out a bottle of claret, handing it to Malcolm, along with two tin cups. He uncorked the wine and poured as she spread a blanket on the ground and settled there, tucking her legs beneath her.

He folded himself down next to her, clinking his cup to hers. "Cheers to adventure and drinking much more wine than tea."

They sat for a while in companionable silence, enjoying the pastoral beauty of the countryside. The sun was a sultry glow in the distance, turning the skies to a streaming, mottled fuchsia and the distant hills to the shade of plum worn in mourning. Great birds of prey shrieked and called as they chased one another, darting and diving into the feathered heads of Queen Anne's lace and yarrow before night forced them to their nests. The wind, with its earthy midsummer fragrance, brought a redolent sensuality to the moment. Eliza reached up to remove her hat, then unbound the twist of hair from her nape, letting her thick waves fall free.

"A proper lady would never let down her hair in front of any man but her husband, you know. It's incredibly seductive."

Eliza lay back with a sigh. "Well, I'm not a proper lady and I'm tired of rules and etiquette. It's all I've heard since I was a girl and my mother began grooming me for society."

"Mothers only want what they think best for their children, don't you agree?"

"You're far too generous. My mother only wanted what was best for herself. I disappointed her as a daughter. She wanted me to marry a wealthy Creole planter from an old family—to have a fine house and well-dressed children she could trot out to her society friends."

"And yet here you are in the hinterlands, mingling with the mongrel nobility and defying her still. You should set your sights a bit higher. A London duke, perhaps." He smiled, the corners of his eyes crinkling. His features were almost feminine in their fineness—there was something of the Renaissance in his face. Eliza imagined his lips pressing against her own, and her skin warmed at the thought.

"I'm certainly not an Astor. But if you happen to know a London duke in need of a wife, perhaps you could be of assistance. It seems I'm to find a husband after all, although that was the least of my concerns upon coming here." Eliza was stunned at the flagrance of her own words. Words any suitor would take as an invitation.

"Isn't it common for a woman of your age to be searching for a husband?"

"That's the usual story, isn't it?" Eliza rolled onto her side, propping herself on one elbow to regard Malcolm. "I'd always imagined myself as a bluestocking, traveling the world and taking lovers at a whim. I am irascible and decadent. A bit whiny, too. Hardly the qualities most men favor in a wife."

"You certainly are forthright." He cocked an eyebrow at her. "And perhaps a bit spoiled."

"One of my many flaws, I suppose." Eliza plucked a daisy from the grass and put it to her nose, gazing at Malcolm above its petals. "What, or rather whom, do *you* see for yourself, my lord? An actress or an opera singer? Perhaps a continental mistress that you need only see twice a year?"

"My." He laughed. "Your candor is outlandish, but refreshing all the same. My father wanted me to settle down with one of the local girls, but I've always imagined marrying someone more adventurous. Someone a bit less inhibited."

"Less inhibited?" She gave a coquettish grin. "I'd be curious to hear how I differ from the ladies of Hampshire. And no more of this American girl business, if you please."

Malcolm leaned back on an elbow and looked up at the sky, thinking. "I'd say it's your snap, your disregard for propriety, and your marvelous hair." He wound a strand of it around his finger. "It's the color of the best kind of marmalade, and I rather like marmalade." The coil of hair sprung from his grasp and fell back onto the striped cloth of their shared blanket. "And do you find anything at all fascinating about me, Miss Sullivan?"

So much. "Your title," she teased. "And only that."

"How disappointingly predictable. Do be serious."

"You'd want me to show my hand already? Where's the fun in that?"

He met her gaze, his eyes holding hers captive. "I'm quite adept at games, but I'd prefer not to play them with you, darling. I haven't had cause or desire to call on a woman for quite some time. You may read my hand however you wish."

The heady tension that had marked their very first encounter crackled between them. Suddenly shy, Eliza turned her attention to the daisy in her hands, shredding its petals, then tossing it aside. Malcolm sat up and pulled his long-stemmed smoking pipe from his jacket, and without lighting it, let it dangle from his lips. Out over the heath, a thin scrim of golden light was all that separated day from twilight.

"We're moving into the gloaming, I'm afraid." Malcolm gestured toward the darkening sky. "Our time together shan't last much longer if we're going to care at all about being proper."

"I'm not concerned. Are you?" Eliza said.

He smiled. "Very well then. Tell me about your New Orleans. I've only ever been to New York, when I was just a boy."

"It's a strange city, unlike any other, I'd say—embraced by a great, roping river like your Thames that gives and takes life. There's a white cathedral facing the water, with three spires and bells that chime a carillon on top of each hour. Springtime is my favorite season, when the bougainvillea begins to bloom. The petals dance over the streets, all pink and scarlet. It's so humid in the summer that to sleep in clothing is foolish, but in wintertime, snow never falls. Autumn is horrid. That's when the winds come. They howl and shake everything in their path. The floods come after—bringing fevers and death."

"It sounds terribly dramatic, but you make me want to leave everything I know and go there. Won't you miss it?"

Eliza swallowed the catch in her throat as she remembered the stench inside the Metairie farmhouse and the greedy buzz of flies in the darkened, sweltering sickroom. She shook her head. "No, my lord. There are certain things I will remember with fondness, but I will never return. I'm a bit like Lot—I'll only push forward and dare not look back." She shifted uneasily and studied the scuffed toe of her riding boot. "There's nothing there for me anymore."

Malcolm gave a remote smile, as if an old memory had chimed somewhere in his heart. "I admit I've wondered if I'd feel the same about Hampshire and Havenwood Manor if I ever left. Everyone sees a crumbling, tired mansion and a scandal. It all feels a bit like a jailer's chain at times, but I remember when the manor was grand. I have hope that it will be again. Houses have a certain power, don't you think? Almost as if they're people—or perhaps characters in a play."

"Your home reminds me of a house from a fairy tale."

He chuckled. "Don't you mean a ghost story?"

"I'd imagine it has all kinds of stories caught up within its eaves. I confess I've gone smitten with what might be hidden beyond your gates."

"I promise there's nothing more exciting knocking about Havenwood than a few squirrels and bats. Your romantic sensibilities might be disappointed if you're expecting Northanger Abbey." Malcolm tucked his pipe into his pocket. "Still, it's not without its charms." He was pensive for a moment before looking at her again, a mischievous smile playing at the corners of his mouth. "Would you like to see it?"

A frisson ran through Eliza. "Do you mean tonight?"

He laughed at her girlish excitement and helped her to her feet. "It's rather brash, but then again, so is our picnic. The scandal has already been made, I'm afraid, but I'm quite used to scandal. One truly begins living once they no longer hold the opinions of others in high regard." He pushed a wayward strand of hair away from her eyes, and Eliza shivered under his touch. "And besides . . . I'm finding I'm not ready for our night to end just yet. Only do wind your hair up, lest the good people of Cheltenbridge think I've led you completely down the path of debauchery."

Eliza did as he asked, knotting her hair back into her tortoise-shell comb with shaking fingers. They packed up the remains of their repast and mounted their horses. Malcolm led the way back over the heath and onto the lane. The moon had risen over the trees, glowing full and bright as they rode past Sherbourne House, its warm lights shining within. Eliza imagined Lydia watching anxiously through the windows—ever concerned with propriety and caution.

When they reached Havenwood Manor, Malcolm dismounted and produced a ring of keys from beneath his waistcoat. He unlocked the latch on the gate, the jeweled eyes of its twin serpents glittering, and took the reins of Eliza's horse to lead her through. As he pulled the gate closed and locked it behind them, a brief wave of dismay rose up in Eliza at the thought of confinement and all it implied. What if the stories about him were true?

"I can see your concern. I only value my privacy, darling." Malcolm offered his hand as she dismounted. "Despite all reports to the contrary, I *am* a gentleman. Your virtue is safe."

Eliza took his arm as they made their way up a sloping rise, past a silent fountain with algae greening the curves of the maiden who stood at its middle, her hands raising a chalice overhead. The shrubbery grew close on the path, thorns reaching out to grasp at Eliza's riding habit. Within a few yards of the gate, they emerged into a courtyard, knee-length grass sprouting between the pavers. The mansion loomed before them like a vast ship, much larger than it had seemed from her window, its chimneys pushing high into the purple sky.

The heavy door creaked open. A pale face floated in the dark chasm. "Oh, it's only you, m'lord."

"I've brought Miss Sullivan around to see the house, Turner. She believes it to be full of vampires, ghouls, and all manner of fantastic creatures."

The butler smiled down at Eliza. "Good evening, miss. We don't have much in the way of all that, I'm afraid, but we've a splendid whisky that will warm you right up. Bit of a chill in the air for June. Shall I wake Mrs. Duncan to chaperone?"

"That won't be necessary, Mr. Turner," Eliza answered. "Although a dram of your Scotch sounds perfectly delightful."

The butler ushered them inside, and Eliza's eyes widened in covetous wonder. They stood in an elegant foyer, three stories high, punctuated by a skylight that shone like a great eye, spilling moonlight instead of tears. A grand staircase dominated the room and broke into two galleries over the yellow-veined marble floor. The plasterwork ceiling was as magnificent as any cathedral—vaulted arches curved from each corner and leapt with seraphim. The wood-paneled walls and dentil molding harkened back to the last century, and while there was a faint hint of must and dampness in the air, the front drawing room glowed welcoming and warm. A fire crackled in the hearth while an unseen gramophone played Puccini from another room. Eliza felt as if she'd entered a dream in which every fantastic thought of the house she'd imagined had manifested. As if she'd cast a spell and made it her own.

The butler brought their Scotch, and Malcolm poured a tumbler of the whisky for Eliza, his lips curving into a smile. "Welcome to Havenwood Manor, Miss Sullivan. I do hope it won't disappoint."

CHAPTER 7

As Malcolm led her through the house, pausing to describe the renovations his predecessors had made through the years, Eliza's curiosity was piqued at every turn. Each room felt like opening a treasure chest, each discovery more extraordinary than the last.

First there was a magnificent library with books shelved neatly to the ceiling and the gramophone she'd heard from the hall. Beyond, she glimpsed a cozy study with a handsome desk and leaded windows. The dining room boasted a long, polished table with high-backed, throne-like chairs. Eliza imagined men with devilish, pointed beards sitting around it, clutching tankards of ale. "It's been in my family since the Reformation, when my father's ancestors lived in Yorkshire," Malcolm said, brushing its shining surface with his fingertips. "We hid Catholic priests in the foundation of that house, as it's rumored, all while pledging support for our Protestant king. The Winfields have ever played both sides of the coin."

He led her up the curving staircase, its newel post illuminated by an angel holding a lantern aloft. High above the landing, elaborate stained glass windows winked promisingly. Eliza could only imagine the brilliance of their tableaus spilling across the stairs in the light of day.

Malcolm opened a set of ornate carved doors on the landing and, apologizing for the lack of electricity, turned a key set into the wall.

He produced a long match from his pocket and raised it to a sconce on the wall. With a pop, it ignited, and light crept into every corner of the long, narrow room. Eliza's imagination did not go unrewarded. As Malcolm lit the candelabras one by one, the portraits of his ancestors emerged from carved niches. He introduced them all, from the bewigged Scottish lord who had survived the Jacobite rebellion by selling secrets to the English, to the known counterfeiter who had won his earlship from Henry VIII during a card game. "Philanders, fools, and unrepentant thieves—the very lot of us," he said playfully.

"And deadly charming, I daresay." In the corner, half-shrouded by shadow, Eliza caught a glimpse of a portrait. In it, a striking woman wore a dress the color of emeralds. She was a sylph—tall and regal, with luminous skin and dark hair. Her pale-green eyes stared back at Eliza. It was as if the painter had captured her in the midst of some unknowable secret. "And who is this ravishing beauty?"

"Ah," Malcolm said, stopping before the portrait, his hands clasped behind his back. "*That* is my lady mother."

"You favor her. She's lovely."

"She was beautiful, wasn't she? But very sad, I'm afraid." Malcolm grew quiet, his countenance falling. It was a look Eliza recognized—one she'd worn for years—her hollow eyes peering out from mirrors veiled in black.

After turning down the lights, Malcolm led her through a set of doors at one end of the ballroom. They emerged onto a wrought iron balcony. They were in the two-story conservatory she'd seen from her room at Sherbourne House. Eliza tilted her head back, unable to restrain the gasp of delight that escaped her lips. Stars glittered through the glass ceiling, and the moon shone above them, round as a Chinese lantern. It was enchanting.

Malcolm offered his arm, and they walked down the spiral staircase to the brick-paved floor. They trailed along the hothouse path until they came to a wicker settee where he invited her to sit. He took the chair facing her, removing the globe from a garden lantern and lighting it with a match. The smell of sulfur bloomed as the flame leapt about wildly, illuminating his eyes with tiny pinpoints of light. His features were sharper in the flickering glow—wolfish and feral.

"Your home is every bit as lovely as I'd imagined, Lord Havenwood."

"I've only shown you the best of it, I'm afraid. I would show you the rest, but it's far too dangerous to go into the south wing. After the fire, the structure was compromised."

"I saw the burned rafters from my room. What happened?"

Malcolm gave a contemptuous sniff. "You mean to say no one has told you about our fire? It's the favored story to be tossed about over brandy."

"Polly Whitby told me a little, but she seemed reluctant to say much," Eliza lied.

"That was kind of her."

"She did tell me that your father and your brother died that night. I'm sorry. I know what it's like to lose your family—my parents died of yellow fever a few years ago. It was gut-wrenching. I don't think I shall ever recover from the memory of it."

Malcolm nodded. "Wretched, isn't it? Our fire was horrific. It started suddenly, at midwinter, in the wee hours of morning. By the time I woke, Father had already died trying to save my brother, whose chambers were in the south wing. The balcony gave way as he ran to wake Gabriel, and the roof collapsed in on them."

"And your mother?"

"She made it out of the house with me, and we went to an inn in the village while the fire crew and our staff worked to salvage as much of the house as possible. When I woke the following morning, she was gone. I believe it was all too much for her. She has—*had*—a fragile constitution."

"They've never found her?"

"No, but that isn't unusual in these parts. She could have fallen into a ravine. Drowned in the river. There are wild animals about . . ." Malcolm looked away, shifting in his chair. "Quite the bubbling conversation for our first outing."

"Forgive me," Eliza said. She reached for his hand, and he gave it, his fingers warm in her own. His vulnerability touched her, made her long to offer the kinds of comforting words she'd never received. "I only wanted to hear what happened from you, not someone else."

"I do appreciate that. The vilest rumor, which you will hear soon enough if you haven't already, is that I started the fire on purpose to secure my position as viscount."

"Whyever would anyone think that?"

Malcolm stiffened and pulled his hand from hers. "It's rather a long story." He stood, helping her to her feet. "I'm so sorry. It's been such a long time since I've had anyone to talk to, and I've kept you too late as it is. Doubtless your sister thinks I have you trussed up in a dungeon."

Malcolm's mood was somber as they made their way back through the house, the awkwardness between them lingering as she bid goodnight to his kindly butler. She cast a look toward Havenwood's tower window as they crossed the courtyard. A lingering sense of sadness emanated from the house as the wind whistled through its eaves.

At the gate, Malcolm helped her into her saddle. They rode in silence back to Sherbourne House, where Lydia stood in the lantern light beneath the portico, her arms crossed. Malcolm went to greet her and they exchanged a few hushed words. Eliza strained to listen as she busied herself with picking brambles out of Star's mane.

After a few moments, Lord Havenwood's long shadow fell over her. "Your sister is quite protective of you."

"Yes, Lydia takes her role as the much wiser younger sister seriously," Eliza said, laughing. "Perhaps too seriously."

"Right," he said, smiling. "After I was scolded for keeping you out late, she graciously extended an invitation for me to call on you again—so long as she can chaperone." Malcolm's eyes held her own as he took her hand. "I should very much like to see you again, Miss Sullivan, if you'd do me the honor. Please know I have nothing to offer, other than a paltry title and a crumbling mansion, but my intentions are earnest. You have a true and honest heart, I think. A rare thing in a world such as this."

Eliza's words tripped over her tongue. "I . . . I should very much like that, Lord Havenwood. Yes. I believe I would." A feverish glow rose to her cheeks as he lifted her hand to his lips and kissed it.

Casting a long look at her before turning, he mounted Apollo and cantered away. Eliza watched until the darkness of horse and rider became one with the darkness of the night sky.

CHAPTER 8

High summer in Hampshire was a thing of verdant beauty, and Sherbourne House gleamed like a golden coin within it. Eliza and Lydia had made the house their own, and every vinegar-polished windowpane and wooden chair rail shone with proof of their housekeeping. It had become an airy, restful place, with light and freshness spilling into every room. Clarence Fawcett, who had taken rather keenly to Lydia and had a habit of dropping in for dinner every evening after his rounds, enthused over their care of the mansion, even going so far as to say it rivaled the cleanliness of his own hospital ward. At this, Lydia had beamed with pride.

Even still, for Eliza, Sherbourne House was no match for Havenwood Manor and the man who lived within it. It had been over two weeks since her outing with Malcolm, and Eliza was worried. She'd received no further correspondence from him, and as July stretched onward, her anxiety grew. Each night, she cast a pensive look toward the manor, watching its lights flicker on as dusk lay over the day like a heavy cloud.

As for Lord Eastleigh, he'd sent a card and flowers—a mass of love-lies-bleeding accented with the hideous white lilies that reminded her of death. Eliza threw the garish bouquet into the rubbish heap. She was quite decided. Whether Malcolm continued to court her or not, and despite the looming threat to her inheritance, Charles Lancashire did not wear the shoes of a future husband, earl or not. She only hoped he hadn't been meddling in her affairs behind the scenes as he'd threatened, and that Malcolm's absence wasn't the result.

Eliza was filling her mop bucket at the outdoor pump when Nigel came up the path, wearing his cap low over his eyes. After greeting him, she said, "Nigel, I've been wondering about something. It seems as if my business is getting out, and it hasn't been me sharing it. Would you have any idea as to how Lord Eastleigh might have known about my other callers?"

The boy took off his cap and twirled it in his hand, avoiding her gaze.

"Nigel?"

"I'm sorry, miss. I wouldn't know anything about Lord Eastleigh." He shuffled his feet in the gravel. "It's only. Well. It's just that Miss Moseley pays me to tell her the comings and goings on the lane. And me ma can't work, so I do need the money."

Ah. It *hadn't* been Polly, as Lydia had suspected. It had been Una Moseley. But why? Something wasn't adding up.

She offered Nigel a careful smile. "It's all right, Nigel. I'll gladly pay you double what Miss Moseley does to keep my correspondence confidential." His eyes widened, the skin behind his freckles blanching. "Now, what does she pay you, darling?"

"A thruppence, miss."

Eliza laughed. Sold for a pittance!

"I'd say your kind of superior confidentiality is worth at least ten *shillings* a month."

"Really?"

Eliza winked. "Absolutely." She pulled the coins from her apron pocket and placed them in the boy's outstretched hand. "Now, should I hear you've been telling my secrets . . ."

"I'll do no such thing, miss! I swear it. You can trust me to be true."

"I'll hold you to it. Now, do you have anything for me?"

"Only a letter from Lord Havenwood."

Eliza took the envelope from Nigel and excitedly broke Malcolm's seal. Inside was a handwritten note, folded around a charcoal sketch. It showed her in profile, sitting on the heath, her features finely rendered. His talent was formidable.

> *Miss Sullivan,*
>
> *I've become spellbound, I'm afraid. You did not tell me you were a witch. That would have been the kind thing to do, as you now have me in the worst state of distraction, and my fate seems perilously sealed. I've thought often of our most inappropriate outing . . . and of you. I do hope you'll enjoy my sketch. It may not do you justice, but I was inspired to set it upon paper all the same.*
>
> *I'd like to invite you and your concerned sister for a constitutional by the Avon tomorrow. This will no doubt enforce the blight upon your good reputation, being seen with me in public, but it is my solemn duty to give the townspeople something to talk about.*
>
> *In all seriousness, I am attempting to convey my irrepressible desire to woo you, only you, exclusively and in earnest. I'll meet you on the promenade at half past two Saturday if you still find me agreeable.*
>
> *Fondly,*
>
> *Malcolm*

Eliza's face went wild with color. His words nearly had her in a swoon. *Irrepressible desire, spellbound* . . . It was all too heady and delicious. With a smile, she folded the pages and tucked them into her bodice. She bid Nigel farewell, went inside, and bustled down the hall to the kitchen, where Lydia stood chopping onions. "Sister, Lord Havenwood has invited us to take the air tomorrow afternoon!"

Lydia looked up from her work, wiping her streaming eyes with the tail of her apron. "Oh? How delightfully proper. You must wear your blue lawn—the one with the ruffles and Alençon lace. It draws the eye so much better than any of your others."

Whatever her reservations about Una's snooping and Lord Eastleigh's veiled threats, her courtship with Malcolm was about to become common knowledge within Cheltenbridge.

❦

Eliza and Lydia strolled arm in arm along the river promenade, the feathers in their wide-brimmed hats casting nodding shadows on the pavers. There was a weekend fair going on, complete with roving jugglers and carnival games. The delicious aromas of roasted peanuts and fish and chips made Eliza's stomach rumble. Truthfully, her appetite had suffered of late; she'd been far too consumed with ardent feelings and fantasies—the kind of romantic nonsense that made schoolgirls doodle in the margins of notebooks and whisper their beloved's name beneath their breath. She was growing far too old for such things, but heavens, this infatuation was a pleasant surprise, all the same.

And there he was, the object of her affection: dressed in dark blue, his silver-topped walking stick swinging in a jaunty fashion as he came down the path, his straw hat tilted at a rakish angle.

"He's a bit of a dandy, isn't he?" Lydia said. "Far too pretty for a man, in my opinion."

"Oh, Lyddie. Don't be so cutting. I think he looks smashing. They can't all be Dr. Fawcett."

Malcolm's face brightened as he drew near. "Ah, Miss Sullivan and Miss Tourant," he said, sweeping his hat from his head. "I do hope you've been well. You're looking twice as lovely as I imagined you would."

"I've been well—but I was even better upon receiving your note, Lord Havenwood," Eliza said, dropping a quick curtsy as her lips tilted into a flirtatious smile. "Your talent is superb, and your rendering of my countenance too kind."

"Yes, well. Only something I dabble in when I'm feeling inspired." Malcolm offered his arm and they walked on for a bit, following the curve of the river. Townspeople craned their necks to watch as he led them to a gazebo overlooking the water.

"People are certainly paying attention, if that's what you wanted," Eliza said. "We're quite the sideshow."

"I don't often make public appearances. It's much easier for me that way." Malcolm motioned to the wrought iron benches in the middle of the gazebo. "Please sit. The barmaids from the Rose come around with ale and cider, if you'd fancy a pint."

They sat, Malcolm facing Eliza as Lydia sank down at her side. Below, children were splashing in the shallows of the river, screaming and laughing in their play. An unbidden memory flashed through Eliza's mind and she closed her eyes briefly against it. She took a breath to center herself, focusing on Malcolm and the way his dark hair curled so becomingly around his face.

"Are you enjoying Cheltenbridge?" he asked.

"It's been delightful so far. Wouldn't you agree, Lydia?"

"Indeed. We're settling in well, Lord Havenwood."

"If there's something I admire about American women, it's your plucky fortitude. Quite a thing to leave one's country behind to make a life in a new one."

"Yes, but I'm glad to have hazarded the risk," Eliza said. "It's already brought so many unexpected delights."

As promised, a young barmaid with full, reddened cheeks and impressive arms came around, carrying a tray loaded with glasses of frothy ale. Eliza took a pint and offered it to Lydia, then took one for herself.

Malcolm shifted on the bench, crossing one leg over the other and drawing his pipe out from his coat. "Do you mind if I smoke?"

"Not at all," Eliza answered. "I happen to enjoy a fine cigarette on occasion, myself."

"Really?" Malcolm said flatly. He pursed his lips and pulled a tin from his pocket, then packed the bowl of his pipe with cherry-scented tobacco. "I saw no servants when I called upon you. Is it true you've been managing the property all on your own? It's looking splendid."

"We only manage the care of the house ourselves," Eliza said. "We've kept Giles Mason, who lives in our carriage house and maintains the grounds. He's managing our livery for now, though we'll eventually need a proper groom. I've plans to expand the stables and increase our livestock. I'd like to bring in three Thoroughbreds as early as this fall—a stud and two broodmares."

Malcolm leaned forward with interest. "Is that so?"

"As I mentioned, my family owned stables in Louisiana. I'm an expert at racehorse bloodlines. I've been studying the sales sheets for horses derived from our line."

"Fascinating! There's still money to be made in horses, then?"

"Yes, my lord. Even though trains and motorcars are overtaking transportation, they will have no effect on gaming. As long as men bet, horses will run."

"I see." Malcolm took a puff off his pipe. "And how is it with your estate? Did Lady Sherbourne leave things in satisfactory order?"

Lydia nudged Eliza, and they shared a knowing look.

"I've settled the bequest with my aunt's solicitor . . . ," Eliza offered cautiously.

"How many acres came with the estate, then? Three hundred? Four?"

Lydia put a hand on Eliza's arm and gave Malcolm a tight smile. "Never mind Eliza's property. How many acres do *you* own, Lord Havenwood?"

Malcolm tilted his head and arched a dark brow. "One thousand acres with twenty tenants connected to Havenwood Manor, Miss Tourant, and a London townhome in Hyde Park. Shall I bring out my ledgers?" His tone was teasing, but there was a hint of scorn behind his words. "As I told Miss Sullivan on our last outing, my estate has been poorly managed. Your sister has seen for herself the state of Havenwood Manor. And as for the townhouse, rats have taken over the attic and the plumbing remains irretrievably busted. As my pension is greatly lacking, I do not have the means to begin repairs on either property." The green of his eyes deepened as he regarded Eliza. "And there's something else, darling, which you'll hear soon enough from others if you haven't already. I'm indebted to Lord Eastleigh. He holds four mortgages against my properties—gambling debts my father accrued well before I inherited the title. He makes a healthy profit absconding with my rents and filching off my estate. It has nearly crippled me."

Eliza let out a breath. So, the source of the rivalry between Malcolm and Eastleigh concerned money. The earl had a great deal to lose if she accepted Malcolm's suit. And Malcolm had much to gain.

"My goodness," Lydia murmured, "I had no idea things were so *dire* for you."

"I'm nothing if not honest, Miss Tourant." Malcolm sighed and leaned back, blowing a perfect ring of smoke through his lips. "Feels rather good to have it all out there, I daresay."

"Your honesty gives me a great deal of comfort, sir," Eliza said, reaching out for Malcolm's hand. He took her fingertips in his own, grasping them fleetingly. "If we're to continue our courtship, I feel it's only fair to reveal our assets and liabilities early."

"Spoken like a pragmatic woman who knows her mind's value as well as her purse," Malcolm said.

Eliza paused for a heavy moment before continuing. There would be no going back once the next words were freed from her tongue. Even though she wanted to be certain Malcolm was pursuing her for her companionship, her money would go far in sweetening the eventual prospect of marriage. A marriage that had to happen, and soon. Yes, they were practically strangers. But her attraction to him was undeniable, and happy unions had been founded on less. His honesty about his finances was enough to encourage her to level the conversation. But he needn't know the extent of her promised fortune. Not yet. Not until a true betrothal had occurred.

She pulled in a sharp breath. "To answer your question, my lord, the estate has four hundred acres of arable land with ten tenants, who have promised to stay on. *Were* I to marry, I would happily cede the earnings of my estate to my future husband, so long as my sister is allowed to manage Sherbourne House while I build my stables and raise my horses as I see fit. I'll not entertain any offer of marriage unless I can be assured of some measure of continued independence—for myself *and* for my sister."

Lydia let out her breath with a hiss. "You say too much," she rasped.

Eliza shot Lydia an annoyed glance. "*Cher*, these matters must be discussed. It's only practical."

Malcolm's narrow lips quirked at their corners. "I assure you, Miss Tourant, your sister's appeal has very little to do with her inheritance, if that is your concern. She's the most charming creature I've yet had the pleasure of encountering. If I'm to eventually ask for her hand, her estate would be the lesser of my reasons for doing so, although as we all know, marriage in the upper classes is a financial agreement as well as a matter of the heart." Malcolm absently stroked the side of his face. "Well then, now that we've done the accounting and you've discovered I'm a penniless pauper, let's talk of more pleasurable matters, ladies. Shall we . . ."

A sharp scream interrupted Malcolm. A scream of distress instead of play. Eliza leapt to her feet, her glass of ale tumbling to the floor of the gazebo. Down the hill, there was a commotion at the water's edge. A little girl, no more than ten, stood there crying, her hands clawing through her strawberry-blond hair. In the river, Eliza saw the face and thrashing arms of a small child briefly emerge from the swift current, and then disappear beneath the water.

Not this. Not again.

Even as Eliza's head spun with panic, she lifted her hem and ran, her skirts tangling around the heels of her boots as she hurtled down the hillside and scrambled toward the muddy banks. "Move!" she screamed, pushing through the gathering onlookers. Her vision tunneling, she pulled in a deep breath and dove headfirst into the cold, green-tinged water.

Once submerged, she opened her eyes wide and scanned the murk for the boy's gleaming blond hair. She saw nothing but a ruby shimmer of schooling bream, startled by her flailing. She pushed herself deeper with powerful, long strokes, fighting against the Avon's current. Watercress tangled in her fingers and obscured her vision, but she pressed onward until her lungs were brittle with pain and the need to breathe was no longer a choice. She fought for the surface, her drenched clothing heavy as an anchor. Her hair streamed in slimy rivulets over her face as she gulped air. Malcolm and Lydia called her name, but she ignored them, arcing back into the water once more.

Albert! Where are you?

Eliza swirled frantically beneath the surface, straining toward any glimmer of movement as she swam. At last, she saw him. He was trapped against the roots of a tree, his braces wound around a blunt limb, his chin tucked to his chest. Her corset-bound lungs burned and demanded filling, but Eliza pushed onward. She pulled and tugged at the snaking yellow tree roots, her head spinning as her need for air threatened to take her consciousness. Finally, she yanked the boy's leather braces free from their buttons, and he became buoyant. Eliza clawed toward the rippling surface and broke through, gasping and choking, the boy clasped beneath her arm. His skin was cold, his lips a grim shade of violet she remembered all too well.

"It's too late!" someone cried, their words desperate.

"Poor mite!"

"God rest his soul."

"Why weren't his sister minding him?"

Malcolm was suddenly in the river next to her, taking the child from her and helping pull her to shore. He laid the boy gently on the grass, and Eliza rolled him onto his side, smacking his back with the heel of her hand. "Wake up, Albert! Wake up!" She struck the space between the child's shoulder blades, again and again, while his sister cried and the villagers murmured their infuriating, useless platitudes.

"Enough." Malcolm seized her hand, midstrike. "I'm afraid he's gone, darling." Lydia took hold of her elbow and together they tried to pull Eliza to her feet.

"No! I can save him yet. Get away from me!" She slapped and fought free of their grasping hands like a wild animal. Once more, she drove her fist hard against the little boy's back. For a few seconds, there was nothing. Then a sputtering, choking rattle came from deep in his chest, and a stream of water clogged with river grass and mud erupted from his mouth. His lips and cheeks pinked as he coughed, his eyes fluttering open. Eliza wailed and covered his body with her own, rocking him and rubbing his arms with her hands to warm him. "Albert, my darling, *mon petit chou*, I'm so sorry. You're going to be all right. I'm here."

The sister, her chubby face streaked with tears, looked down at Eliza with mournful eyes. "I should have been watching him. He canna swim."

"No!" Eliza said. "No, cher. It wasn't your fault. You're only a child. Albert is going to be fine, do you hear?"

The little girl's lip trembled. "His name's Patrick, mum, not Albert."

"Of course." Eliza nodded. She saw now that he was a brunette, not a blond. *Not Albert.* It was too late for Albert. It always would be. *And it would always be her fault.* Her breath came in sharp, wheezing gasps, her throat closing like a vise. It was as if she were seeing the scene from above, hovering over everyone—the townspeople, Lydia wringing out her hair, the little boy coughing and groaning at her feet.

"Run along, Mary. Find your mama and I'll send for the doctor." Malcolm's rich baritone suddenly sounded as if it were coming through a tin can. A high, intense whistling screeched behind Eliza's eardrums. She was fading into the darkness again—a darkness she'd pushed aside and buried on a warm day in September, so many years ago. "Tell her mother it wasn't her fault," Eliza managed before the world went black, her voice falling to a whimper. "Please."

CHAPTER 9

Eliza woke to a darkened room, her head throbbing so painfully it sickened her stomach. She pulled the chamber pot from beneath her bed and retched into it, then gagged again at the smell. Her eyes were swollen shut from crying, the flood of memories too raw and real to shove back into the locked box she'd constructed of her past.

Her guilt was a prison that would always follow her.

She pressed her thumb against her forehead to quell the sparking pain behind her brow and stumbled to the washbasin, wetting a cloth for her face. The cool water streamed down her heated cheeks and dripped from her chin onto her nightgown.

Eliza parted the drapes and peered out, looking toward the shadowy hulk of Havenwood Manor. A single light shone from one of the upstairs windows and slowly moved back and forth before blinking out. She imagined Malcolm inside, settling beneath his covers. Perhaps he was imagining her doing the same. But sleep would be as elusive as a *feu follet* tonight.

Her own house was quiet, save for a familiar soft snapping coming from belowstairs. Eliza lit a hurricane lamp with trembling hands and went down, her knees weak.

Warm candlelight glowed from the dining room, silhouetting Lydia's pert profile. "I thought you were still sleeping." She was laying out a spread from Mimi Lisette's old tarot deck, the cards well worn around the edges but still vibrant. "Lord Havenwood helped me carry you up the stairs. Do you remember what happened today?"

"I remember," Eliza said, sitting at the table and leaning her head on her hands. "I remember everything I've tried so hard not to." The feel of Albert's limp body in her arms as she dragged him from the water, her new dress clinging to her legs. Her mother's soul-piercing wail. His tiny coffin and the noxious scent of white lilies that to this day turned her stomach. Yes. She remembered all of it.

"I wondered how long you'd push it back." Lydia gave a sad smile. "It wasn't your fault, Liza. But I can tell you that until we're both streaked with gray and it won't matter one bit until you forgive yourself."

Eliza squeezed her eyes shut as a jolt of pain jumped across her eyebrows and tightened her scalp. "Is the boy going to be all right?"

"Clarence says he'll make a full recovery."

The room was suddenly so cold. Eliza gathered her dressing gown around her shoulders. "How is your reading?" she asked, motioning to Lydia's cards.

"This is the third spread. Same results."

"Good news, I hope?"

Lydia shrugged. "I suppose it depends on how you view it, doesn't it?"

Eliza glanced over the cross made of cards. Death. The Three of Swords, the Empress, and the Queen of Cups.

"Do mine, will you?"

Lydia paused, her hand hovering over the cards. "You should wait—it's been a day."

"Yes, but I need a distraction. You know I don't take it as seriously as you."

"You *should* take it seriously, but all right." Lydia sighed and swept her spread back into the deck, then shuffled the cards deftly, her delicate fingers fanning them out in an arc before Eliza. "Think on what you want most before you draw."

Eliza quickly chose three cards.

Lydia raised a dark eyebrow in question. "Would you like me to read for the past, present, future?"

"Yes."

Lydia flipped over the first card, representing the past. Death's skeletal face stared up at them. "The same card was in your spread," Eliza said.

"In the same position."

"It makes sense, then, doesn't it?"

Lydia nodded. "Change. The end of the old ways and the start of the new. You're excited about the future, aren't you, Liza?" She turned the next card and smiled. It was the Fool, with his tiny dog yapping at his heels as he danced. "Le Fou. You always seem to draw this card."

"It's true. It's a happy card, isn't it?"

"Yes, but you know it's also a warning. As carefree as a fool may think he is, he doesn't always see the edge of the cliff until it's too late." Lydia passed her hand over the Fool's dancing feet, her fingers light as a feather. "I don't know that I trust Malcolm. He acted a bit strange today after your spell. He was polite, but he seemed less concerned than I thought he should be. He was in a blind hurry to leave after we'd gotten you home."

"How funny. He's English, after all. I don't think they're as doting as our southern men. A bit of a chill in their marrow."

Lydia shook her head. "It's just that . . . after all that talk of money today, it was a bit disconcerting to see him stiffen up."

A knock came at the door. Eliza looked at Lydia in surprise, then to the clock. It was well past eight. "It's a bit late for callers."

"Perhaps it's Clarence. He did say he'd check in after he got the Cook boy settled in at home." Lydia straightened her skirts and eyed herself in the glass over the fireplace. Once she turned the corner, Eliza lifted the edge of the last card in the tarot spread. She had only to glimpse the flames and falling bodies to know which card it was. The

Tower. A portent of catastrophe. A chill passed over her arms, and she hurriedly swept the card back into the middle of the deck, replacing it with another.

"Eliza!" Lydia called. "You've a guest."

She stood, steadying herself against the high back of the chair before walking out to the foyer. Malcolm stood next to Lydia, his eyes lighting up as he saw her. In his hands, a bouquet of fragrant lavender bloomed. Eliza's heart jumped with sudden happiness. She went to him, clutching her dressing gown over the thin cambric of her shift. On impulse, she rose up on her tiptoes to kiss his cheek. "Lord Havenwood. Thank you for seeing us home and helping Lydia care for me."

"I'd hardly have been a gentleman if I hadn't. I'm so sorry I had to leave in such a rush. I'm chuffed to see you on your feet." He removed his hat, his dark curls fanning around his collar. "And please, darling. I'd prefer it if you'd start calling me Malcolm."

"I'll put these in some water," Lydia said as she took the flowers from Malcolm. "Y'all go visit in the parlor."

Eliza led Malcolm into the sitting room, where red, fractured light shone through the perforated globe of the paraffin lamp they kept lit in the evenings. He sat on the velvet settee by the window, and Eliza sank down next to him. "I'm sorry I became faint today," she said. "Things were going so well . . ." A sob choked the rest of her words. "The truth is, I'm a bit of a mess."

"Please don't apologize, darling." His manner was so tender, Eliza was suddenly flooded with an urge to be embraced by him. As if he sensed her longing to be held, Malcolm's arm went around her shoulders and drew her closer. He took her bare hand and pressed a kiss to the nest of old scars on her wrist. At the touch of his lips there, she flinched. "Your sister told me about your little brother. You left that part out, I'm afraid, when last we spoke."

Eliza worried at the fringe on her sleeve, pulling it over her wrist. "I don't talk about it. It's my biggest shame, the reason I could no longer abide New Orleans—well, one of the reasons. Here, I could pretend it never happened. I could start fresh." She gave a rueful smile. "But I'll never be able to outrun my guilt, no matter how far I go. I blamed myself for his death. I still do."

"And I blamed myself for what happened to my own family." Malcolm squeezed her hand. "If I had been awake, I might have saved my brother. If I'd been home more, instead of at sea chasing my ambition, I would have been a better son to my mother. I could have protected her. And then, to be implicated as her murderer . . ." He blinked and shook his head. "Well. It seems we're broken in many of the same ways, doesn't it?"

Eliza melted into his embrace, lacing her fingers through his. She'd never felt so understood. So safe. "My mother never recovered after Albert died," she murmured. "He was her shining light. After I was born, she lost one baby after another. Some were born blue and fully formed, others died in her womb within weeks of her confinement. The doctors could never say why. After each loss, her grief turned darker." Eliza studied the flaming wick of the oil lamp, the crackle of the burning paraffin filling the heavy silence between her words. "I began to dread Maman's fits of melancholy. She often neglected me and turned to her cups for solace. Mimi Lisette, Lydia's grandmother and our housekeeper, was truly the one who raised me.

"My father seemed to weather things better, but I didn't know that he slaked his own sorrows with other women, including Mimi's daughter—which is how Lydia came to be. My parents raised her as their ward and my companion, but Papa never claimed her as his daughter, even though she was. I think Maman might have known about his affairs, but she hid them from me, although they argued like mad for years. Lydia and I were at the middle of it all. And then, whether out of guilt or genuine feeling, I cannot say—Papa began wooing Maman like he did when she was young. She was soon with child again. Nine months later, Albert was born, fat and healthy. Our house grew happy again. There were parties and picnics, and for a brief time, I felt the fullness of my mother's love. Until . . ." Eliza's face crumpled.

"How old were you? When the accident happened?"

"Twelve. Maman had gone to the market with Mimi Lisette. I was put in charge of Lydia and Albert. He had just turned three. It was a lovely September day, and I wanted to go down the hill to our pond to daydream and read my new novel. Lydia was napping, but I brought Albert with me. I should have been watching him more closely. One moment, he was pawing through the cattails looking for frogs, the next he was gone. I didn't even hear a splash. I looked up from my book, and he was just . . . gone." Her voice broke and she took a long, shaky breath. "I dove in and found him, but it was too late."

Malcolm lifted her chin. "It wasn't your fault, Eliza. You were only a child. Isn't that what you said to little Mary Cook today? Why shouldn't you say that to yourself?"

"Because I took my mother's happiness. Her only son. She never said it aloud, but she blamed me, all the same. How *can* I ever forgive myself, Malcolm?" She began to sob afresh, her grief tearing from her throat like a bird with razor wings.

Malcolm pulled her close, letting her tears soak the fine silk of his cravat. When she had finally quieted some minutes later, he stroked her hair from her forehead and then kissed her there. "I have an idea."

She wiped her face with her sleeve and looked up at him, the angular planes of his face softened by the lamplight. "What?"

"You could do with some cheering."

Eliza laughed. "I suppose I could."

"Would you like to go out? I've heard Sarah Bernhardt is appearing tonight at the new theatre in Southampton."

"But won't we be late? And I look a fright!"

"Nonsense. At any rate, it's a tragic piece. Everyone will think your tears are due to Miss Bernhardt's superb acting. Go put on a pretty frock and I'll meet you outside."

CHAPTER 10

The Grand Theatre stood as stalwart as a brick castle on a plaza surrounded by lavish rose gardens, their fragrance cloyingly sweet. Malcolm circled his creaking, poorly sprung trap around the drive, then handed Eliza down. It was a balmy night, and as they made their way toward the lighted marquee, he plucked a white rose from one of the shrubs and tucked it into her coiled hair with a winsome smile. The long queue advanced quickly, and as they neared the ticket window, Eliza admired the image of Sarah Bernhardt on the playbill pinned out front. The photograph showed the actress in a lace-trimmed gown, her Gallic features accented by a mane of crimped dark hair. The play was *Camille*.

"Two tickets for the loge, please," Malcolm said, palming pound notes toward the clerk.

"I'm afraid we're sold out, sir," the young man said, scratching beneath the brim of his round cap. "The curtain's about to open to a packed house. Miss Bernhardt is here for one night only, you see."

Malcolm's lip twitched. "Most unfortunate."

"My apologies, sir."

Malcolm reached into his pocket. Eliza caught a glint of something metallic and shining in his hand. He slipped it beneath the opening. The clerk quickly swept it into his lap. "I suppose there are two seats available in the balcony, after all. Go around back. My mate'll be by the stage door and he'll take you to your seats. Enjoy the show."

"What did you give him?" Eliza asked.

"Only an old watch chain I meant to pawn, darling. Sometimes one must add a bit of encouragement to get things done, eh?"

As they went around the building, a uniformed usher waved by the rear door. "Come this way, sir, madam. One of our patrons has a vacant box tonight. If anyone asks, I'll say you're his guests."

They followed the usher up a set of carpeted steps and down a hallway. He parted a red velvet curtain and Eliza and Malcolm ducked inside just as the house lights began to flicker. Below, the theatre was teeming with people dressed in varying degrees of finery. Eliza glimpsed Una Moseley's high, gleaming coiffure in the seats facing the orchestra. Before Eliza could look away, their eyes met for a moment. Una smirked and whispered something to her companion, who erupted in a fit of laughter. Eliza threw them an overly friendly smile and raised her gloved hand in greeting. Una only scowled and flicked open her fan.

"I saw that," Malcolm said as they took their seats. "You should know it doesn't bother me. I'm rather used to it after all this time." He motioned toward the audience below, where the other latecomers were greeting one another with presses of the hand and cheek. "Their shunning is the least of my concerns."

"Well, I don't like it." Eliza gripped the curved railing, clenching her teeth. "It's incredibly rude. You're a peer of the realm and they should show deference."

Malcolm laughed. "You'll have to grow used to it if you aim to be seen in public with me."

The lights flickered once more, then faded to black as the scarlet curtain parted. A rush of poignant music ascended to the arched ceiling of the theatre, and Eliza brought her opera glasses up in anticipation as the cast strode onto the stage. The play was an engaging one, with many dramatic moments. Halfway through the second act, after they'd finished a magnum of champagne, Malcolm took her hand in his and held it throughout the rest of the play, sending a wave of ardor through her.

After the final act, Eliza found herself weeping for the tragic Camille, played so regally by Miss Bernhardt. She and Malcolm gave their ovations, then went out to take the air in the garden. Her head was teeming with amorous thoughts as Malcolm drew her into a cloistered arbor crawling with scarlet, cherry-scented roses. He removed her opera glove and brought her hand to his face, nuzzling his cheek against her wrist, his lips cool and soft as he kissed the place where her pulse beat like the wings of a hummingbird.

"Eliza," he whispered. "It's madness to confess my feelings when we've known one another for so little time. But something in your manner speaks to me . . . I find I am stirred by the most tender and passionate feelings when I am in your presence. I won't consider being parted from you."

"Nor will I," Eliza said breathlessly. "I've been drawn to you from the first moment I saw you."

"Will you put away your other suitors, then, and see only me?"

"On my word, I already have. Lord Eastleigh was the only other."

Malcolm's face grew sharp as a blade. Eliza drew back, a small gasp escaping her lips at the sudden change in his demeanor. "Blasted Eastleigh," he spat. "I should have known he'd come panting round your door."

"I carry no fondness for him. I swear it, Malcolm."

"Eastleigh is a wicked, wicked man, my darling. Trust that. I cannot promise an easy time of it when I declare my intentions publicly, but I'm quite ready to take him on."

"Then let him try to stop this. Let him try to stop *us*." Eliza brushed her thumb over Malcolm's mouth, tracing his lower lip, then rested her thumb in the sculpted hollow beneath. He sighed, his momentary rancor dissolving under her touch. A rushing sound filled Eliza's head against the muzziness of the champagne. His mouth was mere inches from her own. "I have never wanted to kiss someone as much as I'd like to kiss you," she murmured. "Won't you kiss me, Malcolm?"

His lips found her own in the darkness with a sweet, questioning hesitancy that set her knees trembling. She wrapped her arms around his neck, rising up on tiptoe as he deepened their kiss. His tongue tasted of crisp champagne and cinnamon, his breath hot against her skin as his lips left her mouth and trailed down her neck. "Yes," she whispered. She pressed her hips against his and felt the wildness of his desire for her there. Mon Dieu, how she wanted him. How quickly he had unmoored her feelings! How on earth could this be wrong when every nerve in her body quickened to his touch?

"Eliza . . . we must stop," he said suddenly, pulling back. His eyes shone like twin jewels. "If we do not, I will be overcome." He rested his forehead against her own, his breath coming in short gasps. "I should see you home. Your sister . . ."

"Will be fine," Eliza said, her body radiating warmth. "I'm twenty-five, Malcolm. A grown woman." She drew in a breath. "And it's time I told you—no virgin. I crave you, in the most carnal and natural of ways."

"In all my scandalous thoughts, I have never imagined you a shy maiden, darling." He chuckled, his hands running along her back, tracing the seam of her dress. "You're giving me the most tempting fodder for my dreams . . . and I *shall* dream well tonight. But you've had far too much champagne, and the sort of day that makes one's senses unsteady." He pressed a kiss to the top of her head. "I'll return you to your sister and your own bed, with much reluctance, but with an ardently settled heart."

❧

Eliza stumbled through the front door of Sherbourne House, giddy from Malcolm's kisses, her earlier tears forgotten. Lydia met her at the door, her lips tightly drawn, her dressing gown tied in a loose knot. "How was the play?" she asked.

"It was wonderful!" Eliza removed her wrap and hung it in the cloakroom, then pulled out her combs, her scalp smarting as her hair tumbled free. "Tragic at the end, but Bernhardt really *is* as divine as they all say. We'll have to go together when she comes back through."

"You smell of his cologne."

Eliza laughed. "And?"

Lydia rolled her eyes. "I turned the final card in your spread. Don't you want to know what it was?"

"Oh. I'd forgotten all about our reading. It didn't go badly, I hope?"

Lydia pulled the worn tarot card from her pocket and handed it to Eliza. She turned it over and her belly lurched. Against all rational explanation, despite her earlier subversion, the Tower card lay in her hand—the falling bodies, the flames, and the forked tongue of lightning flashing through an ink-dark sky, promising peril and ruin.

CHAPTER 11

Eliza tried to concentrate on the words in her hymnal, but it proved impossible to keep up with the portly choirmaster, who seemed unable to sustain a beat. She finally gave up and closed the little book in her hands, observing instead the townsfolk gathered in the white cocoon of the country chapel.

A few of the ladies from Lady Gregory's ball were sprinkled among the congregants, their youthful muslin standing out in a sea of dark clothing. Many of them met her eyes with furtive glances, but only Sarah Nelson smiled at her from the forward pew to her right, raising her hand in a polite wave.

"Sarah's quite comely, isn't she? Like a soft-eyed little deer," Eliza whispered to Lydia as they sat for the sermon. "I think we could become fast friends, don't you?"

"I think so, too."

After the service, the congregants spilled out into the courtyard, greeting one another and giving invitations to tea. Sarah met Eliza and Lydia with a press of her hand. "I'm hosting a game of croquet this afternoon if you'd like to come. Dickie's away on one of his fishing trips and my house has gone much too quiet. It would be wonderful to have you there."

"We'd be delighted, Sarah," Eliza answered.

"I'm certainly glad!" Sarah leaned forward to kiss Eliza's cheek. "We'll have fresh lemonade and you can tell me all about how things are going with your beaus. Would you like to ride in my carriage?"

"Thank you, but we'll enjoy the stroll."

They left Sarah and walked toward the churchyard. It was a fine day—fair and bright, with puffy clouds scuttling along the horizon. Half-wild forest ponies grazed between the sun-bleached gravestones, their shaggy heads searching through the overgrowth. At the end of the path, a stately mausoleum stood well away from the rest of the monuments, flanked by urn-topped pillars and adorned with the Havenwood crest. Surrounded by juniper hedges and myrtle, the tomb seemed out of place and monolithic—as if it had been set down by some Stygian deity. It was a somber irony that the beguiling man whose company Eliza had been enjoying would someday take rest inside its walls. She looked at the crypt's metal door and wondered how many Havenwood wives lay beyond it.

"I was hoping I'd see Lord Havenwood at church today," she said.

Lydia made a sharp little sound. "Perhaps he's a dirty papist like us. Or an atheist."

"Atheism wouldn't put me off. I must admit, I have grown tired of religion. With all its depressing talk of damnation and hellfire, it's no wonder people go off it. Perhaps I'll become a naturalist. Darwin's hypotheses make far more sense than half the blathering I've heard from the pulpit."

"I find my faith gives me a great deal of comfort. You're a bit snippy this morning. Do you want to talk about your reading last night? The final card seemed to have rattled you."

Lydia was right. It *had* rattled her, mostly because of the calamity it implied. She'd only drawn the Tower from Mimi Lisette's deck once before, and Albert had died not even a week later. The worst part was not knowing how the card had gotten back into the spread. She had no way of explaining it, unless Lydia had done it on purpose. But deceit wasn't in her sister's nature. "Do you think it's a bad portent?"

Lydia shrugged. "Well. It wasn't the best kind of draw, but the future is never set solid by a tarot card. You know that. Be that as it may, I still have reservations about Lord Havenwood. I'm not sure he's the right one for you. I've been making offerings to Erzulie for our love matches. She leaves the milk in my dish as sweet as the honey I've flavored it with, but for you, she curdles it sour as vinegar. It's a warning, Liza."

"You know I don't believe in voodoo anymore, Lyddie."

"You should. Mimi taught us never to ignore the spiritual wisdom of the loa. Especially Erzulie."

They made their way past the final tidy rows of grave markers, each topped with a lamb in repose—the graves of children. Albert's grave had been marked just the same. Eliza averted her eyes and quickened her pace until they came to the wagon-rutted lane. Soon they were crossing over the broad expanse of Sarah's lawn, where her Georgian mansion rose three stories, built of trimmed limestone and flanked with hedges of yew.

Lydia trotted off to join the croquet match, where the other ladies greeted her and quickly pulled her into the game. Instead of joining them, Eliza meandered through Sarah's gardens, admiring their orderly French parterres and pergolas, each section planned with as much care as if it were an outdoor room. She sat at the edge of a trilling fountain, its chubby satyrs cavorting beneath a canopy of water, and watched the game from a distance.

"Ah, there you are!" Sarah's voice chimed from behind, and Eliza turned to see her friend balancing a tray of sweets upon a pitcher of lemonade as she tried to spread a cloth over a cast-iron table. "Come help me with this before I ruin everything, will you? I'm not very domestic, I'm afraid."

Eliza laughed and went to help, taking the cloth and spreading it out over the table. Sarah set the tray of refreshments upon the linen and took a seat in one of the caned chairs facing Eliza. "I take it things are going well with Lord Havenwood?"

"Yes. We went to the theatre last night and saw Sarah Bernhardt. She was superb."

"I heard. So has the rest of Cheltenbridge. Una Moseley saw you there."

Eliza blanched, her smile fading. "Una doesn't like me. You were right to warn me about her. I discovered she's been spying on me—even paying Nigel to bring her my business. I'm not sure why."

"Oh? Malcolm hasn't told you, then?"

A nervous tickle ran through Eliza's stomach. "What is it, Sarah?"

"You've made an enemy, my dear." Sarah poured lemonade for Eliza and pushed it toward her. "Drink up, darling. There's gin in that." Eliza took a sip, tasting the warm tingle of liquor beneath the lemons. "Una is spying on you because she's jealous. She and your Malcolm were once engaged."

"Really? He mentioned something about his father wanting him to settle with a local girl, but he didn't tell me who it was or that they were engaged. How shocking."

"Well, none of it was Malcolm's choice. He and Una had been betrothed from the time they were children—all arranged by their fathers. And Lady Havenwood never liked her; she saw Una for what she was—a social climber. True to form, as soon as Una found out Malcolm had nothing but a title to offer her, that's when it went off."

"Then what reason would she have to be jealous of me?"

"Darling, I know you're not naïve. It's the way of women to be jealous when others gobble up the scraps they've flung from their table."

"I suppose you're right." She'd felt the same unfair twinge of jealousy toward Jacob's new love, after all. "I'm relieved she has a reason. Until now, I'd no idea why she hated me. I'll do my best to avoid her."

"Good. She's a sandwich short of a picnic, that one."

They sat in amiable silence, watching the croquet players flit about the lawn like butterflies made of pastel gauze. Polly and Lydia seemed to be engaging in a friendly rivalry, the former's feathered hat bobbing excitedly each time Lydia failed to make her shot. Their girlish laughter carried over the grass.

Eliza reached into her dress pocket and gave Sarah a conspiratorial grin. "Would you mind if I smoke? Lydia hates it and I have to sneak my cigarettes when we're at home."

"I'll only mind if you don't offer me one, too."

Eliza held out the tin of black Sobranies she'd purchased at the local apothecary, and after Sarah exclaimed over their novel color and scent, they lit them, drawing in the flavorful smoke.

"How do you find him? Malcolm?" Sarah asked, leaning forward and propping her chin on her hand. "He's always seemed so stoic."

"I'd warrant he's anything but." Eliza blushed, remembering how Malcolm's kiss had thrown her into a frenzy of unladylike arousal. "His lordship is proving to be quite the charming gentleman, despite rumors to the contrary."

"Indeed." Sarah took another drag off her cigarette, her lips curling at their corners. "I'm not at all surprised you're smitten. There's something endearing about his reserve, isn't there? His brother was quite charming. Both boys served as midshipmen under my father—he was captain of the HMS *Prentiss*. Gabriel loved the sea and would have eventually had the helm of his own ship." Sarah topped off Eliza's glass with more of the gin-spiked lemonade. "Malcolm wasn't suited to the military. He preferred numbers and letters. He left the navy behind to help run his father's estate, which was in dire need of his abilities."

"He told me a little of why."

"Yes. The debt. The late Lord Havenwood was a gambler and an outright cad. He was horrid to those boys, and to his wife."

Eliza thought of Malcolm's portrait of Lady Havenwood and her mirthless beauty. "I'm becoming more and more intrigued by his mother. Was she really mad?"

"Calling her a madwoman would be unkind—she was only shy and far too young to be a mother or even a wife. We always got on well. People thought she was strange because she didn't like parties. She'd draw up a chair and sit, watching everyone with those fantastic eyes and making them nervous. It took effort to get to know her, but it was effort well spent."

"It sounds as if she was incredibly lonely."

"She was. Old Lord Havenwood was hardly sparkling company, and he could turn the corner onto cruelty with enough drink."

Lydia broke away from the croquet game and trudged toward them, her mallet dragging the ground. Eliza stubbed out her cigarette and threw it beneath the table, sweeping it under her skirt. Sarah giggled, giving her own butt a final puff before putting it out.

"Has Polly bested you, sister?" Eliza teased, handing Lydia a glass of lemonade.

"I'd prefer not to say."

"Eliza and I were just chatting about Lord Havenwood," Sarah said. "What are your thoughts, Lydia?"

"The rumors bother me a great deal, there's no doubt. He's charming, but I feel as if he's holding something close to his chest."

"You're wise to be cautious. Many men have impure motives, after all. But the rumors about his having murdered his mother are only that—rumors. What on earth would his motive have been? It makes no sense."

"Lord Eastleigh mentioned something about her knowing dark things about Malcolm," Eliza said. "Things he wouldn't have wanted out in the open. But he didn't offer much more. It all seems so weakly conjectured."

Sarah sighed. "Right. If I may be frank—Charles is an old rival and would say anything to put you off Malcolm. I was most concerned when I heard you were entertaining Eastleigh's interest. He's much more problematic." Sarah covered Eliza's hand with her own. "Malcolm has never been anything but kind to me and my own family. There's a good bit of talk that goes on, but most of it is idle gossip. Ghosts and curses and such." Sarah laughed. "Nonsense. All of it."

"I'd agree. Why don't we turn the conversation to *your* beau, Lydia?" Eliza said, arching an eyebrow. "She's gone over completely for Clarence Fawcett."

Lydia brightened. "Yes. Dr. Fawcett has been calling on me. We've many common interests. We've even talked at length about my becoming a nurse."

"Lydia has the stomach for such work," Eliza said. "She's rather adept at bossing people around as well, if you hadn't gathered."

Lydia gave a playful swat to Eliza's arm. "Only when they *need* bossing."

"Certainly, it's a noble calling. More and more women are working these days, it seems," Sarah said. "Our daughters may not even have to marry to secure their futures. Imagine a world in which men might become redundant! We'll be like Sappho and inhabit a solitary island, filled only with beautiful women."

"An entertaining thought, that," Eliza agreed with an ironic smile. She yawned, covering her mouth with her lace gloved hand. Her headache from the day before still throbbed dully behind her right eye. "If you'll pardon me, ladies, I'm feeling a little tired from yesterday's excitement. The sun and your delicious lemonade have gone to my head, Sarah. I think I'll walk home and draw a bath." Lydia rose slightly from her chair. Eliza patted her shoulder. "No, cher—stay. Enjoy the game." With a kiss to Lydia's cheek, she left the bright garden nook behind and pushed through the bushes onto the wooded lane. She was very seldom alone—Lydia was ever hovering in the background, interrupting her solitude to go on about Clarence or talk about something she'd over-heard at the market. As much as she loved her sister, Lydia's youthful energy made Eliza weary at times. They'd relied only on one another's company for far too long.

Eliza sighed with contentment and took a slow path through the forest, enjoying the singsong call of the birds. After a while she came upon a light-filled clearing in the woods she'd never noticed before. It occurred to her she'd walked well past Sherbourne House and was now deep within Lord Havenwood's estate. Sure enough, the manor's south façade loomed to her left, and to her right was a path leading down a flower-strewn hillock. Wooed by her curiosity, Eliza followed the trail until she reached the bottom of the rise.

A stone circle stood in the little valley—a ring of ancient mono-liths just taller than her own head. Tiny blue cornflowers sprouted between the slabs. She walked around the ring twice and knelt to pick the flowers for a bouquet. As she rose, Eliza had the distinct feeling of being watched. She looked up at the windows of Havenwood Manor. A shadow moved within, as if someone were peering down at her from parted curtains. She tented her eyes with her hands to see more clearly, but where there had been a hint of movement moments before, there was now only the reflection of clouds and sky on the surface of the glass.

She resumed her flower gathering, finding a trove of purple fox-gloves behind the tallest stone, which was figured with ancient symbols. As Eliza ran her fingers over the carved surface, the sun ducked behind a cloud, sending the cairns into shadow. A soft spatter of raindrops landed on her cheeks. If she'd learned one thing about England, it was that the weather had more moods than a woman during her courses. She made her way toward home, eager for a warm bath and a nap.

As she climbed the hill to the path, the feeling of being watched set-tled between her shoulders once more. She paused to listen. There was only the wind soughing through the birches. Eliza walked on, brushing aside her unease. As the twin chimneys of Sherbourne House came into view, something scraped on the dirt path behind her. Footsteps. A chill settled in the marrow of her bones. She whirled to face whoever was stalking her, her heartbeat thudding in her ears.

There was no one there.

Eliza stood stock-still, her eyes darting through the undergrowth. The raindrops became larger, plopping onto her white lawn dress and soaking through to her skin. A shriek of laughter came from the direction of Sarah's house, but all the birds had gone silent. Out of the corner of her eye, movement. A shadow parted the undergrowth.

Una Moseley came onto the path, lithe and slinking. She was dressed in dove-gray muslin, her expression deep and glowering within the fine contours of her face. "I know what you've been doing, Miss Sullivan," she rasped.

"Miss Moseley. What a pleasant surprise." Eliza kept her tone measured, though the flowers in her grasp trembled. *You've made an enemy, my dear.* "Out for a ramble?"

"I saw you, last night. With *him*. In Lord Eastleigh's box." Una's mouth screwed into a mocking twist. "Charles knows all about that now. And he's none too pleased."

Eliza wavered. "We hadn't a clue it was Lord Eastleigh's box. They were the only seats left in the house."

"Malcolm knew they were Charles's seats. He knew he'd be upset, too. He knows a lot more than he lets on," Una said wistfully, twirling from side to side. "A trickster full-up with pretty lies, that one. He has such sweet kisses, too—but I'm not the only one who knows."

"What on earth are you talking about?" Eliza stepped backward and dropped her flowers to the ground. Her fingernails dug into her palms. She'd only been in one tussle with another girl—a redheaded bully who had stolen her lunch pail in finishing school, but she had bested her within moments. She could do it again, if it came to it.

"You think I'm jealous, don't you?" Una crossed to Eliza's side of the path, peering at her through lowered lashes. "You think our betrothal ended because of money. That's what Sarah told you. But Sarah doesn't know what *I* know." Una waggled her fingers in front of Eliza's nose.

Eliza widened her stance and fixed Una with an unflinching glare. "Look, Una. I know you've been spying on me, and I'd thank you to mind your own business, as I mean to mind mine. I don't know what happened to spoil things between you and Malcolm. Nor do I care."

"You'd better have care, Miss Sullivan. You'd better." Una's eyes grew frighteningly dark as the light grew even dimmer. "Else Malcolm will break more than your pretty heart."

CHAPTER 12

The sky tore open with a fierce crack of lightning, charring the air as a mixture of rain and hail pelted to the ground. Eliza flew down the path away from Una, her skirts knotted in her hands. She undid the latch to her rear gate with clumsy, wet fingers and bolted up the hill, drenched and shivering.

Mr. Mason stood beneath the shelter of the rear veranda, his fingers hooked in his braces. Something was wrong. She could tell by the set of his angular chin as she drew near. "There's been some trouble, miss."

"What is it?" Eliza asked, unpinning her hat. It was ruined, the papier-mâché roses on its band weeping dye in lurid pink rivulets. "Do we have a leak?"

"No, miss. Nothing with the house." Mason squinted. "Lord Eastleigh was by, in rather cross spirits. Demanded to be let in."

Eliza's stomach twisted and dropped. "Is he here?"

"No. When I wouldn't allow him entry, he threatened me." He crossed his arms, and she got a glimpse of what Giles Mason must have been like as a younger man. "I came through two wars, miss. I lived through the Battle of Balaclava. I do not stand down when some prancing, toffy boy threatens me."

Eliza couldn't help the smile that spread across her face. "Indeed, sir. To your great credit."

"He won't be bothering you again. You can be sure of that, so long as I guard your gates. But there's something else." He pulled a folded envelope from his trousers pocket and handed it to her. "The Phelps lad—Nigel—delivered this shortly after."

The envelope had been hastily addressed, her name an illegible scrawl. Eliza tore it open, her dye-stained fingertips marring the paper.

My darling girl, I must see you tonight. Discretion is in order. Watch by your window.
Malcolm

Eliza crumpled the note in her hand. A bitter taste crawled up the back of her throat.

Malcolm's note was related to Eastleigh's visit, there could be no question. Una had surely contributed to their rivalry by sharing the results of her spying with Eastleigh, but Eliza had a feeling there was more at stake than Una's jealousy and Malcolm's debt. Despite Sarah's comforting words that afternoon, the mysteries surrounding Malcolm's past still weighed heavily on her mind.

Could she truly trust Malcolm? Were Una's words merely the ravings of an addled rival, or a warning against something far more sinister? Eliza crossed her arms over her chest and rubbed them. She needed her bath. And time to think. "Mr. Mason," she said, "can I trouble you to stay awake late tonight? I've a feeling I may need to call upon your help."

He gave a rare, ragged grin. "Certainly. I'm happy to be in your service, miss."

❦

Eliza knelt over the spigot to the high-backed copper tub and opened the tap, waiting while the basin filled with warm, steaming water. She undid the buttons of her day dress and shrugged it into a sodden heap on the floor, then stepped out of her undergarments. Outside, the rain still spat against the windows. She imagined Sarah had convinced her sister to stay out the storm. They were probably huddled over a game of pinochle or playing drunken charades with the other girls. Well, good.

After her bath, she donned her nightdress, made tea, and sat in the open window to comb out her hair. The skies had ceased their weeping, leaving the grass a brilliant green and bringing a cleansing freshness to the air. She chose a book of poetry from Tante Theo's sparse collection and read until twilight had fallen. The cuckoo clock downstairs rang nine, then ten. She looked toward Havenwood Manor. All the windows were vacant and dark. Still she waited. And still, there was no sign of Malcolm. As night descended, seamless and black, weariness settled deep in Eliza's bones, and the softness of her downturned bed beckoned.

She had just pulled the coverlet to her chin when she heard the sound of hoofbeats.

Eliza sprung out of bed and pulled open the sash, her heartbeat quickening. Malcolm clattered through the copse of trees surrounding his manor, steam billowing from Apollo's nostrils as he jumped the stone wall separating their estates. He slowed when he saw her at the window, easing Apollo into a trot.

"Eliza! Thank God you're still awake." He came to rest beneath her window, his face shadowed by the brim of a crofter's hat. He was dressed like a farmer, in rugged trousers and a corduroy jacket. "I realize this is stupidly dramatic, but please come down and I'll explain."

"I'll meet you in the rear gardens, by the dovecote."

She reached for her dressing gown and stepped into her house slippers, then padded down the stairs and through the hallway to the rear terrace doors. Malcolm stood beneath the eaves of the dovecote she and Lydia had converted to a gardening shed. She ran to his side and he gathered her into his arms, kissing both her cheeks and then her mouth. "We must be careful," he murmured. "I cannot stay long."

"No one will know you're here. I asked Mr. Mason to guard the gate all night. Eastleigh paid an unexpected visit while I was out."

"He came to me soon after."

Eliza breathlessly took him by the hand and led him through the dovecote's low door. Dry leaves scuttled across the dirt floor as they ducked under the lintel and into the small room. The scents of rosemary and thyme wafted from the drying bouquets Lydia had strung from the ceiling. Eliza reached for the kerosene lamp and matches they kept on the shelf above the door and lit it. Malcolm removed his hat, his curls falling over his forehead in disarray. She pulled him to the rustic wooden potting table, where they sat, the lantern throwing weak, orange light across the walls.

"Eastleigh has demanded I vacate Havenwood Manor within a fortnight, or he'll begin legal proceedings to force me out. I'm being evicted, after all this time."

"What? Why now?"

Malcolm raked a hand through his unruly hair, grimacing. "I suppose, since he's aware you've rejected him in favor of my suit, he's getting back at me the only way he knows how."

Eliza's heart dropped. Not the house. Not before she even had a chance to become its mistress. "Well, we can't let that happen. How much do you owe him?"

"Forty thousand pounds."

Merde.

"That much?" Eliza stuttered.

"I'm afraid so."

Eliza pulled her hand from Malcolm's and stood, walking to the latticed window opposite. Her skin suddenly felt clammy and her stomach roiled fitfully. It was astonishing. He owed Eastleigh the equivalent of almost a quarter-million American dollars. How could his father have been so reckless?

Apart from the eighty thousand pounds she was set to inherit from her aunt's estate upon marriage, she still had enough left from her father's inheritance that she could afford to give Malcolm half of what he owed as a loan. Money she'd set aside to buy her horses. Or . . .

She felt him behind her, his breath warm on her hair.

"I won't accept your charity, Eliza," he said quietly. "I'll go to Scotland. Our family has a hunting lodge there. No one knows of it—I've made sure of that. He will leave me in peace so long as I swear to never see you again."

She turned, her eyes filling. "And *would* you swear such a thing?"

"You deserve better than I can give you, Eliza."

How bitter those words. The very same words she'd written to Jacob in a letter bound for Cuba the year before. Tears trickled over her cheeks, unbidden, and she angrily wiped them away. "You'd give up so easily? Why woo me with your words and company if this is the only end that could come of it? How cruel of you!" Her words pierced the air, brittle as ice.

Surprised by her anger, Malcolm took a step back. "I did not know my enemy was courting you until it was too late. I couldn't help myself falling in love. I was not thinking of your best interests, or of what might happen if things went as far as they have. I was overcome."

"And I feel like a steak torn between dogs! *If* you loved me, you would fight for me. You promised as much last night!"

"He will ruin you, Eliza. He said as much. His anger was so great today that he shoved Turner to the floor and accosted me in my study. We nearly came to blows. He has the power to do great harm to you, and I cannot let that happen. It would be selfish."

"You are *already* selfish!" Eliza drew back to slap him and he caught her by the wrist, clasping her to him with a force she felt helpless to fight. Her arousal and anger surged as he seized her lips and kissed her so deeply her breath left her lungs. Eliza pushed him away. "No!" He searched her face. Eliza knew how she looked in a temper—desperate, flushed, manic. "Do you truly never wish to be parted from me?" she demanded. "Or were your words among the roses before you kissed me a pretty lie? I hear you're quite good at lying to women."

Malcolm heaved a sigh. "Una has found you, I see. What did she tell you?"

"That I shouldn't trust you with my heart."

"Una and I have a long history. She had a false impression of something that happened between us once. She's a troubled soul. I was never in love with her. Our engagement was of our fathers' making." He took her hand. "With all my heart, Eliza, I swear that I love you. Only you."

"Then prove it." Her heart thudded so loudly she was sure he could hear it. Suddenly, she didn't care about anything but the burgeoning heat she saw in his eyes. "Marry me. Marry me and you'll never have to worry about money, or Eastleigh, or being alone in the world again."

"So soon? Do you trust me that much?" His voice was thick, choked with emotion. "Do you trust I am not the man others have said I am?"

"Against all my better judgment, God help me, I do!"

He gave a blunted laugh. "Oh, my own darling . . . many would say you are a fool."

"I know that I am!" Eliza laughed, her tears falling freely as a torrent of emotion washed over her. "Will you make me your wife, Malcolm? All I want is to be yours. To share my fortune, my body, and my life with you."

"How under heaven could I say no?"

Malcolm claimed her lips again, his kiss fierce and carnal. Eliza knotted her fingers through his hair, returning his passion with her own. He gripped the fabric of her velvet dressing gown and pulled it free from her shoulders. The ruched neckline of her nightdress followed, spilling down over her bosom. He bent and kissed her there as she swayed, breathless in his arms.

"Do you want me?" he rasped. "Here and now, like this? Not in our marriage bed like a lady?"

A proper lady *would* have pushed him away, denying him until after their wedding. But Eliza wasn't proper. She never had been. She arched wantonly toward him. "There will be time for vows and marriage beds later. Right now, having you ravish me is all I can think about."

A wicked grin spread over his lips. "You're driving me mad."

"Good," Eliza said. "Show me just how mad I make you."

He lifted her by the hips, carrying her to the potting table. His eyes traveled over her plump thighs and belly, burning her with their heat as she offered herself to him in a haze of rampant lust.

When they came apart, flushed with their exertions, Eliza cupped his face in her hands and held his gaze. The rain had started up once more, steady and soft against the window. She pulled in a steadying breath. "Meet me at the carriage house in an hour. I don't care where we go or how we do it. I want to be your wife by morning."

CHAPTER 13

Eliza pulled her trunk from beneath her bed and mindlessly shoved stockings, drawers, and shifts into it. She had no idea where they were going or how long they'd be gone, only that Malcolm had reassured her he'd find an authority to oversee their vows. As she was buttoning her summer wool traveling suit, she heard the front door creak open downstairs. Lydia's step whispered on the marble floor below.

"Liza! Are you awake?"

"Upstairs, cher!" Eliza called. "I have news."

Lydia appeared in the doorway, her hair a wreath of frizzing ringlets. A glossy sheen winked in the whites of her eyes. Her chin and cheeks were the color of claret. Eliza smirked. "You're drunk."

Her sister frowned. "No, ma'am. I am not," she slurred. She wobbled over to the foot of the bed and sat. "Sarah is, though. I put her to bed after the other ladies left. She was wretched."

"See, you're already practicing at becoming a nurse."

"It's the middle of the night. Why are you getting dressed?"

Eliza crossed the room and took Lydia's hands. "Sister, Malcolm and I are eloping."

"What?" Lydia made a dry clucking at the back of her throat. "No. You're not going to marry *anyone* until banns have been read and you've the blessing of a priest."

Mon Dieu. "We *are* eloping. It's settled. You told me to give marriage a chance, and I am."

Lydia stood, her breath huffing from her nose. "You are making a terrible mistake, *ma soeur.* You hardly know him. You have almost two whole months before the clause must be satisfied. Why not wait and have a proper wedding? Be practical. Be *sensible,* for once in your life!"

Eliza dropped Lydia's hands. "We cannot wait. Lord Eastleigh has threatened to file notice of eviction by the end of the month. Malcolm will lose his house, everything. We must be married quickly in order for me to pay the debt and save Havenwood Manor. He can't lose that house."

"What about *your* house?" Lydia gestured to the room, her eyes feverish. "You can live here. Hmm? What is wrong with that? If he loves you, your house will be just as suitable."

"I had planned on giving Sherbourne House to you." Eliza turned away and sat to tie on her walking boots. "You and Clarence will be betrothed soon. I can feel it. I meant to give it to you as a wedding gift."

"There's room enough for all of us here! I can't understand." Lydia stalked through the room. "I don't know what you see in him or that godforsaken house with its bad mojo." She made a dramatic sweep with her arms. "It rolls off that place, Liza. I feel sick to my stomach just walking past its gates."

"You're being ridiculous." Eliza stood and straightened her jacket. "It's only a house."

"*Mais oui!* It is only a house." Lydia's face glistened with tears. "And what of the man? He's the same ilk as Eastleigh, only in more clever clothes. Of that, I am certain. Oh, Liza. I beg of you—please do not do this."

At Lydia's tears, Eliza melted. She went to her little sister and pulled her into her arms. Lydia pushed against her at first, and then stilled. "Do you know? I still remember the day Mimi Lisette first let me hold you."

"Don't talk about Mimi. Not now."

"You were so small, and I felt so big compared to you." Eliza remembered Mimi's soft hand in hers as she stood next to Lydia's crib, looking through the slats at the big-eyed baby with the red face and angry little fists. Mimi had lifted Lydia from the mattress and led Eliza to the rocking chair, where she carefully placed the swaddled babe in Eliza's arms. *Rock her gently, my little Liza. She is your petite fleur. You will always have one another.* With Eliza's steady rocking, Lydia had quieted and drifted into a contented sleep, her little hand curled around Eliza's thumb.

Tears sprung to Eliza's eyes. She drew back to look at Lydia and pushed the rain-crinkled curls away from her face. "We will always have each other, cher. Mimi was right about that. Just because I'm marrying Malcolm doesn't mean you're losing me. That's what you're most afraid of, isn't it?"

"Well. You'll be too busy keeping company with your new husband to think about me anymore."

"I'm only going to be down the road—a quick Sunday stroll away."

"It's going to be lonely here. Too quiet."

"You'll have your nurse training to keep you busy. And Clarence!"

Lydia's face softened. "I suppose you think you love him, or at least you love the idea of him. I just . . . I worry. Something doesn't feel right."

"The rumors aren't true, Lyddie. Malcolm has only had a difficult life. A life just as full of sorrow as our own. It's made him a pariah, and it's unjust. I can right some of his wrongs. His debt is such a small thing, after all. I want this marriage, and him, more than anything I've ever wanted. I *know* it's right. Please believe me."

Lydia drew in a shaky breath, her lips curving into a sad smile. "You must learn to see these things on your own, in time. I will do my best to lock my worries inside."

"Do I have your blessing, then?"

"As much as I can give."

"Good." Eliza kissed Lydia's forehead. "Do you know the very best part?"

"What?"

"Tomorrow, you'll have this entire house to do with as you wish. You can finally take down that damned cuckoo clock."

CHAPTER 14

"You are my *wife*." Malcolm kissed Eliza's bare shoulder and pulled her close. The rains had returned, beating against the gambrel roof of Havenwood Manor, soaking the ground and chilling the air enough that they'd lit a fire in the hearth, illuminating Eliza's new bedchamber with jumping, coppery light.

"Our secret wedding is bound to cause a stir."

"We'll deal with the ridiculous society mess later," he said, rolling her onto her back. He took her hand and played with the simple pearl ring on her finger before kissing it. "For now, I only want to enjoy the fact that you're really here, and not some pleasant dream I'm bound to wake from."

They'd married shortly after midnight, following a frenzied ride to Basingstoke, where one of Malcolm's old schoolmates worked as a magistrate. The wedding had been hastily done and uneventful, witnessed only by the magistrate's sleepy wife and Mr. Mason, who had driven them in his farm wagon as they hid in the back. After their covert return through the service gates of Havenwood Manor, Malcolm had carried her up the stairs. They'd spent every hour since in bed, much to Eliza's delight, even though she was now starving.

"Have you ever wondered how many times a person could make love in a single night before they're overcome with hunger and exhaustion?" she asked.

"My, but I'd enjoy finding out. Wouldn't you?"

She ignored the rumble of hunger in her belly and pushed Malcolm onto his back. "I long to do wicked things with you, husband. All over this house."

"How on earth did I get so lucky? If I didn't know better, I'd think you'd been trained in a brothel," he said, laughing. "You're sinfully eager."

"We're well-matched, wasn't that what you once said?" she whispered, pitching forward to nip at his neck.

"Yes, we are. Twin flames, brightly burning."

"Such a poet," she teased.

With a playful roar, he tumbled her into the soft eiderdown and covered her neck with kisses. Sensation raced through her at the feel of his lips on her skin, until her blood sang with the wildness of him. She wound a strand of his dark hair around her finger, her eyes roving over his chest and the lean, solid plane of his belly, memorizing every inch of him. How fine he was, and he was hers. Truly hers. "I never imagined I'd be anyone's wife. Yet here I am, and I couldn't be more delighted."

He smiled down at her, his eyes sparking with gold from the firelight. "My long days of loneliness and chastity are forever gone, my heart, and I've never been happier."

❦

Eliza rubbed the sleep from her eyes and reached for Malcolm. He was gone—his side of the bed empty, the covers drawn back. She sat up and stretched, the mild soreness between her legs a reminder of the pleasures from the night before.

She rose and crossed to the high, arched window. The morning sun lit the tops of the trees and warmed her skin as she unlaced her nightgown and shrugged it over her shoulders. She washed herself in the basin, then went to her armoire to choose a dress from her hastily packed clothes. She'd have to send Turner to fetch her finer garments sometime this week. She hadn't packed a single dinner gown.

There was a sharp knock on her door.

"Yes, what is it?"

"It's Turner, m'lady. His lordship is requesting your presence in the morning room."

"Thank you, Mr. Turner. I'll be down shortly."

She shook the wrinkles from her favorite tea gown—a periwinkle-blue frock enhanced with ribbons crossing beneath its bust. She glanced in the mirror over the dressing table and gathered her sex-frazzled hair into a loose braid. There was a rather lascivious gleam in her eye, and her cheeks were flushed more than usual. *I'm married now.* A woman in full.

And soon to be a very rich one.

Eliza glided down the stairs. Just as she'd imagined, the stained glass windows above the landing threw fractured light over her hands as she rested them on the bannister—crimson, violet, and a brilliant blue that reminded her of agate. This was the first time she'd seen her new home in daylight, and it shone as brightly as a kaleidoscope to her eyes. How many hidden delights did it have yet in store? She could hardly wait to explore its seemingly endless warren of rooms. Thoughts of summer socials and lavish galas in the magnificent ballroom made her head spin with giddy anticipation.

Malcolm stood from the breakfast table as she walked into the sun-filled morning room, the windows open to the cheerful sounds of birdsong from the gardens. He was dressed in handsome blue serge, his cravat pierced with the emerald pin he'd worn on the night they'd met.

"Ah, there you are, darling. Did you enjoy your lie-in?" He pressed a dry kiss to her forehead, and Eliza leaned wantonly against him, clasping his hand.

"Yes, although I'd much prefer your company while I'm abed."

Malcolm pulled away, arching an eyebrow. "I rise each day at six o'clock, on the nose, my dear. Always have done." He sat, flicking open the newspaper and scanning it.

Eliza took the chair opposite. She poured her tea and flavored it with milk and honey. She sat watching Malcolm for a few moments, studying the way the light played over the angles of his face. *Her husband.* She could still hardly believe it.

He noticed her staring and gave a tight smile above the leaves of his paper. "I thought we'd take a ride into town this afternoon, see your solicitor to finalize the matter of your estate. Would you have any objections?"

"Not at all. I'd rather have this business with Eastleigh settled as soon as possible."

Malcolm cleared his throat and turned the page. "Quite ready, myself."

Eliza smiled over the rim of her teacup. "Perhaps after, we can celebrate by taking our dinner in bed."

He met her gaze, his dark eyebrows knitting together in a pained expression. "Darling, let's leave such talk for our chambers, and not where the servants can hear, hmm? You're a viscountess now. A *lady.*"

"I couldn't care less about my silly title. I'm only happy to be your wife."

"Right. In any case, there are a few matters concerning the house and our marriage we need to discuss."

"Oh?"

"For one thing, the south wing is to remain locked. It's far too dangerous to inhabit, and until the necessary structural repairs are made, you're not to go into that part of the house for any reason. When it comes to the rest of the estate, you are not to go wandering beyond the rear gardens without me—there are traps and snares set in the birchwood, and only I know their locations." Malcolm cleared his throat again. "And . . . as far as our marital duties, I shall only ever come to *your* chambers. Please do not be forward about seeking me out at night. My rooms are my own."

"All right," Eliza said, wrinkling her brow. Rules. What a strange conversation for the morning after their wedding! She tucked into her breakfast, a potato and leek tart adorned with pastry doves in flight. Mrs. Duncan came bustling out of the kitchen, her friendly, round face a welcome distraction. She laid a platter of fresh fruit between Eliza and Malcolm. "Thank you, Mrs. Duncan. This pie is delicious," Eliza said. The rotund little housekeeper beamed and curtseyed before going back to the kitchen.

"No need to thank the staff," Malcolm said curtly. "They're only doing their jobs."

"I show gratitude to anyone who extends kindness to me, husband. Especially to servants. It's how I was raised. Noblesse oblige."

"As charming as they are, you'll find that many of your Creole sensibilities will merit polishing here. Speak pleasantries to the staff and they begin to feel as if they're your equal. We can't have that, can we?"

"I suppose we can't." She hurriedly finished the rest of her breakfast and stood from the table, irritation burning her ears beneath her untamed hair. "I think I'll go to my rooms now," she said sharply. "I need to dress for our outing and finish my toilette. I'll have to send Turner to Sherbourne House to fetch the rest of my clothing, but I do have my daywear."

"Very good." Malcolm stood, scanning her bosom. He scowled. "Something a bit more modest would suit you, I think. I'll come for you at one."

⟢❧⟣

Their trip into Cheltenbridge was lovely, so long as one was talking about the weather. Malcolm was silent most of the way there. He drove Apollo harder than she would have liked, freely employing his crop.

The matter at Mr. Brainerd's office took most of the afternoon, with Eliza having to watch Malcolm sign endless documents, while Monty lay across her feet, his shaggy head nudging her hand for pets, which she willingly gave.

She asked only one question, when the time came for Malcolm to put his pen to the deed for Sherbourne House. "My sister will be able to stay on, as we discussed. Isn't that so, husband?"

"Miss Tourant may stay on until she marries, at which time I'll let out the property to tenants. No need to maintain another household within walking distance, is there?"

Eliza blanched. "I'd hoped she and Clarence might stay at Sherbourne House, even after they marry. I've promised the house to them as a wedding gift. That way, I can visit her whenever I'd like. Lydia is the only family I have left. We've never been apart for longer than a day."

Malcolm turned to her. A slight tremor of irritation quivered between his brows. "Look, darling. I've agreed to let her stay on for now. She isn't even betrothed to Fawcett yet. We'll see, won't we?"

Eliza bit her lip. A drop of ink plopped onto the parchment from Malcolm's pen. Mr. Brainerd shot an annoyed look over the top of his spectacles.

Malcolm scratched his name—Malcolm Aaron Winfield, fifth Viscount Havenwood—across the page next to her own, and it was done. Her house and her fortune now belonged to him as much as herself.

He was positively giddy at the sum, chattering about his plans for renovating the manor the entire way home. All the while, Eliza's head pounded with a sudden, blinding migraine. She did her best to smile and be agreeable, even as a wave of nausea threatened to bring up her breakfast. She skipped the lovely tea Mrs. Duncan had laid out and chased away her headache with a dram of whisky and a nap.

That evening, dressing for dinner, Eliza searched her armoire. She hadn't packed a single suitable gown. Or had she? She gave a noiseless laugh, remembering the long-forgotten parcel in the bottom of her trunk. Her mourning gown. She'd wrapped the black lace and bengaline atrocity in brown paper and twine and buried it beneath a riot of colorful ball gowns when she packed for England, swearing never to wear it again. It wasn't ideal, but it would do. She knelt on the floor in front of the high-legged Chippendale armoire and pulled her steamer trunk from beneath. She took the packet out, ripping the twine and paper loose. The gown bloomed like a black orchid in her hands, smelling of stale church incense. She pulled it on over her petticoats and corset. Its ruffled neck came just below her chin, where the stiff lace flared like a Renaissance collar. The puffed, gigot sleeves narrowed to a sharp point, covering the scars at her wrist. She smirked at her reflection. He did say he preferred modesty, didn't he?

She stood before her dressing table and coaxed her ginger hair into ordered ringlets with bandoline, then piled it atop her head. She finished her ablutions by clipping a pair of jet earrings onto her ears. She looked as tame as she was capable of looking without her full wardrobe.

The gong rang for dinner. Eliza gave herself one more appraising glance and went down, the beaded hem of her gown hissing on the wooden stairs. Malcolm was standing beneath the winged seraph at the base of the staircase, dressed in white tie. He turned, a teasing smile playing at his lips. "My beautiful wife. Looking rather more like a widow than a bride, but lovely all the same."

Eliza pinched the lace collar between her thumb and forefinger. "Well. I had to work with what I had. And you mentioned you prefer modest dress."

He ran his fingertips down the row of tiny buttons up the back she'd had to contort herself into fastening with the help of a crocheting hook. "I suppose I did say that, although I may have to resort to scissors later," he whispered, his breath hot against her cheek. "Your charms are much too hidden for my liking."

The dining room table was laid out *à la russe*, the silver gleaming over pressed white linens. Turner pulled out a chair for Eliza at the foot of the table, and Malcolm put a hand on his shoulder. "Thank you, Turner, but I'd have my wife sit close to me at the head. This old table is rather too long as it is."

Unlike their morning meal, dinner was filled with witty conversation and laughter over Madeira and a sumptuous roasted squab, lightening Eliza's mood. During dessert, Malcolm's hand found its way beneath the table and rested on her knee, then moved higher, his fingers brushing where the boning of her corset met the delta of her thighs. Boldly, she held his gaze and opened her legs. Even under a layer of petticoats, he'd be sure to gather her intentions.

"I'm quite full, aren't you, darling?" he asked.

"I'm not as hungry for dessert as I'd anticipated," Eliza said, her lips curving into a slow smile. "And I'm suddenly so tired."

"Perhaps I should see you to your chambers."

They were hardly over the threshold before Malcolm was clawing at her gown. "You're wearing far too many clothes," he teased, biting her earlobe. "It's driving me mad."

"Then take me out of them."

Without hesitation, he spun her around, hooking his fingertips in the back of the gown and ripping the buttons free. They fell and scattered on the floor like black, glistening rain.

"Goodness. I'll need a lady's maid if I'm to have any clothing left," Eliza teased.

"That dress is no great loss, I assure you." Malcolm loosened her corset with practiced fingers and pulled her petticoats free from her hips. She turned slowly to face the heat flaring in his eyes. "I've been thinking about this all day long, wife. Thinking about you."

Eliza nearly swooned, the memory of his strange words from that morning fading as desire replaced her doubts. His fevered mouth found her throat, where her pulse hammered against her flesh like a bird trapped in a room. "You're mine now," he whispered. "Do you know that? Mine."

They fell together into the welcoming bed, soft and fragrant with lavender. Within moments he was driving her over the edge, and he knew it, damn him—his lips curving into a vulpine grin as he watched her with lamplit eyes. "Tremble for me, my darling," he rasped. And as if he had command over her very body, Eliza came undone.

After he'd met his own crisis, he wrapped her in his arms. She turned to stroke the fine-boned planes of his face, her eyes closing and opening drowsily. As a deep, satisfied torpor crept into her every muscle, Malcolm gently took her forearm and ran his fingertip over the jagged scars that snaked across her inner wrist. "You've been clever—concealing this with your gloves and sleeves—but I saw this mark after that awful incident with the Cook boy. What happened?"

"It's nothing, my love," she said, turning from the searching look in his eyes. "An old injury. I scratched it while mending fences on our farm."

"Eliza, please don't lie to me. I'm your husband."

"It's shameful."

Malcolm's pupils darkened, growing large in the dim light. "Tell me, darling. Please."

"It happened when I was eighteen. For years after Albert died, I had horrible fits of melancholia. My mother was too deep in her cups to comfort me, and Papa was always away because of her drinking. I had little to make me happy besides lessons with my harp teacher, Giselle. Maman thought I was becoming too close to her, so she sent her away. It was heartbreaking. Then Jacob came to work for my father. He was two years older and I was curious what it would be like to be with a man. We soon became lovers. With Jacob, I had some respite from my sadness."

"Yet you did not marry him?"

Eliza shook her head. "We had talked about running away. When Maman found out about our trysts, she had Papa write his severance that very day. I hated her for that, but I hated myself more for not standing up to her. Without Giselle, then Jacob, I fell into my deepest hysteria, fraught with nightmares and wicked thoughts. I felt unwanted. A burden. One morning, I broke my hand mirror and used a shard to . . ." Eliza ran her thumb over the old marks. "Well. By the time Lydia found me, I was barely conscious."

"Promise me, my own heart, that you will never do such a thing again."

"I won't. I was young and in an awful state then." Eliza smiled sadly. "If it hadn't been for Lydia, I wouldn't be here. I love her, not because we share blood, but because she is the truest of friends. She understands me in ways no one else ever has. She sees all of my flaws and loves me despite them."

"I see now why she's so protective of you."

"And I of her. Which is why I couldn't bear it if you ever put her out of Sherbourne House."

Malcolm propped himself up on his elbow, his brows gathering. "Why would you ever think I would do such a thing?"

"We spoke about it at the solicitor's today, remember? If Lydia marries, you said you'd let out Sherbourne House and she and her husband would need to find another home."

Malcolm's eyes narrowed. "Well . . . I've changed my mind. Lydia must stay on. I insist. I want our children to grow up surrounded by their cousins. A big, joyful family, spending Christmases and summer holidays together. It's all I've ever wanted." Malcolm pressed a kiss to her forehead. "Put every thought of being separated from your sister out of your mind. I'll hear nothing of the sort."

"You've made my heart light again," Eliza said, her concerns from earlier in the day flying free. "You are the most beautiful and rarest of creatures I've ever laid eyes on, do you know that?" She reached out to trace the crisp line of his lips with her finger. "I could have chosen a man with feet of clay, but I reached high into the heavens and brought down an angel."

Malcolm gave a sad smile. "I'm hardly that, my love."

⚜

Eliza flew awake, gasping and sputtering. Her heart slammed against her rib cage. She disentangled herself from the circle of Malcolm's arms and breathed in and out, counting in rhythm with the steadiness of his breathing. It had been weeks since she'd last had the nightmare. Weeks of restful, blissful sleep. Doubtless, their conversation the night before had revived her unbidden memories. Memories that would never fully leave her.

She swung her legs over the side of the bed. Her shift clung to her body, soaked with sweat. She rose on unsteady feet and crossed to the dressing table, startling at her reflection in the glass—all haunted eyes and tangled hair. She rummaged through her drawerful of cosmetics until she found her tin of cigarettes. She went through to her sitting room. Moonlight spilled through the mullioned casement, dotting the floor with discs of prismatic light. Eliza cranked open the narrow window, the blast of cool air soothing to her fevered skin.

She lit a cigarette and drew in the rich tobacco, leaning her elbows upon the sill. Within moments, the tremor in her hands had quieted and her pulse had slowed. Downstairs, the clock chimed thrice. Three in the morning. *The witching hour*, Lydia always called it. The time when the veil between worlds was thinnest. Eliza wondered how her sister was faring, alone in that big house. She needed to visit soon. If for no other reason than to assure Lydia she was well.

A sudden quiver of movement drew Eliza's eyes downward. Among the birches, a light bobbed between the slender trees, as if someone were wending their way through the woods, carrying a lantern. But who? And why at this hour? The light danced and jumped erratically, like a will-o'-the-wisp. She had often seen these sorts of illusions in the bayous around Lake Pontchartrain. There, it was merely swamp gas. But there was no swamp around Havenwood Manor.

Eliza pitched herself forward to get a closer look, stubbing out her cigarette and tossing it through the window. The lantern stilled, as if whomever was carrying it had seen her at the sash. Her impulse was to call out a greeting, but she didn't dare wake Malcolm at this hour. Instead, she waved. The light moved nearer, and then stopped again. Eliza drew in a sharp breath. Her eyes strained in the darkness, trying to discern a form within the halo of light.

There was a stirring from the other room, followed by a yawn. "Eliza . . . where are you? Come back to bed."

Eliza turned at the sound of Malcolm's voice. "In a moment, love. There's someone in the forest."

"What?"

"Yes, I just saw . . ." Eliza turned back to the window, but the light had gone. All was dark. The trees stood tall and silent, keeping their secrets close.

CHAPTER 15

August came through in a rush, bringing a relentless, steaming heat that made the inner rooms of Havenwood Manor intolerable by noon. Eliza lingered long in her bed, shedding her nightgown as she had in New Orleans, stretching out on the sheets with the windows thrown wide. While she was as lustful as a courtesan at night, she remained as demure and well mannered as her husband had asked during the day.

The truth was, it was an easy thing to accomplish, because Malcolm was hardly home during daylight hours. He was ever off doing business in Winchester or Southampton, or in his study with the door closed, drawing up plans for the renovations to Havenwood Manor. Eliza spent her solitary afternoons exploring the jigsaw puzzle of interconnected rooms inside the mansion. She relished every detail—from the friezes in the small parlor depicting a unicorn hunt, to the burlwood escritoire in her room. As she walked the maze of halls, she traced each baroque line of trimwork with worshipful fingertips and cataloged the martyrs depicted in the stained glass windows. Saint Sebastian had become her favorite, his torso pierced with arrows, his head thrown back in ecstasy. Despite the damp and the mildew that remained tucked in the corners of certain rooms, the house was as much a bridegroom as her husband, and she adored both with fervent admiration.

Eliza was happy. But there was one matter, in all of this decadent fog of newlywed rapture, that concerned her to distraction.

Two weeks after her wedding, she knocked on the doors of Sherbourne House. Her sister opened them, dressed in plummy linen. "You look awful," Lydia said archly. "You're not sleeping, are you?" She stood aside to let Eliza through the doorway. In the front parlor, Tante Theo's porcelain samovar steamed on the console. Next to it, a tray laden with Eliza's favorite jam-filled sugar cookies beckoned. She greedily chose four, stacking them in her hands as she sat.

"If I'm not sleeping, sister, it's only because my husband insists on making love to me all through the night," Eliza said. "I'd no idea men could be so . . . enthusiastic."

"That's exactly what you wanted, isn't it? It seems my concerns about your husband were unfounded." Lydia searched Eliza's face. She had a way of looking at a person and seeing the things they wanted to keep hidden. "Still, there's something bothering you. Isn't there?"

"Yes. There's something I would ask of you, if you're willing." Eliza took a drink of her tea and set it down with a clatter. "I don't want to have a baby. At least for a good long while."

"Why? If you love this man so much, why wouldn't you want to give him a child? He'll be expecting you to provide him with an heir. And you aren't getting younger."

Eliza closed her eyes. "I just don't want to, cher. I'm not ready for that sort of responsibility. Perhaps someday. But not yet."

Lydia sighed. "I suppose I can make you Mimi's herbal tonic. It may cause cramping, and there's no guarantee it will work. It also tastes of piss and quinine."

"I remember. She made it for me once." Mimi had concocted the bitter draught after Eliza had confessed the loss of her virginity. *Foolish child. It may be too late, but I will make something that should right your wrongs. You better damn well pray it works, otherwise your maman will murder you and that poor boy both.* "I'll endure the cramps gladly. I'd rather that than face the confinement of motherhood." Eliza shrugged. "It's a mercy, really. You and I both know I'm not suited to motherhood. Besides, I'm anxious to build my stables."

Lydia cleared her throat. "And does your husband know your opinion on motherhood? You should talk of such things with him."

"Merde. I will give him a child. Someday. Just not now."

"Fair enough." Lydia gave a petulant huff of breath. "Are you coming to Sarah's party?"

"I hadn't heard she was having one."

"It's only a small gathering. This Friday night."

Eliza paused before answering. Apart from their hasty trip to Brainerd's office, they'd made no public appearances since their elopement. "Does anyone besides you and Mr. Mason know Malcolm and I have wed?"

"I haven't said a word. Not even to Clarence."

"Good. I want our nuptials to remain a secret for the time being. We're filing paperwork against Eastleigh's notice of eviction, and Malcolm wants to make sure the legal protections are in place before we announce our marriage."

"Still, you should come to Sarah's party. Why not? Everyone already knows you're courting, after all. You have to be getting bored in that drafty old house."

Eliza winked. "Sister, I assure you. I am *anything* but bored."

❦

Eliza dressed for Sarah's party, choosing a new gown made of watered-silk douppioni. It draped about her figure like a sheath made of shifting ocean waves, bringing out the aquamarine tones in her eyes. She clasped the pearl necklace her father had given her for her debut about her neck, and swept her hair up loosely, letting a few wild curls escape around the edges. As she was finishing her toilette, something flickered behind her in the glass, just for a moment—a blunted streak of light. She pivoted on the stool, but there was nothing there. How funny. Perhaps it was a moth, flitting between the arms of the chandelier. Since she'd seen the mysterious light in the woods, which Malcolm had dismissed as one of the crofters checking snares, a kind of vigilant, hopeful curiosity had enlivened her explorations of the house. What if? What *if* some of the stories were true? Her skepticism could be made to waver, with enough proof.

Malcolm strode into her room, his white tie freshly starched. He rested his hands on her shoulders as she rouged her cheeks, and then her lips. "Tonight's a bit of a coming-out party for us, isn't it?" he said. "Our secret won't last much longer."

"Knowing how gossip travels in this town, you're probably right. But perhaps they won't guess just yet." Eliza took off her pearl wedding ring and placed it in the dish on her dressing table. A shiver went over her shoulders as she pulled on her gloves, remembering Eastleigh's threats. "Do you suppose Eastleigh will be there?"

"He's not a favorite of the Nelsons." Malcolm knelt at her feet. "But, if he does come, we'll have quite a surprise for him, won't we?" He placed her shoes on her feet and fastened her gilded buckles, then slid his hand up her calf to the soft skin of her inner thigh.

Eliza's breath caught in her throat. "Keep that business up, husband, and we'll be unfashionably late."

When they arrived at the Nelson's mansion, Sarah answered the door, dressed in a handsome tuxedo with a glen plaid waistcoat and white cuffs, her chestnut hair down around her shoulders and her cheeks rouged. Her gaze lingered warmly on Eliza before she turned to lead them inside. "I've never seen a finer-looking sight, I daresay. Like a siren of the waves. It's good to see you out after all this time, Malcolm. Especially with such pretty company."

"Our Sarah might steal you away if I'm not careful," Malcolm teased.

"That I may," Sarah said with a wink. "Pistols at dawn, sir."

Malcolm chuckled. "I remember Sarah and I were at a dance in Somerset once, I believe in our sixteenth year, and there was a girl with hair the color of new flax . . ."

Sarah's brows gathered in confusion. "Really? Your memory must be better than mine."

Just then, Polly came whirling into the foyer in a flurry of blush silk and rhinestones and pulled Sarah aside. "Cora says you're up as dealer. I'm losing terribly and could use your luck."

"Now how can I resist a plea like that?" Sarah linked arms with Polly and gave Eliza a knowing look. "Do come talk to me in a bit, darling. I hear we've a bit of catching up to do."

"She fancies you," Malcolm whispered after she'd gone.

"What?" Eliza asked.

"Sarah. She's an invert, dearest. She prefers women. We often chased the same girls in our youth. She was much more successful than I."

"Really?" Eliza giggled, thinking of all her stolen kisses with Giselle so many years ago. Kisses that had eventually landed on collarbones and bosoms and could have easily become something more. At times, she still ached for the easy companionship she'd enjoyed with Giselle. She could understand Sarah preferring the same and admired her boldness. "How incredible. Yet she's married?"

"Yes, well. Her husband is just the same. His summer fishing trips to Bath are a ruse. He goes there to meet his male lovers."

"My goodness. What other secrets are you keeping?"

Malcolm's lips curved in a wry grin. "Tons."

As they moved into the drawing room, a string quartet began tuning up by the hearth. Lydia came to her side, resplendent in scarlet satin. "You look like you're up to something," she whispered. "If you're truly wanting to keep your secret, quit smirking like a cat in the cream. I can always tell when you're thinking naughty things."

"Perhaps," Eliza rasped. "But it's so fun. Besides, I think Sarah already knows."

"I'm not at all surprised."

Clarence Fawcett came forward wearing cleverly patched evening dress, his hair slicked with pomade. He made a crisp bow to Malcolm and took Eliza's gloved hand in greeting, then whisked Lydia into a rollicking mazurka. Several familiar faces were among the people gathered around the dance floor. Eliza was most relieved to see that neither Eastleigh nor Una Moseley was among the guests.

After they'd had champagne and made polite conversation, Malcolm and Eliza joined the other dancers for a breathless waltz. When the song ended, he guided her from the room as the guests looked on, whispering behind raised fans. They went down the hall and through a doorway hung with lavish fringed curtains. In the secluded alcove beyond, a tufted chaise sloped against the wall, a portrait of a naked nymph above it.

"Did you see their faces?" Eliza giggled. "We're beyond scandalous."

"It's quite fun, isn't it?" Malcolm pulled her onto the low couch, stifling her laughter with his hand. He lifted her wrist and parted the fabric between her glove buttons, then brought the keyhole of bared flesh to his mouth, flicking her skin with the point of his tongue. A lascivious heat spread from the junction of Eliza's thighs to her belly. "I wonder how much we could get away with, hidden here," he said. His fingertips teased her through the fabric of her dress, the heat from his breath warming the skin on her neck.

"Yes," she murmured, arching her back. God, how he made her weak. Wanton. She ached to have him touch her. His mouth sought hers in the darkness as she guided his hand beneath her petticoats.

"Liza! Come out here."

Merde. It was Lydia. Through heavy-lidded eyes, Eliza could see her flickering silhouette against the wall outside the opening of the curtains.

Malcolm withdrew his hand, a sigh of frustration hissing through his lips. "Your sister has impeccable timing."

"Stay here. I'll see what she wants," Eliza rasped. She stood, smoothing out her skirts. She pressed a hand against her cheeks to cool them and walked out into the drawing room.

"What were you doing?" Lydia gave an appraising look to Eliza's flushed cheeks and bosom. "All saints. Never mind. I don't want to know."

"Is something wrong?"

"Eastleigh is here, in the rear gardens with Polly. She's trying to calm him, but he knows y'all are here and he's none too happy."

Eliza felt Malcolm's presence behind her. "Miss Tourant, would you care to show me out so I may address the earl? His quarrel is with me."

Eliza shook her head. Panic twisted in her gut. "Malcolm, don't. Please."

"Darling, I'm sure his mood can be lightened after a snifter of whisky and a hand of cards. Eastleigh isn't the sort to make a public row." Malcolm's voice was tense as steel. "Miss Tourant, please."

Lydia flounced down the wide central hallway and led them onto the terrace facing the garden. Polly and Eastleigh stood a few yards away, near a fountain of Neptune shooting arcs of silvery water from his trident. Polly's face was wet with tears. "Charles! Forget her. She's made her choice and she wasn't worthy of your attention to begin with. It's my father's fondest wish, and mine, to see us married. He sent his blessing, just this week!"

Eastleigh had his back to them, but Eliza heard every word. "Marry *you*?" he slurred. "Surely you didn't think I wouldn't set my sights higher than a half-witted admiral's daughter?"

Eliza gripped Lydia's hand. "Poor Polly," she whispered. "I'd no idea they were courting."

"I don't think they were," Lydia whispered. "I think she's a bit delusional."

Polly pushed past Eastleigh and hurtled toward them, her pale hair mussed and her eyes streaming. "Ah! Here she is now, Charles. Did you enjoy witnessing my humiliation, Miss Sullivan?"

"Polly, please. I am no rival for Lord Eastleigh's affections. I've only ever wanted to be your friend." Eliza reached out for the distraught girl's hand. Her gesture was met with a stinging slap to the wrist. Two bright spots of color flared on her cheeks.

"Do you know?" Polly spat. "I've had my cap set toward Charles for years. From the time I was a girl. And he wouldn't so much as glance my way." Polly's hands clenched her skirts, her mouth twisting into a sardonic smile. "And finally, I'd charmed him. He was lately round for tea every Sunday. And then you come here, with your slatternly American ways, and all the lords of the realm fall at your feet."

"That's not true, Polly. I do not love him, I promise you. Malcolm owns my heart, and only Malcolm."

"Miss Whitby," Malcolm said gently, his arm going around Eliza's waist. "Charles is not worthy of your tears. Your honor is high above his own, I assure you. You've no rival with Eliza."

Polly cackled. "Have you told your Eliza the full story, Malcolm? I'm quite sure her pretty face and fine figure aren't the real reason you're wooing her."

"Havenwood! I'd have a word with you." Eastleigh rounded the hedge, reeking of liquor, his white tie rumpled and his hat askew. Eliza's heart gave a sickening twist.

Malcolm stepped in front of Eliza and lifted his hat. "My lord, how pleasant it is to see you this evening."

Eastleigh glowered. "I was feeling rather the opposite."

"Look, Charles . . . I realize in matters of the heart we share the same interest, but Eliza has made her choice."

"Indeed. I have," Eliza said, coming out from behind Malcolm. "Good evening, sir." She took a deep breath and released it through tight lips. "Malcolm and I are married. We've been so for over two weeks."

Polly gasped.

"Married!" Eastleigh sneered. He gave a bitter bark. "Really? I've seen no banns. I'd warrant the thing, if indeed it happened, is far from legitimate."

"I have the paperwork from a magistrate in Basingstoke saying that it is."

"Bloody hell. Rather fast, after a fashion. I suppose you let him have a run up your skirts and there's a child in your belly he didn't want born a bastard. They do say you Americans are loose."

Malcolm tensed next to her. "Sir, you'll not address my wife in such a coarse manner. Apologize."

"Or what?"

"Or I shall be forced to challenge you."

Eastleigh rolled his head back and laughed. "Bold to be challenging the one who holds four mortgages against your estate, sir."

"Not for long. We've filed an injunction against your notice of eviction." Eliza's words were as sharp as cut glass. "I'll soon be clearing my husband's debts with my fortune. We've more than enough to cover it, I assure you."

Eastleigh tore his hat from his head and tossed it to the ground, where it rolled in a crooked circle. "You righteous little whore."

"Right. That's enough. Let's go, then." Malcolm unbuttoned his jacket, his jaw clenching.

"Malcolm, please! It isn't worth it," Eliza cried. Malcolm ignored her protestations and handed his jacket to Lydia, then pushed up his shirtsleeves. A cold sweat broke out along Eliza's brow. It seemed a chivalrous thing in a romance novel, having two men fight over you, but in reality, it was anything but. It was nauseating.

"Look, I don't rate a fight, little Havenwood." He made a mocking bow to Eliza. "I'm ever so sorry for offending your honor, my *lady*."

"Coward," Malcolm spat. "More gratifying to insult a woman than face your equal, is it?"

"You may have claimed your prize, but her money won't take the tarnish off your name." Eastleigh gave a slow, devilish grin. "Do you know? Your father was never proud of you. Called you his soft, pretty lordling. I suppose you've got something to prove then, haven't you?"

Malcolm went after him with a roar, tackling Eastleigh to the ground. They tangled in a heap down the hill, Malcolm's fists hammering the smug look from Charles's face. Polly screamed and sat upon the ground, covering her face with her hands, looking for all the world like a ruined, wilting rose. The door to the mansion flew open. Sarah came running out with a horrified shriek, the rest of the guests trailing her. With some effort, Clarence and the other men pulled Malcolm off Charles, who lay rolling on the ground, laughing, his nose bloodied. "Should've been your brother that lived, Havenwood. Real man. Unlike you, crying for your mummy when you so much as scratched your knee."

"Enough, gentlemen!" Sarah boomed, her usual good humor gone. "Lord Eastleigh, Lord Havenwood, you'd both do well to leave immediately, else I'll be forced to fetch the constable."

Charles stood and straightened his jacket, wiping his nose with the back of his hand. "Fine, fine. I'll be heading out, straightaway." He tipped his hat to Eliza. "You'll soon live to regret your choice, Lady Havenwood. You can set a wager on that."

CHAPTER 16

It was a week after Sarah's party when Eliza first heard the tapping. Thanks to Lydia's tonic, her menses had arrived on schedule, and though she was loath to admit it, she was glad for the respite from Malcolm's attention. He was proving to be insatiable. Their amorous activities left her breathless with pleasure, but she was hardly sleeping. She was relishing the chance to read alone and drift off to sleep, taking up as much of the bed as she liked.

Tap, tap, tap.

She looked up from the book propped against her knees, a rather dry history of the Napoleonic wars, and took her spectacles from her nose, listening. For a moment, she thought it was merely a tree limb knocking against the side of the house. But when it came again, too steady, too measured to be anything wrought from nature alone, Eliza threw back the covers and went to the window, lifting the sash and peering out. There was no wind. Only the sound of tree frogs and the distant baying of a dog met her ears. "How strange."

There were three more knocks, then a breath of silence. Eliza looked up at the ceiling. The attic was above her, with nothing in it but dusty trunks and discarded furniture. It couldn't have come from there. Eliza crossed the floor and flung open the door, peering down the hallway.

Only the dim, gaslit sconces hissed along the wall, throwing shadows on the carpet.

"What on earth?" she asked the room, turning to climb back in bed. She picked up her book once more and, after fluffing the pillows behind her head, went back to her reading. An hour passed, and then another. Just as Eliza was falling asleep, her book dipping perilously close to her chin, the rapping started up again. Eliza's heart pummeled out of her chest, and she jumped free of the eiderdown. She knelt on the floor, confronting her childhood fear of monsters beneath bedsteads, and lifted the dust ruffle. She closed her eyes, counted to three, and opened them wide as she ducked her head to look.

There was nothing there.

Just as she was about to climb back under the covers, it sounded again. This time louder, more insistent. Eliza stumbled backward, nearly knocking her washbasin off its stand.

"That's it. I'm sleeping in Malcolm's room, no matter what he says."

She tore across the gallery connecting her wing to Malcolm's and rapped on the door, her breath hitching. "Malcolm! Something's happening in my room."

She heard him swear. There was clicking and turning on the other side of the door as he undid his latches. He opened to her, his face drawn and tired, his pinstriped pajamas wrinkled and buttoned to the collar. "What are you on about, darling? You've woken me from a perfectly good sleep."

"There's a knocking in my chambers. It moves, just as if there's someone walking around in the attic or the hall. It taps thrice, stops, then changes places and starts up again. Always in a pattern of three."

Malcolm passed a hand over his hair in irritation. "It's only the pipes. They clang awfully at times. The plumbing runs over your ceiling and behind the walls."

Eliza shook her head. "No, this wasn't the pipes. My walls were fairly jumping with it, Malcolm!"

He pressed the back of his hand to her forehead and yawned. "I think you might have a fever, dearest."

"I was wondering if I might sleep in your room tonight. I'm frightened."

"Darling . . . you know my rules about the house. Proper gentlefolk do not share bedrooms."

"Yet you've no problem sharing *my* room."

"But that's the way of it, don't you see?"

"Well, I'm afraid."

"Eliza, you're not a child. Go to bed—take some laudanum if you must. When you're finished with your"—he waved his hands about—"*lady* time, I'll be back in your chambers once more, protecting you from the scary pipe beast knocking about your room."

"You're being priggish, husband."

"You'll not be the first to say as much. Now, go to bed."

Malcolm shut the door in her face, and Eliza groaned in frustration, banging her fist against the door and then kicking it. "Jackass!" she screeched and stalked back across the gallery. "It's all well and good to share a bed when you're betwixt my legs. Well, two can play at this merry game."

Eliza slammed the door to her room and angrily batted the covers back on her bed. There was a muted thud from across the room. The door to the armoire creaked open. Eliza gave a shriek and climbed atop the mattress. She crouched on all fours, expecting a mouse to come scurrying across the floorboards. Instead, lying beneath the edge of the wardrobe was a book, no bigger than a deck of cards, figured on its cover with the letters *A* and *M*.

Eliza woke the next day to more rapping—this time the unmistakably human sort. "Mum, it's Mrs. Duncan. I've brought your tea and a note from your sister."

The little diary lay next to her on the bed. Eliza slid it beneath her pillow. "Come in, please," she said, pushing the heel of her hand against her eyes. Her head was still fuzzy from the dose of laudanum she'd needed to calm her nerves the night before.

The housekeeper scurried through, her face flushed beneath her lace bonnet. She set the tea tray upon the mattress and pulled a card from her apron pocket, handing it to Eliza.

Sister,
I suppose you're enjoying all the delights of married life,
but I have news. Come this afternoon.
Yours,
Lyddie

"I'd reckon your sister is lonesome, m'lady," Mrs. Duncan said, her Scottish burr warm as she poured Eliza's tea with a steady hand. "I've a sister meself, back in Aberdeenshire. Been a fair bit since I've seen her, my Maggie."

"Well then, we must do something to remedy that," Eliza said, offering a smile. "Say, I have a question for you. Last night, I heard a curious tapping inside my room. His lordship said it was the pipes. Have you ever heard such a thing, Mrs. Duncan?"

The housekeeper paused, lifting the spout of the teapot. It dribbled on the napkin below, spotting brown. "I wouldn't ken any such thing, mum."

"Are you sure?" Eliza prodded. "It's all right, you know, talking to me. Despite what his lordship says. I spent the better part of my childhood belowstairs, and I much prefer the company of maids and cooks to lords and ladies."

Mrs. Duncan gave a dry laugh. "Och, I'll not tell his lordship a word. He's gone to Winchester for the day, at any rate."

"He's always gone to Winchester. Please, sit." Eliza patted the top of the counterpane. "And have a cookie while you're at it so I won't feel badly eating in front of you. You do make the very best shortbread."

"Thank you, m'lady." Mrs. Duncan made a little hop and perched on the edge of the bed, her toes barely touching the floor.

Eliza helped herself to the refreshments, her belly growling with hunger. "How long have you been on staff here? And what on earth is your first name? Malcolm hasn't told me."

"Shirley, mum. The last housekeeper, Mrs. Galbraith, hired me on as a chambermaid at sixteen and I'm now six-and-forty."

"You knew my mother-in-law, then. Tell me about her."

"Oh, dear Lady Havenwood—Ada, that is. She was from Scotland, too. We got on like a house afire." A sheepish look passed across Shirley's face at the gaffe. "Sorry."

"Don't be silly, I'm not easily offended. That explains why Malcolm sometimes whispers his endearments in Gaelic. I wondered where he learned it."

"Aye. He loved his mum. My but she was bonny. So fair it'd make your eyes hurt to look upon her too long. The house was happier with her in it. But the old Lord Havenwood didnae treat her right. He took his moods." Shirley looked down, picking at the lace tatting on her pinafore. "He struck me on occasion. 'You make the beds all wrong, stupid girl,' he'd say."

"I'm so sorry."

"'Tis the way of it with some masters. Your own husband is kinder. He'd do no such thing."

"He's a bit stiff and proper, my husband." Eliza took a sip of her tea. "Until the lights go down, that is."

"Aye, mum, but he cares for ye. I can see it. He's not been happy in so long. He was an awkward lad. Quiet and studious—always in a book. He didnae deserve the way his father treated him." Shirley shook her head. "Neither one of the lads did."

"This tapping I heard last night . . . did Lady Havenwood ever mention it? This was her room, wasn't it?"

"It were, mum, yes." Shirley shifted her bulk. "At least, until the years before the fire. She moved into the south wing then. As I recollect, she did mention the pipes creaking a time or two." Shirley stood, shaking the crumbs of shortbread out of her apron and into her reddened hands. "Well, I'd best be minding the dishes before his lordship comes home. If there's anything at all you'd like, m'lady, just ring."

"Thank you, Shirley."

"Only, please doona call me by my Christian name around your husband, mum. He's keen on keeping things proper."

Eliza winked. "It'll be our secret, I promise."

After the housekeeper left, Eliza pulled the diary from beneath her pillow. She'd thumbed through enough of the pages to know it was Ada's diary. She'd been too afraid and exhausted to read it the night before, but now, in the light of day, her curiosity overrode her fear. "What secrets are you hiding, little book?" she asked, running her fingertips over the embossed cover.

One thing she knew for certain: pipes didn't make walls shake. Pipes didn't tap in patterns of three. Something was being kept from her, and she was going to find out what.

CHAPTER 17

Eliza sat tucked inside the bay window of the morning room as Shirley bustled about, clearing the breakfast dishes and doing the dusting. She'd concealed Ada's diary between the covers of a dog-eared copy of *Sense and Sensibility*. It felt good having a secret—something decadent to keep for herself. If Malcolm was going to have secrets, she could have some too, after all. She opened the journal's crinkled, fragile pages and read.

> *August 18th, 1873*
>
> *Jennie adores parties. She pulls me out to every ball and soirée until my ears ring from the noise. I have been introduced to so many bachelors this Season I can no longer tell a duke from a baronet. They're all 'my lord' or 'your grace' or sir this-or-that and I cannot keep up! Jennie is the most devoted of companions, and I am grateful. Being an American, she isn't as stodgy as the sassenach girls, and she's so lovely to look at, with flashing dark eyes.*
>
> *I have been presented to the queen, and met the crown prince, Bertie. He's quite a flirt. He wants to have me come to Marlborough House for one of his famous parties. I have heard they turn into bacchanals as the night creeps into the wee hours. It all sounds positively scandalous.*

As for suitors, there's a viscount who seems fond of me. He owns a country manor in Hampshire, and a fine townhouse in Hyde Park. I met him on the Isle of Wight on the same day Jennie met her beau. He's quite old—at least forty—although it would relieve Papa's burdens to see me engaged to such a grounded and mature man, especially during my first Season. Living in Hampshire would mean I'd be close to the sea, which would make me happy. I do not think myself suited for life in London. Things move much too quickly, and the skies are ever blackened with soot.

I will be journeying home to Scotland soon for hunting season. I shall be chuffed to be back at Brynmoor, cozied up by the fire with my dogs after a good run in the gorse.

September 4th, 1873
Lord Havenwood proposed before I left London. I've a pretty ring—a wee pearl. Papa is pleased to see me engaged. I have no thought as to how I will fare with the delicate matters of marriage. I wish Mama were alive to speak to me of such things. My intended has yet to even kiss me. In some ways I feel I shall be more his daughter than his wife, which seems rather fine by me.

Jennie keeps asking if he's taken liberties, which makes me blush. I often feel set apart from the other girls in London—as if I am an outsider, looking in. They're always going on about their wedding nights, and while I'm curious, I do dread it. I pray my husband will be merciful and tender.

Eliza fiddled with the pearl ring Malcolm had given her, twisting the narrow band. Why hadn't he told her he'd given her his mother's ring? If he and his mother were so close, wouldn't that be something he'd share? Ada's journal was only creating more questions. Though her vision was strained from reading the childish, messy scribble of words written on the tiny pages, Eliza adjusted her spectacles and read on, eager to learn more about her predecessor.

December 31st, 1873

It is my favorite night of the year—our annual ghillies ball at Brynmoor! Papa has declared it fancy dress, and I'm keen to wear my Cherubino costume. I've been working on it all month. It's rather more comfortable than the stiff party taffetas I have to wear in London. I may well shock the elders, but it's all in good fun. Lord Havenwood won't be attending, as he's away on business of some sort, so I shall dance with whomever wants to turn me out in the reels, whether they be larder boy, prince, or shepherd. I don't fancy loud parties—but o! how I love our ghillies.

Eliza read on, delighting in the little sketch Ada had drawn in the margins, showing a Christmas tree and a pair of hounds reclining by a stone hearth. Malcolm had gotten his artistic talent from his mother.

She turned the page. Several of the leaves had been ripped from the journal, their jagged remnants deckled against the binding. The next entry was very short:

April 20th, 1874

I am married.

The clock in the foyer chimed twice. Eliza shut *Sense and Sensibility* and tucked the little journal into her apron pocket. It was time to meet Lydia for tea.

"Clarence proposed. We're to be wed at Christmastime." Lydia extended her hand. A heart-shaped ruby on a slender gold band glinted on her finger.

"Oh, Lyddie, I'm so delighted! We must start planning."

Lydia shook her head. "It will only be a small affair—at the chapel. Clarence has his heart set on a proper church wedding. He's promised he won't have me convert, so long as I agree to baptize our children Anglican. I've agreed."

"You confessed your faith?"

"Of course, Liza. As well as everything else. He's quite open, my Clarence. And you can't very well base a marriage on lies, can you?" Lydia sat across from Eliza and took a drink of her tea. Her eyes darted to the carpet at Eliza's feet, her brow creasing. "What's that, on the floor?"

Ada's diary lay there, its embossed cover gleaming in the afternoon light slanting through the window. Eliza reached down to pick it up, flipping her thumb through the pages. "It's my mother-in-law's old diary. It must have fallen out of my pocket when I sat down."

"How intriguing. Where did you find it?"

"It's the strangest thing," Eliza said. "Last night, I was reading in my room when I heard a tapping sound. I never found the source, but this diary came tumbling out of my armoire. It must have been shaken loose by the racket."

"Tapping, you said? Was there any rhyme or reason to it?"

"It came in a series of three, as if someone were walking about and pausing to rap thrice before moving on and doing it again. It happened at least five times."

Lydia's brows knit together in concern. "Have you seen anything? Heard anything else or felt strange sensations of any kind?"

"Not especially. Nothing but the house settling, as all houses do. Creaking doors and such. Malcolm said it's only the pipes clanging through my walls, but it sounded . . . intelligent."

Lydia held out her hand. "Can I see the diary?"

Eliza bridled. "Why?"

Lydia tilted her head, fixing Eliza with an annoyed expression. "You know why."

Eliza reluctantly handed the book over. Lydia took it and sat back in her chair, closing her eyes. A distressed frown crossed her face, and within just a few seconds, she gasped and dropped the diary as if it were a hot coal. It landed on the carpet with a muted thunk.

"What? What did you see?" Eliza asked, her hand darting out to retrieve the little book.

Lydia pushed her fingers against her forehead. "Blood. Fire. Rage. I didn't want to go any further. The person who wrote this was deeply distressed."

"Everyone I've met but Sarah says the same—that she was mad."

A humorless smile twisted Lydia's lips. "That's not the worst of it. I've tried to warn you. You need to be careful. Protect yourself with charms and pray the Rosary every day without fail."

A shiver ran through Eliza. "Are you talking about ghosts?"

"It could be more. Perhaps it's only the spirits of the deceased, but it might be something worse." Lydia reached out and grasped Eliza's wrist tightly, pressing in with her fingertips, and then let go. The impressions left by her fingers remained on Eliza's wrist, glowing whiter than the skin around them. "When something traumatic happens, it leaves a mark. That energy—that blackness and anger—remains in a place the same way a bruise lingers long after an injury. Whatever happened in that house, the evil created by it may still be there, Liza."

CHAPTER 18

September came to Hampshire, and with it, near-constant rain. The storms rumbled through in daily succession, turning the ditches to swollen rivers and drenching the ground until it was sucking soft. Fat droplets raced down the leaded glass panes of the library windows, casting tearful shadows over Eliza's hands as she did her needlework. Even though a fire roared in the hearth, a chill had settled over her. Fall was her least favorite time of year—the changing leaves and colder weather only brought memories of fever, death, and wooden coffins carried through doorways. Everyone she'd ever loved had died at the waning of summer.

Seven years and two weeks after Albert's drowning, a strong hurricane had ravaged the gulf coast of Louisiana, tearing shingles and clapboards from the Metairie farmhouse and sending the household into a blind panic. The day after the storm made landfall, the banks of Lake Pontchartrain began to overflow. Eliza watched the storm surge creep closer and closer to the farmhouse. Soon ugly brown waves were lapping at the raised decking of the front porch. Her father waded out to the stables to lead the horses to higher ground while Lydia and Eliza helped Mimi move their best furniture to the second floor. Maman only took to her bed, watching the endless rain and dosing herself into an alcoholic stupor.

After the rains ceased, the paddocks and pastures remained flooded for nearly a month. Mosquitoes swarmed in thick clouds below the trees. No matter how hard Mimi Lisette scrubbed, she couldn't remove the dark line showing that the foul-smelling floodwater had risen half-way up the downstairs walls of the farmhouse. The scent of mildew emanated from every room.

And then one evening, Eliza and Lydia were rolling Maman's fine Aubusson carpets over the warped wooden floorboards when her father came in from his chores. He mopped his sweat-slicked face with a hand-kerchief, his eyes bleary and bloodshot. Suddenly, he rocked back and forth on his heels and promptly fainted at Eliza's feet. It took three farmhands to move Nicholas Sullivan to the rear of the house, where Mimi set about arranging a sickroom. He shook so uncontrollably and vomited so much Eliza was certain he would die within the same night. As the late hours wore on, she busied herself mopping the floors with vinegar and boiling water. She scrubbed her hands with lye soap until her knuckles bled and traded vigils with Mimi until she nearly collapsed from exhaustion.

Just as suddenly as Papa had taken ill, he rallied. Though pale and weak, his good humor returned within days, and Eliza was soon push-ing him out to the rear veranda in a wheeled chair to take the air. They made plans for sowing rice in February and selling the foals at market.

It was only a brief reprieve.

The next day, Papa fell shivering into another fever, then into a deep sleep he never woke from.

As Papa's skin yellowed and every breath became a fight, Maman fell sick on a miserably hot Sunday, her delirium so profound it was terrifying to be in the sickroom with her. Helene shrieked at unseen demons and clawed at Eliza's arms when she offered her water. She died a few days later, crying crimson tears and vomiting black blood. Papa followed peacefully the next morning, silently drifting from his coma to meet Maman in the afterlife.

The undertaker was too overtaxed with the epidemic in the city to come collect the bodies. Four days passed. By that time, the stench in the farmhouse had become unbearable. After the hearses finally came to take away the fetid, swollen corpses, Mimi Lisette—who had never grown sick with the yellow jack in her lifetime—took ill, shaking so hard with rigors that the bed frame she lay upon broke under the weight of her body.

After Mimi died, Lydia and Eliza emptied out every room of the farmhouse and towed as much as they could carry to the far pasture. The bonfire they created rose so high into the night it seemed to lick the stars. They held tight to one another as it burned and made promises they were unsure they'd be able to keep.

If I get sick, Lyddie, promise that you'll shoot me. I don't want to die like that.

And if I die before you, will you find my maman and tell her, Liza?

A killing frost came after the funeral and plunged New Orleans into winter, putting an end to autumn's fevers. The epidemic of 1893 had ended as quickly as it started. And by some strange mercy, she and Lydia had survived.

Just then, the bell clattered at the front entry, startling Eliza from her memories. Turner strode down the creaking hallway and spoke a few terse words to whomever was at the door, then went past her to Malcolm's study. Eliza put aside her needlepoint and crept to the paneled door. She put her ear to it, listening.

"Lord Eastleigh's footman is here, sir. He's requesting an immediate response."

There was the crisp sound of paper being unfolded.

"Christ," Malcolm swore. "Tonight?"

"Yes, m'lord."

Eliza's mind swam. Eastleigh. What could he possibly want now? Their debts had been settled weeks ago.

"Tell him we'll be there."

"Right, m'lord."

Turner's footsteps shuffled toward the door, and Eliza ducked around the corner, taking her seat again. Malcolm came out a few seconds later, running a hand over his hair. His brows were knotted together, his face creased with worry.

Eliza stood and went to him. "What is it, husband?"

He gave a weary sigh. "It seems we've been invited to dinner tonight with Lord Eastleigh and his wife, and I've accepted."

"His wife?" Eliza asked, incredulous. "I'd no idea he'd married."

Malcolm laughed sharply. "Yes, well, funny enough, it seems he's married Una Moseley."

"Una! How queer."

"I've a notion he's married her out of some ulterior motivation. At any rate, we're still negotiating the terms of the London townhouse. It seems as if there's some question about the terms of repayment in the original mortgage."

"If it's a matter of inflation, we'll pay him whatever it takes to be off his chain. And perhaps it's only dinner, after all."

"With Eastleigh, it won't only be dinner, darling. I think you know that."

⁘

The wind tore at the carriage like a wild beast as Malcolm and Eliza made their way to Clairborne Hall, the ancestral home of the Lancashire family. Despite the muddy roads and overflowing ditches, they were soon splashing up the drive to the gaudy, overblown baroque mansion that resembled a layer cake made of limestone brick. Electric lights shone aggressively through every window, blazing in starbursts through the streaming rain.

"I'll go in first," Malcolm said, his hand on the butt of the pistol he'd holstered beneath his waistcoat. "I'm not expecting anything untoward, but with Eastleigh, we can't be sure."

She'd tried to prevent him from bringing a gun to the dinner table, but he was insistent. Eliza's stomach lurched as she envisioned the possibilities Malcolm was anticipating.

Turner pulled up to the porte cochere at the side of the lumbering manse and hopped down from his perch to open their door. His derby was rimmed with water, only his heavy-lidded eyes visible above the scarf he'd gathered about his face.

"I'll wait here, m'lord. If there's any trouble . . ."

"There won't be, Turner," Malcolm said confidently. "But if you do hear anything, remove her ladyship to Havenwood, posthaste."

Malcolm handed Eliza down from the carriage and she followed behind him, lingering at the edge of the rain-puddled terrace. A purple silhouette appeared in the doorway. Una stood in the double-hung doors of the threshold, looking as regal as a queen. Her eyes skimmed over Malcolm, then came to rest on Eliza, her lips forming a foxlike smile.

"Do come in, Lord and Lady Havenwood. We've been ever so anxious for your company."

❦

Eliza's head spun as Una took Malcolm's arm, smiling up at him in a way that turned Eliza's thoughts momentarily to violence. She imagined them in the days of their betrothal, Malcolm hovering over Una and kissing her in the places where she now enjoyed his attention. *Malcolm has such sweet kisses . . .*

They made their way into a sumptuous drawing room hung with French green silk. Eastleigh's butler took Eliza's cape from her shoulders, revealing her blue velvet gown and the generous amount of décolleté it afforded.

"Lovely dress." Una's voice was hollow as she gave the compliment.

"You're looking well yourself, Lady Eastleigh. Marriage agrees with you," Eliza answered, bobbing a quick curtsy. It was true. Una's cool, dignified hauteur suited her new station as countess.

"My husband will be down shortly, but we'll go through without him."

Una led them into the dining room, her hips swaying beneath her snug gown. Eliza wove her arm through Malcolm's, jealousy at Una's beauty seizing her heart in an unbecoming vise.

The varnished mahogany table was laden with sparkling crystal and silver chargers, each place setting pristine with its matching gold-rimmed china. Gardenias spilled over the sides of gilded chinoiserie vases, their fragrance smothering. Eastleigh had spared no expense. Eliza could only imagine how much of Malcolm's extorted money had gone into the impressive display of wealth surrounding her.

"Strange amount of rain we're having," Malcolm said, filling the uncomfortable silence as they waited for their host. "I hope it won't interfere with the winter wheat."

"I rather like a good storm, Havenwood. It suits my mood." Eastleigh's sibilant baritone floated toward them as he strode into the searing brightness of the room, dressed in immaculate white tie. He paused to greet Eliza, taking her fingertips as his eyes walked all over her. "Lady Havenwood. Delighted to have you at Clairborne Hall at last. It's the finest house in the county, you know. Made even finer by your company."

"It's an honor to be invited, my lord." Eliza's mouth went dry as he kissed her gloved hand, his lips lingering uncomfortably long.

Her husband's eyes could have cut glass.

They sat, and liveried footmen approached, offering oysters on the half shell and caviar. Eliza was thankful for food as a distraction from Una's dark scrutiny. The weight in the room was unbearable—like a heavy, silent sword of Damocles poised overhead.

After their dessert had been finished—a decadent charlotte russe—Charles stood. "Darling, please take Lady Havenwood into the parlor for a digestive. Lord Havenwood and I have private matters to discuss."

Eliza looked to Malcolm, her heartbeat quickening. The last thing she wanted was to be left alone with Una. And what if Eastleigh became violent?

Malcolm gave her a tight smile. "Go on, my love. It's all right."

Una swayed down the hallway, leading Eliza into a high-ceilinged drawing room lined with portraits. Eastleigh's ancestors glared down with hawkish faces, every bit as unfriendly as her present company. Una tugged the bellpull near the mantel and a frantic maid came scurrying in with a decanter of brandy and a tray of ginger wafers.

Una poured a glass and handed it to Eliza. "Have you been presented to the queen? If not, I'd be willing to sponsor you. I was brought before Her Majesty several years ago. Your mother-in-law did the honors." Una winked.

"I'd rather not pretend at civility, Lady Eastleigh. I already know you don't care for me." Eliza sniffed her brandy suspiciously, then took a tiny sip.

Una put her hand to her chest. "My. I'll give it to you Americans—you're certainly forthright."

"My candor is one of the many things my husband finds charming about me."

"I'm not so sure about that. Your kind of charm will wear thin after a time. Malcolm is traditional and prefers modesty in a woman."

"*Does* he?" Eliza smirked and took a braver sip of her brandy. It was so sweet it made her cheeks ache. "I had no idea you and Lord Eastleigh were courting. News of your wedding was quite the surprise to Malcolm and me."

"Charles is moneyed, powerful, and handsome. A good catch. I've admired him for years. We've many common interests. What kind of fool would turn him down?"

"I'm quite happy things played out the way they did."

"Are you?" Una waggled her finger at Eliza. "It doesn't look like you're sleeping well, if I'm to be honest. But how could you, in a house with such a dreadful past? Have you found out about the others?"

"What do you mean by *the others*? If you're implying Malcolm has lovers . . ."

Una laughed. "Oh, it's much worse than that."

The tops of Eliza's ears caught fire beneath the upswept waves of her hair. She wanted to throttle the smug look from Una's face so badly her hands shook. "Come out with it, Una. Ever since that day on the path, you've wanted to say something foul and unforgettable to me."

"But it'll be so much more fun to watch you find out the hard way!" Una narrowed her eyes. "I'll just give you one teensy-tiny little clue."

"I'm enthralled," Eliza spat.

"You should look around the south wing of your new home. Your husband hasn't let you back there yet, has he? It's all locked up, I'd reckon." Una took a sip of her brandy and held the glass up to the light. The crystal etching threw prismatic sparks over the walls. "I'd imagine he has some story about it being dangerous."

Eliza remembered how often Malcolm had admonished her about the dangers of the south wing, beginning on the very first night of their courtship. She thought of the heavy key ring he always kept beneath his waistcoat—how he'd not yet given her a copy of the house keys. His strange rules. Were there secrets within the hidden wing she wasn't meant to uncover? Secrets about Malcolm that might reveal motive enough for him to murder his family?

"I can see you thinking about it now," Una said. "It's delightful to see your face twist up and get all red. Do you know how you look when you get nervous? Don't ever play cards. You'll be as wretched at it as your father-in-law was."

"I'm quite finished with your insults. If we were in America, I'd have you down on the floor, pulling your bloody hair out of your head."

"Wouldn't *that* be the scandal?" Una leaned forward. "You're already an odd duck here, but you should go to London with your husband when the Season opens. You'll see what everyone else thinks of you. You may look the part of a lady in your jewels and expensive gowns, but you and I both know you're nothing but a cheap Yankee trollop."

Eliza stood, clenching her fists. "I am not a goddamned *Yankee*."

Malcolm strode into the room. "We're leaving," he said, firmly taking Eliza by the elbow. "Lady Eastleigh, please never speak to my wife with anything less than civility again."

"I wouldn't dream of it, Lord Havenwood," Una said, her eyes widening in mock alarm.

"It's not in my nature to be cruel, but you should know I've loved Eliza more than I could have ever loved you in ten lifetimes."

Una sighed. "Oh, Malcolm, you and I both know who and *what* it is you really love."

Malcolm turned on his heel, pulling Eliza along with him. He snatched his hat and cane from Eastleigh's butler as Eliza swept her cape over her shoulders. They marched out to the landau, where Turner waited with the door flung wide. As they pulled away, Eliza sensed the fury seething beneath Malcolm's demeanor. They rode in silence all the way to Cheltenbridge, until she could no longer resist the question that had been on her tongue.

"What did Lord Eastleigh say to you, my love?"

"I don't wish to talk about it, Eliza." His eyes met hers and narrowed. "I want you to go to your room when we get to Havenwood. I want you to take off your dress and make yourself ready for me."

CHAPTER 19

Eliza woke to a narrow finger of cold light shining through the window. Malcolm stood within it, dark as a sentinel, looking out at the seamless gray sky. Though he seemed calm enough, he'd been like a ravenous beast the night before.

She had done as he'd asked, removing every stitch of her clothing and letting her hair loose while she waited for him, her pulse pounding in her ears. When he came into the room, she sensed a primal change in him. He crawled over the mattress toward her, feral and hungry, kissing his way up her body until he hovered over her. "Do you want me?" he asked. She bucked her hips in answer. He laughed. "Good. I mean to have you begging, darling."

He had teased her to the edge, then denied her until she twisted and pleaded beneath him. He'd finally taken mercy, and their coupling had left her breathless and quaking afterward. She'd learned her husband was all fire once the sun went down, but there was none of that fire left as he turned to look at her now. His eyes were tormented, his mouth drawn into a grim frown.

"Malcolm, what is it? What's wrong, my love?" Eliza scrambled out of bed and went to him. She put her palms on each side of his face, and he turned from her gaze, as if ashamed.

"You asked what Eastleigh and I spoke about last night."

"Yes?"

"It seems the money for the mortgages wasn't enough for his liking. He's holding the title to the London townhouse unless I give him what he wants."

"What is it? My land? Sherbourne House?"

Malcolm's lips twisted into a bitter smile. "The price is much dearer than that, darling."

Eliza's stomach dropped, and a stinging nausea crawled up her throat. "What do you mean?"

"He bid me take you to the Gryphon Arms this very evening, to a private room where he could do with you as he wished."

Fear and helplessness pulsed in her chest. "Did you refuse?"

"Of course! What would you take me for?" Malcolm's eyes flashed. "He'll seize the townhome instead. He can have it, rats and all. I told him if he gave one more lecherous thought to having you, he'd face the barrel of my pistol. Coward that he is, I've no worries he'll heed my warnings." Malcolm turned from her, passing a hand through his unruly curls as he studied the mist-shrouded countryside. "There are many old grievances between our two families. There always will be. No amount of money will heal them."

More dark secrets. "I think you'd better tell me what you mean, Malcolm."

"Eastleigh and I have history. Being six years older, he bullied me constantly when I was a child, and I've already told you how he and his father cheated at cards and robbed our livelihood, but our feud goes much deeper than that. Our families have been rivals for nearly two hundred years. To the time of Queen Anne. It all started with a pig."

"Really? That sounds a bit ridiculous."

"It was likely a Berkshire pig. The lands around Havenwood Manor once belonged to the Crown—dating all the way back to the Norman Conquest. It was used as a hunting ground for the aristocracy. When my great-great-grandfather Reginald Winfield was granted the title I now hold, Queen Anne parceled off the land and gave him one thousand acres as payment for his service during the War of Spanish Succession. Eastleigh and his three sons continued to hunt here, ignoring our boundary lines, tracking anything they wanted to set their guns upon. Even our livestock."

"They were poaching, then."

"Yes. A capital offense. One day, Eastleigh's eldest son and heir was chasing a pig through the underbrush. Reginald was waiting with his musket. Blew his head clean off his block, without hesitation."

"God."

"Lord Eastleigh was just as belligerent and vengeful as you'd imagine— it's an unfortunate family trait. He kidnapped Reginald's eldest daughter, Abigail, his favorite child. His two remaining sons had their way with her, then took her out on the moors to die of exposure. It's said that before she was abandoned, she cursed the land around Clairborne Hall to become barren. And it still is, to this very day."

"Poor Abigail. What an awful story. Do you really believe in that kind of blood magic, though? Curses and such?"

"Perhaps. Crops that had once flourished withered, and cattle dropped as soon as they set foot on Eastleigh's estate. It was all rather biblical."

"Couldn't science explain it? Perhaps it was a blight."

"I'm sure there could be any number of rational explanations. In any event, the first Lady Havenwood was so distraught she took her own life. Reginald never remarried."

"Goodness. All of that over a pig!"

"Indeed. The corn depression of the last forty years hasn't helped Eastleigh's plight, which is why he's been loath to let go filching from my land. My crofters have always gained healthy profits for themselves and the estate—profits and rents Eastleigh has seized for years. Until now." The downstairs clock chimed six times, and Malcolm crossed the room to give Eliza a lingering kiss. He pulled back to search her face, his fingers stroking the hair back from her brow. "I must be going, love. I aim to find workers to begin repairs. We've much work ahead to restore this old house to its former splendor, but I'd say Captain Reginald Winfield would very much approve of my choice of wife."

Eliza smiled. "Let's only hope I meet a better end than the first Lady Havenwood."

"You're just the type to buck a trend, darling."

CHAPTER 20

An unshakable sense of unease had fallen over Eliza since Eastleigh's dinner party. It crept behind her as she went about her day, slinking over her thoughts as she remembered Una's words. She often found herself standing before the locked entrance of the south wing, as if drawn there by some mysterious force. What was worse, a latent mistrust had begun to grow between her and Malcolm. She'd asked for a copy of the house keys one evening after they'd made love—a time when she found him the most malleable. Malcolm had stiffened and pulled away, muttering an illogical excuse beneath his breath.

What was he hiding?

Her new husband was an enigma. He'd been curiously obscure about the basic details of his life, revealing only the facts he felt were pertinent to their marriage and estate. His moods were increasingly mercurial, his tastes unpredictable. It was both frustrating and fascinating. And if she were being honest, more than a little concerning. If there were some sort of hereditary psychopathy that ran in his family, it was entirely within the realm of possibility her husband had fallen victim to it.

Eliza once more returned to his mother's diary, seeking answers in Ada's cramped, tiny words.

May 1st, 1874

'Tis Beltane. I have been biliously sick in my confinement, bedridden with cramping pains and headaches keen as a hatter's needle. Thomas has gone to the crofters' cottages to celebrate with a bonfire and ale, but I am left alone with Mrs. Galbraith—her beady eyes darting from corner to corner as she whispers and laughs to herself over the mending.

Yesterday I was feeling better and wanted to take the air. I rode with Galbraith to market, and on the way back, she told me a bit of gossip: 'Every Lady Havenwood has met with a bad end.' She said it lightly, as if it were a trifle about the weather. As if I didn't sit there, beside her, the fourth of my kind. Galbraith has a cruel streak.

'First there was Mary, the wife of Reginald, who slit her own throat. Charlotte fell in front of a carriage after drinking too much wine. She was the daft one!' She clicked her tongue against the roof of her mouth and laughed. 'But Laura—sweet, angel-voiced Laura—she found the childbed fever after the birth of your husband. Took her three days to die, I hear.'

She stopped talking then, Galbraith. But her grin stretched wider.

'And you will meet a bad end as well!' That's what she meant to say—her unspoken words poisoning the silence between her next breath and mine. I sickened again and heaved my breakfast over the side of the wagon. I had to spend the rest of the day in my room saying prayers to settle my mind.

How horrid is this house, and everyone within it!

So that's what Una had meant by *the others*. The other wives. The ominousness of the passage sent a twist through her gut, but Eliza pressed onward.

> *September 21st, 1874*
> *My perfect darlings were born late last night. I was sleep-ing when they were delivered, as surgery was necessary to bring them safely into the world. There was some degree of complication—I am told I nearly joined the rest of the unfortunate Ladies Havenwood in the halls of eternity. I can just imagine Galbraith telling everyone, 'And Ada, only sixteen, bled out in childbirth.' I'm happy to report I have lived, mostly to vex her.*
>
> *Upon waking, weak and dizzy with my loss of blood, I was greeted with the most serene and ecstatic vision. My bairns, with their ebony curls and skin like milk, were placed in my arms, where they nuzzled their way to my breast. Though tired, I wept for joy. I was unsure of my fitness as a mother when I first learned of my condition, but now I am filled with new purpose!*
>
> *I have called them Malcolm, who will be my protec-tor, and Gabriel, who will be my warrior.*

Given the dates in Ada's diary, she'd been well into her confinement on her wedding day, which was surprising, given the virginal tone of her earlier entries. Tonight Eliza would be pressing her husband more about his family—especially about Ada. She tucked the journal beneath her mattress and dressed for dinner.

Malcolm was waiting for her at the foot of the stairs as always, beaming up at her as if she was a new revelation to his eyes. "Did you have a good day, darling?" he asked, taking her hand.

"I did indeed. Mrs. Duncan and I went to town to choose new draperies for the front drawing room. I was thinking a gold velvet with copper fringing. Won't it match the green damask well? They have the most fanciful tiebacks at the mercantile—they look like human hands! I found them most curious."

"Purchase whatever delights you, my love. My day wasn't nearly as successful as your own, I'm afraid. I'm having a bit of trouble."

"Oh?"

He pulled out her chair and kissed the back of her neck as she sat, sending a shiver from her spine to her toes.

"It seems none of our local craftsmen want to work on the manor."

Turner poured their wine while Eliza helped herself to the cheese on her plate. Creamy, crumbly Stilton. Her favorite. "Did they say why?"

Malcolm gave his wry grin. "No, but I wouldn't be surprised if Eastleigh had something to do with it. That, or they've heard our old stories."

"That's preposterous," Eliza said. "We've perfectly good money on offer and it's mostly the roof, isn't it?"

"The wallpaper will need to be pulled down and the plaster will have to be refinished due to the smoke and water damage. There are a few broken windows that need replacing, but yes—the roof is by far the worst of it." Malcolm took a drink of his wine, twisting the long-stemmed goblet in his hands. "I'll go into Southampton and see if any men are willing to come out. There are plenty of sturdy Irish there who don't mind a bit of hard work. They shouldn't care to know anything other than that they'll be paid well."

"Perhaps we can have them take a look at the pipes too," Eliza said.

"Pipes? Why? Are we having issues with the plumbing?"

Eliza was beginning to wonder just how hard her husband had been knocked about the head when he was a child. "Really? You honestly don't remember the night I came pounding on your door?"

Malcolm laughed. "Oh, yes. Something about the rapping in your room, wasn't it? I was barely awake, darling."

"You were a complete ass." Eliza smirked and took a drink of her wine. "I nearly clobbered you with my bed slipper."

"Well. Let me make it up to you. I was thinking we'd go for a ride this evening. Would you like that?"

Eliza's eyes widened. "Yes, you know I would!"

"I was thinking we'll need to find a saddle horse for you. Perhaps a Friesian mare to have as a match for Apollo. She can be your wedding gift. And we'll begin with building your stables after the repairs to the house are complete."

A new horse! She'd left Star with Lydia and missed her daily rides ever so much. Eliza jumped up and kissed Malcolm on the cheek. Despite his frustrating moods, he knew her so well.

❦

Malcolm was waiting beside the fountain of Leda and the swan near the pergola, its bowers heavy with red grapes. Apollo pawed at the ground and tossed his ebony mane when he saw Eliza, and she palmed a handful of sugar cubes beneath his velvet mouth. He snuffed and gently nibbled them from her fingers.

"I knew you were going to spoil him. He's anxious for a run. He hasn't been on a proper ride since we married," Malcolm said.

"It's because you've been far too occupied with other diversions."

"With no regrets on my part." He swatted her playfully on the rump.

Eliza swung herself up onto Apollo's back, and Malcolm settled in behind her. They flew through the rear gates and onto the wooded lane behind the mansion, galloping down the hill toward the stone circle Eliza had discovered on a summer walk that now seemed a lifetime ago. As they neared the stones, they slowed to a trot and Malcolm pulled

Apollo over to a patch of clover, where he promptly lowered his head and began to graze. Malcolm helped her down from the saddle. The stars were bright pinpricks in black paper, their beauty undimmed by the waning crescent moon.

"This is my favorite place on the estate," Malcolm said, drawing Eliza by the hand to the table-like slab at the center of the circle. "My mother, being of the north, where superstitions about stone circles are rife, was always frightened of it, but I've found myself drawn here since I was a boy, time and again."

Eliza sat on the stone, giving Malcolm a mischievous grin as she leaned back on her hands. "Tell me about your mother. You've not offered much about her, and I want to know what she was like. I don't even know her name." The lie fell so easily from her lips.

Malcolm took off his hat and sat next to her. "Her name was Ada. Ada Miriam MacCulloch, the belle of Oban. She met my father when she was just a girl. She was quiet, but a bit wild around the edges. She loved to fish and hunt. She was a hell of an archer and a crack shot."

"She sounds quite spirited."

"She was, but she changed a great deal, over time. Mostly the fault of my father. He had a tendency to drain a person's humor—to get inside their head. She faded a bit as the years wore on. There's something of hers I've been meaning to give you, by the by." He undid the button of his waistcoat and drew out a gleaming brooch. Its twining rowan branches formed a heart of gold, with his clan badge at the juncture, the arrow pointing upward, its tip elongated like a key.

"What is that?"

"It's called a luckenbooth. It's tradition for a Scottish groom to give one to his bride. This is the luckenbooth my grandfather MacCulloch gave to my grandmother. And my mother gave it to me, for the bride she knew I would one day wed." He pinned the clasp to the bodice of her riding habit, where it rested below her shoulder. "Now you've the key to my own heart, *mo chridhe*. Always keep it with you."

"It's beautiful." Eliza smiled wistfully and leaned to kiss his cheek. "I do hope your mother would have approved of me. Now that I've heard all about your mother, what was Gabriel like? You didn't tell me you were a twin, by the way."

A shadow seemed to pass over Malcolm's countenance. "Yes. We were twins. But even so, we were different in many ways. Things between us often were not so well." A familiar expression etched itself in the corners of his eyes. "I loved my brother, but at times, he was more like my rival. He was adventurous and free, where I was more careful and studious. I admired and envied his easy way with people. You know how it is with siblings. Their petty jealousies. Well. I've said enough. He's gone and I'm still here, and there's no use hashing out our flaws." Malcolm went silent, looking down at his hands.

His sudden reserve spoke volumes. Eliza chose not to press things further. "The druids used stone circles like this for human sacrifice, isn't that right?" she asked, changing the subject.

"That's one story. There are also tales of the fair folk traipsing among them."

"You're talking about fairies? I didn't take you for the fanciful sort."

"The fae are nothing to mock in this part of the world, darling. They're quite real to us Britons. Terrifying, rather."

Eliza laughed. "Surely you can't be serious? I'll admit my disbelief may be tested when it comes to ghosts and spirits . . . but fairies are a bit of a stretch."

"My mother told us stories that would make your hair stand on end."

Eliza scooted closer to Malcolm, leaning against his shoulder. He was warm and solid next to her, the scent of tweed and damp moss filtering from his jacket. "I love a good scary story. Tell me. Please."

Malcolm chuckled. "Well, if you insist. It's a tale about a lass who lost her way in the forest beneath Ben Nevis, the tallest mountain in all of Scotland."

"I want to go to Scotland someday. Will you ever take me?"

"Someday, mo chridhe, but first, our story." He put his finger to her lips, quieting her, and a frisson of heat ran through her at his touch. "This pretty lass, we'll call her Bess"—at this, he winked—"had been promised to a local minister—a fine young man with a pure heart toward God. The banns had been read, her dowry had been paid, and all of her family were gathering for her nuptials. She'd decided only the wildest mountain roses would do for her bouquet, so she trekked to the foothills of Ben Nevis the day before her wedding to gather her posy."

"She sounds a bit reckless, doesn't she? Walking out all alone without a chaperone."

"Rather." Malcolm smiled at her in the low light and wove his fingers through her own. "After Bess finished her gathering, she headed back. It was the summer solstice, the longest day of the year, but the sun had already fallen well behind the mountains, and from there, it dropped quickly. Once she'd gotten into the woods, she found the path harder and harder to see."

Perhaps it was the hushed tone in which Malcolm was speaking, or the way the wind had picked up, tossing leaves into a whirlwind between the stones, but Eliza's skin began to cool and prickle. "Our poor lass was well and truly lost. With only the light of the moon coming through the trees, she began to cry. She wandered about, looking for anything in the shadowy forest to help guide her way. As she pushed through the trees, into a clearing a lot like this one, she saw the flicker of firelight."

"Someone friendly was there, I hope."

"Oh, yes. Quite friendly indeed. Bess came into the light to see a tall man sitting by the fire. When he saw her, he stood and pulled back his cloak. She stumbled backwards, her wedding roses falling to the ground."

"Was he a monster?" Eliza said, clutching at Malcolm's sleeve. "A troll?"

He shook his head. "Not at all. In her dreams and fantasies, Bess could never have imagined a more seductive man than the one who stood before her." Malcolm snapped his fingers, the crisp sound making her jump. "In an instant, every thought of her first love—her true love—was wiped from her mind. The glamour he'd put upon her was irresistible."

Malcolm looked at her for a long moment, his face a breath away from her own. He still drove her to such distraction! Eliza leaned forward to kiss him and he leapt to his feet, pulling her with him. He spun her in a circle, and then dropped her into a dip, her head coming perilously close to the stone beneath her. He lowered her onto it and crouched over her, a gleam in his eye.

"The handsome stranger took Bess into his arms and loved her so well that she trembled beneath him until dawn." Malcolm nuzzled her neck with the pointed tip of his nose, drawing a sigh from her throat. "When the sun came up, he whispered pretty lies into her ears and set her on the path toward home. Her groom waited for hours at the altar in tears. His bride never appeared. Bess, on the other hand, was aglow with the ecstasy of new love. Alas, her happiness was to be short-lived.

"Though she trekked to the foot of Ben Nevis each day, hungry for the fairy lord's touch, her strange lover never returned to the stone ring as he'd promised. He'd seduced his prize and abandoned her, just as he'd seduced many maidens before her. Our bonny lass withered and grew weak—even her mother's prayers were futile. After a time, she died. The hunters and trackers say her shade haunts the forests and the mountain to this day, screaming and weeping for the gancanagh who stole her heart."

"And are you a gancanagh, my love?" Eliza arched her back as his hands roved over her.

"Perhaps I am. And if so, you should be very frightened."

"Why?"

"Because I'm about to ravage you into ruin."

CHAPTER 21

Tap, tap, tap.

Eliza gasped, panic seizing in her chest as she woke. She blinked and looked about the room, wavering lines of color shimmering in front of her eyes. The laudanum she'd taken hours before still clouded her senses, making the shadows wickedly long—the silhouette of the stag's head above the mantel loomed like a manitou.

Malcolm was gone to Southampton, his side of the bed cold and empty. Lately, especially at night, every wall seemed to breathe and move. An unsettling sense of being watched haunted her in the small hours—a feeling of being stalked like prey.

Even though she didn't want to believe Lydia, even though the possibility of spirits went against everything in her skeptical nature, as the night stretched onward, it went from absurd to entirely plausible.

The knocking came again.

Fear filled Eliza's mouth with metal. Whatever it was, it was now above her. And this time, as she watched, a dark shadow skittered over the plasterwork, crawling as quickly as a many-legged insect over the laughing mouths of the frolicking cherubs. Eliza felt for the lamp next to her bed, a whimper escaping her lips. She turned the key, gas hissing through the jets before it ignited. Finally, thankfully, the spark caught, and the room was bathed in soft yellow light.

She lay in bed, frozen in place. Waiting. Listening.

But there was nothing more.

Unable to sleep, she rose and paced about the room for over an hour, her ears pricking at every sound until exhaustion overtook her. She turned down the lights and climbed back beneath the covers. As she was creeping toward the fringes of sleep, she felt Malcolm turn the covers back next to her.

"I'm so happy you've returned, my love . . ." She smiled and reached for him, hungry for his embrace, but felt only the smoothness of the linen sheets next to her. She opened her eyes.

There was no one there.

But she could feel *something* there, looking at her.

Something cold, brittle, and faceless.

With horror, Eliza watched as the frigid darkness next to her bed grew deeper and began to take form. An icy wash of panic scalded her throat as a sudden cacophony of tapping began all around her. She ran down the stairs and banged on Mrs. Duncan's door. "Shirley, please! Open up. There's a ghost in my room!"

⁓✦⁓

"I didnae want to tell ye, mum," Shirley said, holding Eliza's trembling hand in her own. "I was afraid to say anything. His lordship bid me not to."

"His lordship doesn't want to tell me anything, it seems," Eliza said. She rested her forehead on her hand. Mon Dieu, how her head pounded. "I've never believed in such things. My sister tried to tell me about evil spirits. I thought she was being silly."

"If I may, it might bring comfort to know this particular spirit is nae evil. Just a bit . . . lost."

"What do you mean?"

"Sometimes a soul gets confused, especially if they were wrenched out of this world unexpectedly. Now, I've never seen anything meself, but I've felt things. A sadness. It hangs over this house at times. Not always. Things only get a bit stirred up, like the dust in quiet corners, and the veil parts a wee bit. You seem to be the one doing the stirring this time."

Eliza thought for a moment, remembering the first night she'd visited Havenwood Manor and the inexplicable sense of loss she'd felt. "Yes, I think I know what you mean. I've felt the sadness you speak of, only I'd no idea why."

"This spirit must feel a kinship to ye, m'lady."

"Then why couldn't it be *kinder* about telling me? Instead of rapping all over the walls and staring at me in my bed? I don't know if I have the fortitude for communion with spirits. The only sort of spirits I fancy come in a bottle." She dug her fingers through her hair, tugging at her tight scalp. "I could certainly do with a drink right now."

Shirley winked. "I've a wee flask, just here in my dresser. I sneak a tipple of your husband's fine Oban whisky now and again."

Eliza gave a conspiratorial grin. "Care to share?"

❦

Muzzy-headed, both inside and out, Eliza woke in Shirley's narrow bed, her neck stiff from the lumpy pillows and hard mattress. The little housekeeper had already gone from the darkened, tiny room—her cheerful banter rippling from the kitchen.

Eliza crept into the great hall, ducking to the side of the stairs as Malcolm walked out onto the landing. So, he had come home early after all. The dressing-down she'd receive if he found she'd spent the night in Shirley's quarters was something neither her head nor her nerves could bear at the moment.

"Good morning, Turner." Malcolm's voice was boisterous, excited. "I've news for her ladyship. Please go upstairs and wake her. I'd have her company at breakfast before I go."

Merde.

"Very good, m'lord."

Eliza listened as Turner trudged up the stairs. She waited for his knock on her door, hoping he wouldn't turn to look back over the gallery, and tiptoed through the open foyer to the library, careful to avoid crossing in front of the morning room. She peeked through a crack in the pocket doors and saw Turner walk across the landing and back down the stairs.

"I'm afraid her ladyship is not in her chambers, sir," he called, the hint of concern in his voice endearing.

"What?" Malcolm asked, incredulous.

Eliza pushed through the doorway, pulling her dressing gown tight over her nightdress. She glanced at herself in the full-length mirror in the foyer, and immediately wished she hadn't. She looked like a sea witch—her hair standing out from her head in tangled, ropy knots.

"I'm here, husband," she called, sweeping into the morning room. "I was in the library. I'd no idea you were already home."

"Oh?" Malcolm turned in his chair at the sound of her voice, his eyebrows arching skyward when he saw her. "Oh, my."

"I regret my appearance isn't to your liking . . . I did not sleep well."

"I can see," he said, his eyes trailing over her messy curls and the puffy circles beneath her eyes. A single feather floated to the floor, garnered, no doubt, from Shirley's sad pillow. "Well. At any rate, please join me."

Eliza sat at the breakfast table and fiddled with the crocheted doily at its center, relieved when Shirley swung through with coffee and a steaming plate of scrambled eggs. She gave a sly smile to Eliza before going back to the kitchen.

"I thought I'd share the good news. Work on the south wing will begin this very week." Malcolm beamed. "I hope you're as excited as I am."

"Certainly," Eliza said. "It will be good to have full use of the house."

"Well . . ." Malcolm's lips pursed.

"What?"

"It's quite a lot to open up the entire house. More than Mrs. Duncan can handle on her own."

"Then we should hire more staff. Mrs. Duncan is overworked as it is, being both cook and housekeeper. There's plenty of room in the maids' barracks for at least two chambermaids. And while we're at it, we should look into remodeling the servants' quarters."

"That's being overly charitable, wouldn't you say?"

"What would be wrong with a bit of charity? A well-cared-for staff is better suited to serving their masters, don't you think? Have you seen the state of their mattresses?"

"Yes, but all of that business gets expensive, darling."

"Right." Eliza bit the inside of her cheek. Her eyes went to the suit Malcolm was wearing—one she'd never seen before, his pinstriped trousers at the height of fashion. "New suit, husband?"

"Yes, do you like it? I visited the tailor when I was in Southampton. I've had it on order and had the final fitting yesterday."

"I'd imagine a fine bespoke suit is much more important than comfortable quarters for our staff, isn't it?" she said scornfully. "Shirley and Turner could both do with raises and a day off now and then."

Malcolm folded the paper and smacked it down upon the table as if he were crushing a gnat. Eliza flinched. "Shirley, eh? I see you've been getting on. Look. You are now a member of the aristocracy and must act it. Not like a bloody Marxist. Appearances rate more than how one treats their servants." Malcolm cleared his throat and adjusted his cravat. His voice softened. "Our family has been under enough scrutiny. Since we've lost the townhome to Eastleigh—gossip, no doubt, that will soon make its way to the London scandal sheets—it's ever more imperative that you make an effort to fit in. You must do your best to dress well, show impeccable *English* manners, and ingratiate yourself with the wives of my peers. This is your duty as a viscountess. You're not meant to be cavorting with the servants."

Tears welled in Eliza's eyes. "But this is where I become confused, husband. I behave and dress modestly during the day, as you've asked, only to have you tear my clothing off me in my chambers. I show concern over my sister's housing situation after you say she can stay on at Sherbourne House only until she's married, and then you say—that very evening!—of course Lydia must stay on, regardless. Surely you'll forgive me if I'm feeling a bit . . . flummoxed." Eliza took a deep breath. "And then there's the matter of the bloody *pipes*. And my hearing things that supposedly aren't there. I heard it again last night. Something was in my room, Malcolm. Something inhuman. I'm beginning to question my sanity!"

"You're becoming hysterical." Malcolm's voice rose and he shifted in his chair, shaking his head. "It is nothing more than the settling noises of an old house. Your fits of passion do not suit your station. You must endeavor to maintain a sense of dignity."

"And *you* must endeavor to be consistent! You go from being the most ardent and sensitive of lovers to being an insufferable toff who keeps secrets from me and implies I'm mad for thinking there's a ghost in my chambers. Well, there *is* a ghost! And none of your lies will convince me otherwise!"

Eliza stood and flounced out of the room, ignoring Malcolm's platitudes. She raced up the stairs to her room, where she threw herself onto the mattress and screamed into her pillow like a spoiled child. After indulging in a few moments of self-pity, she wiped her eyes, washed her face with rose water to calm the redness, and rummaged beneath the bed for Ada's diary.

June 9th, 1876

Today, I was informed my allowance has been diminished to two shillings a week. Two shillings! What can one buy with so little a sum? My husband has lost again at the card tables, I'd wager. He is a wicked, wicked man, ruled by his impulses and possessed of a foul temper.

At this, Eliza laughed.

My angels are my keenest joy. They are growing much too quickly. I can no longer keep up with Gabriel, who went from crawling to running and hopping about like a tiny jackrabbit. He torments his brother so, and I am worn thin by their wee battles.

July 1st, 1876

Thomas finally tired of my complaining and put in an advert for a companion. Our new Beatrice is such a blessing. And so merry! Her presence takes me out of my dark thoughts. Best of all, she loves my bairns nearly as much as I, and with much more patience. At long last, I have a friend, one who endeavours to know me as I am.

July 30th, 1876

I had quite a conversation with Bea today. She thinks Galbraith and my husband are lovers. Malcolm had toddled into the library, and she went to fetch him. The door to Thomas's study was cracked. She heard giggling and peeked through. There was Galbraith, engaged in a state of undress with her pinafore off, big, sagging breasts falling over the top of her corset. Thomas was all red-faced in his chair watching her pinch and pull at them, his old poker in hand, abusing himself.

Am I foolish for being relieved? If it keeps that awful old man distracted and away from me, I am ever so glad. Have at him, brave Galbraith! You are a far more formidable woman than I. And ugly, besides.

August 8th, 1877

The Isle of Wight reminds me of home. I covet Scotland. I long for mist-veiled mountains and the sound of the waves crashing over the firth. This house is irredeemably dark and close. Even the brightest noonday sun cannot pierce its gloom.

Beatrice came with us to the regattas today. I dressed Malcolm and Gabriel in their matching sailor suits and did my best to cover my bruises with my yellow lawn. It's stiff and itches so, but it has long sleeves. Beatrice wore blue. It suits her well. I tried to convince her to sit for the portrait the boys and I made, but she demurred, saying her hair was too mussed by the wind. She's a silly little hen, but we take great pleasure in one another's company. We converse only in French around Thomas and whisper our secrets behind Galbraith's back like naughty schoolmates. It's great fun.

After the races, we took the boys for strawberry ices and sat watching the yachts move back and forth over the water as the sun fell like a stone and painted the Solent crimson. Bea told me she has a bloke back home on Guernsey, a longshoreman named Dan, but he's stopped

writing. It's made her a bit maudlin. I tell her there are
many loves in life. And she is yet so very young.
      I pray she will have much better fortune in love than I.
      I only hope she won't leave me when she does find a
husband.

Eliza closed the diary on her finger. The more she read Ada's words, the more she felt a certain kinship to her. It was almost as if Ada were speaking aloud in the room—her presence felt that real. "Where are you? What happened to you?"

CHAPTER 22

Eliza was planning an experiment. Tonight, if the ghost knocked again, she would answer. She'd refused to go downstairs for tea, even though Malcolm had lingered by her door for a ridiculous amount of time. Instead, she'd spent the better part of the afternoon coming up with a code and key she could use to commune with the spirit. Even though hunger gnawed at her stomach, she was determined to avoid the kitchens until the rest of the house was sleeping. She was being petty, and she knew it, but spending another tense hour across from her husband at dinner was not her idea of a pleasant evening.

She'd nearly finished reading Ada's diary—the pages toward the end had been ripped from their binding, and there was a gap in entries from shortly before the twins' third birthday to their twelfth year, as if Ada hadn't cared to journal their childhood. Strange for an otherwise devoted mother. Eliza had begun a chronology of events within her notebook, carefully constructing a timeline from the evidence in Ada's diary as well as the anecdotes she'd gathered from Shirley and Sarah.

The final entries were almost illegible. Ada's messy handwriting was now a shaky scrawl that showed growing evidence of a tremor. Eliza scrutinized the words with her magnifying glass.

March 25th, 1887

My sons are growing into young men.

Malcolm is ever by my side. The old man says he is mollycoddled, but what am I to do? He's a quiet lad, of delicate nature. I do my best to protect him from his father, but the old bastard persists on tormenting the boy as if he were a nuisance and not his first son and heir.

My Gabriel, on the other hand, is strong-willed and stubborn, though he hasn't an ounce of guile—when I catch him at his boyish crimes, he confesses and never lies about having done them. Instead, he seems rather proud of how clever he is. He's too much like me, that one.

What will I do once my wee ones are grown and gone away, and I'm left with old Havenwood? Miserable thought. I am most relieved he no longer attempts his poking. His staff will only rise to half-mast now, thanks be to God. I made the mistake of laughing. Once.

December 18th, 1887

Havenwood has betrothed Malcolm to a local girl— the middle daughter of George Moseley—and he's gone behind my back to do so. I was furious when I found out. Moseley is a duplicitous and cunning shill, with a mind only for money. Una is to be wed to Malcolm when he turns twenty-one. I got myself into such a state upon hearing this news as to require a heavy dose of laudanum.

The old man is doing this to punish me. He'd a notion to start up his poking again after all these months of celibacy and found his way to my room the night before last. Malcolm had taken to my bed—the poor bairn had only had a night terror and wanted my comfort. Old Havenwood threw back the covers, and finding Malcolm there, pulled him down upon the floor and began to beat him as I watched. I climbed onto the old bastard's back to try to pull him off—he struck me full across the face and tossed me across the room. I now bear a bruise under my eye that no amount of tincture or cosmetics will cover. I believe I've a broken rib as well. Each breath feels as if I'm being stabbed in the side by a hot poker. I am not allowed to see a physician, so who can know? I bind myself with my corsets and Beatrice makes cool poultices to soothe the pain. I must heal soon.

My papa is not well. He is plagued by returning tumors and fits of fatigue. I plan to journey to Scotland to care for him, as I believe he is not long for the world. I will take Malcolm and Gabriel with me and devise a plan to remedy the situation I now find myself in. I am wretched with it.

Eliza's stomach turned. In this very room, where Malcolm made love to her, his own father had beaten him. And how many times had Ada felt Thomas's unkind touch on the same bed in which Eliza slept? The thought sickened her and brought a newfound sympathy for her husband at the same time. Was it any wonder he sometimes struggled with showing affection and empathy? That his moods were as unpredictable as a storm at sea?

The final two pages, loosened by the threadbare binding supporting them, slid free onto the surface of her secretary. There was another long gap between entries. Ada's handwriting trailed haphazardly across the pages, blots of ink scarring the paper.

January 5th, 1888

My poor papa has died. I was not allowed to travel to Brynmoor to see him during his illness. I've even been forbidden from going to his funeral. Old Havenwood found out about my plans to leave him. No doubt it was due to Galbraith's snooping and prowling. How I hate that woman.

February 3rd, 1893

I am now locked within the south wing, day and night, with a set of keys that are never within my grasp. The chill creeps . . . as the wind pushes through the weak spots within the walls. Shadows whisper and taunt, crawling over the ceiling like insects. My mind is no longer sound, nor trustworthy. I have turned to my old friend laudanum, as its velvet comfort is the only way I can take rest.

May 1st, 1894

At long last, when I had found love—truest, purest love in spite of my captivity!—I am now left broken by it. I find myself desolate at my memories of such a brief, golden time. Now that I have tasted passion, I would give such riches to have it again! I partook of heaven—and knew what it meant to be whole and loved for who I am. But now, my kindred spirit has left me.

I wish that my husband would d . . . I pray for it. My fantasies concerning the painful and inventive ways it might happen are of great comfort. My own darkness frightens me.

Ada had taken a lover, it seemed. But who? Could it have been Beatrice, or someone else? And if so, what had happened to part them? Eliza opened her notebook and scratched, *Took lover between February 1893 and May 1894.*

Tap, tap, tap.

At the sound of the ghostly rapping, Eliza jumped from her desk, pushing Ada's diary to the side. Her hands shook with excitement as she opened her chalk tablet. She'd transcribed the alphabet across its surface in a neat row, a series of dots beneath each letter. The sound came again, and Eliza answered, tapping on her blotter with her knuckles.

An echoing knock replied immediately.

"Hello there," Eliza said. Her lips spread into a smile. "What would you like to tell me?"

Three hours later, her mattress was strewn with paper. Some of the communication had been successful; some of it had not. But one thing was certain: the spirit she'd been speaking with wasn't malevolent old Havenwood, but a woman, and she had died in this house.

CHAPTER 23

Eliza reclined like a torpid odalisque on the veranda of Sherbourne House as Lydia rifled through the ghostly messages she had copied down the night before. It was the kind of warm autumn day in which the cloudless sky arched overhead, blue as a robin's egg. The yellow leaves of the ancient oak towering over the terrace were already beginning to fall, rattling across the stonework at their feet.

"What do you make of it?" Eliza asked, yawning. She sat up from the chaise to reclaim her tea. She hadn't gotten a wink of sleep.

"I've heard of spirit dictation, but I've never attempted it. Many people think it's only a parlor trick." Lydia held up a sheet of paper. Eliza's handwriting looped across it: *I was murdered.* "Your key was clever. How did you come up with the idea all on your own?"

Eliza raised her eyebrows. "Really? I'm quite smart about such things. How else do you think Jacob and I communicated so long without Maman ever knowing?"

"I can tell you're very proud of yourself." Lydia smirked. "Who murdered this woman?"

"She didn't tell me. I believe the answers might be in the south wing of the house. Ada was locked within that wing for years before the fire. Una mentioned secrets, too. Malcolm won't allow me back there, but the workers will be starting on repairs soon, so it will have to be opened while they're in and out. I plan on sneaking through and exploring."

"Do you think someone killed Ada, and this is her ghost?"

Eliza narrowed her eyes. "I know who you mean by *someone*. I'm still not sure what Malcolm's motive would have been, at any rate. In all our conversations, he seems to hold his mother in the highest regard. Perhaps she ran off with a lover. This ghost could be one of the other Ladies Havenwood. Many of them had tragic lives. Although, if I *can* find out for certain what happened to Ada, it would go a long way toward proving Malcolm's innocence."

"Sarah told me he and his brother were twins."

"Yes. What are you implying?"

"If birth order was in question, and he was hungry enough for the title, he'd have reason to eliminate their mother. She was likely the only witness to their birth besides the doctor . . ."

"I see what you are saying, and I've thought of that as well. But Gabriel died before Ada disappeared, eliminating the need to prove primogeniture. It's true that Malcolm and Gabriel *weren't* always civil. Malcolm has been honest about that. But you and I can be a bit contentious at times, as well." Eliza took a sip of her tea. "There's always a bit of hair-pulling between siblings."

Lydia shook her head. "There has to be something more with his mother. Women of her station rarely abandon their households. Did she have any enemies, do you think?"

"She had an ongoing rivalry with the housekeeper at the time— Mrs. Galbraith. They hated one another. Ada and her lady's maid were convinced Galbraith and old Havenwood were lovers. Perhaps Galbraith had something to do with Ada's disappearance."

"Well, be careful with your digging and investigating. Especially concerning the supernatural," Lydia admonished. "I'm glad you finally believe me about spirits, though. How long have I been telling you?"

Eliza sighed. "You so enjoy gloating when you're right, don't you? You've done so since we were children."

Lydia wrinkled her nose and took a sip of her tea. "I'm *always* right."

Eliza lay back with a yawn and twirled an oak leaf between her fingers. "I'm curious about this ghost. She frightened me at first, but our latest interaction didn't seem menacing at all. I feel as if I've a new friend."

"Do be careful, Liza. Spirits can be deceptive. The bad kind can play especially well at innocence."

"Right then," Eliza said, eager to change the subject. "How is your Clarence?"

"I've been volunteering at his clinic. We've started my formal training."

Eliza sat up to grasp Lydia's hand. "Oh, Lyddie! I'm so proud."

"I've learned how to splint broken bones, and next I'll be learning how to assist in surgery. Soon, I'm to be helping Clarence call on expectant mothers in the village."

"Speaking of such things, or the prevention thereof, would you make me more of your tonic? I'm nearly out."

Lydia nodded. "Yes. I'll need to purchase another packet of black cohosh from the apothecary and dry some tansy. These tonics aren't meant for continual use, Liza. They can be dangerous."

"I realize that. I'll use it sparingly and look into other methods, at least until things are more settled between Malcolm and me."

Lydia lifted a brow. "You're not as opposed to motherhood as you once were, then?"

"I'm still not keen. But I suppose I'm coming around to the thought. Both of our lives have taken some unexpected turns, haven't they, sister? Things are certainly different than we anticipated here in England."

"Different is certainly a way of putting it."

When Eliza came home, her mind spinning with all the mysteries she longed to unravel, Malcolm was waiting in the foyer. As Eliza passed him, her eyes fixed on the marble floor, he put his hand out to stop her. "Still avoiding me, wife?"

"I'll not speak to you until you apologize for the way you addressed me yesterday morning," Eliza said churlishly, pushing his hand from her shoulder. "You scold me as if I'm a child."

"Darling, sometimes you behave like a child that needs scolding." Malcolm grinned. "Come into the study. I've a feeling I have something that'll make you less cross."

Eliza was dubious, but the sight of his smile never failed to weaken her tempers. She followed him through the library into his squarish study lined with hunting trophies. His desk dominated the center of the room, its base carved with elaborate gryphons. Building plans lay scrolled upon the velvet blotter. Malcolm spread the first one out flat. It showed the rear elevation of the house, rendered with mathematical precision. Arch-topped windows nestled in the dormers, and a new scalloped slate roof was a crowning finish over it all.

"I've just come from a meeting with the builders. Our workmen will arrive tomorrow."

Despite herself, a smile tickled the corners of Eliza's mouth. "How exciting."

"And . . ." Malcolm rolled up the first set of plans and unrolled another. This set showed a long, low building punctuated by a row of stalls. "I finished the plans for your stables last night."

Eliza gasped and put her hand to her mouth. The stables were beautiful—with green-paneled doors and ornate Corinthian pillars, the Havenwood crest perched on the keystone above the entry.

"I thought we'd break ground this spring. Still cross with me?"

Eliza turned to Malcolm, all of her remaining anger fading. She thought of the sweet, studious young man who only wanted to read and work at his figures. The quiet boy who only ever wanted his father's approval and had never gotten it. She reached out, her hand cupping his jaw. At her touch, he closed his eyes for a long moment, then opened them again.

"Eliza . . . I'm sorry. I know I'm not always kind, but please try to understand. I have reasons for the things I say and do. I only mean to protect you. Not only from Eastleigh, but from anyone who would question your honor. *Our* honor."

"Shhh . . . husband. I understand," Eliza said, pulling him close. When their lips touched, it felt like a first kiss—hesitant, soft, shy. He slowly eased, melting into her with a ragged moan, his hands tangled in her hair.

"I'll come to you tonight, darling," he said, gently pushing her away. "I cannot do this right now."

"Why, Malcolm? Hmm?" she said, nuzzling against him. "We're alone. There's a lock on the door." Her hand went to the fork of his trousers. "I've missed you. Let me show you how much."

"Eliza, please. I . . ."

Ignoring his protestations, she pushed the building plans aside and perched on the edge of the desk, rucking up her skirts. Malcolm's cheeks blazed with color. "My God," he murmured. He closed his eyes and stumbled backward as if he were drunk. He stood staring at her for a long moment before turning away to hastily unbuckle the closure on his trousers. She sensed what he meant to do.

"Come, husband. There's no need to pleasure yourself. Let me satisfy you. The hours have been too long since we last enjoyed one another." Eliza lay back and raised her hips in offering.

"I can't, Eliza," Malcolm said, with a ragged sigh.

"I'll be quiet. I promise. No one will ever know what we're getting up to."

"Is that so?" He gave a bitter laugh, then turned and crossed the room in two strides. He braced himself over her, gripping the edges of the desk. "What torment this is! You are so lovely," he murmured, his eyes lit with lust. His fingers hesitantly traveled from the inside of her knee up to her thigh, then higher. Eliza closed her eyes with a soft sigh, her body responding to his touch.

There was a knock at the door.

"What, what is it?" Malcolm called, pushing away from her. Eliza stood, smoothing her skirts, her body jumping with arousal and frustration.

"There's a delivery here, m'lord." Turner's voice. "Lumber. They need you to sign."

"Blast it," Malcolm spat, his face florid. He angrily fastened his trousers, then passed a shaky hand through his hair.

"Shall I wait here?" Eliza asked.

Malcolm waved his hands, his irritation displacing the desire she'd felt only moments before. "No. And please do not try . . . *that* business again. Such vulgar displays of seduction are meant for common prostitutes, not ladies." He sneered. "Bloody hell, Eliza. What were you thinking?"

What was *she* thinking? How dare he shame her! Her husband was a beast. More harsh and cruel than she'd ever thought possible. Almost as cruel as the man who raised him.

Eliza bit her cheek against her threatening tears and pushed Malcolm out of the way with an angry shove. Damned if he'd see her cry! She threw open the door, swept past a befuddled Turner, and went through the house to the gardens, where the sounds of Leda's fountain drowned out the ragged, heaving sobs she could no longer contain.

CHAPTER 24

As September curled more deeply into autumn's bosom, the pounding of hammers and rasp of saws rang through Havenwood Manor in a near-constant symphony, beginning shortly after sunrise and carrying on until sunset each day. Malcolm kept watch at the entry to the south wing, supervising the workers as they went about their repairs. Eliza's plans of sneaking into the south wing unnoticed had been thwarted by his vigilance.

He hadn't visited her chambers in almost a week. Her isolation was by choice, the sting of his rejection still fresh as a whip's lash. After the second night, he'd stopped knocking on her door.

Shirley brought breakfast, tea, and dinner to her room, perching on the edge of Eliza's bed while she picked at her food. In the evening, Eliza turned to her laudanum, dosing herself into a delirium that made the walls heave like the bellows of a blacksmith's forge. In her dreams, she heard arguing men, voices raised in an unknown language. At other times, an unseen hand stroked her hair as tenderly as a mother would. Eliza liked to think this was the kindly spirit, come to comfort her in her loneliness. Was the spirit Ada or one of the other tragic Havenwood wives? Or perhaps Beatrice? If it *was* Bea, who had murdered her? And why?

Eliza had taken to strolling the perimeter of the property during the day to banish her omnipresent tiredness, puzzling over her thoughts and observing the improvements to the house from the outside. She enjoyed watching the workers. Their easy banter and lack of airs reminded her of her father. They were most grateful for her deliveries of apples, smoked herring, and Shirley's shortbread, which she placed in tin pails to haul up to them. It was good to feel useful and appreciated.

The new beams coaxed the voluptuous curve of the mansard roof back to life, the brightness of the fresh yellow wood replacing the dark, scorched rafters she'd first seen from her room at Sherbourne House. Little by little, her home was being made ever finer, at least to the outside eye.

She was taking her daily deliveries to the workers when a young man with clever, sun-creased blue eyes smiled down at her, dangling from the scaffolding. "How're ya, maum?" he said, doffing his cap. His dark hair waved in sweaty tendrils around his forehead. "You're the famous missus, right?"

"I am," she said, shielding her eyes with her hands. "I bring you men your cookies each day." She lifted the tin bucket.

"What are cookies, maum?" he asked, scratching his head as he climbed down and took the bucket from her hand.

"You call them biscuits."

"I'll call them whatever you like, so long as you smile at me the way you're doing right now. I'm Freddie."

"Well, Freddie, you're a flirt. I'm Eliza. But around my husband, it'll have to be Lady Havenwood, or my lady, or your ladyship, or any of that other proper nonsense."

He grinned. "Hey, do you know you've a spook?"

"What?" she asked, squinting at him.

"A ghost."

"Really?"

Freddie nodded and took a bite of his shortbread, wiping his mouth with the back of his hand. "I don't figure it much likes us working on your house. Keeps stealing our tools."

"I'm sorry. My husband will certainly replace anything that's gone missing."

"That's just it, maum—they ain't exactly missing. Only moved around, like. Shepherd's plaster trowel was stuck in the side of the house the other day, and my hammer was left hanging from the rafters. It nearly fell on the foreman's head."

Eliza shivered, despite the warmth of the mid-September sun. "I see. Perhaps you could try locking everything up once you've finished for the day?"

Freddie laughed nervously, brushing his hands clean on his trousers. "Right. That's the funniest thing of all. We put everything into a trunk with a padlock last night, just to test it. And this morning, all the tools were pulled out and lined up in rows, neat as chessmen. Now ain't that queer?"

⁂

Someone was watching her. She sensed it. A shadowy form, looming over her. Her heartbeat ratcheted and her limbs went rubbery soft . . . until her eyes adjusted, and she came fully out of her slumber. It was only Turner, his face shadowed by the noonday sun. She blinked up at him from the hammock. She'd been spending most of her days in the gardens of late, resting in the shade of the chestnut trees. It was an effective way to avoid Malcolm.

"Mum, so sorry to wake you. You've a visitor. Miss Whitby. Shall I tell her you're indisposed?"

"Polly's here? How unexpected." Eliza sat up and patted her hair. "Bring her around back. We'll visit in the gardens."

Turner gave a crisp nod. "I'll have Mrs. Duncan bring refreshments."

Eliza stood and shook the fallen leaves from her skirts. She wondered why Polly was coming to call now. After their acrimonious words over Eastleigh at Sarah's party, Eliza had dismissed their chances of ever becoming friends. But they were still neighbors, after all. And, as Polly was the local gossip, it would be pleasant if they could come to some sort of accord to temper the scandalous talk about town. It would be nice to be welcomed at the market with smiles instead of spiteful whispers about her loose American morals.

Polly rounded the corner, trailing Turner. She was wearing another one of her fluffy concoctions, this time in yellow, her eyes flitting nervously over the topiary until they finally landed on Eliza.

"Hello, Miss Whitby," called Eliza with a friendly wave. She closed the gap between them and offered her hand. Polly took it, bobbing an awkward curtsy.

"He . . . hello, Lady Havenwood," Polly stammered. "Lovely day to be out-of-doors."

"Yes. I'm ever so glad you decided to call," Eliza said with an ingratiating smile. "Please sit. And please call me Eliza." She motioned to the table and chairs beneath the pergola. "I find the gardens a peaceful respite from the noise these days, what with all the construction going on."

Polly took her seat, sighing with what Eliza took to be relief. What had she been expecting? A shunning? Polly turned her attention to the rear elevation of the house, where the workers were taking their lunch break on the scaffolding. "It's impressive what you've been able to accomplish in so little time."

They'd made notable headway that morning on the fascia and soffits, which gleamed with new copper gutters. "We've a good crew. And Malcolm has been overseeing it all."

Freddie caught Eliza's eye and waved, then nudged his friend. Doubtless Polly's arrival had created a stir among the young men.

"My lady . . . I mean, Eliza," Polly began nervously, "more than anything, I've come to apologize."

"Polly . . ."

"No. I behaved atrociously at Sarah's party. There are no excuses for it." Polly pressed her lips together. "I made myself look a fool over Charles. It was terribly embarrassing."

Eliza reached for Polly's hand. "Darling, you've no reason to apologize to me. I've been young and in love. I know what it means to lose your head over a man."

"Well. You've heard the news, I suppose." Polly's voice grew tight as a lute string—her smile even tighter. "About Charles and Una."

"Oh, yes. They had us to dinner recently so they could gloat about their match. It was awful. I'm afraid I don't know how to be pleasant to either one of them."

"I was gutted to hear of it." Polly absently fiddled with the ruffled cuff of her dress. "I suppose I always made things too easy for him, though. Men like Charles fancy a challenge."

Where was Shirley with their tea? The last thing Eliza wanted to do was spend the afternoon sawing on about Eastleigh. "I think you're better off not having married the likes of him. You're a lovely girl. He wouldn't have treated you well at all," she said, thinking of the obscene proposal he'd offered Malcolm. "You would've been quite unhappy with him, in fact. Una and Charles belong together. They're equally loathsome."

"It's just that my papa always wanted me to marry well, to elevate our place in society. He's only the second son of a baronet—which is nothing really special, you see, but it was enough for him to become an officer. He received several commendations, which put him on the path to promotion at a younger age than most. He's worked very hard and is quite proud of being an admiral. His daughter marrying an earl would have secured his estate and livelihood into old age. A man without sons becomes desperate."

"Your father sounds a great deal like my own," Eliza said. "A self-made man."

"Yes, well. He's not very happy with me at the moment." Tears sprung to Polly's eyes. "I'm nearly twenty-four, Eliza! My hopes of finding a good match are dwindling."

"Nonsense! Haven't you ever thought it ridiculous that a woman must marry before twenty-five to escape the stigma of spinsterhood, yet a man can marry at whatever age he likes? It's preposterous."

Polly wiped at her eyes. "You sound like Sarah."

"Well, it's true."

"Oh," Polly said, glancing over Eliza's shoulder. "There's a young man coming, and he's bringing tea."

Eliza swiveled in her chair. Freddie approached, a bashful grin on his face. "Pardon me, maum. Your housekeeper was flustered about a pudding she thought was burning, so I offered to bring this out to you."

"You're a jewel and a gentleman, Freddie. I may convince my husband to let me keep you. You'd make a fine footman."

"I wouldn't know about that, maum." He set the tray down, with its lopsided Victoria sponge and hastily assembled tea service, then took his cap from his head to greet Polly. "Good day, miss . . ."

"This is Miss Whitby, Freddie. Polly, this is Mr. . . . oh, I'm sorry . . ."

"O'Riordan, maum."

Polly glanced at Freddie's proffered hand, with its dirty fingernails and calloused palm, and made a simpering sound at the back of her throat. "Charmed," she said disdainfully, and pulled her hands into her lap.

Eliza's eyes nearly rolled to the back of her head. Seeing the lay of things, Freddie turned with a nod and trundled off, hat in hands. "Polly!" she scolded after he was out of earshot. "That utterly charming boy brought our tea so that he could be introduced to you. If anything will prevent you from marrying, your own snobbishness may well do the trick! Not every good man you meet comes with a pedigree."

Polly sniffed. "An admiral's daughter could never entertain a carpenter's attentions. And an Irish one at that! Imagine the gossip!"

Eliza sighed and sat back in her chair. "Yes. Imagine the gossip."

"Speaking of, there's loads more gossip about town," Polly said, eagerly slicing a wedge from the sponge. "Do you want to hear it?"

"Oh, why not?"

"The Tates have sold half their estate. Can you believe it? They've lost three tenants, just this year. It seems many of our lot are doing the same. Parceling acreage and selling. Some of the lower gentry have even started working in the city. Hard times for many, I suppose. Desperation will drive you to that sort of thing, but it's better than thievery. Do you remember that highwayman that was terrorizing the countryside when you arrived? He seems to have gone with the summer. Lady Gregory claims she saw him east of Alton in late August, but that was the end of it. At least we can travel at night again without worry, thank goodness." Polly took in a breath. "Her palsy is worsening. Lady Gregory's, that is. Sarah doesn't think she'll live to see in the new century."

"Terrible news," Eliza said, doing her best to muster a sympathetic look, remembering the disdain Lady Gregory had shown to her and Lydia at the ball.

"And there's talk about you and Malcolm, of course. They say you were with child before the wedding." A pause. "Are you?"

Eliza snorted. "No. I am most certainly *not*."

"I didn't think so, of course." Polly shook her head. "And then one of the local farmers said he saw you and Malcolm engaging in a vulgar, pagan ritual amongst the standing stones."

Eliza bit her lip to stifle a laugh. There might have been some truth to that one. They'd been rather flagrant that night, after all. She longed for more of the sort—her winsome, spirited husband, so bold as to take her breathless beneath the stars. Lately, he'd become a prudish shadow of himself. "They'll be calling me a witch soon enough, won't they?"

"Oh! They already are. But if you'd like news of your wicked ways to spread even further, I'm sure I can manage to help."

Eliza laughed, and Polly joined in. "I'm so glad you came, Polly. Aren't we friends now? In full?"

Polly reached across the table to squeeze Eliza's fingertips. "Yes. Friends indeed."

CHAPTER 25

Someone was screaming.

Eliza tossed her book aside and ran from the library, her heart racing. Another scream cut through the echoing vestibule. It was a man, his pained cries coming from the south wing. Malcolm was no longer at his post in the doorway. Fear funneled through her. Was he hurt?

She burst into the south wing, the fragrance of freshly sawn wood all around her. Despite the repairs, the evidence of the fire was everywhere, from the smoke-streaked plasterwork to the singed curtains still hanging from the windows. Up ahead, the workers huddled together below a two-story section of scaffolding. She lifted her hem out of the sawdust and hurriedly made her way toward them.

It was Freddie. He lay crumpled at the foot of the scaffolding, his leg oozing blood. A thick shard of wood pierced his dungarees. Eliza pushed the workers out of the way and knelt at the young man's side, taking his hand. His eyes rolled in his head as he groaned and arched his back. Eliza flinched at the fresh spurt of blood that came streaming from his thigh. "Freddie! Please do try to be still, darling. I'll fetch Dr. Fawcett."

"Your husband's already gone for the doctor, mum," the foreman said, a grizzled man named Hicks. He held his cap to his chest. "He was here when it happened."

"What happened?"

Hicks looked down, his moustache twitching. "Freddie fell, m'lady. That's all."

"'Tain't right to lie, Mr. Hicks! He were thrown!" The young man who'd just spoken was tall and as thin as a water reed, his eyes wide with fright. "And it weren't no human what did it."

Eliza gasped. "Where was he when he fell?"

He pointed with a knobby finger. "All the way up there, mum."

Eliza followed his gaze to where the scaffolding butted up against the curved walls and newly framed ceiling. In what was once the attic, an empty section of lath stood out from the soot-stained wall. Below it lay a pile of ragged boards and chunks of plaster tinged with Freddie's blood. If the shard of lath now lodged in his leg had pierced him somewhere vital, he'd surely be dead.

"He was up against that wall, scraping, and something grabbed hold of his shirt and yanked him over the edge. I saw it with mine own eyes!"

"He lost his balance and fell, Cecil!" Hicks roared. "That's enough, I say."

Freddie cried out again, and Eliza squeezed his hand. "Please, gentlemen. Try to stay calm. We'll get to the bottom of things, but first we need to think of Freddie."

Cecil knelt at her side, lowering his voice. "See, mum, my mate here's sure-footed as a cat. He's been climbing on roofs since he could walk. He were thrown. And your ghost was the one what did it."

⊱⊰

Clarence and Lydia came out of the surgery room, Lydia nearly unrecognizable in her starched pinafore and buckram cap. Clarence's once-white apron now resembled a butcher's bib. "The young man is stable," he said, taking off his spectacles and wiping his face on his gartered sleeve. "Breathing steadily and sleeping."

"Will he live?" Eliza asked, rising.

"So long as infection doesn't set in, I'd say he has a fighting chance. He has a broken femur and that splinter nearly pierced his femoral artery. Had that happened, I'd now be dealing with a corpse."

The door to the clinic swung open, and Malcolm strode in, his hat in his hands and a grim expression etched across his face. Lydia's eyes narrowed at the sight of him. "It wasn't an accident, Liza," she whispered. "You know that." She offered Malcolm a stiff curtsy and turned on her heel to go back into the ward.

"Ah, Lord Havenwood. I was just telling her ladyship the young man should recover," Clarence said. "Lydia's put him on a morphine cycle for sedation and pain. I've notified his family via telegram, but as they're in Dublin, he's not likely to receive visitors."

"Well, we must make sure he has visitors while he's confined," Eliza said. "I'll check in, and perhaps Sarah and Polly can drop by as a charity. It's dreadfully sorry not to have the comfort of family while undergoing such a trial."

"Very good, my lady. My lord." Clarence gave a crisp nod to Malcolm and went back to his surgery.

"Don't go to any trouble, darling," Malcolm said. "I'll see to it that he's compensated for his troubles. It's enough."

"We should at least look into what happened. What if one of the other workers becomes injured? Perhaps there's an instability in the scaffolding that needs to be addressed."

"That won't be necessary, Eliza," he replied, his lips tightening over his teeth. "There *are* no other workers."

"What?"

"After they'd loaded your carpenter onto the ambulance, the men packed up their tools and presented a bill for their final day of work. It wasn't the foreman's wish, but he couldn't keep his crew there against their will."

Eliza's shoulders slumped. "How unfortunate."

"Indeed."

"They said you were there when it happened. What did you see?"

"I saw a young man stumble and lose his balance."

"One of the workers said it looked as if he'd been pulled or pushed by unseen hands. What do you make of that?"

"I'm quite sure of what I saw, darling." Malcolm's jaw clenched. Tension swelled between them. "At any rate, it's pleasant to have a conversation with you, despite the unfortunate circumstances. I have sorely missed your company." His eyes remained fixed on a spot on the far wall, his voice hollow. "Won't you join me for dinner tonight?"

Eliza worried the buttons on her gloves. "I suppose I'd better."

Malcolm laughed, a harsh sound in the cavernous room. "You make it sound like a trip to the gallows. Am I truly that monstrous?"

"Sometimes."

"Look. I am wretched over what happened between us, Eliza. I saw the shadow of my father in the way I behaved that day in my study. I hated myself for it."

Eliza's heart caught at his earnestness. She reached out and took his hand. "I shall join you for dinner, on one condition."

He lifted her hand to his lips. "Anything."

"Promise me you'll allow me fully into your world and your heart. You're still hiding so much from me, Malcolm—ever pulling out of my reach when I only long to be close to you. If we're to have a happy marriage, you *must* learn to trust me. With everything."

He smiled sadly. "I'll admit it's not in my nature to be free with my feelings, but I will at least endeavor to be less of a prig, darling." He pressed a kiss to her brow. "I'm going to head back to the manor to close up the south wing. Will you come with me, or would you rather stay on to visit with your sister?"

"I believe I've lost Lydia to the wonders of modern medicine. She's much too busy with her patients for a chat. I think I'll walk home. I've been needing some exercise, and it's such a fine day, at least as far as weather."

They parted at the curb, Malcolm folding her into a stiff embrace before he climbed back into the carriage. Eliza turned to the west—choosing the long way home, through the pastures, where their tenants were threshing the last of the summer wheat. The air was crisp as a harvest apple, giving clarity to her mood and thoughts.

Malcolm had promised better days, but Eliza was no less troubled than she'd been hours before. Their marriage seemed to be unraveling almost as quickly as it had begun, and no matter how desperately she grasped at the threads of their affection, her weaving was proving to be an exercise in frustration. For every kiss he lavished upon her, there soon followed a harsh word. For each night spent in passion, there was a day spent in awkward silence. It brought back painful memories of her parents' unhappy marriage and the chilly indifference they'd eventually shown to one another. Chasing Malcolm's affections was like trying to hold water in a sieve.

She was lost in her thoughts when a motorcar came rattling past her, then pulled to a stop along the verge. Sarah leaned out, her face beaming beneath the brim of her hat. "Ho there, if it isn't my long-lost Lady Havenwood!"

Eliza jogged to catch up. "How fortunate! I was just thinking about you."

"And I think about you far too often for my own good," Sarah teased. "I've just attended my first suffragist meeting in Basingstoke. Lots of womanly shouting and high passions. I daresay it won't be my last. What news from town?"

"I've just come from the hospital."

"Oh? Is everything all right?"

"There's an Irish boy named Freddie there. He was injured at our place today. I thought you and I, and perhaps Polly, could pay him a visit soon. His family is in Dublin and your kind of merriment is just what he needs."

"Goodness! I hope he'll be all right."

"Clarence seems to think he'll come through it."

"If anyone can bring him back to health, it's our fastidious young doctor. Say, when are you going to have a party and invite us to that fresh new home of yours? I've been watching the work being done. What a fine slate roof you've got! I told Dickie we should scallop our roof just the same. In different colors, of course."

Eliza squinted up at Sarah. "The roof is about the only thing done, I'm afraid. All of our workers have quit. It seems they think this boy's fall was no accident."

"How curious," Sarah said. "But I'm sure you can find more men. Perhaps in Dorset. Heaven knows there's nothing to do down that way when the watercress goes dormant. Or Essex." Sarah stuck out the pink tip of her tongue and shook her head. "Dreadfully boring and wet, Essex. That's where Dickie's from. Full of doddering aunties asking when we're going to set a baby loose."

Eliza grinned. She'd certainly missed Sarah's merry wit. "I'm not sure Malcolm will want to be doing anything with winter coming on so soon, but at least the weather will be kept out with a proper roof on. He's been so glum lately. It has me in a state."

"He was born glum! Hop in," Sarah said, patting the seat next to her. "You look like you could do with some cheering yourself, and I'd love to have your company on such a fine afternoon. But do hang on, because I like to go fast."

While "fast" was relative concerning automobiles, most of which any farm nag could outpace, Sarah made true on her word. No sooner had Eliza settled into the leather seat than they were off, the Duryea's narrow tires flying over the rutted lane. Eliza gripped the edge of the seat with one hand and held her hat to her head with the other. Once they were out over the moors, the way became smoother and Sarah slowed to a puttering idle.

"My, that was just what my spirits needed," Eliza said.

"I'm chuffed, then! Have you really been so low?"

Eliza paused for a moment. "My marriage isn't quite what I anticipated. That's all."

"Oh?" Sarah asked, her round brown eyes searching Eliza's face. "How do you mean?"

"Malcolm is often moody and talks to me as if I'm an idiot child. And then, just as quickly, he'll turn the other way, and be as charming as he was during our courtship. I just don't understand it. I don't understand *him*. It was intriguing at first, but now it's a source of frustration. I'm afraid I know very little about my husband, and all my efforts to learn more have led to a game of hide-and-seek I'm not keen on continuing."

Sarah pulled the car over to the side of the road and turned to Eliza. "I've known Malcolm since I was a child, and his brother was my very best friend. I spent a good deal of time at Havenwood Manor when I was young. I saw a lot. Ask me anything, and I promise I'll be honest with you."

"Anything you'd care to tell me is welcome. Was their father as awful as everyone says?"

Sarah nodded. "When it came to the boys, the expectations he had were ridiculous. He had Malcolm rise every morning at six, and if he wasn't up by then, he'd drag him out of bed by the ear, calling him a lazy brat. He beat him to 'toughen' him up. I saw it once. It was so bad I'm surprised your husband made it to adulthood as comely as he is."

"Merde," Eliza said. "I didn't know the beatings were such a regular occurrence."

"Yes. And to many, it seemed as if he favored Gabriel, but that's pure rubbish. The only reason Havenwood *stopped* beating Gabriel was that once he was old enough, he'd hit back even harder. The old bastard could mold Malcolm, bend him to his will. With Gabe, he had to be more subtle. Havenwood gave him two choices: become a vicar or choose a military career. I can tell you—my Gabriel wasn't suited to a priest's collar." At this, Sarah smiled sadly. "I miss him so. Everyone thought we'd marry—my father would have loved that—but my marriage with Dickie suits me perfectly. He lets me be myself."

"That's what anyone should hope for in a marriage." Eliza sighed. "I wish I knew more about what happened to their mother. She's an enigma. I've found her diary, but the entries are a bit of a riddle. The puzzling thing is, she didn't seem to have any true enemies who'd want to see her dead, apart from that housekeeper . . ."

"Yes. Mrs. Galbraith. Hideous woman. Face and manner like an axe. She was certainly awful and there was talk she had designs on old Lord Havenwood, but she died in the fire as well. It couldn't have been her. We'll likely never know what happened in that house, fully. And Ada was a mystery to most who knew her. She and I had many things in common, but even still, she would only let me get so close before pulling away." Sarah looked out over the moors. "I only hope she's happy, wherever she is."

"You don't think she's dead?"

"Not for a minute, darling."

CHAPTER 26

The downstairs clock was chiming. Eliza counted six bells, and then seven, but for once, Malcolm remained in her bed. They'd made up in full after their dinner together, indulging in the leisurely kind of lovemaking that soothed Eliza's frustrations. But while Eliza had been satisfied, Malcolm had barely slept afterward, his body racked with nightmares. Long after he'd drifted into his fitful sleep, she stayed awake next to him, stroking his back and whispering endearments until he quieted.

As the clock chimed eight, he finally woke, his eyes blinking drowsily. "You're still here."

"I was just going to say the same to you. I miss you when you leave me so early." She pushed his dark curls from his face. "You were troubled last night. You cried out in your sleep, several times."

Malcolm closed his eyes, deep creases forming at their corners. "I had a dream you'd left me. Well and truly. I was searching for you everywhere, but all the light had gone from the world, and fanged beasts tore at me from every dark corner. It was hellish."

"You sound a bit like Dante searching for his lost love." Eliza chased the drifting thread and barely caught it. "Beatrice. There was a maid here at one time called that, wasn't there? Just like Dante's love?"

Malcolm sat upright in bed, fully awake. Something akin to panic glinted in his eyes. "How on earth did you find out about Beatrice?"

"Mrs. Duncan told me about her once, in passing. Why does it matter?"

Malcolm ran a hand over his tangled hair and reached for his trousers. "It doesn't. She was just a young woman my mother hired on as a lady's companion and nanny. Did Duncan say anything else about her?"

"No, nothing at all." How funny. There was something about Beatrice—she could see it on his face, the sudden way he'd flinched at her name. She had caught him unawares, but pressing her husband wasn't the way to get him to open up. She'd leave it . . . for now. Eliza sat up against the headboard and pulled the sheets around her bare bosom. "What are you up to and about today?"

"I've an appointment in Southampton. I should have been on the road an hour ago."

"Are you looking at hiring more men to finish our work?"

Malcolm buttoned his shirt over his chest and shook his head. "No. This is something else. A surprise." The hint of a smile tugged at his mouth. He sat in front of the chair by the fireplace and pulled on his boots. "You'll still be here when I return, won't you?"

"Of course. Mrs. Duncan and I are planning on working in the garden this afternoon. She insists the carrots must be pulled." Eliza stood, letting the sheets fall away.

Malcolm's eyes roved hungrily over her bare flesh. "Come here, wife."

She walked to him, her pulse quickening. He cupped her breasts, kneading their fullness in his palms, his tongue flicking over their hardened peaks. "Like so much ripe, delicious fruit," he murmured.

Eliza sighed, her head rocking back. "Shouldn't you be going?" she asked breathlessly. "Don't you have somewhere to be?"

"Do I?" He gripped a hank of her hair, pulling her onto his lap as his lips found the soft curve of her throat, drinking her skin.

"I thought you were late . . ."

His fingers trailed down her belly, spreading heat in their wake. "It seems something much more pressing has come up at home."

⬥

Eliza bent to her work, weeding the rows of red lettuce in the kitchen garden as the sun warmed her back. A delicious ache still rested between her legs from Malcolm's attentions that morning. Even though their lovemaking had been a pleasant distraction, his strange response to her mention of Beatrice's name had piqued her curiosity.

Eliza eyed Shirley, who was busy shaking a flurry of dirt from a bundle of carrots. She placed them in the basket at her feet, then moved toward the row of parsnips.

"Say, Shirley?" Eliza called.

"Yes'm?"

"I've been considering adding to our staff. Malcolm mentioned he'd like to hire a maid for me, and I thought someone already familiar with the manor would be a good fit, wouldn't you think?" In reality, Malcolm hadn't brought up any such thing. "Sarah Nelson and I were talking the other day, and she mentioned Ada's maid. I believe her name was Beatrice?"

"Aye, mum. I remember her." Shirley paused, the ruffled top of a parsnip within her chubby hand. "He's said he wants to hire another maid? Really?"

"Yes. Did Beatrice leave a forwarding address or ever send for a reference?"

"I wouldn't ken where to find her, mum. She left in a rush quite a few years ago. I believe she said she was going home to Guernsey or some such." Shirley's voice had risen in pitch from her usual alto rumble. "Nae, I've no help for ye on that count."

What was it with Beatrice that had everyone in such a state?

Eliza sighed and stretched her back. "It's just that I'm considering having a party, and I wouldn't want you having to do all the work."

Shirley brightened, her relief in the change of subject apparent. "Dinnae fash about my working. I'm built to the task. I've been managing things for many a year."

"I'd want dancing and a buffet, and all the rest. That gorgeous ballroom has been closed up for far too long."

Shirley brushed her hands on her apron. "It'd be nice to have a bit of merrymaking in this old house again. His lordship's mother held a ghillies ball each fall before the hunt. She didnae care for parties, not usually, but she liked to keep her Scottish traditions."

"Do you think we could pull off a ghillies ball at Havenwood Manor? By mid-October, perhaps?"

"Oh, mum. We most certainly could. I could help you plan the menu after tea! We *could* bring in a pair of village girls to help with the cooking, I suppose. Just for the day. His lordship surely wouldn't mind that. And unless the moths have gotten to it, I've yards of tartan bunting up the attic."

"That all sounds marvelous."

Just then, their happy plans were interrupted by a commotion of hoofbeats from the flagstone drive. Eliza shook out her skirts and went around the side of the house. She was greeted by the unexpected sight of Malcolm driving a fine new carriage—a varnished ebony wood landau with sweeping French lines and purple tufted upholstery. Apollo was hitched to the shaft, and next to him trotted a beautiful Friesian mare, black as coal shards, her crimped mane tied with violet ribbons. Malcolm pulled up to the terrace, his face breaking into a proud grin.

"Husband, what have you done?"

"I've retrieved your wedding present, darling. As promised."

Eliza covered her mouth with her hands. "But this is *trop cher*! It must have cost a fortune."

Malcolm hopped down and pulled her into his arms. "It's also my apology. It's not too dear at all, considering. Do you like it?"

Eliza laughed, incredulous. "How could I not?" She ran her hand over the beveled edge of the carriage door. "It's gorgeous!"

It was more than gorgeous, it was extravagant—a carriage meant for a duke or a prince. A gilded *H* adorned the front fender, and its well-oiled wheels gleamed with gold plating along their spoked rims. But for all the landau's finery, it was the new horse she was most anxious to see. Eliza went to the mare's side, sweeping a hand over her velvet flank up to her neck. The horse turned her fine head to study Eliza with long-lashed, dewy eyes.

"She came all the way from Holland, with the very best bloodlines. Her ancestors carried kings."

Eliza's tears welled. "Hello, Artemis." She placed a kiss on the horse's muzzle and was rewarded with a soft huff of hot air against her cheek. "Oh, Malcolm. I love her already."

"She'll carry you well. And now you won't have to walk to town when I'm away."

"You made excellent time to Southampton and back. This carriage must be swift as the wind."

He gave a puzzled look. "Did I? I've been gone since early morning."

"I suppose for most people, nine in the morning *is* early." She winked. "You seemed rather unconcerned with the time."

Turner came onto the terrace, his hands clasped behind his back. "Mrs. Duncan is readying tea, m'lord. Shall I have her hold off for a while?"

Malcolm turned to Eliza. "Would you like to take a ride in your new carriage before tea, darling?"

"Shouldn't I change first?" she asked, poking an errant curl behind her ear. "I'm sure I look dreadful."

"Nonsense. You look as fresh and lovely as a spring day." Malcolm pinched her chin and smiled. "Turner, have Mrs. Duncan pack a picnic basket instead. Her ladyship and I are going on a ramble."

∽❀∾

The new carriage was indeed as fast and nimble as Eliza had imagined. They rolled along the lane, past Sherbourne House, where Mr. Mason waved to them and called a greeting as he trimmed the shrubbery. Lydia was rarely there these days. Eliza had learned if she wanted to hold congress with her sister, she'd need to go to the hospital. Nursing had become Lydia's driving passion in life, and Eliza was glad for it.

They rambled through the thicket of spindly birches on the outer edge of the forest glen. Malcolm guided the horses onto the same mounded knoll where they'd lingered on their first outing. Instead of summer's daisies and yarrow, red grass and purple heather now crested the hill in colorful runnels.

"Taking me back to where it all began, I see," Eliza said.

Malcolm slowed the horses to a stop and looped the reins over the carriage's lantern post. "It's one of my favorite places, after all." He gave her hand a gentle squeeze. "We'll walk on for a bit, if that's all right. I want to show you the mill."

She gathered the quilted blanket and picnic basket Shirley had packed for them and handed both to Malcolm. They walked arm in arm over the grass, the wind ruffling Eliza's cotton skirts. When she first glimpsed the edges of the millpond, a brief moment of terror shot through her belly. It was nearly identical to the pond Albert had drowned in, down to the narrow jetty angling toward its center. The only difference was the windmill slowly turning at the far end, its wooden blades creaking.

"Are you all right, darling?" Malcolm asked. "You've gone a bit pale."

"I'm well. It was just a moment."

"Memories of your brother?"

Eliza nodded. "They come unexpectedly. Small things, rippling through like a finger placed in a puddle of water. Sometimes I hear him crying in the call of a bird or see a glimmer of his hair in the way the sun shines on a plume of sedge. He's ever out of my reach, yet ever present all the same."

"Memories of my brother often come in the same way."

Malcolm spread the quilt out on the ground, and Eliza sat next to him, hugging her knees until her breathing steadied. He poured tea for them out of a squat, lidded carafe and sweetened hers with honey before handing it to her. Eliza cupped it in her hands, savoring its warmth. "Tell me about Gabriel."

Malcolm smiled sadly. "As I've said, my brother and I were as different as we were alike. Much of our trouble was due to how differently our parents treated us," he said, removing his tweed derby and reclining next to her. "Our mother seemed to favor me. 'Mollycoddled' was what my father said. Perhaps he was right. Gabriel was a difficult child. Independent, rash. Our father admired his spark but knew he wouldn't be suited to play the subtle politics of a country lord. Still, I became jealous when Papa would crow about Gabe's military accomplishments. He was made one of the youngest lieutenants in the Royal Navy, you know. He would have been a captain someday."

"But *you* are so clever, Malcolm! Talented and quick of mind. It's one of the things I admire most about you. And you're an artist. The plans for the renovations are superb. You're an accomplished architect."

Her husband turned bashful, fiddling in the pocket of his coat until he drew out his pipe. "I do find great comfort in the orderliness of numbers and geometry. It's predictable and reliable. Unfortunately, my father never saw the merit in my interests until it came time for me to manage the estate's ledgers."

"We're opposites in that regard. My papa always treated me as his heir and reassured me I was capable," Eliza said. "He was too indulgent with me at times, I suppose, but Maman's criticisms brought me back down to earth. No matter how hard I tried for her approval, I would never be as graceful as she, or as talented at singing and the harp. She saw me as an impulsive little girl with hopeless manners and knock-knees. And then after Albert . . ." Eliza turned away, looking out over the water. "I should have never been made responsible for his care. I wasn't suited to it. I've never thought I'd make much of a mother. I still don't. I'm sorry."

"That's utter nonsense! You show the utmost care when it concerns the feelings of others. I see it in the way you treat our staff. You'll make a fine mother, darling." Malcolm packed his pipe and lit it, a curl of smoke streaming from his nostrils.

"You say that now." Eliza looked down and took a steadying breath. It was time to lay her own fears bare, in the hopes that her husband would reciprocate. "But what if one of *our* children dies, Malcolm? What if I get distracted and turn away at the wrong moment, and your son and heir wanders out into the road? What if he pulls a kettle from the hob, or falls from a tree? Will you truly be able to forgive? Or will you blame me? Will I suffer the removal of your affection and your silent disregard?" She shook her head. "I couldn't endure that. Not again. If I'm ever to happily bear your children, I must be assured your love is evergreen, come what may."

Malcolm put down his pipe and grasped her hand. "My dearest wife, if the worst were to happen—which I've the utmost confidence it will *not*—you have my word we'd shoulder it together. I promise you."

He pulled her down onto the blanket, his lips meeting her own in a chaste kiss. She sighed and nuzzled beneath his chin, inhaling the earthy fragrance of his skin. He undid her hair from its long plait and combed through it with his fingers, holding it up so the sun's rays sparkled through. "You remind me of our wild Boudicca, with your fire-bright hair."

"I was always teased for it, as well as the freckles that come along with it." Eliza sighed. "Maman made me scrub my face and arms with lemon water and wear long sleeves in summer to prevent the damnable spots from multiplying."

"Spots and all, I've rather come to appreciate your rustic kind of beauty."

Eliza frowned. "Your compliments need a bit of tuning, husband. I'm not a log cabin or a grizzly bear, after all."

"Fair enough." He smiled and cupped her jawline, his thumb tracing her cheekbone. "I'd no idea I could feel so happy. You've brought me back to life, Eliza."

When they'd returned from their drive, Eliza went upstairs to her dressing table. She withdrew the amber bottle of herbal tonic Lydia had given her. She grasped it for a moment, briefly wavering, then went to her water closet. As the last dregs dripped into the flush toilet, a well of calm resolve settled over her. If deception were to truly be undone in their marriage, she would no longer play the hypocrite.

CHAPTER 27

Dressed in worn linen dungarees, Eliza hefted a length of MacCulloch tartan over her shoulder, pins bristling from the cushion on her wrist. Shirley held the tail of the fabric as Eliza climbed the ladder to reach the ballroom's crown molding. There she gathered the satin in billowing puffs, pinning the bunting to the trim. She dropped the remaining lengths of green-and-red plaid and left them to pool on the freshly waxed floor.

The preparations for their ghillies ball had gone swimmingly. The guest list had been made, the menu was in its final stages of planning, and they'd ordered a magnificent three-tiered cake from the best bakery in the county. Polly and Sarah had shown up that afternoon to help, and Eliza had put them to work on the invitations. Polly was addressing each placard with her immaculate penmanship, then handing them off to Sarah, who sealed each envelope with red wax. They sat in the corner of the ballroom at a narrow table, talking in quiet whispers as Shirley and Eliza bustled about.

"His lordship will be right pleased with you for going to all the effort, mum," Shirley said, poking branches of spiny thistle and purple heather into a vase. "It's a noble thing to open a great house to guests. Reflects well on your station."

"I certainly hope he'll be pleased," Eliza said, climbing down from the ladder to survey her work. She'd learned not to predict her husband's reactions to anything. "It's a bit of a coming-out party for us both."

Polly looked up from her writing. "You've got the house looking grand again. It needed a woman's touch."

"Shirley deserves most of the credit, if I'm to be honest." At this, Shirley clucked and shook her head. "You know," Eliza continued, "it's funny when I think about it, but I believe I fell in love with the house before I fell in love with Malcolm. Living here is a bit like opening up a present every day."

"Don't the ghosts bother you?" asked Polly.

Eliza feigned ignorance. "Ghosts?"

"Sarah and I have been visiting your Freddie. He won't tell us what happened, but rumors are flying about town that he was injured by an evil spirit. There's been rumors about ghosts for years, though."

"Oh, you know how people like to talk." Eliza laughed dryly. "How is Freddie? I've been so involved with planning this party I haven't been round to see him."

"He's recovering well. Clarence says he'll be out of hospital soon."

"Oh, that's fantastic news!"

"It's mostly thanks to your sister. The hospital is much improved for having her."

"Polly's often enough about the ward to know," Sarah said, winking. "Isn't that right, Miss Whitby?"

Eliza caught on, her eyes widening in surprise. "Polly! Have you taken a shine to the Irish boy, after all?"

Polly shifted in her seat, a red stain creeping up her fair bosom to her chin. "Well. He's very charming."

"And handsome," Sarah prodded.

Polly's face grew scarlet as a poppy. "Well, at any rate, one must move on." She rested her pen on the table and flexed her fingers. "Speaking of moving on, I'm quite relieved to see Lord and Lady Eastleigh aren't on your guest list."

Eliza laughed, picking up a dustcloth and running it around the frame of Ada's portrait, its corners carved with acorns. "If I never see Una and Charles again, it will be too soon."

"Do you know? They bought another townhome in London," Polly said. "In Hyde Park. Now they have two. Una must have come with a healthy dowry."

"I daresay *bought* is a generous term," Eliza scoffed. *Stolen* would be more apropos. The forfeited townhouse was still a sore subject under their eaves. "You know as well as I that he only married Una to spite Malcolm."

"Well. Enough about that," Sarah said, clearing her throat. "Do you have a tiara to wear to the ball, Eliza? If not, you can wear one of mine. I have a lovely emerald one that would look ravishing with your hair."

The doorbell chimed from downstairs. "I wonder who that could be?" Eliza said. "We aren't expecting visitors."

"I'll go see who it is," Sarah said, standing and stretching her arms behind her head. "I could do with a smoke by the by."

A few minutes later, she returned, her eyebrows drawn together. "I'm so sorry. Turner just got your husband from the library. I'm not sure what's going on, but he had an official telegram in hand. From the look on Malcolm's face, it seemed urgent."

Eliza went into the hall and caught the sound of Turner's wavering tenor on the steps. She hovered near the doorway of the ballroom, listening.

"What'll we do then, sir? Shall we send her ladyship with you?"

"As we've lost the townhome, she'll need to stay on to manage things here in my absence, Turner. Just mind the south wing stays locked."

She swept onto the landing and into their view. "What's going on, Malcolm?"

Malcolm's head jerked toward her in surprise. His mouth flinched, then settled into a taut line. "The Boer army is on the move. We've been given an ultimatum by their president, Paul Kruger, to remove our troops from the Transvaal border. It's likely we will not comply with his demands." He offered the telegram to Eliza. "It's likely it will result in conflict."

She scanned the brief message. "We're going to war?"

"It very much looks like it," Malcolm answered. "I'll need to report to Parliament. I'll leave for London first thing tomorrow."

"But, our ball . . ."

Malcolm's jaw clenched in irritation. "Will have to wait, darling. I'm so sorry."

Alongside her disappointment, a thought needled in the back of Eliza's consciousness. The south wing. "Will I be left alone, then, to manage the house?"

"Turner and Duncan will remain here with you, but yes. For a time. I have every confidence I can rely on you to maintain the household. I've no doubt it will flourish under your care."

Eliza sucked in a breath to fight the smile twitching at the corners of her mouth. "Though it may be a challenge, husband, I will endeavor to do my best."

CHAPTER 28

Eliza's breath puffed in a cloud as she and Malcolm stood on the railway platform in Winchester, awaiting the first train. The temperatures had taken a precipitous dive, and she'd had to don her wool cape for the first time that season. Winter would come early this year.

Malcolm had been troubled all night, pacing and talking to himself as he and Turner packed trunks and made arrangements for managing the estate in his absence. Eliza had played the dutiful wife, helping Shirley fold clothes and handkerchiefs, all the while plotting an internal list of investigations to engage in during Malcolm's absence.

The rumbling locomotive pulled into the station, blasting a loud hiss of steam. Malcolm stooped to kiss her brow. "Try not to worry about things, love. I'm hoping to be home by Christmas, at the very latest. It will likely be a brief conflict."

"Where will you lodge?"

"I'll stay at the club for now, but if our session is extended much more than a month, I'll look into letting a room. I'll strive to make it home now and again in the meantime."

Silence swelled between them, full of words Eliza was afraid to speak. A porter with a braided cap and handsome scarlet livery came to claim Malcolm's valise. "First class, sir?"

"That's right, mate," Malcolm answered. He kissed her once more. "I need to be going now, darling. Take care of yourself until we're reunited."

Eliza stood watching until Malcolm's train was only visible by the plume of smoke threading from its stack. She pulled her cloak tight against the buffeting wind and turned to go back to the station. There, leering like a goon, was Lord Eastleigh, dressed impeccably in a caped Astrakhan greatcoat and wool hat. Eliza's stomach dropped.

"Ah, Lady Havenwood. I've missed the seven o'clock, haven't I?"

"I'm afraid so," Eliza said, making no attempt to mask the chill in her voice. "On your way to London?"

"Indeed. Bloody business with these rebel colonists. I'm assuming you've just seen your husband off?"

"Yes. I'm only sorry I couldn't accompany him. I'm needed at Havenwood."

He nodded. "Lady Eastleigh will be remaining at Clairborne Hall as well."

"Oh? She isn't going with you?"

"It's her ladyship's condition that makes her unfit for travel at the moment."

"Is she unwell?"

"Yes. I suspect she's in the family way," Eastleigh said with a grin. "You should call on her. I'm sure she'd be glad for your company."

She gave a sharp little laugh. "I'm not so sure about that, my lord. But congratulations, all the same."

Eastleigh took two steps toward her, close enough that the breath steaming from his mouth collided with her own. He took her gloved hand. "I was hoping we could mend our rift, Eliza. That we could endeavor, at least, to be friends."

She narrowed her eyes. "I'm quite sure that's impossible. After what you asked of Malcolm, I cannot fathom the thought of our ever being civil, much less friends."

"Do you really know *everything* about your husband, Eliza? It's an easy thing, to paint me as the monster. But have you asked him the troublesome questions? Or is your mind still clouded by the tragically romantic idea you have of him?"

Eliza's heart hammered as he studied her—searching her face for the doubt she knew was there. The ground beneath them began to shake. A mournful wail pierced the silence between them as the train bound for Dorset arrived. Eliza jerked her hand from his. "I'd better be going, Lord Eastleigh."

"Very well." He lifted the brim of his hat. "Good day, Lady Havenwood. I'll be sure to keep an eye on your husband. He acts a different person entirely when he's in London."

✲

With Malcolm gone, Eliza had two goals in mind. The first was to pay Freddie a visit. Her errand would serve mostly to cheer Freddie as a charity, it was true. But she also wanted to hear his version of the accident in the south wing. Malcolm had been curiously obtuse about the events of that day. There was something he wasn't sharing, and Eliza meant to find out what.

The second endeavor, which would require much more creative enterprise, would involve breaking into the south wing to investigate the clues in Ada's cryptic diary. Eastleigh's words at the station lay heavily on her mind. In order to feel settled and safe in her marriage, she needed to know whether her husband was innocent of murder. If Malcolm wouldn't willingly divulge his secrets, she would find out what he was hiding in the south wing. On her own.

The morning after Malcolm's departure, she dressed in a simple plaid shirtwaist and woolen walking suit, then gathered a basket from the pantry and filled it with ginger tea biscuits, shortbread, and a carafe of coffee.

Instead of riding Artemis, Eliza walked to the village along the back lanes. A rare sunny morning in October was enough cause for a constitutional. It also afforded her the chance to smoke. Her old habit rankled Malcolm, and while he hadn't forbidden her smoking entirely, he certainly cast aspersions. *Unbefitting a lady of rank*, he'd said one morning as they breakfasted together in the conservatory. She'd ignored him, idly puffing her Sobranie while enjoying her coffee. Even though she acted cavalier, Malcolm's casual criticisms wounded her more than she let on. He couldn't see her unfitness now though, could he? She smirked and blew a steady stream of smoke toward the treetops.

When she arrived at the hospital, Lydia was bustling around the atrium, her arms laden with hot-water bottles. "I forgot to fetch the pushcart before I filled these," she said, an errant curl falling into her eyes. "Here to check up on Freddie?"

Eliza nodded. "Let me help you, sister." She adjusted her basket and unburdened Lydia of one of the bottles. They were much heavier than they looked. "Goodness. Are you here all alone?"

"Yes," Lydia said. "Clarence is in surgery, and Dr. Gilmore has gone to Godshill for the day. A small outbreak of cholera started there before the frost. Probably an infected farm pond, I'd imagine. I'm left here doing everything else, and the arthritics are whinging because of the cold snap."

Eliza grinned at the nascent English accent Lydia was developing. "It's certainly lucky for those gentlemen doctors that you're so capable."

"If there were such a thing as women doctors, I could run this place all on my own," Lydia said proudly. "Although Clarence has made me nurse-midwife, which is almost as good. He means to turn the delivering of babies over to me."

"Oh, that's fantastic! I'm pleased you're so happy in your work."

"I certainly am. Come this way," she said, motioning to the left. "Freddie's just here, in the recovery ward. I'll drop you off before I see to the other patients."

Lydia led the way through the swinging doors. The room beyond was clean and sterile, its pale-green walls reflecting the sunlit windows opposite. Freddie sat in a narrow cot, propped up with pillows, his injured leg elevated. A screen separated his bed from the one next to it, which held a sleeping elderly man whose right arm was bound up in a splint. They set their water bottles on the wheeled cart inside the door and pushed it through the ward.

Freddie's eyes lit up when he saw Eliza. "Lady Havenwood, aren't you in fine fettle."

"Hello, Freddie. Would you like a hot-water bottle for your feet? My sister is making the rounds."

"I sure would, maum. Your sister is right bossy, but she takes good care of me."

Lydia snorted. "You can have a hot-water bottle for your good foot, Mr. O'Riordan, but you can't suffer the weight on your injured leg."

Freddie gave a playful grin. "See what I'm on about?"

"You're not telling me a thing I don't already know," Eliza said. "Lydia's taken charge of every situation she's ever been in, since birth." Lydia took a water bottle and applied it to Freddie's foot before moving on to check the patient next to him. Eliza pulled a chair close to Freddie's bed and sat. "I'm so sorry I haven't been by. How are you, darling? Are you feeling any better?"

"A bit. They won't let me walk with crutches just yet, but the doc said I could try next week. He thinks I'll be fully on my feet again within a few months."

"That's good news." She rustled around in her basket. "I've brought you some coffee and shortbread."

"Sugary sweets are hardly good for his recovery. He's not supposed to have any outside food unless Dr. Fawcett approves," Lydia scolded. "Don't tempt him. He's ever begging for more to eat as it is."

Eliza rolled her eyes and gave Freddie a conspiratorial look. "Ignore her," she said in a stage whisper.

"I heard that." Lydia shot an annoyed look at Eliza and left to resume her rounds. Eliza waited until the squeak of the cart and the swish of Lydia's uniform could no longer be heard on the other side of the door. The silence was broken only by the quiet snoring of the elderly man next to them.

She cleared her throat, unsure of how to begin. "Say, Freddie. Your friend—that tall fellow—I think his name is Charlie? He told me something quite concerning after your fall."

"It's Cecil, maum. Cecil Wright."

"That's it. Cecil."

"He told you I were pushed, didn't he?"

"Yes. What happened, exactly?"

"Right." Freddie shifted in the bed, wincing as the covers pulled tighter over his leg. "Your husband asked me not to tell anyone how it all happened. He gave me a great deal of money to make sure myself and the others would keep things quiet."

So Malcolm *had* lied. Again. Eliza pressed her lips hard against her teeth. "My husband and I have no secrets between us, Freddie. He's told me what he saw. I only want to hear things from your perspective."

"Fair enough. I'd been working along the back attic wall all morning. I kept hearing sounds in the wall—scratching and scrabbling, like."

"Like rats?"

"Yes, maum. Just that." Freddie nodded. "That's a problem, see. When rats get between the inner and outer walls of a house, it's bad. Dangerous. I started tearing through the lath and plaster with my hammer. The lath was all rotted out, so it was easy work. As I was at it, the air around me started getting cold." Freddie passed a hand over his jaw. "But it wasn't cold at all down by my mates. And you'll remember, it was a warm day, otherwise."

Eliza remembered the unnatural chill in her room on the night she'd felt the presence beside her bed. Had this been the same spirit? "Go on, please."

"I started to wonder if I was taking ill, seeing as I got real sick to my stomach. But I kept on working, as it were almost the lunch hour. A few minutes went by. Some sort of crazed, wavery line flickered at the corner of my eyes, all different colors."

"Like a migraine aura?"

"I couldn't say, maum. All of a sudden, I felt something stinging the back of my neck, like a cat had sunk its claws into my skin. I cried out and clapped my hand to my neck, and that's when it jerked me over the scaffolding. Grabbed me by the shirt, just like a bloke does during a brawl." Freddie shook his head. "I didn't just *fall*, maum. Whatever that thing was, it meant to hurt me. I don't figure it liked us working on the house. The misplaced tools and all, that was a warning, right. And when we didn't heed it . . ."

Eliza reached for Freddie's hand and gave it a gentle squeeze. "Rest assured, Freddie, I mean to find out what's going on. And should you need more compensation to tide you over until you can work again, come to me, not my husband." After turning his mood happier with talk of Polly, Eliza bid Freddie farewell and left the ward.

Lydia met her at the foot of the stairs. "I see from your face he's told you what *really* happened."

"I don't know what to make of it, Lyddie."

"He won't talk to me about it now, but I heard enough on the day it happened. His friend was in a state." Lydia pressed her lips together, blanching their color. "It's what some call a poltergeist . . . or a demon. The bad energy I was telling you about. If it's strong enough to toss a man from a scaffold, it's mortally dangerous. I'm worried for you."

Eliza grasped her sister's hands. "You've enough to worry about here, with your work. I won't go poking around, trying to stir things up. I promise," she lied.

Lydia wrinkled her brow. "I wish I could believe you. I will pray for your protection, Liza."

CHAPTER 29

Eliza peered out her window through branches furred with hoarfrost. A ragged chill ached through her wool stockings, cramping her toes. Shirley knelt before the grate, humming to herself as she stoked the embers, but the meager fire did little to dispel the cold as Eliza dressed. It now felt like true winter, even though they were only a fortnight into October. Eliza had spent the three days since Malcolm's departure watching the shadows grow long across the floor as the sunlit hours grew shorter. Even her favorite books were no longer a distraction. She'd been too consumed with thoughts of malevolent spirits and Lydia's warnings to concentrate on anything else.

The truth was, for all her protestations otherwise, Freddie's story had rattled her. His distress as he relayed his account of the accident had been enough to demonstrate his honesty. Whatever happened in the south wing, it had frightened him terribly. It was one thing to have spirits that played at games. It was quite another to know it was done with malicious intent.

That evening, Eliza took her solitary dinner early, then went up to her rooms. She was settling down for the night, doing her mending by the fireplace in her chambers, when a creaking sound, as if a door were slowly being opened, sounded from the other side of the wall. She paused, listening. The unmistakable sound of footsteps came down the hallway. Eliza glanced at the mantelpiece. The clock read eleven. She rose and went to her door, peering out. The shadow of the winged seraph at the foot of the main staircase loomed like a great dragon over the gallery leading to Malcolm's chambers. There was no one about that she could see.

Perhaps it had only been Turner, tending to his last few chores before going to bed. Yes, that was all. Surely. Eliza slowly closed the door. She settled back into her chair and picked up her sewing. Her hands shook slightly as she strained to keep her stitches in a steady row.

There it was again. Footsteps.

She put her work to the side and rushed to the door like a blood-hound with its nose to the ground. The sound was further away now—the distant clicking of heeled shoes on marble flooring. The ballroom. Eliza went into the hallway and crossed the gallery to the ballroom's entrance, her heartbeat jumping in her throat. She put her ear to the door and listened. The tapping was dainty—delicate. The footsteps of a woman.

"Shirley, is that you?" Eliza called, her voice wavering. The footsteps stopped immediately. But no voice answered in reply.

Eliza closed her eyes and drew in a deep breath. She flung the door open wide and then stepped back as if she were expecting a ghostly cavalry to come charging through with swords drawn. She cautiously peeked over the threshold. The room was empty apart from the decorations for their abandoned ghillies ball, the plaid bunting shrouding the corners. The wet scent of fallen leaves wafted through the room, as if carried on an invisible breeze. "Hello?" she questioned. "Shirley?"

The distant sound of footsteps came again. On the floor, just visible in the wan light from the windows, a faint tracery of damp footprints led to the doors to the south wing. Eliza raced across the room, nearly slipping in her haste. "Shirley, are you in there?" She shook the doorknob and twisted it. Locked. As usual. She ran her hands along the edges of the molding, feeling for anything that might indicate a weakness she could use to her advantage. The wood was as smooth as vellum, the joining solid. She tried the latch again, but the lock held fast.

"This is ridiculous. I'm finding my way in here, one way or another."

She went back to her room and rifled through her writing desk until she found her pearl-handled letter opener, its edge as sharp as a surgeon's scalpel. She flew back to the doors and wedged the pointed tip into the lock's opening. She leaned on the handle as she worked the letter opener in a circle, trying desperately to engage the lock's tumbler. After going through various maneuvers, she gave up, groaning in frustration. A locked door was not going to keep her out for long. Someone was in there. Someone corporeal enough to leave footprints on the floor.

She had the momentary thought of going through the windows from the outside, as only two of them had been replaced during construction. But that was risky. If she injured herself, no one would know until it was too late. She needed a better plan. One that Malcolm would never find out about.

༺✿༻

Eliza was helping Shirley clean the larder when she decided to bring up the matter of the keys. "His lordship didn't happen to have a copy of the house keys made for you, did he, Shirley?"

"He did. Mr. Turner has his set and I've one, too."

A frisson of excitement ran through Eliza. "Is Turner here?"

"Nae, mum. He's gone to the village for the weekly errands."

"After we've finished the larder, let's go into the south wing and freshen it up a bit. I'm sure it's still a mess from when the workers were here. With winter coming on early, I'd like to at least cover the broken windows."

Shirley stopped her scrubbing and slowly turned. "His lordship told me we weren't to go into that part of the house, m'lady. He said it weren't safe."

"Malcolm doesn't think my crossing a mud puddle is safe, Shirley. I've learned not to listen to my husband on every account, especially when he isn't here."

❦

Eliza stood before the doors to the south wing, going through every key on Shirley's chatelaine, twisting and turning from left to right. When she became frustrated, Shirley tried them herself, huffing and puffing with the effort. "I'm sorry, m'lady, but none of these are a fit."

Eliza sighed, her shoulders slumping. "Do you think any of these would fit the downstairs entrance?"

"Nae, mum. The locks are cut just the same. We can ask Mr. Turner for his if it's so important."

The house keys were always in Turner's possession, either buckled to his waistcoat or locked in the desk in his room. The loyal butler was kind and deferent, but Eliza had the sneaking suspicion he relayed all her activities to Malcolm. "No, no we can't do that. I've another idea."

"I'd figured as much, canny as ye are."

Eliza gave a sly grin. "I know you're sweet on Turner. I can see it when you look at him."

"And here I thought I was doin' a better job of hidin' it. He's right charming, after all."

"I'll tell you a little secret," Eliza whispered, pulling Shirley down the hall. "I've caught him looking at you when you're unaware. I've a *feeling*, with a little encouragement, he could be persuaded to confess his longing for you."

Shirley's round little cheeks turned scarlet beneath her curls. "And this late in life! The very thought of it."

"Why not? You're not too old, and neither is Turner. Now, I've found his lordship's cache of Oban whisky, which I know you're fond of."

"Indeed, it sets the senses to tingling, doesn't it?"

"I can certainly tell when his lordship has had it," Eliza said, smiling slyly. "He paws at me like a jungle cat."

"Goodness me."

"After dinner, you and Turner can go into the library. You'll put some music on—perhaps something French to set a mood—and I'll pour the liquor."

"Sounds lovely," Shirley said. "I've not played the coy hen for many a year. I'll have to practice."

"The only thing I'll ask is that you swap your keys for Mr. Turner's. Do you think you can manage that?"

"That won't be any problem at all, m'lady. They look exactly alike, apart from the one key. He won't likely ken the difference."

"And I can trust you never to breathe a word of this to his lordship, or Mr. Turner?"

"You can, mum."

"Good. After you've finished with your little tryst, come upstairs and rap on my door. You can pass me the keys. That's all you'll need to do."

"Aye, are ye sure, then? Rather late to be doin' the dustin' is all, m'lady."

"Yes, but I've always been a bit of a night owl."

⁂

Eliza poured the amber whisky into two glasses and handed one to Turner and the other to Shirley. Shirley had dressed for the occasion, wearing a purple silk kimono over a simple lavender dress, her auburn hair piled high. Turner, still in his livery, perched on the edge of his chair as if he'd soon be called into action. He was avoiding looking at

Shirley. Eliza was growing ever more confident his reticence was proof of his ardor.

As Jenny Lind crooned from the gramophone, Eliza poured herself a finger of whisky and knocked it back in one swallow. They obviously needed a bit more help. "Doesn't Mrs. Duncan look fetching tonight, Turner?"

"I wouldn't know, mum. Wouldn't be polite to say so, even if I were to think it."

"Turner, you're certainly entitled to give your opinion. Besides, if we're to run this household well while my husband is away, it starts with harmony between the two most important people in the house."

"M'lady, I'm quite unsure what you're talking about," Turner said, fidgeting in his chair.

"It's just that, with all these years working beneath the same roof, Mr. Turner, I barely know ye," Shirley said. "I'm keen to be your friend."

"Well then." Eliza clapped her hands together and stood. "The two of you should enjoy your whisky and get to know one another—I'm sure you have much more in common than you realize. I'm going to put myself to bed and read for a bit."

Eliza ducked around the corner. She stood listening as Shirley began recounting stories of her youth in Aberdeen. In a few moments, Turner began to chuckle, and there was the sloshing of more liquor being poured.

"You little minx." Eliza smirked. She crept up the stairs to her room on catlike feet.

After an hour or so, she heard the telltale squeak of the floorboards outside her room. She put down her novel and slid into her bed slippers. "Come in, Shirley."

Shirley poked her head in the door. "He's out like a light, mum. I dinnae think he'll wake 'til morning." She shook the keys in her hands.

"How was it?"

"Oh, it was delightful. Mr. Turner is right charming once he lets off his airs. He'll nae likely remember it tomorrow, but we had a wonderful conversation."

"Nothing more?" Eliza asked, arching her brow as she took the keys.

Shirley giggled. "Not yet at any rate, but perhaps in time. Are ye sure ye won't be needin' me to go with ye tonight, mum? It's nae entirely safe."

"It's best if I do this alone, to keep his lordship from blaming you should he ever find out what we were up to while he was gone. I'll be fine, Shirley."

"Och. I'll not say a word to his lordship, but I won't be takin' any of the blame if things go pear-shaped, ye strong-willed lass." She gave Eliza's hand an awkward pat, then ambled down the hallway, weaving a bit as she walked.

Eliza waited, listening to the house creak and settle. Content that all were asleep who should be, she lit one of the Tilley lanterns Malcolm had placed in each bedroom for emergencies and crept to the ballroom. She muffled the clanking of the keys in the folds of her nightdress and stood her lantern on the floor to work by. The jumping flame illuminated the portraits of Malcolm's ancestors, creating the unsettling feeling of being watched.

She went through each key in an ordered fashion, eliminating them one by one. After four tries, she found it—a bronze key with a carved, crown-shaped fob at its base. The lock engaged with a satisfying click and turned. The door swung open. Eliza drew in a steadying breath to push past her fear, lifted her lantern, and stepped inside.

CHAPTER 30

Eliza didn't even dare to breathe.

The south wing was just as dangerous as Malcolm had said it would be. Had she been foolhardy enough to charge through the doorway without looking, she'd have toppled straight over the edge of the make-shift plank she now stood on, falling onto the marble checkerboard of flooring far below. Instead, she stood balanced like a tightrope walker on a rough-hewn beam no more than twelve inches wide, spanning the chasm of missing balcony. Her muscles tensed like a cat's. She hugged the wall with her back and slowly sidestepped along the board to the section of balustrade with its railing intact, the lantern clutched in her hand.

Though the rafters and roof had been repaired by the workers, great swaths of soot still muddied the wallpaper from floor to ceiling and smudged beneath the broken windows. Cold air channeled through the ragged shards of glass, causing her flesh to pimple.

A double waterfall staircase streamed down either side of the atrium. Other than that, this foyer was an exact mirror image of the one in the north wing. From Eliza's vantage point, she could see the section of flooring Freddie had fallen on, its surface now cleared of debris. She closed her eyes for a moment to center her equilibrium, then worked her way to the staircase on her left. She put a slippered foot out to test it, carefully proceeding until she'd reached the bottom.

At the back of the house, beyond a series of arched French doors, the rear gardens with Leda's fountain glowed in the moonlight. Eliza had a sudden vision of the windows flung wide to the summer air, music streaming in from the gardens while ladies in white lawn swanned about. The picture was so well formed she even heard a string quartet and caught the cherry-sweet fragrance of roses in full bloom.

There were two large drawing rooms facing the main foyer, their double-hung doors wide open. Eliza went to one, then the other, but they were empty, with not a scrap of furniture within, their floors crazed with moonlight. The fireplaces had been swept clean, with only the lingering scent of old ashes serving as a reminder these rooms once enjoyed life.

Seeing no other doorways on this level, save for the one leading to the main part of the house and the servants' quarters, she made her way toward the stairs. A whisper of sound met her ears, like a dry leaf skittering across the floor. Her eyes flitted from the broken balcony above her to the statue of Cupid and Psyche in the center of the room. "Is anyone there?" Eliza called. Only her own voice echoed back.

For a moment.

"Eliza."

She gasped. Her name. Someone had just whispered it. She was sure of it. She whipped her head from side to side and peered up at the balcony.

"Who's there?"

Again, only an echoing of her own voice. Cupid grinned at her from his marble pedestal, his blank eyes indifferent to her fear.

"Time to quit the laudanum," she whispered, and went back up the stairs.

There were several doorways lined up on either side of the gallery, equivalent to the bedrooms in the main part of the house. She tried the first door she came to, the cut glass knob twisting easily in her hand. This was a small room, no bigger than a closet, meant for a maid or nanny—empty save for a set of blowing lace curtains and plaster flaking off onto the floor.

The next room was connected to the first by a pocket door. It was a nursery. Eliza's heart clutched at the sight of twin cribs set on either side of the casement window, their headboards carved with thistles and roses. She imagined Ada leaning down to look at her sleeping babies. She thought of how often she'd done the same when Albert was new—in those brief, halcyon years before the drowning, when her little brother was safe and the house on Metairie Road was happy. She closed her eyes for a moment, steadying her breath.

There was a small Chippendale bureau against the wall with a water-stained tintype on top. Eliza picked it up and held it in the beam of the lantern. Malcolm and Gabriel—chubby babies both—seated in a pram with stoic expressions. She studied the photo for a long moment before replacing it. In the drawers beneath, she found nothing but the dusty wings of a dead moth and a few old postage stamps.

She stepped into the open corridor and paused. For a moment, around the corners of her eyes, there was a flickering—not unlike the wavering hallucinations she often had with her migraines. The same sort of flickering Freddie had mentioned. She turned her head, trying to re-create the phenomenon, but the walls remained still. "How queer."

When she lifted her lantern and went through the remaining door, her breath caught in her throat. Inside, it was as if the wings of time had been held down and punctured with a lepidopterist's needle. The room was a shrine—so much so it felt like Ada would emerge from behind the silk dressing screen in the corner of the room, her green eyes widening in surprise at Eliza's intrusion. The bed was turned down, its duvet pushed aside, as if someone had just risen from it. A china teacup sat on the nightstand, rings of evaporated tea staining the inside. Eliza opened the drawer beneath, and her stomach dropped. Inside was a novel. The very book she'd been reading when Albert drowned: *The Portrait of a Lady.*

Despite the sickening jolt the book triggered, she was drawn to take it. She slid it into the pocket of her dressing gown, alongside the precious keys. As she did, she had the sudden, uncomfortable feeling of being watched. She slowly turned.

Someone else was in the room.

Eliza jumped, her heart pummeling.

And then she laughed. She wasn't seeing anyone else at all, but her own reflection in Ada's dressing table mirror, her hair frizzing around her head like a lion's mane. She took a moment to calm herself, then went to examine the items on the vanity. Long strands of black hair were caught in a silver brush, untarnished despite its age. Eliza picked up a beautifully etched perfume atomizer and spritzed it. This was how Ada had smelled—like attar of roses and warm cinnamon.

Next to the toiletries, a portrait of the twins and their mother by the seashore sat in an oval frame. They were older in this photo— around three, by her reckoning. One of them gazed up at Ada with a rapturous expression while the other scowled at the camera, his arms crossed beneath the bib of his sailor suit.

In the photograph, Ada's face was placid, inscrutable, the mere hint of a smile playing on her lips. She was so young. Fragile.

"Where are you?" Eliza whispered. "What happened to you?"

There came a soughing hiss from the hall, like something being pulled across the floor. Too late, Eliza realized the flame inside her lantern was dying, its paraffin spent. After one final flicker, she was plunged into deep and total darkness.

❦

In the dark, blind, all of Eliza's other senses came to life. Her eyes picked up every shadow, her ears perked at every sound. She drew in a shaky breath and pushed her back against the wall, her hand still clutching the useless lantern. With a whimper, she felt her way to the balcony, the peeling wallpaper coming off in her hand like a corpse's leathery skin.

The hissing sound came again.

As if drawn by a magnet, Eliza's head swiveled to follow the noise. It had come from the right side of the gallery—the section she had yet to explore. One of the doors stood open there, its portal a blackened maw in the already dark space. That door hadn't been open when she'd first entered, she was certain of it. Her heart thudded in her ears, in her throat, in her head. Shirley was right. She shouldn't be in here. Not alone. Not at night.

Suddenly, a painful, very human groan echoed from the open door. Eliza's adrenaline surged. She dropped the lantern and hurtled toward the entrance of the ballroom, relying on memory to take her over the broken section of the balcony. She slammed the heavy door behind her and leaned against it to catch her breath, passing a trembling hand over her hair.

There came a hollow thud from the other side, as if someone had struck the door with the heel of their hand. A growl, feral and low, vibrated through the wood. Fear climbed through the soles of her feet and threaded through her limbs, cold as a January day. Eliza ran to her room, found her long-forgotten rosary beads in her dressing table, and knelt at the foot of her bed to pray as fervently as a frightened child.

CHAPTER 31

Eliza brushed her hair in the glass, judging her reflection harshly. She looked wretched. Her eyes bore dark, puffy circles beneath them, their rims red. She hadn't slept well since her night in the south wing. The house, now that she was alone with only Turner and Shirley, seemed to be closing in around her. Malevolent whispers, whether real or imagined, followed her down the halls, day and night. She often stayed awake until morning blushed over the horizon, too frightened of the spirits to sleep once the lights had been turned down. She was no longer a skeptic.

It had been nearly a fortnight, and she hadn't received word from Malcolm since he'd left for London. She had no way of knowing where he was staying. He'd sent no forwarding address or contact. The war, despite his optimism, looked to be a long one. The papers screamed out their headlines, relaying news of grueling warfare and a growing body count in the Transvaal. The empire had won its first battle at a harrowing cost. Though she was relieved Malcolm was not in any physical peril on the front, Eliza was beginning to lose hope she'd see her husband anytime in the near future.

There was a knock at her door, and Eliza put down her hairbrush. "Yes, what is it?"

"Your sister is here, mum." It was Shirley. "Shall I tell her to come back later?"

"No, no, that's quite all right. I'll be down in only a moment. Have her wait in the conservatory. I could do with some sunshine."

⟨❧⟩

Despite the October chill, it was warm and humid inside the conservatory. The fragrance from the tropical flowers surrounding Eliza and Lydia gave the illusion of an exotic summer paradise.

The high gothic arches of the hothouse ceiling sparkled with dew, and condensation clouded the glass walls, making the courtyard beyond an impressionistic blur of yellow and red. Somehow, Lydia had managed to procure coffee with chicory, and Eliza was now enjoying her first real café au lait in months. She took a long drink, savoring the sweet taste.

Lydia shifted in her seat and looked at a spot over Eliza's shoulder. "I'm sorry to call on you unannounced. I only came because I have news."

"Don't be silly. You know you're always welcome. Now, tell me your news."

"I've received a letter from my mother."

Eliza's coffee cup hovered before her lips, the steam curling around her face. "Really?" That answered the question of where the coffee had come from. "She's well, I hope. How did she come to find you?"

Lydia gave a rueful smile. "All this time, she's been in New Orleans, Liza. She went to the farm, looking for me, and spoke with the new owners."

"I'm surprised she hadn't come by before."

Lydia's amber-tinged eyes hardened slightly. "It seems your father set her up with a yearly stipend. It was conditional, of course. She wasn't allowed to speak to Mimi Lisette or see me, ever again. So long as she kept her end of the agreement, I'd be raised as a lady instead of a

230

servant and given every opportunity you had. She hadn't a clue about his death until his lawyer contacted her when her stipend expired at my coming-of-age this year."

"God." Eliza sat back, thunderstruck. How many lies had Nicholas Sullivan told over the years? The more she learned, the harder it became to reconcile her father's good traits with the bad. Could you continue to love someone, even after you knew they'd done wrong? "Lyddie. I'm so sorry . . ."

Lydia put up her hand. "I've tried not to be angry, but I find my resentment has grown claws and teeth over the years. And I *should* be angry, Liza. I knew there was something false about all the stories they told, from the time I was little. Starting with that preacher whose name changed depending on who you asked. I think my maman *did* come to the house, once. You probably don't remember it, but I do. I was five, maybe six. She stood by the fence rail and waved at me while I was playing with my dolls under the elm tree. I had on a white dress, tied with a green sash. Even my dolls were white." Lydia voice wavered. "Your maman did the best she could, I suppose, raising us as equals, but I always knew we weren't. It was in every moment of every day—how you were served first at dinnertime and how your dresses were just a bit finer than my own."

"Maman could be unwittingly cruel."

Lydia shook her head. "Perhaps she meant to be, perhaps not. It's a tall order to be given, to raise your husband's illegitimate child as your ward. Especially after losing so many babies. I'm sure she knew the truth. Still, I've found reason to forgive her. But I can't, not in a thousand years, forgive the man who took my mother from me." Tears sparkled in Lydia's eyes, then spilled over and ran down the full curve of her cheek. "I'd always thought she'd abandoned me. That she didn't want me. Mimi Lisette was only trying to protect me from the truth so she could be near me. To protect me. But now that I know . . . I owe my maman the chance to see me. I need to set things right between us. As best I can."

"What are you trying to say, cher?"

"Please promise you won't be angry with me."

"Why would I be?"

"I've decided I'm postponing my wedding. I'm going home for the winter. To New Orleans."

"What?" The ocean roared in Eliza's ears. Her coffee cup trembled in its saucer, and she hastily set it down.

"I'm going, Liza. I told Clarence last night."

"I—" Eliza choked on her words, her mouth closing and opening like a fish. "When?"

"I leave in two days."

"Can't you wait until the storms have gone? It's dangerous to make the crossing now." Eliza was grasping, helplessly holding on to anything that might keep her sister with her, if only for another day. "I was hoping we might at least have Christmas together. With Malcolm gone, this house . . ."

"Perhaps you should go to Sherbourne House. Stay the winter there, at least until Malcolm returns." Lydia took both Eliza's hands in her own. "With the war on, there likely won't be another passenger ship until winter is over and I don't want to wait. Clarence has asked I return before March, to tend to the injured soldiers returning home. But this is something I must do for myself. To have peace and the answers to questions I could never ask before. If I'm to be happy . . ."

Eliza gasped, choking back tears. "I think I understand, sister. I do."

Lydia gently squeezed Eliza's fingers. "You can't understand, Liza. But I love you all the same for trying."

⟨⟨❧⟩⟩

The same steamship that had brought Eliza and Lydia to Hampshire bellowed alongside the pier, its twin stacks smoking. A cold, drizzling rain sprayed over the slick wooden gangway. The raucous carousel was silent now, its horses frozen in place. Whitecaps lashed at the pilings and the wind bit at Eliza's face beneath her hat.

It was a miserable day. In every way.

"Write to me when you arrive home, cher," Eliza said, straightening Lydia's coat collar as she'd done when she was little. "And if you come upon a semaphore station on your way, please send me a telegram. I'll worry if you don't."

"I'll be all right. I'm the one who worries, remember?" Lydia's voice broke. "You'll pack up and go to Sherbourne House tonight, yes?"

"Yes, I will," Eliza said, her eyes downcast. "I love you. So very much." Eliza kissed Lydia's cheek and tasted the salt from her tears. Her throat clenched, threatening to steal her words. "I don't know what I'm going to do without you."

"You're stronger than you know. It's well past time you learned it." Lydia clasped Eliza's hands. "I love you, my silly little fool. It's not forever. You'll only be a prayer away."

Eliza stood on the pier until the *Evangelina* was a shining dot on the horizon. She'd kept her tears hidden from Lydia, but as Turner drove her back to Cheltenbridge, she wailed her grief inside the curtained landau. For all of Lydia's consoling words, their parting felt as final as death.

CHAPTER 32

Eliza didn't go to Sherbourne House the evening after Lydia's departure, or the days after. While the guilt over lying to her sister niggled at her conscience, Havenwood Manor and its secrets would not relinquish their hold. She was driven to find out the truth.

October was nearly spent, and Malcolm still had not written. Despite Turner's assurances he was alive and well, the sense of dread Eliza felt whenever she thought of her husband sickened her stomach. Shirley had attempted to keep Eliza occupied with carving jack-o'-lanterns and crafting brooms out of straw and birch branches "to sweep the Evil One away." But no matter how diligent the little housekeeper's efforts at cheering her were, Eliza's mood remained sullen and dark.

That morning, she'd finally gotten the nerve to open the copy of *The Portrait of a Lady* she'd found in Ada's room. Instead of the pages of the novel she was expecting to find, she discovered the book had been hollowed out with the blade of a knife and filled with memento mori—a locket inlaid with plaited dark hair and a time-worn photograph. When Eliza turned the photograph over, her heart lurched to her knees. Her husband lay in a coffin, his hands folded over his chest in the semblance of serenity, his dark hair curling around his pale face. She dropped the book and its contents to the floor and cried out, sending Shirley running into her room.

"Where in heavens did you find this?" Shirley asked, picking up the photograph. As the housekeeper tucked the celluloid image back into the book, Eliza noticed the neat script printed on its border: *Gabriel Winfield, 1896*

Not Malcolm. Gabriel.

"There now, mum. We'll have done with that. What a terrible thing for ye to find."

"It was in the south wing."

"Aye, I was afeared you'd find only unpleasant things there. Poor hen. Come down to the kitchen with me and have a spot of sweet tea for the shock."

"I think I'd rather go for a ride instead, Shirley."

Within minutes, Eliza was flying through the bare, rain-blackened forest, the steady tattoo of her mare's hoofbeats on the cold ground a pleasant diversion from her bleak thoughts. She stayed out until the hours grew long, riding past the millpond and over the heath until the sun became a saffron glow in the western sky and the lashing wind numbed and reddened her cheeks.

She cantered back up the drive to the manor, where it loomed like a hulking beast, its dim gaslit windows weeping with melted frost. Nigel stood on the front steps and Eliza's heart quickened with hope and fear to see him there. She trotted to the terrace and dismounted, tying Artemis to the hitching post. "Nigel! Have you any news from my husband?"

He gave a bashful smile. "I'm not sure, mum. But I check every day, just as you asked."

He handed her a gray parchment envelope, figured around its edges with elaborate scrollwork. She turned it over and recognized the seal immediately—Eastleigh's lions. Why in heavens was *he* writing to her? She tipped Nigel, went over the threshold, and tore open the seal.

19 Rutland Court, Knightsbridge
London, West

My dearest Lady Havenwood,
I hope this letter finds you well. I fear our encounter at
the railway station may have left you at odds with myself,
and I can no longer endure your disregard.

You say that you know what was asked of your hus-
band. I cannot fathom your thinking I intended any
harm or insult toward you. Whatever he has said, it
was false. I assure you, upon my honor, any thought I
have—and I do think of you often—holds no lack of
respect.

I shall come to it now: I have been watchful for your
husband, yet he eludes my presence. I have only seen him
in the Lords once since my arrival to London. Should I
hear he is engaging in any of the salacious behavior he
was known for in the past, I will surely make you privy
to my knowledge. You may reach me in London at the
address above.

With fondness,
Charles Lancashire
Earl of Eastleigh

How dare he. Eliza clenched her teeth and rent the paper in half.
She tossed it into the grate, where the flames raced to consume it. She
raced to her room and dosed herself with enough laudanum to ensure
a sleep as velvet deep as death.

Someone was in her room.

Eliza bolted awake, her breath clouding the air in front of her. Candlelight flickered from the corner. She turned toward the shifting light, blinking in confusion.

"Ah, you're awake." Malcolm lounged in the chair by the fireplace, one long leg crossed loosely over the other. "I can't stay long, mo chridhe."

"Am I dreaming?"

He floated to her side, his eyes catching the reflection of the candle flames as he leaned over her. "Perhaps, my darling." His lips met her own, the sweetness of the kiss bringing forth a sigh. "But if you were dreaming, could you feel this?" He nuzzled her hair from her shoulders, her pulse racing as he pushed the fabric of her nightgown down over her breasts and caressed her. Her senses exploded just as they would have if she were awake.

She turned her face into the pillow, closing her eyes. Malcolm plucked at the delta between her thighs, coaxing her to open for him. Sweet, delirious pleasure tightened in her belly with each expert movement, and Eliza's hands fell above her head in surrender. This was what she wanted. What she *missed*. His touch. Unmerciful and unyielding. Eliza twisted in the tangled sheets as he brought her climax shuddering through her body.

As her breathing slowed, her flesh grew too tender to bear his continued attention. "It's too much, my love." She reached for his hands to push them away. Only instead of human flesh, she felt undulating, rippling scales.

She opened her eyes. And screamed.

It wasn't Malcolm.

It was a monster.

A massive, hooded serpent leered over her, its scales an iridescent greenish black. Thick coils wrapped around her wrists, holding her fast.

Eliza thrashed to find the edge of the bed, but the creature only tightened around her as if she were a helpless, tiny mouse caught in its grasp. The snake's jewellike eyes flashed with intelligence as its forked tongue flickered over her throat. With a low hiss that sounded like laughter, it opened its jaws and lunged to strike.

CHAPTER 33

Eliza woke the next morning, the sheets tangled around her, the waxen odor of extinguished candles wafting through the room. She was naked, her nightdress heaped on the floor beside the bed. She shivered at the memory of her nightmare. Though it had only been a dream, it felt all too shameful and real.

Her head rang like a gong. She pushed the heels of her hands against her eyes to quell the throbbing, then stood on shaky legs. Her stomach turned and she hastily rushed to her washbasin, but as she'd slept through dinner, nothing came up but water.

Shirley rapped on the door. "Mum, I've a warm toffee pudding downstairs. I'm dreadful worried you're not eating enough."

Her stomach lurched at the mention of food. "I'll be down shortly, Shirley. I'm feeling a bit unwell this morning."

Eliza put on a simple day dress made of silver-gray wool, then went downstairs on leaden feet. She hadn't even bothered to brush her hair.

Turner was in the morning room, filling a dish with almonds on the sideboard.

"Mr. Turner, have you heard from his lordship?"

"No, my lady. But that isn't at all unusual when he's in London. Politics in a time of war is a full-time endeavor. Our men over there are struggling, I'm afraid."

"Yes, but I received a letter from Lord Eastleigh yesterday. He claims he's only seen Malcolm at the Lords once. And I had an awful dream last night. I could have sworn Malcolm was in my chambers." Eliza shuddered. "And then he turned into a gigantic serpent and tried to devour me. It was horrid."

Two bright spots of red appeared on Turner's wrinkled cheeks. "How strange."

"I've been more than a little troubled by sleeplessness and horrid dreams lately. They've the feeling of portents—bad omens. If you know something I don't, Mr. Turner, you must tell me. I haven't heard a word from Malcolm, and you must at least know where he's lodging." Eliza crumpled her napkin in her hand, her voice rising. "Is he in trouble or hurt? I feel as if I'm the last to know anything about my husband, when I should be the first!"

Just then, as if she'd been summoned by the fervor in Eliza's voice, Shirley swung through from the kitchen. She and Turner exchanged a look. "Now, dinnae fash your head, ye wee dove." Shirley patted her shoulders and poured more tea into her cup. "His lordship is only right busy, that's all. Now, have some pudding. All's well, I promise."

"You should get out for a bit, m'lady," Turner offered dismissively. "See your friends. Have your mind on other things. It's no good for a soul to be cooped up inside all the time. As soon as I've heard a hint of a word from London, I will pass it directly to you. I can assure you of that." With a crisp about-face, he left the room, Shirley trailing him.

Eliza slumped in her chair. Whatever they were keeping from her, she wasn't going to find out anything by asking questions.

⚜

"We should have a séance!" Polly clapped her hands together and beamed across the checked tablecloth. "On All Hallows' Eve!"

Having grown tired of the gloom inside the house and her pointless worrying over Malcolm, Eliza had taken Turner's advice and invited Polly and Sarah to dinner out at the Rose. The little pub was bustling with activity, the farmers' purses fat with their harvest profits. Eager to help the villagers escape the grim news from the foreign front, the barkeeps were generous with their pours, and bawdy jokes were in abundance. The air was clouded with a warm, pleasant fug, scented with tobacco and wood fire as a band pounded out a jig, making the wooden tables bounce with the beat.

"If we're to have a séance, then you must play medium, Miss Whitby! Or should I say Mrs. O'Riordan?" Sarah smirked. She was dressed in a tailored suit and a felt derby adorned with a jaunty quail feather, handsome as any swell.

"We're not yet betrothed."

"*Yet*," Eliza teased. "Polly, I am so very happy for you."

"Save your celebrations. Papa may well forbid it. I still have to write to him."

"Then you'll do the same as Eliza and elope. He can't very well steam home from India in time to stop you," Sarah said. "Besides, you're as good as living together with him staying in your guest house. It's not as much of a well-kept secret as you think. You should hear her brag about Freddie's kisses, Eliza. I've heard he's kissed more than her pretty rosebud mouth."

Polly turned scarlet. "Oh, do hush up, Sarah!"

"I'd wager he's not as good at pleasing your quim as I am, though." She leaned back in her chair and took a drag off her cheroot.

"You go too far!" Polly exclaimed.

Sarah grinned. "Polly pretends to be demure, but I brought her first paroxysm."

Polly's mouth formed an O, and she crossed her arms over her bosom. "Sa-rah! Please!"

"Yes, as I recall, that's exactly what you said."

"We have had far too much ale, ladies," Eliza said, laughing. Her head was growing lighter by the moment with drink, but she hadn't felt this carefree in weeks.

"Back to your ghosts," Sarah said. "Who do you think is haunting you?"

Eliza shook her head. "I'm not sure. But I'm certain at least one of the spirits is female. There's a lady's maid no one seems keen to talk about—a woman named Beatrice. As for the other, the bad one, Lydia thinks it may be old Lord Havenwood. Or a demon."

"Ah, I remember Bea. She was always kind. I believe she went back to Guernsey to get married. I think one of your ghosts is Gabriel. Pulling your covers off at night and such. Sounds like something he would do. He would have fancied you." Sarah gazed at her through half-lidded eyes. "He was keen for a ginger cat."

"I found his funerary portrait the other day, tucked into a book. It startled me."

"Fastest wake in all of Hampshire, that one," Sarah said, taking another draw off her cigarette. "Straight to the tomb after an hour. People implied it was because Malcolm murdered him before the fire even happened and he didn't want people staring at the corpse too long. Not a hair was singed on his head."

"It was likely the smoke that killed him. I suppose a funeral was a lot for Malcolm to manage on his own. I've buried my family. It's something you're only halfway present for." An image of her parents' wake flew through her memory, their coffins raised on crepe-shrouded plinths in the front parlor of Anaquitas, white lily petals against their jaundiced, swollen skin. She shuddered, eager to turn the conversation away from funerals and murder and back to ghosts. "Won't Freddie be concerned about your being in the same house as the ghost that toppled him, Polly?"

"Freddie may not want to set foot inside your house ever again, but *my* curiosity must be satisfied. What he won't know, he can't forbid." Polly smacked her palms down on the table. "It's settled, then. An All Hallows' séance. We'll get soused on rum punch and consult the spirits."

CHAPTER 34

Lit by hearth fire and candlelight, the front parlor leapt with long shadows. Eliza looked out at the lowering sky through the fog-shrouded window and pulled her shawl tight over her shoulders. Thunder rumbled steadily in the distance. Though glum, the dreary weather had set a perfect mood for their séance.

They'd arranged a summoning table in the middle of the room, an octagonal spirit board with an alphabet and Roman numerals at its center. Eliza poured herself a steaming mug of spiced rum from the samovar and sat, warming her fingers as she drank.

Sarah fidgeted in her chair. A look of uncertainty flitted over her usually cheerful face. "Are we so sure this is wise? Without having a true medium present?"

Eliza thought of Lydia's admonitions. "My sister would say it's not. She believes trifling with spirits without proper knowledge is incredibly foolish. She may well be right."

"Don't be silly. We're only having a bit of fun," Polly said. "Besides, I'm happy to play medium." She was dressed like her idea of a mystic, her blond curls covered by a black lace scarf, her dark-purple caftan a parody of a fortune-teller's costume. She lit a bundle of herbs and bustled through the room, waving the smoke to waft through the air.

"Isn't the veil supposedly thinner on All Hallows' Eve?" Sarah asked, lighting up a cheroot. She was dressed in smart tailored brown wool, a scarab brooch pinned to her lapel. She'd cropped her hair to her chin since their night at the Rose, her chestnut waves gleaming with brilliantine. "Who knows who might come through tonight?"

Eliza drew a Sobranie from her dress pocket and Sarah lit it. The combined smoke of herbs and tobacco wreathed the table in swirling eddies.

"Let's begin, Polly," Eliza said. "Duncan and Turner won't be at the pub all night."

"Oh, all right. Fuddy-duddies. I was only trying to create some atmosphere." Polly smudged out the crackling bundle of herbs and sat. "Join hands and close your eyes."

They did as she asked, Sarah gripping Eliza's hand as Polly began chanting nonsense about portals and parting the veil. After a few moments, they opened their eyes. Nothing had changed.

"What now?" Sarah asked.

"We rest our fingers on the planchette, and we take turns asking it questions," said Polly. "I'll go first." They placed their fingertips on the teardrop-shaped piece of wood. "Who is here?" When she received no response, Polly gave the planchette a shake and wrinkled her brow. "If there are any spirits about, tell us your name."

Nothing happened. Not even a wiggle.

"Can I have a turn?" Eliza asked.

"Right," said Polly. "Couldn't hurt."

"Ada, are you here?" For a brief second, the planchette quivered beneath their fingertips. Eliza gasped, looking across to Polly and Sarah. "Did you feel that?"

"Yes—give it another go!"

"Ada, are you here?"

The planchette jerked and slid across the board, landing on the word *no*.

"Oh my God," Eliza said, a laugh escaping her lips. "It's working."

Sarah's eyes widened. "Heavens. It seems to only want to talk to you, darling. Ask it something else."

"Did you die here?"

The planchette slid smoothly to *yes*.

"Quick! One of you fetch paper, so we can mark the answers as they come," Eliza said, her heartbeat stammering.

"I'll do it," Sarah said, hopping up to gather a piece of newsprint from the basket by the fireplace. Once she'd settled back in her chair, pencil poised to write, Eliza began again.

"When did you die?"

The planchette nudged at the line of numbers at the top of the spirit board. 1896—the year of the fire. Sarah piped up. "Are you Gabriel?"

The planchette answered a decisive *no*. A sudden clap of thunder rattled the windows and brought a shriek from Polly.

"Are you the spirit I spoke to in my room?" Eliza asked.

The planchette darted to *yes* briefly and then jerked to the opposite side. It rested, trembling, on *no*.

Confused, Eliza pressed on. "Did you die in the fire?"

The planchette vibrated, but did not move from *no*.

Polly had gone pale. "Maybe we should stop," she whispered with a little squeak. "I'm becoming afraid."

Eliza shook her head. "If you'd like to sit things out though, Polly, I'll understand." She could have been imagining it, but she felt a slight tingle run across her shoulders, as if someone had walked behind her and brushed her with their fingertips. It was an intimate, uncomfortable feeling. "If you're not Ada or Gabriel, who are you?" she asked.

The planchette quivered again, then sped across the board to a row of letters. It landed on the letter *T* and stayed there.

"Who is T?" Sarah asked.

The planchette went wild, going from one letter to the other until it had spelled out a name: *Thomas*.

"That . . . that was Malcolm's father," Eliza stammered. "The old Lord Havenwood." The planchette rocketed to *yes*. A sudden sickness ran through her belly. She stubbed out her cigarette and took a drink of her punch.

Polly lifted her hands from the planchette and scooted back from the table. "Well. I'm quite finished. Yes, I think I am." She retreated by the window and sat in an armchair, huddling in fright. "You should stop, too. I'm feeling rather sick."

"As am I," Sarah said. "Rather queer that it came on so suddenly. D'you think it's the punch?"

"No," Eliza said. "Freddie felt the same way, right before his accident. It's the spirit. Thomas. He's the bad one."

The table vibrated, sloshing their rum onto the white tablecloth.

"What the bloody hell?" Sarah grasped the candelabra to steady it, the flames guttering.

"It's just old Havenwood. Trying to intimidate us." Although fear lanced through Eliza, she was undeterred. This was her house. She was not going to be driven off by a dead man. "I'm not afraid of your parlor tricks and games, Thomas, but I don't understand why you're still here. Why did you pull Freddie from the scaffolding? Why are you so angry and mean?"

The planchette quivered and raced to spell out another word: M-U-R-D-E-R.

Sarah stood and backed away from the table, genuine fear crumpling her face. The room grew eerily quiet.

Eliza wrinkled her brow. "Did someone kill you?"

For a moment, there was nothing, and then the mirror above the fireplace began to judder as if an omnibus had driven by. It rattled against the wall for a good minute, then stilled. The planchette whisked over the alphabet once more. It spelled out the same word. *Murder.*

"If not from fire, how did you die?" Eliza asked, incredulous.

Shot.

"How strange. Malcolm told me his father died when the balcony collapsed as he was rushing to save Gabriel."

"I've heard the same," Sarah said quietly. "Old Lord Havenwood and Mrs. Galbraith, the housekeeper, were both recovered from the debris the next morning, terribly burned. Gabriel was found in the hall outside his room."

"Perhaps this is someone else coming through now, then."

"Heavens!" Polly sprung to her feet and ran to Sarah's side. "Look at the window!"

As if a child were standing before the fogged glass and using it as a chalkboard, letters appeared, illuminated from behind by the lanterns on the veranda.

B, B, be, beeea, B

The candles were blown out by a sudden whoosh of cold air, plunging the room into darkness. Polly wailed and Sarah pulled her close to comfort her. Eliza's eyes strained to adjust to the light, her pulse rushing in her ears.

"Who is B?" she asked, projecting her voice over Polly's fervent praying. "Are you *B* for Beatrice? What happened to you? Who killed you? Did someone shoot you?"

The answer didn't come from the spirit board or the window. Instead, it was a sibilant whisper in her left ear, coaxing every hair on the back of her neck to stand on end.

"Leave us or die."

CHAPTER 35

Eliza was no longer sleeping. Instead of retiring to her chambers in the evenings, she remained on the chesterfield in the library until she heard Shirley's door open at five in the morning, her eyes bared to every flitter of movement. Once the house was bustling with activity, she could finally rest, but her sleep was far from restorative. Her skin had lost its characteristic flush and her fingers trembled from exhaustion. Even her appetite had become abysmal—the tea tray Shirley brought for her hours earlier, stacked with squares of her favorite shortbread, remained untouched. Every bite of food she took in lately seemed to turn to ash in her mouth.

The séance had stoked even more questions. Who were the spirits they'd spoken to? One seemed to have clearly been old Havenwood. Was the other the mysterious Beatrice? Or someone else?

The sonorous chime of the doorbell interrupted her thoughts. Shortly, Turner appeared in the library, presenting an envelope on a silver tray. Eliza recognized Lydia's looping, graceful hand right away. Taking note of the address and the fineness of the paper (Lydia's mother had married well, it would seem), she tore the seal carefully and read.

Dearest Liza,

I have arrived unscathed and in good health. The passage was a bit choppy, although we experienced no delays. Maman Justine met me at the port with her husband, George Fontaine. He's a railway engineer and very kind. They've a lovely home with green shutters in Uptown, near the park. Best of all, I have a brother and sister! Margot is fifteen and a bit spoilt and headstrong, like you. Hugo is twelve and so quiet I hardly know he's about. I must admit, a piece of my soul has moved back in place. I do miss you, though. Terribly.

How is Sherbourne House? Pray, tell me you've gone there, at least while Malcolm is away. I do worry so. Have you heard news from London? The papers are saying the war in Africa isn't going well, although there is much more sympathy for the Boers' plight here, as you can imagine. I expect the soldiers will be returning to England soon. I'm going to volunteer at Charity while here, to insure my skills will not founder. I mean to improve in surgical assistance and midwifery, so that upon my return I will be primed to begin my work with Clarence anew—and I will return after the year turns, I promise you, sister. Have faith! Ask after Clarence for me, would you? And please write soon.

All my love,
Lyddie

Eliza wasted no time in replying. She rushed to her room, took out her finest stationery, and wrote.

Cher Lyddie,
I miss you. A thousand times a day I think of you! Sarah and Polly are fine company, but they could never replace

your fond governance over me. It seems you are more settled having gone, and that is no small thing. I am happy for you, even if, selfishly, I wish you were here at my side.

I have not heard from Malcolm. Not a single telegram or letter. I am more than a little concerned by this, but Turner says this is not unusual when he is away. I will remain optimistic and try not to worry.

Sherbourne House is in good order under Mr. Mason's care, although I have not left the manor. Things are as quiet as a church at Havenwood. There has been no activity from the spirits, and I am safe. Please do not be angry with me for staying, sister. It is my duty, as mistress of this house, to remain in my husband's absence. As he continually reminds me, I am a viscountess now, and must act as such. Please write again . . . your letters are sustenance.

I love you,

Liza

Eliza sealed the envelope. Lying to her sister was no easy thing, but it was much more readily done in writing than in person, where Lydia could search out a falsehood in every glance and gesture Eliza made. At least she'd told half the truth.

Eliza bundled up in her fur muffler and cape, then walked the short distance to the post road, where the postal office stood like a stalwart little fortress among a zigzagging maze of telegraph wires. Inside, she was greeted with a blast of warm air, and Nigel sorting mail at the counter. He was wearing a smart new uniform, with a gleaming badge on his breast.

"Good afternoon, Nigel," Eliza said. "You've gotten a promotion, I see."

"Yes, m'lady. Assistant Branch Postmaster Phelps now, it is. I'm looking to hire a boy to help with deliveries, as I'm needed here in office.

I'm fifteen now, you know." Nigel smiled, sending her thoughts once more to Albert, who would have been about the same age, had he lived.

"Well, Mr. Phelps, congratulations."

"I see you've a letter to send?" he asked. Eliza offered the envelope. Nigel glanced at the address. "To America! I hardly ever get to use that stamp." He placed it to the side with a stack of mail, then reached into a cubby behind the counter. "You've saved me a trip down the road, mum. A wire came through from your husband a few moments ago."

"Oh, what good news!" *Finally.* Eliza took the telegram from Nigel and opened it with shaky fingers. To her disappointment, it contained only two lines of text:

> Will return Nov 6 (stop) Send Turner to Winchester Station that morning (stop) War is going poorly and I am weary (stop)—Malcolm

Malcolm was coming home! Her relief tempered the momentary irritation she felt at his lack of endearments. He was safe and well, and that went a long way toward lifting her bad humor. But it meant she only had a few more days to freely investigate the strange happenings in the house. She had to hurry.

When she got back to Havenwood Manor, sending Turner and Shirley into a flurry of preparations for their master's return, Eliza went directly to her room. She took the hollowed-out book she'd found in Ada's room and sat on the edge of the bed, holding it in her upturned palms. She closed her eyes, hoping for a psychic impression. Nothing but dizziness and a wave of nausea coursed through her. Unlike Lydia, divination wasn't one of her gifts.

She took out the items within the book, laying aside the macabre image of Gabriel and flipping it over so she wouldn't have to look upon it again. She picked up the locket and ran her fingertips over the front. It was heavy and well made, with its inlay of plaited dark hair woven into a flat herringbone pattern, a heart-shaped medallion made of polished silver at its center. She pushed the clasp, and it sprung open with a click. Inside there was a portrait, not of Gabriel—as she'd expected—but another man. He wore a derby, its brim tilted, the crisp line of his jaw accented by a high, starched collar. His full lips held an easy smile.

Eliza turned over the locket. Engraved on its back was an inscription: *Mon coeur est à toi, pour toujours.* My heart is yours, for always.

Eliza's weariness was replaced with sudden excitement. This wasn't memento mori at all, but a love token. Had this man been Ada's lover?

She closed the locket and picked up the book again. Shook it. Nothing. But some pages seemed thicker than others, especially toward the back, past the clever hand-cut cubby. She ran her fingers along the binding, her thumb flicking through the pages near the end. Her intuition proved right; instead of Henry James's words, thin pieces of onionskin tracing paper adhered to the original pages and flyleaf, their surface figured with letters. The lines were printed neatly, without break or punctuation. Eliza smiled.

It was a code. Now *this* she could manage.

She rushed to her escritoire and gently prized the vellum from the book's pages using her letter opener. She pulled out her notebook, hurriedly flicking past her other notes. Within an hour, she'd deciphered the crowded, encoded writing. The letters corresponded to the alphabet, in reverse. Only, instead of English, the words were written in French. Her excitement growing by the moment, she translated the messages. They were love letters—erotic, intense, gloriously descriptive love letters.

I think of you, spread across the whiteness of your bed on those long summer days when the great house grew quiet and still around us, your body an invitation for my lips to kiss. How I long to ply you through your cries, your eloquent whimpers of pleasure maddening me to my own end. Are you touching yourself now? Are you remembering how well I loved you as you read these words? Hasten to me once more, my darling, when the harvest is done.—M

How I long for you, my sweetest love. The taste of your lips. The feel of your soft breasts and the press of your hips against my own. Our love is pure. Do not let them keep us apart. They will not. You are my only joy—a need that courses through me, demanding satisfaction. What torture it is to be kept from you!—M

I went to Winchester, as always, but you did not come. I waited in our little room at the top of the stairs as the hours grew long and my patience grew short. I waited until my obligations to this hellish life forced me to leave. Have you abandoned me altogether? I am lost. If you do not come to me soon—I cannot fathom what I should become capable of in my grief!—M

Eliza drew in a shallow breath. The pieces were falling into place at last. Her intuition had been correct. She opened the locket and traced the picture of the man in the derby hat with her fingertip. If this mysterious "M" was indeed Ada's secret lover, these concealed love letters could be proof of a motive for murder.

CHAPTER 36

In anticipation of Malcolm's return, Eliza took more time with her toilette than she had of late, winding a strand of black pearls through her neatly braided and coiled hair. She felt and looked haggard, despite her rouged cheeks and mouth—as if she were cheap fabric torn in half. She spritzed on her favorite lilac perfume and went down to the drawing room, where she took up her needlepoint and arranged herself on the chaise in what she hoped was an alluring fashion.

Malcolm came through the door a little after twelve o'clock, followed by a puff of frigid air. She sprung from the chaise to greet him, standing on tiptoe to kiss both his wind-chilled cheeks. His hair was neatly combed, and he'd grown a moustache since she'd seen him last. It gave him a devilish air. She wasn't keen.

"Did you miss me, darling?" he asked, giving her a tight-lipped smile.

"I have! But I'm not sure you missed me. I was hoping at least for a letter. Your telegram was rather spare."

"Drat. I'm so sorry. I'm ever doing things to make you cross, aren't I?"

"Yes. And I'm not so sure about your new moustache, husband." Eliza arched a brow. "You look a bit like a villain in a vaudeville."

"Oh? A bare upper lip isn't the fashion in London, I'm afraid. I was only endeavoring to fit in. If it displeases you, I shall shave before dinner." He kissed the top of her head, his brows drawing together. "You look frightfully pale, darling. Have you been unwell?"

Eliza sighed. Ever one with the stunning compliments, wasn't he? "I haven't had much of an appetite lately, that's all. But Shirley's made a wonderful luncheon in celebration of your return. Come see."

They went to the dining room, where the table waited with a tureen of lobster bisque. Malcolm pulled out her chair and Eliza sat, snapping her napkin open. "How was London?"

"Dreadful. The past week has been just a bunch of old men sat round smoking cigars and whinging about the defeat at Ladysmith. I'm glad to be home, although I'll likely have to return before the week has gone."

Eliza frowned. "So soon?"

"Wars are tedious business, love, and we must do our part. As I'm no longer in the military, this is my way of serving the empire."

"Seems as if it would be the easier thing to let the Boers have their full independence," Eliza murmured, garnering a sharp look from Malcolm. "Surely the loss of life isn't worth gaining a few gold mines in the queen's interest."

Shirley swung through with a platter of fresh, crusty baguettes. Her eyes lit up at the sight of Malcolm. "Good to have you home, your lordship." She spooned soup into their bowls and ground fresh pepper over the top.

"Ah, good day, Mrs. Duncan. Have you been keeping my wife occupied?"

"Oh, she's been right busy indeed, sir. Keeping company with the local ladies. She even hosted a party on Samhain."

Eliza cleared her throat and shot a pointed look at Shirley.

"It were only a *small* party, sir. Embroidery and such."

"Excellent!" Malcolm said. "I'm ever so glad you're making social connections, darling. I shan't have to worry about you being lonely when I'm gone."

Eliza took a drink of water. "Yes. We were making christening gowns for the orphaned infants at the mission. Polly's stitches are very neat and even. Do you know, the boy who fell in our south wing is courting her?"

"Is that so?"

"Yes, he's quite recovered. I visited him at the hospital. He told me you paid him a generous sum for his troubles."

"Right." Malcolm dabbed at his mouth, his moustache twitching. "Never mind that. How is your sister? Is she finding her new station as Fawcett's nurse satisfactory?"

"She's well enough, I suppose. She's gone back to New Orleans for the winter. Her mother wrote to her and she went to be reunited with her."

"She'll return, though?"

"She's said she'll be back before March."

"Fair enough." Malcolm nodded. "I'll have Mr. Mason look after Sherbourne House this winter. We'll need to let it out if she lingers much longer, however. It would bring in a goodly revenue for the estate. The middle classes are keen at pretending to be us these days. And we wouldn't want squatters coming in."

"Mr. Mason wouldn't let that happen. And if Lydia says she will return, she most certainly will," she said, unable to hide the thread of irritation in her voice. "She still means to marry Clarence—their engagement has only been delayed."

"Very good." Malcolm took up a baguette and broke it in his gloved hands, sending a shatter of crumbs across the tablecloth.

Eliza wrinkled her brow in confusion. "Why are you still wearing your gloves?"

"What?"

"Your gloves," Eliza said, motioning to her own, which lay neatly folded to the side of her place setting. "You've forgotten your manners."

"Men have started wearing their gloves at dinner in London, darling."

"How strange," Eliza said. "I've never heard of such a thing."

"Ah, it'll likely make its way to Hampshire soon enough. These sorts of things always hit the countryside last."

While Malcolm was in an amiable mood throughout the rest of their luncheon, chattering on about the newest MPs and the votes they'd made in support of the war, Eliza was suddenly becoming bilious. Heat and cold shuddered through her body in alternating waves. She pushed back from the table, her gorge rising. "I'm not feeling so well, husband. I think I'll turn in for a few hours, if you wouldn't mind. I'll be happy to hear more about London and the war at dinnertime."

Malcolm looked at her warily, arching one dark brow. "Are you quite sure you're all right?"

"It's only one of my migraines flaring up, I think."

"Well, if you're not better by tomorrow, we should have Dr. Fawcett examine you." He stood to press a kiss to her clammy forehead, and she hurried up to her room, where her fine lunch promptly met her chamber pot.

⊰✣⊱

Eliza rolled onto her back, panting and slicked with sweat. She nuzzled into the sheets with a satisfied sigh. Her nausea from earlier in the day had been replaced by an urgent need to lay with her husband that demanded satisfaction. Multiple bouts of satisfaction.

"My." Malcolm laughed. "You're feeling better."

"Indeed. Whatever my sickness was, it was brief."

"I thought you were going to tear me to pieces," he said, looking over his shoulder at the path of scratches she'd left on his back.

258

"I had to mark you as my own, lest the ladies of London get any ideas upon your return." Eliza bit her lip and smiled up at him. "You're *mine*."

"I am that," he said. "Although I assure you, you've nothing to worry about."

"When I didn't hear from you, I began to wonder." Eliza turned her words over in her mind before speaking them aloud. "I saw Lord Eastleigh after I said goodbye to you. At the station. He missed the first train."

"Oh?" Malcolm asked, his voice deepening. "I do wish you wouldn't bring beastly Eastleigh into our bed. What did he say?"

"He said he'd keep an eye on you. That you act a different person entirely while in London. And when I didn't hear from you, not even one letter . . ."

"Ever the architect," Malcolm spat. He rubbed his neck in irritation. "Despite what Eastleigh said, I was no different in London than I am here, although I can venture a guess as to what he was implying." He let a puff of air out of his lips. "Like most young men, I had some wilder days in my youth. I visited a few of the brothels he frequented. And it's expected that men of my station will take a mistress, but you keep me more than satisfied, my love. Likely he was trying to cover his own bad behavior."

"Have you heard Una is with child?"

"No." Malcolm's eyes narrowed. "Rather fast, isn't it? I'm surprised he didn't dangle that before me in London. It's just the sort of thing he'd crow about."

"I've my suspicions they've been enjoying one another's company for quite a while." Eliza thought for a moment, wrinkling her brow. "You know, you say it's expected for highborn men to take a mistress, but what about women? Why is it so taboo for a wife to take a lover if married men enjoy such freedoms?"

"I suppose it goes back to men believing their wives are their property, to be taken and dispensed with as they wish, and a wife cuckolding her husband is an affront to his stature. My father was that sort." Malcolm pulled on his pajama trousers and stood, stretching his lean but well-muscled chest.

"Well, I certainly hope you don't view me as an old leather shoe to be tossed to the side or a heifer you can take to market." Eliza sat up, the sheets falling around her hips. "I'd like a nightcap, wouldn't you? Sit with me awhile before you leave."

Eliza shrugged on her nightdress and they went through to the small parlor adjoining her room, where the dainty crystal chandelier threw multifaceted amber light over the burgundy walls. Malcolm went to the liquor cabinet in the corner and drew out a decanter. He poured himself a dram and smiled over his shoulder. "Whisky or brandy, darling?"

Eliza sat in one of the high-backed chairs in front of the fire. "Brandy, please."

Malcolm brought her drink to her, his fingers grazing her own.

She took a deep breath. "I made some discoveries while you were gone."

"Yes?" he asked. "What kinds of discoveries?"

"Your father was a horrid man, wasn't he? Abusive."

"He was. He could be. His mother died shortly after he was born, and my grandfather was too busy with politics to pay any attention to him. He was raised by nannies, then shipped off to boarding school as soon as he was old enough. I'm quite sure he never learned how to be a proper husband or father because of it."

"Your mother must have been dreadfully unhappy. In her loneliness, do you think she ever took a lover?"

Malcolm blanched. "I'm not sure what you're talking about, darling. Or why you're bringing up such things when we've just had such a lovely time together."

"Because I mean to know, Malcolm. I found a photograph of a young man. Along with some love letters."

Malcolm leaned forward, a shadow slanting over his face. "Really? Where?"

"In my armoire," she lied. "I also found her diary there."

"Darling . . . I . . ." His eyes were flitting about again, looking everywhere but at her. "You found her diary?"

"Is that where she's gone—with this man? This M?" Her voice was staccato, sharp. Determined. "If so, you can tell me. I'd hardly blame her."

"You're jumping to conclusions, Eliza."

"Am I? Did your father really die in the fire, or was he murdered first? Was he shot? Perhaps by your mother's lover?"

"Christ, you're like a bloody courtroom barrister all of a sudden." Malcolm's face had gone red, his eyes glassy.

"And what of Beatrice? No one seems to want to talk about her either, do they? I wonder why."

"I can't tell you everything about the past, darling. Some things must still be kept from you."

"Why?"

"Because there is too much at stake. You can't possibly understand why, but old secrets can still do harm."

Eliza stared at him, her frustration at his obstinance shifting to rage. "Our marriage feels like a game of hide-and-seek, Malcolm. I plead for the truth and you keep it from me. I am your *wife*!"

"You are. And it's my duty to protect you."

"Protect me?" Eliza stood. Blood pounded in her ears. "If I'm in danger, you'd better tell me from what or from whom, because as it stands at this very moment, I'm most afraid of *you*!"

"Do you really want to know the truth?" he asked, walking about like a caged jaguar. "If so, I will tell you as much as I can." He stalked to the liquor cabinet and knocked back the remains of his whisky, grimacing as he swallowed. "But you must promise you will hear me out."

"I will listen and try to understand, husband." She lowered herself back to her seat, her pulse thudding like a timpani.

"You knew of our debt to Eastleigh."

"You were honest with me concerning that. I hope."

"Yes. To a point. The truth is, the mortgages and financial pressure Eastleigh exerted became too much for our father. We contrived the fire as a way to receive an insurance payment." Malcolm squeezed his eyes shut. "I helped him set it. Then things went all wrong."

The matter-of-fact way he stated the truth ran through her, taking her breath. A vision of the south wing, its windows lit with flames, shot across the back of her eyes. "My God, Malcolm . . . to hear you say it!"

"Yes, well, it's a burden I'll have to bear for my whole life, isn't it?" he said. "It wasn't entirely my doing, but the guilt will ever haunt me."

Eliza's mouth went dry. "All this time, you've been lying to me."

Malcolm turned and nodded sadly. "Yes, darling. I have been a liar. From the very moment I first saw you, I've been false. I wish the fire were all I had to confess, but as we're in the process of laying my shame bare, I suppose I'll go on and tell you the rest. We'll start at the very beginning. Perhaps you heard talk of a highwayman terrorizing the countryside when you first arrived in Hampshire? Isn't it queer there've been no reports since we married?" He gave a grim smile. "That night you saw me from your window, I wasn't going on a midnight ride for pleasure. I was going to rob whomever was unlucky enough to meet me on the road. It was the only way I could afford to feed myself or my staff. That's how desperate I'd become. But I never harmed anyone I robbed, I promise you."

Eliza remembered their night at the theatre—the jewelry he'd slipped into the clerk's hand. It hadn't been an old watch chain meant for pawning. He'd stolen it. She was sure of that now. After all the trust she'd shown, after she'd defended him to her sister—he'd been lying. Blatantly. *I'm always right*—Lydia's words rang through her mind like a schoolyard taunt. She'd been used for her money, under the guise of love, and wedded herself to a thief and an arsonist. This . . . this was too much.

"It was my money that drew you to me," she said with a contemptuous sniff. "I should have known."

"No, Eliza. It wasn't your money. Not for me, I swear it." Malcolm crossed the room and knelt at her feet, reaching for her hand. "I was besotted. I married you because I loved you, I *swear* that much is true!"

Eliza flinched, pulling back as if he were a cobra set to strike. As if he were the serpent from her dream. Angry tears bristled at the corners of her eyes. "You'll not touch me, husband. Not now."

"You wanted to know the truth, dammit, and I'm telling you!"

She clenched the arms of the chair, her nails digging into the varnish "The truth! After how many lies? Do you expect me to sit here and nod politely as you confess to highway robbery and an arson that resulted in the deaths of your father and brother? And as you won't tell me what happened to Beatrice or your mother, how am I to know whether I am looking at their murderer right now? I am terrified of you! Of this house!" She sprung to her feet, sending the chair toppling to the floor.

"I did not kill Beatrice or my mother. How it wounds me to hear you say these things! I would never hurt a woman, Eliza. I swear it!"

There was a knock on the door. "Everything all right, m'lord?"

"Yes, yes, Turner. We're quite well," Malcolm called, his eyes glistening as he stood.

Eliza looked at her husband, incredulous. Was he about to cry? Christ. "I cannot fathom this," she hissed. "Any of it."

"I thought perhaps with time you'd understand. I thought with what happened to your own brother . . ."

Her anger overtook her then. "Don't you dare, Malcolm! Don't you dare. It's entirely different. You were complicit. You are a criminal, guilty of an imprisonable offense!"

He seized her wrist and stood. "Do you know? I am already imprisoned! Every day I'm tortured by what I have done. By what I have *seen*. I never wanted to lie to you. It is not in my nature!"

"And how am I ever to trust you again? 'Don't lie to me, Eliza, I'm your husband,'" she mocked, pulling free from his grasp. "Weren't those your words to me, the day after our wedding, about this?" Eliza raked her fingers over the scars on her forearm, a trail of red welts emerging from the path of her nails. "Even though we've both our shameful pasts, I was honest with you about mine!"

"I was afraid you'd think me a monster if I told you the truth, and I was right." He sat heavily, his head in his hands. "I promise you—even though I've done horrible things I will regret for the rest of my life, I could never, ever hurt you."

"But you *have* hurt me, Malcolm. You have! You've wounded me as mortally as an arrow through the heart ever could." Her eyes spilled over with hot, angry tears. How dare he put this on her shoulders! Him! With his limpid green eyes brimming and overflowing with tears of his own. He was a liar, with a clever silver tongue. She despised him in this moment. But she hated herself even more for being tricked and taken in by his charm. No more.

He reached for her again, and she pushed him away, running back to her bedchamber. She flung open her armoire and pulled out her valise.

"What are you doing?"

"I'm leaving," Eliza spat, ripping dresses from their hooks. "I . . . I don't know where I'll go, but I can't spend another moment in this miserable house with you and your bloody secrets."

"I'll tell you everything else, I swear it! We'll go to Scotland, like I promised . . . we can even leave tonight! I'll spend the rest of my life earning back your trust, Eliza. I'm ready to be free of this. All of it!"

"It is too late! People do not lie to the ones they love, Malcolm. I gave up everything for you. I defended your honor and threw myself into proving your innocence because I loved *you*. I loved who I *thought* you were." Her fists clenched at her sides. "I thought, 'Here at last is a man who sees the good in me. Here is a man who has been hurt as much as I have.'" She gave a bitter laugh. "You played your role quite well, sir, and it's a cruel lesson you've taught me. But I've learned it well, all the same. I've been learning not to trust those who profess to love me, over and over again, for my entire life."

"Eliza, please!"

She pulled her coat on over her nightdress and threw open the door, then raced down the staircase shod only in her slippers. Turner stood at the foot of the stairs, his gentle, wrinkled face drawn, his eyes glassy. "Mum, if I may, his lordship only means to protect you . . . He's not . . ."

Eliza shook her head and put her hand up. "Ready the carriage, Mr. Turner. I'm leaving."

CHAPTER 37

Eliza stood before the window, looking out at the spitting snow. It was her second night in Southampton and she had a decision to make.

The memory of Malcolm's tears and the way he'd looked at her in pleading desperation had nearly been enough to send her running back. She'd been harsh—cruel even. She had asked for the truth and he'd given it, only to be met with her rage.

But he'd lied to her. Not once, but many times. How could she ever know the full depth of his betrayal? No. Reconciliation was impossible. She could no longer trust herself when it came to him.

She could return to Sherbourne House, of course. But to think of looking down the hill, each day, wondering what Malcolm was doing— she would never fully move forward. She'd already pawned her mother's diamond necklace—it had given her more than enough money to let this room until she could make passage back to New Orleans, where she might rendezvous with Lydia and come up with a plan. It seemed the best solution. In America, perhaps she would be granted an annulment—so long as she could provide evidence of marital deception.

Could she, though? It was her word against his. And the evidence, if proved, might send him to jail. Or the gallows. The thought sent a chill through her marrow.

Eliza drew the curtains closed over the sash and lay down on the scratchy sheets. Sleep was impossible in this hotel. The other guests stomped down the hallway past her room at all hours of the night, coming in from the pubs or the theatre, the sounds of drunken love-making floating through the thin walls. As she tossed with insomnia, she turned her row with Malcolm over and over in her mind, replaying her harsh words as she stared up at the ceiling, measuring the moon's path across the chipped plaster. As morning light crept over the top of the curtains, Eliza finally drifted into a deep sleep. When she woke, it was already night again. It was a disconcerting feeling, this winnowing of one day into the next, her time spent endlessly scraping the worn furrows of her mind.

Eliza opened the cheap curtains and peered out. The flurries had ceased, leaving a soft blanket of white over the streets. Across the plaza, the theatre's marquee blinked on, spilling long columns of yellow light onto the new snow. Yesterday evening, a vaudeville had been the attraction. But tonight, an opera was touring: Rameau's *Castor et Pollux*. It had been a long time since she'd seen a show—the last had been with Malcolm, the night of their first kiss in the rose garden, when the air whispered a promise of happiness. Eliza rubbed her temples. She winced as another wave of nausea and light-headedness rolled through her. The walls drew in like a squeeze-box. "I need to get out of this room."

A show would be just the diversion she needed.

꧁✦꧂

Eliza swept into the vestibule of the Grand wearing her blue velvet gown. She handed her cape to the cloak girl and joined the milling crowd queueing up at the entrance to the auditorium. Hampshire's finest seemed to be out and about tonight, the rare snow creating a festive mood.

She was studying the program when a gentle tap came to her left shoulder. She turned.

Eastleigh in white tie and tails. God.

"We seem to encounter one another more and more these days, Lady Havenwood," he said, his eyes skimming over her. "Has your husband gone to buy you a posy from the flower urchins? Your dress would be most enhanced with a blushing rose at your bosom."

Eliza couldn't hold back her sullen frown. "I wouldn't know where my husband is, my lord, but he certainly isn't here."

"Well. That's too bad. Has he rushed back to London so soon? We've broken Parliament for an entire fortnight." Was it just her imagination, or did his smile widen?

The usher opened the richly carved wooden doors. The crowd rushed forward in a perfumed mass. Eastleigh offered his arm. "You might get trampled under if you try to find a seat within the orchestra. You should come sit with me." He motioned to the gallery boxes above, their velvet depths ambient with electric chandeliers. "As I recall, you seemed to enjoy my box."

Eliza craned her neck, looking for a glimpse of Una's gleaming, mink-dark hair within the loge. "Shouldn't you ask your wife first?"

He tilted his head. "Now, why would I need to ask Una, when she isn't even here? I'd say fortune has favored us this evening, wouldn't you?"

"I . . . I . . ." She stumbled over her words as he watched in amusement. Her cheeks flared with heat. "Charles . . . I can't. I'm not in the right state of mind for inviting more gossip."

"Oh, darling. It's already too late for that."

Indeed, heads were turning in their direction and whispers rustled behind fans. Charles lifted her hand and kissed it, his sapphire eyes meeting her own. "Come now, Eliza," he whispered. "You're wearing your sadness like a shroud for all to see. If they're going to talk, we may as well have a bit of fun with it, hadn't we?"

Eliza batted her fan to cool her flushed skin. A forlorn sense of guilt rankled at her as the crowd below turned in their seats to stare up at her, although Charles didn't seem to mind their scrutiny a bit. He sat himself so close to her that each time he shifted she felt the nudge of his knee against her own. A waiter brought a tray of fresh oysters and poured bubbling champagne into flutes adorned with the Eastleigh crest rendered in gold leaf. Eliza removed her opera gloves and helped herself to the refreshments, her appetite grown ravenous as the salty-sweet taste of the oysters slid down her throat. She hadn't had a proper meal since she'd left Havenwood Manor.

"Why *are* you alone in S'oton?"

Eliza took a long swallow of her champagne, the bubbles tickling her nose. "We had a fight—a row. A bad one."

"I daresay, for you to walk out alone. How long have you been here?"

"Three nights now." Eliza closed her eyes and let her breath out through tight lips. "I'm considering going home. To New Orleans."

Charles turned, gazing at her with concern. "Surely you can't mean to seek a legal separation. You'd need grounds for such a thing. They're rarely granted to a woman. What has he done?"

"Plenty, my lord." Malcolm's tear-streaked face briefly flashed into her consciousness. She was at the edge of a precipice. Here she sat, with her estranged husband's rival. Anything she said now could be used to Eastleigh's advantage. She clipped her words, biting the inside of her cheek. Still protecting him. Why?

"Is it about his mistress?"

Eliza felt the color drain from her face. "What?"

Charles's eyebrows gathered. "Oh. I take it you didn't know about Annie?"

Eliza barked a laugh. "I should have known there was more, shouldn't I? I might have guessed when he didn't write from London or send a forwarding address."

"She's very ill, Annie. Quite mortally so." Charles took out a tin of cigarettes and offered them to Eliza. The new Pall Malls. "Would you like one?"

"I'd better," she said, her fingers shaking as she gingerly placed the cigarette between her lips. Charles lit it for her, and she drew the strong, acrid smoke into her lungs. "How long?"

"Many, many years. She was his first, I believe."

"Is she a prostitute?"

"*Courtesan* would be a better word," Charles said with a grin. "She had a reputation for training up the young gentlemen of society. At least . . . until she fell ill."

"No wonder he's so bloody talented," Eliza spat, tears pricking at the corners of her eyes.

"Yes. Well. I'd be mindful about yourself. Have you ever noticed any sores?"

Eliza took a draw off the Pall Mall. "What? No, never."

"Perhaps a rash? On his hands, or across his shoulders?"

"No. Not that I've seen."

"Very good. That's good news, indeed. It's likely you're not infected, then."

The chairman stood before the stage, the footlights flaring for the pre-show. "Ladies and gentlemen! Direct from Paris, I present La Troupe Sauvoir!"

A trio of acrobats went tumbling across the demilune stage, dressed in red-and-gold motley. Everything before her began to blur. A mistress! After all his protestations otherwise. "Was that what you meant at the train station, then? When you said he became another person entirely?"

"I'm afraid so," Charles said, his surly frown contrasting with the laughter rocketing through the theatre. "He has a tendency to become

270

quite the vulgar swell at a party. And if he's been with Annie lately, you'd do well not to share his bed again. She's got the French disease. There's no cure."

The acrobats were climbing on top of one another's shoulders now, creating a tower. When the smallest reached the top, he pulled off his cap. A circlet of false flames ignited on top of his head, and he went tumbling off to the side, howling in distress. The audience roared. Eliza's head spun and her stomach dropped.

"Syphilis?"

Hours later, after the interminably long opera was over, Charles walked Eliza across the plaza to her hotel. They stood beneath the beam of a streetlamp, the snow gusting in billowing, feathery flakes around them. The muffled clip-clop of hooves on the slushy pavement and the whisk of carriage wheels were the only sounds. If her mood had been happier, Eliza would have felt as if she were in a scene from a romance. Instead, she felt like a toy dancer in a music box, wound too tightly and left to spin recklessly out of control.

"If you need a place to stay until you've made a decision, you could come to London with me tonight. I'm leaving on the last train," Charles said, winking. "I'd be happy to put you up in my new townhouse."

Eliza regarded Charles coolly. "And what would be the expectation, my lord?"

"Only to lock the doors when you leave and turn down the lights at night to save on my electricity bill. I've even installed a telephone and tiled floors, like a Roman bath. It's all rather decadent." Charles's full lips curved into a smile. "Look, Eliza—regardless of the things your husband may have told you, I'd never force myself upon you, in any way. I'm a married man, and people may very well talk after seeing us together tonight, at any rate. I cannot deny my attraction to you.

Setting you up in a household would help you gain your independence. I'd expect no more. Unless you'd decide otherwise." His eyes narrowed. "And it would be most advantageous if you would."

Ah, there it was. The proposition she'd been expecting.

Eliza laughed. "I hardly think becoming your mistress would solve any of my problems."

"Even with a generous allowance? Until you're granted a separation, you may become destitute in the meantime. Havenwood does have a petty streak."

An uncomfortable silence lingered between them. Eliza wasn't sure what to say next.

Charles scrutinized her face as if he saw the struggle there. "It's a lot to consider. Take however long you wish. There are no other prospects for the position, I assure you. Please say you'll at least entertain the thought. I'd spoil you, Eliza. I'd treat you leagues better than he ever has."

Charles lifted her hand to his mouth. As he did, a surge of unexpected vengeance rolled through her. She thought of Malcolm with his whore in London. He was probably there now, slaking his sorrows in her bed. Eliza shook with anger at the thought, remembering how he'd shamed her that day in his study when she'd tried to seduce him, comparing her to a prostitute. All the times he'd lied to her, then made her question her own mind. He'd never do it again.

The alcohol had gone to her head, just enough.

Before she could change her mind, she pulled Charles to her by the lapel and locked her lips to his, taking his breath as she kissed him, in full view of anyone who happened to be watching. It was a brutal, violent kiss, full of tongues and teeth. Charles returned her affections ruthlessly, his hands grasping and pulling at her as if possessed. When she broke the kiss, her lips felt so raw they could bleed.

He drew back to look at her, his eyes clouded with lust. "I knew it," he growled. "You and I are the same, after all. I shall take your kiss as a promise and meet you at the platform later tonight, eager as a bridegroom."

❦

Nothing.

That's what she'd felt when she kissed Charles. Nothing but her own bitterness, anger, and regret.

And now there would be consequences. The scandal sheets would be flooded with talk of her salacious behavior. Malcolm would know, and he'd be well within his rights to divorce her. Well within his rights to ruin her. Their legal covenant had been broken the moment she threw herself into Charles's arms.

And then there was the venereal disease. What if Malcolm *had* been infected when he lay with her, and her recent nausea and dizziness were the first of much uglier symptoms to come?

Her mother's words mocked. *Who will want you now?*

She wilted against the red brick of the hotel's façade, her vision blurred by tears.

Curious passersby stared at her. Some laughed. She could only imagine how she looked—her face streaked with kohl, her hair speckled with snow, frizzing up like a charwoman's. She stumbled back to her room, her head throbbing with her drunkenness. Instead of packing to join Charles, she ordered up a magnum of champagne and drank it, wishing she had laudanum instead. As the night grew long, she thrashed on her bed, still in her evening gown, her shoes leaving muddy streaks on the white eiderdown. When she woke, hours later, her own vomit cold on the coverlet, she sprung from the bed. Disgusting. Wouldn't Maman be proud?

But no. Even on Eliza's best days, her mother had never been proud of her. With every childish attempt Eliza had made to court her love

273

and attention, she had only shown criticism. If only she'd tried harder, it might have made a difference. Perhaps.

Too late for that now.

She'd failed at everything that ever mattered.

Eliza ran a bath and stripped off her clothing, leaving it on the honeycomb-tiled floor. She climbed into the steaming tub, hugging her knees. In the soap dish, alongside a pristine bar of lemon verbena soap, was a cut-throat razor, its blade closed. It was as if a silent wish had been granted. Eliza picked it up, opening it with wet fingers. What was stopping her, truly? It was a way out of the mess she'd created of her life, once and for all. She could put an end to all her memories and failings with two strokes of a sharp blade.

If she did this, even with a practiced hand, it would be painful—she remembered that well. The water would sting and burn. There would be a slow slide into unconsciousness. And then? She held the blade up to the light, watching water bead and drip from the edge.

How silly she'd been to think she could ever be happy. That she'd ever deserved love, or an easy life.

CHAPTER 38

Eliza was a girl again. She was running hand in hand with Albert, his golden curls bouncing with every jogging step. In the distance, the blue ellipse of the drowning pond glimmered beneath the noonday sun. Albert let go of her hand and bolted for the water. Eliza raced after him, grasping for his collar, his sleeve—anywhere she might find purchase. Her fingers closed on air. The old helplessness rushed through her, and though she tried to scream, her throat choked with silence. He splashed through the shallows, laughing. And like he had every other time before, he disappeared.

Eliza ran to the edge of the water. The pond was as clear as a mirror, and Albert was lying at the bottom, his eyes closed. Eliza dove in, shattering the surface like glass. She clawed her way deeper, the glass-water tearing at her skin as billowing clouds of her own blood obscured Albert from view.

Suddenly, someone drew a curtain over the sun and the darkness around her became absolute. Eliza thrashed and reached out, blind, her mouth open in a soundless scream. The figure on the bottom of the pool had morphed. Instead of Albert, it was now a pale girl clothed in a sodden calico dress, her coppery hair floating away from her face in wavering coils. Her lips were purple. Her eyes were open. Lifeless.

It was Eliza, as she'd been at twelve.

She dove into the darkness, fighting against the shards of razor-sharp water. She grasped the girl she once was by the wrists and pulled. The void clung to the young Eliza's body as if it were a metal filing on a magnet. *Please,* she prayed. *Please don't die. It wasn't your fault. I love you. You must live. You must.*

One by one, a million stars pierced the darkness, each pinprick of light ringing like a bell. She was no longer underwater, but a part of the sky.

Eliza was flying.

༄

"Eliza!"

She bolted awake as if breaching from water, her fingers clawing at the air, her mouth open in a soundless scream.

"Breathe, my darling. I'm here." Malcolm pulled her tightly to his chest, rocking her as she cried. "It's all right. I'm here. You gave me such a fright."

She pushed him away, growling like a wild animal. "Get away from me! Don't you dare touch me."

Malcolm let go of her with a ragged sigh and slumped to the edge of her bed. He looked awful—unshaven and drawn, the lines around his eyes deeper, as if he hadn't slept in days.

A sharp, antiseptic smell wafted through the room and she suddenly realized she wasn't at the hotel. She looked around, blinking in confusion. Sterile white walls gleamed with harsh morning light. Too bright. They were in a hospital ward. Or an asylum. Eliza slid her hands free from the blanket and examined her wrists. There were no marks, her skin flawless apart from the etching of her old scars. "What happened?"

"The chambermaid at your hotel found you. It seems you fainted getting out of the bath and hit your head. She called for an ambulance and the attending physician happened to be a friend of Dr. Fawcett's. He recognized you and sent for me."

The last thing she recalled was opening the razor and holding it to her wrist. But my God, her head pounded like a drum, didn't it? It had to be the truth. "Oh. I don't remember falling at all. I thought I'd died in the bath. I was sure of it."

He gave a dry laugh. As if such a thing could ever be funny. "You've only got a mild concussion, and you were severely dehydrated." Malcolm took her hand, the hint of a tired smile quirking up the corners of his mouth. "And there's something else."

"What?"

"You're going to be a mother, mo chridhe."

The room went into a spin. "What?"

"You're with child."

Eliza rode beside Malcolm in the landau, her aching head leaning on her hand as the country scenery flashed by. The snow had melted during her brief stay in the hospital, leaving muddy, splashing puddles all along the roadway. The trees expanded and contracted like a dizzying forest made of matchsticks, their wet branches dripping onto the top of the carriage with the steadiness of a metronome. She bit the inside of her cheek to stifle her tears and leaned her head against the window.

She couldn't believe her misfortune. The timing couldn't be worse for this baby, but what could she do? Her condition now grievously limited her choices. It seemed a lifetime ago that England had meant freedom and a fresh start. She'd traded the happy, independent years of a spinster for the fetter of false love, and it had cost her everything. She had the feeling if she ever tried to leave Havenwood Manor again, the house would rise up against her, like a cursed castle from a fairy tale, imprisoning her behind a wall of thornlike daggers.

Malcolm stirred next to her, clearing his throat. "Darling, I was thinking, before your confinement is too far gone, we should go to Scotland. Perhaps we can leave this weekend."

"Don't you have to return to London?"

Malcolm stroked his scraggly beard, his hand trembling. "No. I'm not going back. At least for now."

"Why not?"

"They've a majority in the Lords. My vote isn't necessary. I rather think a holiday is in our best interest—some time alone together to mend our disagreement. I want to show you where my mother grew up. Take you to Loch Lomond and Ben Nevis—the mountain from our fairy story."

"Oh." Eliza fiddled with the loop of her reticule. Her fingers were frightfully thin. Malcolm grasped her frantic hand in his own, stilling her nervous movements with his warmth.

"Won't you ever be able to forgive me, Eliza?"

"I suppose I'll need to find a way, given this new . . . revelation. I nearly went back to New Orleans, but because of the war, there were no steamers available."

Malcolm put his hand over his eyes and leaned forward. "God. I don't think I would have survived it if you'd truly left me—I've been wretched."

Eliza ignored his self-pitying comment. "Before I can feel safe enough to live with you again, you must look me in the eye and tell me you did not intentionally kill anyone in your family. Or Beatrice."

Malcolm fixed her with a steady gaze. "I swear before heaven and all of its angels that I did not."

If he was still lying to her, he was doing an excellent job of it. But she wasn't finished. Eliza pulled in a resolute breath. "I saw Lord Eastleigh.

At the theatre. He told me something else about your past." She studied Malcolm's face—marked the sudden twitching of his eyebrow over his red-rimmed eyes and the set of his jaw. "There's another thing that needs clearing before I can ever hope to forgive you, husband."

Malcolm sighed. "Is it Annie?"

"It's true, then?" Eliza bit the inside of her lip so hard her eyes smarted.

"What did he say about her?"

"That she was your first. And now she has syphilis and she's dying."

Malcolm closed his eyes. "All of it is true."

"A whore, Malcolm? Really?" Eliza pulled her hand from his, scowling. "Did you lodge with her in London, then? Is that why I received no letter from you?"

"No. I lodged at a boardinghouse in Piccadilly. I did drop in to see Annie. She's in a bad way." Malcolm leaned back against the seat, passing a hand over his eyes. "I can't help but care about her. It all seems sordid, but Annie was and *is* very kind. At the time I met her, I hadn't a clue about women. Father was keen on making my brother and me into men as soon as possible. Against my mother's protestations, he took us to London for our first Season when we were fifteen. He took us round all the usual places—the Houses of Parliament, Kensington, and countless society balls. And at the end of it all, he took us to a brothel. Annie taught us how to pleasure a woman to help ensure a happy marriage. I promise you I have not had intimate relations with her for many years, and certainly not since her illness."

Eliza sighed, pushing out a rush of air so forceful it fogged up the glass of the carriage window. "So, I am . . . well?"

"Yes, my darling. You'll not be endangered by my past, and neither will our baby." Malcolm kissed the top of her head. "And you've no worries as to my recent activities in London. I have been steadfast. I swear it. Charles was lying to you to raise doubts and get you into his bed. He was a terrible person. More horrid than you can ever know."

Eliza caught the word as soon as it fell from Malcolm's lips. "Was?"

Malcolm looked down, his lips working silently before he answered. "Yes. It seems Lord Eastleigh lost his balance on the train platform in Southampton and fell onto the tracks. He's dead."

CHAPTER 39

They attended Lord Eastleigh's funeral out of a sense of duty, but it was a miserable affair, taking place on the grayest of frigid London days. His family crypt was located in Highgate's prestigious west cemetery, in the most elaborate of funerary gardens adorned with veiled maidens and grief-stricken angels. As Eliza huddled close to Malcolm for warmth, pulling the hood of her fur-lined cape over her head, the funeral carriage rattled through the cemetery gates, pulled by black-plumed horses. The rest of the cortege followed, ending with the polished landau carrying his widow.

As the bell tolled from St. Michael's, Lord Eastleigh's carriage came to a halt at the foot of an ivy-covered hillock crowned by a pillared tomb. At its base, a pair of sleeping stone lions rested, their paws crossed one over the other in repose.

Una descended from the landau, caped in a gloriously figured black bombazine cloak, the pale oval of her face punctuated by her dark eyes. She was both regal and catatonic. The mourners resembled a somber murder of ravens as they queued up along the narrow path, greeting Una with bowed heads and the press of their hands. Eliza was moved to sudden, unexpected sympathy.

"Lady Eastleigh," she said as Una swept past. "I . . ."

Una put up her hand and shook her head.

The crypt was opened, and the pallbearers came to their sad duty, moving the sleek ebony casket down the rails of the hearse and hoisting it onto their shoulders, its coffered top weeping white lilies and roses. Malcolm was as stoic as the stone mausoleum before them, his eyes hard as glass beneath the brim of his hat.

Unbidden tears sprung to Eliza's eyes. She hadn't been fond of Charles, it was true. But it was unfair for his life to have been cut short in its prime, with a young wife left to birth and rear a child all alone. She dabbed away the tears with her handkerchief, turning her face from Malcolm's disapproving gaze.

The vicar said his blessing before the opening of the tomb, made the sign of the cross, and motioned for Una to come forward. She kissed her gloved fingertips and pressed them to the top of the coffin before turning away. The pallbearers finished their duty and the tomb was sealed, wreaths of holly and myrtle left to adorn the steps of the mausoleum. The mourners departed to go back to their warm townhouses or out for a drink at the pubs, chattering quietly among themselves. Eliza gave a final mournful look to the dreary tomb and took Malcolm's arm as a frozen drizzle began to fall. They'd nearly gotten to the gates when Eliza heard Una's voice from behind.

"Lady Havenwood, now that the others are gone, I'd have a word with you."

Eliza turned, lifting the rain-dotted veil of black chiffon from her eyes. Una took two steps toward them and Malcolm gave a quick shake of his head. His arm tightened around her. "No. We've shown her enough respect by being here."

Eliza pulled away. "I need to speak with her, husband. For my own peace. Go to the carriage. I'll just be a moment."

Malcolm tipped his hat to Una and she gave a terse nod before fixing the full ire of her gaze on Eliza. "How dare you," she spat. "You've taken everything from me. My dignity, my husband's honor, my privacy as a widow."

"Una, I . . ."

Again, Una put up her hand. "No. You will listen. The scandal rags came out this morning. On the very same day as my husband's funeral. Now all of society knows you were the last thing on Charles's mind. That your kiss was his final spending of passion before he died." Una circled Eliza slowly, her face a blade. "Do you know I had to go to the morgue to identify his body? Can you imagine what that was like?"

Eliza's heartbeat fluttered in her throat. "I'm so sorry . . ."

"No. You cannot imagine. So, I will tell you." Una gave a mirthless smile. "His face . . . his beautiful face," she said, stopping in front of Eliza. "It was gone! Torn right off his skull. Only bits of his hair remained, stuck to his pate. The rest of him was crushed like raw meat. I'll never forget the smell within that room." Eliza's gorge rose, so vivid was the picture that Una painted. She turned her head to quell her urge to vomit. Una clucked her tongue. "I've spared you the worst. Train accidents are no pretty death."

"I never meant for what happened between us to happen. It was a silly impulse! A mistake. I was drunk."

"I was drunk!" Una mocked. "Yes, it appears you both were. While I languished at home with a fever, you were getting on so well with my husband over champagne that he drank too much and stumbled right over the edge of a train platform. I hate you. I hate you with all that is in me to hate another living creature. So I will tell you the truth about *your* husband."

Anger and shame flooded Eliza's face with blood. "Is it Annie you mean to shock me with? If so, I already know. He's told me."

Una's smile spread slowly across her face, pulling her prim features into an ugly rictus. "No! You're wrong—again! Who cares one flit about Annie? Every boy's first romp is with a whore. This is so much worse."

"Then tell me!"

"Do you really want to know what kind of monster you've married?"

"For God's sake, Una!"

Una's gloved hands balled into fists at her side. She shook with rage. "He lay with his own mother!"

"What?" The wind screamed in Eliza's ears and the tombstones around her seemed to wheel in a careening circle.

"I saw them. Together." Una laughed. "I'll never forget the day. I'd gone out to the rear gardens to gather a posy. When I came back through the south wing, I heard laughter coming from Ada's room. I crept up the stairs and opened the door, only a crack. I saw them there, together."

"I don't believe you!"

"Old Havenwood even caught them in the act once. Cuckolded by his own son!"

"No! I found her diary. He'd only had a nightmare. Ada wrote about it. The old man beat him to a bloody pulp after."

Una cackled. "Are you *really* that daft?"

"I . . . I saw letters . . . Ada's lover was another man. I found his portrait, in a locket . . ." Eliza shook her head. "No, you're wrong about him . . . you . . ." Eliza's words died on her tongue and she sat hard on the stone bench at her back.

Una smirked. "Oh, you really *are* too much. You still want to believe the best about him, even though he's proven himself a liar, time and again. You little fool! He killed his own father so he could freely have his pretty mother. And here you are, right in the middle of it all!"

CHAPTER 40

Eliza cut the leaves of her new book with her sewing scissors and cracked open the spine. Malcolm fidgeted in the seat next to her as the train sped back to Hampshire, checking his watch and returning it to his waistcoat pocket over and over.

He'd been in a cycle of moods since the funeral, his tempers vacillating like a gyroscope. During their two days in London, he'd harangued her about everything from the manner in which she dressed to the way her shoes clicked on the floor of their hotel room, only to praise her moments later for her wit. She'd bitten her tongue so many times she was surprised she still had one.

"What are you reading, darling?" Malcolm asked.

"It's a book of poetry. Walt Whitman."

He gave a disdainful sniff and toyed with his cuff links. "Silly things, poems."

Eliza rolled her eyes. "I don't think so at all. Verse is one of the loveliest modes of expression."

"Always the dreamer, aren't you, pet? Your frivolity is endearing." Malcolm pinched her chin and Eliza flinched away. She could no longer abide his touch.

"Say," he continued, "what did you and Una speak about after the funeral? You've been out of sorts ever since."

Oh, I've been out of sorts, all right. Eliza closed her book and sighed. "She was upset. People in mourning sometimes say unkind things."

Malcolm gritted his teeth. "But I asked *what* she said."

"I don't want to talk about it, especially right now."

Malcolm huffed, his breath fogging on the glass window.

The truth was, Eliza couldn't bear to speak the abominable things Una had said. Nor could she look upon Malcolm's long-fingered hands without imagining them caressing Ada, their bodies wrapped in an infernal embrace. *Had* he shot his own father to have her, then started the fire to hide the evidence, perhaps killing his brother and Mrs. Galbraith by accident? After all, the author of the sordid love letters she'd found had only signed them with a singular *M*. Was that *M* for Malcolm?

She wanted to believe that Una's words had been a vindictive lie. The thought of Malcolm lying with his mother was so abhorrent it physically sickened her. There was a visceral part of her that refused it.

They were crossing the Thames, the red-sailed barges spilling black clouds of smoke. The skies over London were in a near-constant haze from the unpleasant fug. She hadn't been fond of the city. Her soul was most anxious to be back in the countryside, with its fresh air and open landscape. The one thing she had to look forward to in the coming weeks was their Scottish holiday. She had a feeling the Highlands would suit her spirit, and perhaps give her time to be alone in the wild, away from Malcolm. "When are we leaving for Scotland?" she asked. "I was wondering what I should pack. I'd reckon it's much colder there than it is in Hampshire."

Malcolm turned his head slowly. "What did you say?"

"Scotland. You said we'd go to Oban to see your hunting lodge. Brynmoor. We talked about it on the day you brought me back from the hospital. At great length."

A low growl came from the back of Malcolm's throat. His eyes narrowed to slits. "I most certainly did not. Travel in your condition over such a long distance would be anything but prudent."

Eliza sat back against the train car's seat, her mouth falling open. What on earth was wrong with him? He'd been acting increasingly queer. Well, he wasn't going to turn her own mind against her again. If she were to be trapped in this marriage, she would not play a willing sycophant to his delusions. "Malcolm, we *did* speak of it! I remember it well. Are you becoming ill?"

"I am not *ill!*" A sudden roar erupted from his mouth and he stood, rocking back and forth as the train rumbled through the Battersea docks.

The other first-class passengers, startled by his outburst, put aside their papers and sewing to look. Embarrassment flooded Eliza's face with heat. She tugged on the hem of Malcolm's coat. "Darling, sit down. You're causing a scene."

"Liars. All around me. Betraying me," he muttered.

"What on earth are you talking about?" she asked. "What liars?"

"All of you! Even him!" A well-dressed man with a full gray beard glared at Malcolm from across the aisle and snapped his paper, shaking his head. This was beyond embarrassing.

Eliza stood. "There now. It's all right," she soothed, patting and pushing at his shoulders. The train lurched and Malcolm fell against her, nearly knocking her to the floor of the car. A gentleman in the seat behind theirs reached out to steady her arm.

"Get your hands off my wife!" Malcolm screeched.

The man's eyes widened. "So sorry, sir. I was only preventing her from falling."

"Is that so?" Malcolm was sneering now, his lips tight over his teeth. "Look, chap."

"I am no chap, sir. I am a viscount!" Malcolm thundered, going out into the aisle.

Merde. Eliza sank down into her seat, hiding her face in her hands.

"Well, your lordship," the other man said, squaring off with Malcolm, "I'm a baronet and you're bloody well acting far below your station, if I may say so."

Malcolm laughed. "Who are you to tell me how to behave?"

"Malcolm, please! You're going to get us removed."

The baronet rolled up his sleeves and stepped out into the aisle of the train car. He was short and stocky, with broad shoulders. He'd likely best Malcolm, if it came to it. "Very well, my lord. If it's a fight you're after, I'll not disappoint you."

Malcolm began struggling with his coat as the baronet looked on, an amused smirk on his face. As Malcolm was peeling his gloves from his hands, Eliza noticed a constellation of bumps scattered over his palms. They were small—no larger than the barrel of a pencil, with red margins and a clear center like a blister or pustule. She remembered Eastleigh's words to her at the theatre and a shard of raw panic went through her. Was this a sign of the disease he'd warned her about?

"Malcolm, would you please sit down! You're being ridiculous."

"I will not sit until this man has apologized."

"He already has!"

With a resigned sigh, the finely dressed older gentleman Malcolm had accused of being a liar calmly walked up and pinched Malcolm's shoulder from behind. He fell to his knees and went limp as a kitten. The train porter rushed up the aisle and helped the man haul Malcolm to his feet. "Let me go! That man challenged me, and on my honor, I shan't back down!"

"My lord," the bearded man said firmly, "I am a psychiatric doctor. If you keep that claptrap up, I'll see that you're escorted to Bethlem Royal at the next stop."

"I must apologize, gentlemen," Eliza said, trying to salvage what little dignity they had left. "My husband has not been well. We've just returned from the funeral of a dear friend. I'm afraid the shock has gotten to him."

"That is quite apparent," the doctor said. "For the sake of yourself and the other passengers, I'd offer an intervention. I've a tranquilizing vial in my bag. If you'd give me permission, my lady, I'd like to administer it."

"I'll have all of you know, Lord Eastleigh was no friend of mine." Malcolm was shaking now, sweat beading along his hairline. A vein pulsed at his temple. He'd gotten himself into a state, and it showed no sign of improving. "I have no friends. Everyone wants rid of me, it seems! Even my own wife." There was more murmuring throughout the carriage. Undoubtedly the other occupants were working out who they were. Yet another item for the gossip sheets. They were certainly keeping the presses well inked these days.

"Malcolm," Eliza soothed, "no one wants rid of you. Perhaps you'll feel less anxious after a nap. Doctor, if you wouldn't mind? The sedative?"

"Right. Hold his lordship, young man." The porter locked Malcolm's arms behind his back as the doctor produced a vial of clear liquid and prepped a syringe, flicking it with his fingers as he filled it. "This is only a bit of chloral hydrate, sir. It will calm your nerves and give you a nice rest for the remainder of the journey. There's no harm in it, I assure you."

Malcolm strained his neck and gnashed his teeth as the needle went into his arm. Within moments, his muscles went slack and his eyes grew heavy-lidded as sleep took him. "Help me get him to the infirmary car," the doctor ordered the young porter. "His poor wife needs her rest, too."

After Malcolm was taken away, the baronet leaned around the post between their booths with an apologetic smile. "So sorry for all the trouble, my lady. But your husband is a right loon."

She hadn't the strength or desire to disagree. She sank into her seat, her head pounding dully behind her temples. Was this to be her life, then? Chaotic madness, all of it. Even worse, with the papers out, it would only be a matter of time before Malcolm punished her for her behavior with Eastleigh. To bring a child into the mess was cruel. Pure folly. Eliza rested her hands on her belly, absently rubbing, and nestled into the corner of the compartment to hide from the pitying looks of the other passengers. Outside, rain began to lash against the windows. A bone-deep weariness set in, heavy and thick as treacle. She closed her eyes as the train curled on its journey southward.

Sleep had become her only solace.

CHAPTER 41

Eliza's days and nights were now spent in torturous pacing. From the time she rose in the morning until late in the evening, she walked the labyrinthine maze of Havenwood's halls, whispering to herself. The house heaved and groaned as true winter came in, cold and dank and mean. The days were gunmetal, the nights never-ending in their bleakness.

When she felt the first stirring of the child in her womb, as December stretched out its fingers toward Yule, Eliza imagined she was feeling the clawing of a demon.

What if?

Truly, Eliza had wondered what manner of man she had married.

Upon their return from London, she'd gone to a discreet apothecary for a consult, where the pharmacist had tried to be reassuring, but prepared her for the worst. Malcolm's symptoms, as described, fit the criteria for syphilis. With sorrowful eyes, the apothecary told her their child might be born blind and deformed. Or dead. The best Eliza could do would be to rest, pray for the best outcome, and avoid intimate congress with her husband at all costs.

She had no need to worry on the last count. Malcolm no longer visited her chambers, and their interactions were mostly silent, although the clattering of the silverware against china and their careful politeness with one another gave the impression of domestic tranquility. Eliza still hadn't uttered a word to Malcolm about Una's revelation at the cemetery. How did one say *I've discovered you fucked your own mother* over dessert and wine? And what kind of mother would take such liberties with her son? No. It was monstrous. All of it. Better not to speak of such abominations. Better to pretend they'd never happened if she wanted to survive.

For his part, he'd mentioned nothing of the scandal sheets or Eastleigh. Eliza had no intention of raising the subject, though her reticence did nothing to allay her worries over what kind of retribution might be brewing in Malcolm's addled mind. He knew. There was no way he couldn't.

One night, after dinner, Malcolm went into the library to smoke and Eliza followed, unbidden. They sat by the fire and Eliza took up her needlework. She was embroidering twining willow branches on the hem of a pillowcase meant for the baby's crib. She finished a line of stitches, broke her thread between her teeth to change it from green to brown, then rethreaded the needle and pushed it through the fabric. "I'm feeling restless, husband. Since we're no longer going to Scotland, I need something to look forward to. Some purpose, other than my embroidery."

"I had a thought this morning," Malcolm said. "I believe I'll give the staff the rest of the month off for the holiday. Send Mrs. Duncan to Aberdeen and Turner can, well . . . go wherever he'd like. Perhaps we'll redo their rooms while they're away. Like you wanted. That should keep you busy, shouldn't it? Choosing new linens and furniture?"

"That sounds lovely. They do work so hard for us, after all. And then we'll begin planning for the building of my stables?"

Malcolm heaved a weary sigh and rubbed at his forehead.

"Is there something wrong?" Eliza bit her lip. "I thought we were going to break ground in the spring. Isn't that still your plan?"

"You'll be great with child by then, Eliza. Exertions can lead to early labor and stillbirth. We don't want that, do we?" There he went again, talking to her as if she were a child and telling her what she needed.

"I'm feeling much better. And times are changing. Women no longer need to take to their beds throughout their confinement. Besides, I won't be the one doing the work and exerting myself. You promised we would start on the stables in March. We should start looking for workers now, given our past troubles."

He uncrossed his legs and crossed them again, fidgeting with his pipe. "I suppose I can inquire after workers. Anything to please my little wife." He folded his newspaper across his lap and peered at her through a scrim of smoke. "Now, there's a smile. You look so lovely when you smile. Tell me, did you smile so coyly when you went about seducing Eastleigh at the opera?"

Eliza's face fell. So here it came at last. Her punishment. A roil of words rose up in her throat and burned on her tongue, full of retribution for his hypocrisy. Only the gentle stirring of the baby kept her silent.

"You didn't think I'd find out about your little kiss, did you?" He laughed. "It was all over the papers. But it's all right, darling. I've forgiven you. It's all right *now*." There was a demented gleam in his eye as he rose and came toward her. His pupils blackened, nearly swallowing the green of his irises. He leaned forward, his hands gripping the arms of her chair, trapping her. His breath was rancid. Sour. He patted the subtle curve of her belly. "I had a happy thought. As soon as this one has popped free, I'll be crawling upon you to make another, I suppose. You're always keen for a poke and tumble, aren't you, darling?"

Eliza cringed away from him, repulsed by the coarseness of his words. As he stood to go, she spied a faint pinkish rash along the skin above his high collar. "You've a bit of a rash on your neck. I think you may be taking ill."

Malcolm put a hand to his throat, his nostrils flaring. "Most certainly not. That woman only uses the wrong kind of starch. How many times have I told her? Mrs. Duncan, you may *not* use alum in my collars!"

Eliza pulled in a shaky breath. "I'll make sure I remind her."

"I'll be off to bed, then," Malcolm said, suddenly jaunty. "Can you have Turner cover the embers?"

"Of course." He stalked out of the room, his gait swaying as he muttered to himself. Eliza picked up the tumbler from the table by his armchair and sniffed it. There was no trace of whisky. She pulled the bell rope and Turner came through. He knelt to rake ashes over the embers in the grate, tamping out the glowing coals with the back of the hearth shovel.

"Have you noticed anything off with his lordship lately, Turner?"

"I'm not sure what you mean, mum," the butler said, brushing the ash from his livery as he stood. His eyes skittered past her own. Poor Turner hadn't the hint of a poker face. He knew exactly what she meant.

"There was an incident on the train on the way back from Lord Eastleigh's funeral. He took a fit and had to be sedated. And then tonight, he was in a strange mood. Haven't you noticed him acting a bit nutty?"

"I suppose he has a lot on his mind. A man sometimes acts strange when he's to be a father."

"You've served this family for how many years, Turner?"

"Over thirty years." The butler warily eyed her. "And a wonderful assignment it has been, mum."

"Before Ada disappeared, did you ever hear her talk of another man? A man whose name started with *M*? Perhaps he was a Michael, or a Matthew?"

At the name "Matthew," Turner blinked and cleared his throat, then bent to close the damper, fingertips fumbling. "No, mum. Never met or heard of any Michael or Matthew, apart from her ladyship's father. Sir Matthew MacCulloch. He died when your husband was a boy."

"It's puzzling, you see. I'm being told different things by different people, and any clarity you could offer would be ever so helpful. I've a feeling you know more than you're letting on."

Turner heaved a sigh, as if defeated. He lowered his voice. "My lady, if I may say so, you are a right canny lass. This house has many shameful secrets. Some of those secrets were once perilous and needed to be kept for many, many years. That is no longer the case." Turner gave a tremulous smile. "I'll leave you with this: look about your chambers. Look closely. You will find the answers you're seeking. And for your own good, the sooner you do so, the better."

༼༕༽

Eliza went to her room, clapping her hands over her ears to cut out the hissing of the gas jets in the hallway. All of her senses were heightened by her condition and it was beyond vexing. She closed her door and locked it, then turned the key to her overhead chandelier.

With her chambers fully lit, she set out with a methodical determination. She had no clue as to what she was looking for, but if this house had shown her anything, it was that it kept its most precious secrets well hidden. She moved across the room, palms flat against the velvet wallpaper, feeling for any abnormalities. When she came to the area across from her fireplace, she knocked, listening for any difference in the sound, just as she'd done with the other three walls. The surface bounced beneath her hand, as if there were nothing solid behind the wallpaper. Encouraged, she pushed harder. The fragile paper tore down its length, and Eliza nearly stumbled forward. Beyond the torn paper, a hollow had opened up. It was a hidden room.

༼༕༽

Eliza lit her Tilley lantern, this time checking that its fuel chamber was full of paraffin. She slid her house slippers on over her stockings and went through the portal, her heart thudding. Inside, a kind of anteroom with a low ceiling led to a descending spiral of stone steps, the bottom obscured by a darkness deep as an oubliette.

"Old house, you are full of surprises."

She picked her way down, counting as she went. There were thirty-three steps to the bottom, which meant she was probably beneath the main floor of the house. The basement. She was standing on a packed-dirt floor, in a passageway of sorts, the ceiling just a few inches above her head. The walls were made of dank, rough-hewn stone, and as she moved forward, the scent of loamy earth bloomed beneath her feet.

There were two directions she could go, both of them hidden in shadow.

She turned in a circle, holding the lantern at arm's length. To her right, the hallway was lined with cobweb-shrouded wine racks, the necks of the bottles reaching out like blackened fingers. The other direction seemed barren apart from a few empty baskets and old fruit crates.

Beyond the wine cellar, the passageway continued, extending in a long, serpentine curve that canted slightly to the right the further she went. When she reached the end of the corridor, there was another spiral staircase—an identical twin to the other.

Eliza grasped the metal railing and went up, the rusty iron creaking under her hands, each step an exercise in anxiety. When she reached the top, she found a trapdoor closed with a hinged hasp. She set the lantern on the top step and, using both hands, rocked the hasp back and forth until the rust welding it to the peg flaked free. She pushed, fighting against an unseen obstruction. The hatch opened and fell back with a loud crash, kicking up a musty cloud that smelled of ashes.

"Oh my God."

She was in the south wing, emerging into an empty room that was a mirror image of her own.

❦

Eliza craned her neck and hoisted herself through the trapdoor's opening, listening. There was music, soft and low, with an occasional crackle interrupting the sweeping melody. It was a gramophone. Playing Chopin. "Hello?" she called, swinging the lantern in an arc as her voice echoed around her. Her footsteps sent up another cloud of black dust. The entire floor was covered with ash. She tilted her chin back and looked up, casting the arc of yellow-orange light from the lantern above her. Singed, bubbling wallpaper scarred the walls. There was no ceiling; only the attic rafters rose high above her head. Eliza wondered if the fire had started in this room and raged outward from it. Had this been Gabriel's room? Or Lord Havenwood's? She carefully picked her way forward, her feet sliding along the floor, following the muffled sound of the piano concerto.

"Hello?" she called again, projecting her voice. The music abruptly stopped, as if someone had heard her and lifted the stylus from the disc. Her heart fluttered in her chest as she held her breath to listen. Her eyes searched the room, seeking the source of the music. There was nothing.

Until there was.

Eliza heard the ghost before she saw it.

There was a gentle sweeping hiss from the corner of the room, as if the hem of a dress was being dragged across the floor. She froze as a shadow the color of the soot at her feet uncurled and floated before the window, its contours vaguely shaped like those of a woman. Ice ran along Eliza's spine and every hair on her arms stood up at once.

The shade floated past the window, its movement setting the remnants of the fire-scalded drapes aflutter. The moonlight shining through the ragged fabric blinked as the ghost went past, as if a living person of flesh and blood had walked in front of her, blocking out the light.

The cold in the room became a void. Eliza whimpered and stepped backward. The ghost turned its countenance to her, amorphous in the dim light, dark hollows where eyes had once been, and extended its arm.

Eliza followed the ghost's gesture, rooted to the spot, her breath coming in small, sharp pants. It was pointing to the adjoining parlor, where Eliza could see the yawning mouth of a fireplace.

"What is it?" she stammered. "Beatrice? What are you trying to tell me?"

The specter turned away from her with a lingering look. Sadness pierced Eliza, as if she could feel what the spirit was feeling . . . as if she'd lost someone dear to her. The tangy scent of birch leaves briefly wafted through the room. Then, as if it were ash dissolving in a dish of water, the spirit disintegrated, leaving Eliza's heart in a gallop.

She pushed through her fear and dashed to the parlor, nearly stumbling over a toppled, broken chair, its upholstery ragged and torn. She went to the fireplace and peered into it. The damper was open, funneling cold air through its baffles, a rectangle of star-filled sky at its top. She ran her frantic fingers around the brick lining, feeling for anything out of the ordinary.

Ah-ha! One of the bricks above her head felt loose, its edge out of alignment with the rest. Eliza excitedly pried at the brick, rocking it from side to side. With a crumble of mortar, it came loose in her hand. She carefully laid it in the grate, then walked her fingers into the opening, expecting spiders and centipedes. Instead, she felt a smooth metal box. It was a cigarette tin. "Thank you, Beatrice," she whispered.

Eliza hurriedly snatched the box free from the hollow and backed away from the fireplace. Too late, she remembered the decrepit chair was behind her, and she stumbled over it, her hip slamming into the floor. The lantern rolled to the other side of the room. Its molten paraffin sloshed from the globe and the flame within it turned from yellow to blue. Suddenly, a muffled shouting channeled through the chimney. Whoever—or whatever—it was had heard her.

Eliza breathed in and out, the tin clutched to her breast. The acrid fear of a prey animal sliced through her, souring her sweat. Should she run for the hatch? Remain still? With a final steadying breath, she crept toward the trapdoor on hands and knees, her fingers sinking into soot, not realizing until it was too late that the hem of her nightdress had caught on the splintered chair arm. A high-pitched screech came as the chair dragged on the floor behind her. Eliza winced, vowing to chop the wretched thing into kindling.

There was a creaking, then the slamming of a door downstairs—it was the main entrance to the south wing's vestibule. Footsteps pounded, running now, the sound growing louder by the second. Malcolm. Eliza yanked her nightgown free and stumbled to her feet, raw fear propelling her forward. She seized the handle of the toppled lantern and shimmied down the spiral staircase. As her feet hit the ground, a menacing growl echoed from abovestairs.

Eliza took off at a run down the meandering passageway, ignoring the pain searing her bruised hip. What would he do, if he found her here? Poised, as he seemed to be, on the brink of madness? Eliza did not want to find out.

She raced up the groaning secret staircase that led to her room, comforted by the safety of warm light and familiar surroundings. She slammed the door and, with more strength than she realized she possessed, pushed her armoire across the floor to cover the hole in the wall. She piled anything else she could find—books, her dressing table, and even her washstand—in front of it. She stood perfectly still, holding her breath and listening. There was nothing but the incessant hiss of the gas jets and the clicking of a tree limb against her windowpane.

Eliza sat in her armchair to face the makeshift barricade, wielding a fireplace poker like a queen's scepter. Though her eyes grew heavy and sleep threatened to steal her vigilance, she denied its temptation until dawn crept across the floor, blazing silver bright and cold.

CHAPTER 42

The next day, Eliza descended to an empty house. The grandfather clock chimed eight times as she went through the foyer to the morning room, her feet leaden with lack of sleep. A tea tray had been left on the sideboard, stacked with oatcakes and sweetmeats and tented with a folded note. Eliza opened it:

> *My lady,*
> *His lordship was keen to take us to the station early this morning. Said you and he needed some time alone to sort your holidays out. Mr. Turner (Sam) is with me. We've kicked up a wee romance, he and I. We're bound for Aberdeen to see my Maggie and her bairns. I thank you for your kindness and we shall see you when the year turns.*
>
> *Cheers,*
> *Shirley Duncan*

She closed Shirley's note and poured her tea, holding her wrist steady with her other hand. So she was alone then. Alone in a house full of spirits, at the mercy of a husband whose behavior was increasingly unpredictable. A man who was quite assuredly capable of murder. She remembered how often he'd demurred when she'd brought up Gabriel. How their rivalry was his chief memory. His contempt for his brother was palpable. Had Malcolm shot his father, then contrived the fire to eliminate Gabriel and the meddling Mrs. Galbraith? And if so, why hadn't he killed Shirley and Turner as well? Had they helped? It would explain why they were so secretive. And was his mother still in this house, kept like a mistress as Una had implied? *Someone* had been in the south wing last night. A person of flesh and blood who had a fondness for Chopin. It all made sense. Una's warnings. Even Eastleigh's. There could be no more shameful secret in a family than incest. Who was the true monster? Malcolm or his mother?

Eliza moved to the breakfast room. Her place at the table had been set, a lone candle lit next to the silver charger. There, on her plate, tied neatly in a bow, was a scrap of lace from the nightgown she'd worn the night before.

It was a warning.

A threat.

❦

Eliza went to her room and packed her valise. She hurriedly dressed in her worn dungarees and a blouse, then pulled a heavy fisherman's sweater over her head. Her corsets had grown too small as her pregnancy progressed, and she needed to be able to move quickly. She needed to be able to run. As she was rummaging through her drawers for any jewelry she might pawn, her fingers brushed against the luckenbooth Malcolm had given her. She held it in her hands, feeling the weight of happier memories. *Now you've the key to my own heart, mo chridhe.*

Eliza wavered for a moment, then secreted the luckenbooth inside the pocket of her dungarees alongside the cigarette tin she'd found in the south wing, which she had yet to open. No time for that now. She laced up her riding boots and descended to the main floor. All was quiet and still.

She went out the servants' door and hurried through the kitchen garden. The pumpkins and winter cabbage were fringed with frost, their broad leaves glittering in the pale sunlight. Like everything else in this horrible house, they were rotting on the vine. She slung her valise over her shoulder and pushed through the delivery gate, picking up her pace as she approached the thicket of trees surrounding the stables.

As she cut through the birchwood forest, veering off the gravel-paved leisure path, the sagging roof of the stables came into view, its eaves green with lichen. Eliza's walk became a jog. She had no idea whether Malcolm had taken both Friesians to the station, but at least Star would be there, as he had been since Lydia's departure. She'd ride to Sarah for help—practical Sarah would know what to do.

Eliza had nearly reached the paddock fence when her toe nudged something solid among the fallen leaves on the forest floor. She looked down. A metal disc, barely visible, poked through the yellow birch leaves directly in front of her right foot. She stood stock-still, her breath rasping through her lips.

It was the trigger to a snare. Likely a boar trap. If she moved too hastily, she would set it off, sending metal teeth into her ankle.

Malcolm had warned her about snares in the woods, hadn't he? To keep wild dogs and badgers at bay, he claimed. To protect the crofters' livestock. But now Eliza wondered if he'd set them for far more sinister reasons.

Eliza's heartbeat clamored as she slowly shifted all of her weight onto her left leg. If she could scoot her foot away from the trigger plate without touching it, she might be able to escape without injury. She drew in a slow breath and let it out through pursed lips. She carefully inched her leg backward, tensing her thigh muscles until they screamed.

She was almost free.

Almost.

As she watched in horror, her valise suddenly shifted off her shoulder and slid from the crook of her elbow toward the jaws of the trap. On impulse, Eliza grabbed for it with her other hand. In an instant, she realized her mistake. A bone-wrenching snap echoed through the trees. Pain shot through Eliza's leg like cold fire. A sob of rage tore free from her throat. "You bastard!" She collapsed to the ground, the trap tightening around her ankle. Blood began to pool on the yellow leaves beneath her boot.

Eliza clenched her teeth and strove to steady her breathing through the clouds of pain and dizziness. The trap was smaller than she'd expected it to be, but its grip was fierce. With what little she knew about traps, she wagered that the more she struggled, the tighter it would become. She gingerly felt along her shin and ankle, pressing with her fingertips. The way the mechanism was built, only two of the teeth had penetrated her boot on either side. It appeared as if nothing were broken—the thick leather and wool sock within her boot seemed to have protected her from the worst—but she wouldn't know for sure until she could stand again.

She needed to get free. Before Malcolm found her.

Eliza combed the underbrush with her eyes, seeking a large stick or anything else at arm's length she might use to pry the trap free. There was nothing. In desperation, she leaned forward and pushed at the leaf springs with the heels of her hands, trying to leverage all her strength to open the trap's jaws. Her arms trembled with the effort. It was futile. She was only tiring herself and driving the rusty teeth deeper into her flesh.

It was suddenly so cold. Eliza shivered and pulled her cloak over her shoulders. Her child turned within her womb, light as a sparrow's wing. She rubbed at her belly and lay back on the ground, blinking. The treetops spun above her. The world only stopped tilting when she closed her eyes.

Without realizing it, she descended into sleep.

When she woke, the sky had shifted from morning's pale blue to a rosy purple. Her leg throbbed, sending spikes of pain up through her calf when she moved to sit. Fresh blood oozed from her punctured boot.

It would be dark soon. Doubtless, Malcolm had returned by now and discovered she was gone. Eliza could only imagine his anger. She dreaded what would happen when he found her.

As the moon crested the spindly tops of the birches, a rustling came from the underbrush. Eliza turned her head to look. A ghostly orb of light bobbed among the trees, just as the eerie lantern had months before when she'd spied it through her window. She stilled, her heart thudding. *Please be one of the tenants.*

But it wasn't a tenant or a ghost. It was Malcolm, a grim frown drawing the edges of his mouth downward. His eyes landed on her and narrowed. The lantern light carved his cheekbones sharp as sabers. "Ah, there you are. Just as I thought."

Eliza hugged herself beneath the chilling scrutiny of his gaze, silently swearing. How idiotic it was to think she could get away again without his knowing! She should have left the night before and used the time she'd had more wisely. But it was too late for that now. Now she'd have to face the consequences. Alone.

"I only wanted to go for a walk in the forest," she stammered. "I tripped, that's all."

Malcolm calmly strode to her side, his boots kicking up a flurry of leaves. He knelt at her side and raised her face to meet his eyes. A nervous flutter went through her at the tenderness of his touch. "Is that all, darling?"

She nodded.

"It's funny, you see. People don't normally pack valises and leave their rooms in disarray when they go on a walk."

"I . . . I . . ."

"Come now, Eliza. I'm no fool. You meant to leave me, didn't you?"

She flinched. "I'm not sure what you mean."

"Don't lie to me. You've been deceiving me. We both know that." Malcolm turned to her entrapped ankle and ran his long fingers gently over her boot. She winced. "I know all about your scheming. Your plotting and planning. Finding out all our little secrets, aren't you?"

He withdrew something metallic from his greatcoat pocket. Despite the cold, sweat beaded at her temple and ran down her collar. Her heartbeat surged.

"I warned you," Malcolm said, his voice crisp, each word enunciated. "About the traps." He hinged her knee and placed her foot flat on the ground. She howled in pain. "There, there, darling. This might hurt a little. Do try to be still."

Eliza began shaking uncontrollably.

And then there was Eliza, caught in a trap and murdered in the forest. She could almost hear Galbraith's wicked cackle on the wind.

Malcolm bent to his work. Eliza saw that the instrument he held wasn't a weapon at all, but a simple carpenter's C-clamp. He fastened the clamp around one of the trap's springs and twisted its wing nut, sending it spiraling down the bolt. The pressure around her leg slowly began to diminish. After a few moments, Malcolm worked his hands between the loosened jaws of the trap and pulled it open with a snap. Blood rushed to Eliza's head in relief. She nearly swooned. She was free. Alive.

She flexed her knee and tentatively circled her ankle. It rotated normally, but a jolt of ragged pain traveled up her leg, making her gasp.

"I'll have to carry you," Malcolm said. "It's likely your ankle is broken."

He scooped his arms beneath her and picked her up off the ground. Eliza wound her arms around his neck and allowed herself to be carried. She caught the scent of his camphor soap and felt the stubble sprouting from his chin against her cheek. A part of her wanted to nuzzle there and pretend that nothing between them had changed. That they were still the tender lovers they'd been before and he wasn't gone to his madness.

As if reading her mind, he kissed the top of her head and chuckled warmly. "Ah, pet. You needn't worry. All will be right again between us. Soon."

Malcolm trudged through the gate and onto the tree-lined drive. The shadowed shoulders of the manor loomed ahead. Its yellow windows winked, as if they were amused by her misfortune. The house she'd once loved had become both curse and prison.

As Malcolm carried her over the threshold just as he had on their wedding day, Eliza knew with certainty she'd never see the outside of Havenwood Manor again.

CHAPTER 43

She was a prisoner now.

From Ada's bed, Eliza watched the tumbling snow, its downy serenity giving little comfort as it enfolded the hills and clung to the naked branches of the birchwood grove in the distance. Night would be falling soon, and Ada's room was frigid and mean—a room with windows locked and barred from the outside. A room where no one would hear her cries for help. Eliza shivered, running her hands over her arms. She only wore the thin cotton blouse and dungarees she'd escaped in. They stank of sour sweat and chafed against her skin. Malcolm had promised to give her a bath and a change of clothing that evening, but she didn't trust him.

She should never have trusted him.

Her ankle still throbbed dully, like a toothache set into her bones. It had been two days since her injury, by her account. Possibly three. Malcolm had kept her in an opium-clouded stupor. She'd drifted in and out of consciousness so many times she couldn't be sure of the days.

Upon their return to the manor, he'd been ostensibly tender and doting. Too tender. He laid her on the chesterfield in the library and applied compresses to her swollen ankle, all the while plying her with romantic platitudes. He brewed cup after cup of tea she refused to drink, until her thirst became unbearable. Just as she suspected, the tea contained a sedative. After her second cup, the wallpaper began to waver and flow like incandescent water. She dimly remembered the feeling of being picked up again and carried. When she finally woke, her head pounding like a drum, she'd found herself here and realized Malcolm had turned a corner from which there would be no return.

Eliza pushed herself up against the headboard and looked about the room, wiping the crust from her eyes. It looked much the same as it had on her first visit to the south wing. Ada's bottle-green dressing gown was still draped over the screen and the objects on her bureau showed no signs of having been disturbed. That was one mystery solved—if Ada *were* still living in the house, she would have had no reason not to still be residing in this room. She wasn't here.

Eliza suddenly remembered the tin she'd found in the chimney. Had Malcolm discovered it in her pocket and taken it? She patted the leg of her trousers. It was still there, along with the luckenbooth. She brought out the little box, weighing it in her hand. It was so light that whatever was inside couldn't amount to much. Eliza carefully opened the lid. Inside there were several pieces of paper, neatly folded and stacked, tied with a faded violet ribbon.

She pulled at the ribbon's tail and it came loose in her hands. With hollow excitement (what did solving an old mystery matter now?), Eliza unfolded the first paper. It was a drawing. In it, the same young man from Ada's locket sat in the crook of a tree, one leg crossed casually over the other. He was well dressed, with wide eyes beneath the brim of his derby. Eliza turned it over. Written in the bottom corner was: *Matthew, April 1894, drawn by Gabriel Winfield.*

The mysterious M. That explained Turner's reaction when she'd mentioned the name Matthew. And Gabriel had known this Matthew—they'd obviously been friends, otherwise he wouldn't have had occasion to draw him. School or navy chums, perhaps? That would explain how Ada had met him. Eliza put the drawing to the side and unfolded the next item. It was a newspaper clipping.

Havenwood Manor Burns! the headline screamed. Beneath the bold-face, there was a photograph of the house, the south wing's upper floor brimming with flames beneath a pitch-black sky. The article was dated December 23, 1896, and it was short, stating the fire had started under mysterious circumstances attributed to a ruptured gas line. The casualties were listed:

Thomas Winfield, 4th Lord Havenwood, aged 68 years

Lieutenant Gabriel Winfield, aged 22 years

Dolores Galbraith, housekeeper, aged 54 years

There was no mention of Ada or Malcolm. Eliza folded the newsprint and removed the next item. It was a letter. Eliza recognized Eastleigh's perfect, aristocratic penmanship immediately.

November 1st, 1892

Lord Havenwood,
As you well know, upon the death of my father, the estate and the title have fallen to me. Matters have been poorly managed. I have done up our books. My father's laxity regarding your debts has been fully revealed. You are in prodigious arrears, Thomas. I have attached the balance sheet. Perhaps you did not realize these numbers were being kept. Perhaps you thought a hand of cards now and again would not add up to this amount. You were rather free with your bets, and now I must be called to collect upon my father's generosity. You must remit the sum total of your debt by the beginning of January, else I will be forced to lay claim to your estate's rents.

With all sincerity,
Charles Lancashire
Earl of Eastleigh

There were three more letters from Eastleigh beneath.

January 5th, 1893

Havenwood,
We are at an impasse, it would seem. As you are unable to pay me outright, I will begin calling upon your tenants at the beginning of next month. I hold four mortgages against your estate. Lest you see your family fall into penury and your property seized, you will not impede me. This has been an issue of your own making. I am merely the creditor.
Charles Lancashire
Earl of Eastleigh

February 2nd, 1893

Havenwood,
You are sorely lacking, sir. Do you realize how long it would take to resolve your mortgages with your paltry rents alone? Two lifetimes! And I do not wish to wait that long.
There is something else you have which might allay your debt.
I have long looked with covetous eyes upon your wife.
If you will agree to enter into an agreement with me, whereupon I am allowed to visit Lady Havenwood's

chambers and disport myself there, I will apply the sum of fifty pounds per week against your debt. If you agree to this arrangement, apply your signature to the promissory note and send it to me posthaste. I would desire my own key to her room, as well as the assurance she will cheerfully submit to my attentions.

> *Charles Lancashire*
> *Earl of Eastleigh*

February 4th, 1893

Havenwood,

You, sir, you surprise me with your enthusiastic response! Your terms are most curious and unexpected, yet I can see the logic behind your wishes. You may observe my congress with your wife, if it so titillates you. Beyond the keyhole, as it were. I shall make my first visit to her chambers on the morrow. We shall keep one another in check. If anyone should hear of this, we would both see our good names ruined. No one can know of our arrangement. This is imperative.

> *Much obliged,*
> *Charles Lancashire*
> *Earl of Eastleigh*

Vomit flooded Eliza's mouth. She leaned over the edge of the mattress and heaved onto the floor. Nothing but bile came forth. Eliza remembered the feel of Eastleigh's greedy hands clasping her waist, the possessiveness of his slimy kiss. She had been a conquest for him—a challenge and a prize. Just like Ada. Malcolm had at least been truthful about Eastleigh. He'd protected her, only to turn tail and become the serpent in the garden himself. But why?

Eliza took a shaky breath and unfolded the next piece of paper, its edges torn. It was one of the missing entries from Ada's diary.

> *June 18th, 1893*
>
> *Our plan is becoming reality. My long-tormented marriage is almost at an end. Beatrice has played her part well. Eastleigh is as regular with his visits as clockwork. Every Sunday, just before four o'clock, Beatrice climbs into the dumbwaiter in the basement and hauls herself upstairs. As Eastleigh ruts with me, Beatrice spies through the top of the dumbwaiter to make sure his actions are witnessed and that I am as safe as I can be, should he turn violent. Beatrice is so specific in her recounting of Eastleigh's anatomy and the physical nature of the ordeal that I am often amused. As that miserable, grunting fool spends himself within me (it is quite brief, thanks be to God, as is his member), I only think of the day when I will use him to bring my husband begging for mercy at last. If he refuses to grant me a divorce settlement, Beatrice will go to the papers and reveal his and Eastleigh's debauched arrangement for all the world to see.*
>
> *I disguise myself and use the dumbwaiter in my room to sneak out to meet Beatrice in Winchester once a week to go over her records. We have a merry time, laughing at the pub and drinking to old H's ruin. I think of the future, when Beatrice and I will be safe beside Brynmoor's hearth, to love and live out our days in happy companionship, and where I at last can be free. Oh, I cannot wait!*

Realization broke over Eliza. Ada and Beatrice *had* been more than friends. They'd been lovers. She imagined them together, in a cozy hunting lodge made of fieldstone beneath a fog-wrapped mountain. It was a lovely picture—but one that had never come to pass. Something had happened to thwart Ada's plans and bring about Beatrice's death, leaving her spirit to roam restlessly within this house. Eliza opened the final folded paper. A feeling of dread came over her as she read what she already knew in her heart.

> *December 17th, 1896*
>
> *At last, I have discovered what happened to my love. She is dead, my Beatrice, and has been for nigh on three years. Gabriel came to me, weeping in my arms like a child as he told me the truth of what they made him do. Of how they kept him silent, with threats against my life and his own, should their shameful secrets ever be revealed to the world. They shall pay, my enemies. I will take my revenge. For every cruel fist that bloodied my body and broke the will of my sons. For each time I've had to endure Eastleigh's loathsome, crawling touch. For every devious deception. They shall pay. They think me weak. But I have become vengeance.*

There was a creak outside her door, and the crystal doorknob began to twist as a key rattled in the lock. Eliza scooted backward on the mattress and shoved the papers and cigarette tin beneath the pillow. Malcolm pushed through the door, carrying a salver stacked with plates and a tea service. He set it down on the mattress and gave a toothsome grin.

"I've brought refreshments, darling. I've even made you a toasted cheese sandwich." He shrugged. "It's the only thing I know how to cook, I'm afraid."

At an earlier time in their marriage, this sort of proclamation would have charmed her. Now it rankled her every nerve. Her knees shook, whether from hunger or fear, she couldn't know. "How long are you going to keep me in here?" she asked. She reached out for the sandwich. She sniffed it, then pulled apart the bread to inspect the hummocky layer of melted cheese.

"Don't be concerned. I haven't poisoned it. It wouldn't be in my best interest to kill you, seeing as you've my heir in your belly. I've only locked you away to protect you from yourself."

"I don't know what to think, Malcolm. Locking me up doesn't seem like the sort of thing a normal husband does." Eliza bit into the sandwich, the salty taste of the cheese exploding on her tongue. "Hardly conventional."

"I suppose we *do* have a rather unconventional marriage." He grinned and sat on the stool by Ada's dressing table. "I was thinking about the carriage ride we took, that last warm day of autumn. Wasn't it lovely? Perhaps when you're better, we can go again."

Eliza swallowed her tea to chase the dry sandwich down her throat. "Seems a lifetime ago. I thought we'd turned a corner that day. I thought we'd be happy."

Malcolm tilted his chin and looked at her. "So did I. You know, I didn't think much of you, at first."

"You certainly could have fooled me."

"Oh, but I did fool you. Quite well, for my part." He gave a wistful look and clapped his hands on the top of his knees. "Well. I've rats to poison and grates to blacken. I've been rather industrious since our staff left. I daresay we won't need them anymore. Now, isn't that modern of me?" He rose, turning toward the door.

"I thought you were going to give me a bath and change of clothes. And this room is so cold. Can I at least have my sweater back?"

"You're so very spoiled." He frowned and clucked. "I simply haven't the time to give you a bath tonight. Perhaps tomorrow."

"Fuck you, Malcolm," she spat.

He stood and backed away, his green eyes glinting hard as quartz. "Do manage to be good until morning, dearest wife."

The door shut with a snick, followed by Malcolm's key turning the lock. Eliza screamed a string of expletives and flung the porcelain teapot against the wall, where it shattered into creamy shards, the tea splashing onto the dressing table mirror. Her reflection was crazed, her eyes wild with her fury. But there was something else there—something she hadn't felt in a long while—the blazing, heart-pounding will to survive and protect her unborn child. No matter the cost.

❧

To escape her captivity, she'd have to play a game. A game that would likely end with killing Malcolm. *Would* she be able to kill him, if it came to it? She closed her eyes, remembering their courtship. But that charming man she'd met on a summer balcony wasn't him—it never had been. It was all a lie—he was a lie—nurtured by her own foolish naïveté and unwillingness to face the truth.

Yes. If she had to, she would kill him. For her baby. For herself.

As December rolled onward, Eliza made her plan. She had nothing but time, after all.

Her ankle had healed quickly. She'd tested it every day, slowly putting more and more weight upon it. At first, it had been painful and arduous to even manage standing. A sharp hiss of breath would burst from her lips as soon as her foot touched the floor. Now, little more than a week later, she was able to walk in a steady line across the room, almost as well as she had before the trap had caught her. Only a trace of yellow bruising surrounded the scabbed marks where the metal teeth had punctured her flesh. A few more days, and she'd be whole.

But Malcolm needn't know that.

She played her part well. When Malcolm brought her food twice a day, she pretended to be sleeping, or delirious with pain. When he touched her ankle, poking with cool fingertips, she cried out as if he'd whipped her with a riding crop. Her ruse seemed to be working.

On a particularly frigid day, when every joint ached from the cold, she heard Malcolm's step outside her room. She decided she was ready. She arranged her filthy hair on the pillow to make it look as if she had been sleeping. When he opened the door, dragging a triangular shaft of amber light behind him, she sat up, pretending at feverish confusion. Her heart thumped with excitement. He'd left the door slightly ajar. This was her chance.

"I've brought you beef tea, darling. For the baby." Malcolm set the tea tray with its tureen of soup on the bed, then settled on the edge of the mattress. He began swiping butter on soda crackers, chattering away about the weather and the war.

Eliza didn't waste another breath.

She lunged for the tureen and flung the hot broth in Malcolm's face. He gave an enraged roar and covered his eyes with his hands. "You little whore!"

Eliza scrambled clumsily toward the door.

It was a foolish mistake.

Malcolm recovered more quickly than she'd bargained for. With grasping hands, he shoved her back onto the mattress, then extended his leg, slamming the door shut with his foot. Now that her egress was blocked, she'd have no choice. She'd have to fight.

With a scream of righteous rage, Eliza pounced on Malcolm's back like a jungle cat and began clawing at his neck. He spun in a circle as she wrapped her legs around his hips, locking herself to him and pounding his shoulders with her fists. He backed toward the bed, laughing, and lay down on top of her, crushing her beneath him. She thrashed and bucked her hips until he rolled off. He pinned her wrists to the mattress with his hands and crouched over her on all fours. Broth dripped from his ears and hair onto her face. The skin over his cheeks was angry and scalded. His neck bore her scratches, oozing scarlet lines of blood.

At least she'd wounded him. There was some satisfaction in that.

"You think you're so clever, don't you?" he spat. "Try that business again, and I'll have to tie you up." He bent and kissed her neck, his tongue hot against her pulse. She recoiled in disgust. "You'd like that, I think."

"Get off me!" she screamed. Her knees strove to find his groin. He wedged himself between her legs and crushed his hips against her own. Eliza gathered her saliva in her mouth and spat it in Malcolm's face.

He stood, wiping the viscous gob from his forehead, a look of disdain snarling his lip. "You're so very lucky you're with child. But women often die after childbirth, just like my grandmother. Or stumble in front of carriages to be trampled by horses." Malcolm smirked. "Or they drown with their pockets full of stones. Tell me, darling, which would you prefer when the time comes? I know you're rather fond of water."

A blade of panic cut through Eliza, but she wouldn't give him the pleasure of seeing her fear. "I hate you, Malcolm."

He backed toward the door with a contemptuous sniff. "I assure you, Lady Havenwood, the feeling is quite mutual."

CHAPTER 44

That evening, Eliza rose from a fitful nap and looked around the room, her eyes straining as the spare sliver of moon replaced the sun. She needed a weapon—something that would give her better odds than a bowl of hot soup. Malcolm wouldn't be letting his guard down around her anymore. Her mind raced. What sort of weapon would a woman have in her bedchambers? What unconventional method of defense could she concoct in a room full of half-used toiletries and moldering lace petticoats?

As if her baby sensed her unease, it turned and kicked within Eliza's womb, sending flutters through her abdomen. She rubbed her belly through her dingy trousers. "There, little one. All is well."

It was so dark. She needed light to find something to defend herself. Eliza rushed to Ada's dressing table and rustled around inside the drawers. There was nothing within but a few handkerchiefs and underthings. She felt around the edges of the drawers to see if any of them might have a false bottom. No such luck. Finally, tucked beneath a stack of folded stockings in the last drawer, a familiar shape met her touch. It was a tin of matches and a few stale, hand-rolled cigarettes. Ada had been a closet smoker, too. This made Eliza smile. At the very least, she'd get to have a cigarette, even though finding a candle to see by would have been better.

She lit one of the rustic fags. The ember glowed dully in the mirror as she took a tug of smoke into her lungs. The tobacco was bitter with age, but it served to calm her trembling hands and made the cold funneling through the window seem less keen. She sat on the foot of the bed to order her thoughts, her shoulders slumping. She couldn't let despair overtake her. She had to find a way out of here. Tonight.

After a few more rallying puffs, Eliza stubbed out the meager butt against the footboard and went to the wardrobe snugged against the corner of the room. She opened the mirrored doors and searched its compartments, running her hands over the surface of the shelves and along the top. Nothing but dust. She could break one of the mirrored panels, but she'd be just as likely to injure herself in the process. And Malcolm would see the broken mirror upon his next visit and know immediately what she intended. There wasn't a thing in the entire room that she could remotely fashion into a hidden weapon meant to kill or wound.

Or was there?

Eliza's heartbeat picked up its cadence. She remembered Lydia's prescient worry on the night she and Malcolm had gone on their first ride, and the two pins she'd used to fasten her hat to her hair—something all women had at the ready to fend off street harassers and beaus who attempted to take liberties. Hatpins. Surely Ada had them, too! With renewed determination, she searched beneath the mattress and behind the headboard, then pawed through the drawers of the vanity once more, but it was futile. There wasn't so much as a brooch remaining in Ada's jewelry cases. "Dammit!"

And then, just as she was about to lose hope, the silk dressing screen came to mind. Eliza crossed the room and pushed the pleated panels of the screen closed. A pile of carelessly discarded clothing lay on the floor. Eliza knelt and sorted through it, sending dust flying into the air. When she found a wide-brimmed hat at the bottom of the pile, she couldn't contain the shriek of joy that burst through her lips. Sticking out of its crown was a single pearl-tipped hatpin.

Eliza pulled the pin free and clutched it in triumph. She brandished it like a tiny sword, stabbing the air. This, this was a way to improve her odds ever so slightly. She could go for his neck. Or his eyes. Even if she couldn't land a mortal wound, she could at least blind him or cause him enough pain to give herself a fighting chance at escape. She practiced her routine a few more times, then threaded the pin into the leg of her filthy dungarees, hidden from sight, its pearled head against her fingertips.

Tomorrow morning, when he brought her breakfast, she'd be ready.

As midnight chimed in the main part of the house, the tolling of the clock as empty as a death knell, Eliza nestled under the covers, shivering as she fought for rest and warmth. Just as she was drifting off, a thread of sound filtered through the room.

Eliza sat up.

Someone had just said her name. She was sure of it.

"Eliza . . ." It came again. The voice was wan and distant, as if her name were borne on a tail of wind. It seemed to be coming from below—perhaps from the same room where she'd heard the mysterious gramophone? Eliza rose and put her ear to the floor grate nearest the bed. The sound of labored breathing came through, followed by a low groan.

"Hello?" she said, her voice quaking.

"Look . . . ," the voice said, followed by a raling cough. Distinctly male. "Behind the wardrobe . . . way out."

She sat up, her forehead wrinkling in confusion.

It suddenly came to her. Ada's diary entry. The dumbwaiter Beatrice had hidden in had to be in this room. Might it still be there, perhaps behind the armoire? If Ada had used it to escape, so could she. Excitement rallied her strength. She scrambled to her feet and rushed to the hulking piece of furniture, using her hips as leverage to push it inch by inch across the wooden floor. She could have cheered at the sight of the rectangular dumbwaiter door, mounted flush with the wall, its keyhole surrounded by a heart-shaped hasp. She fumbled to open it, but it was locked.

Eliza gave a growl of frustration. To have the possibility of freedom offered and then cruelly taken away was too much. Bitter tears welled in her eyes. She was going to have to fight her way out after all. A fight she would most likely lose.

She was reaching for the tin of matches in her pocket to light another of Ada's cigarettes when her fingertips brushed against the luckenbooth Malcolm had given her.

The luckenbooth whose elongated arrow looked suspiciously like a key. *Was* it a key?

If she was wrong, what more did she have to lose? May as well chase one final folly. Eliza withdrew the brooch and carefully inserted the tip of the MacCulloch arrow into the keyhole and turned. After a few seconds of fumbling, the lock gave a satisfying click and the latch sprung free. Eliza could hardly believe her eyes.

She slid the door up with shaking hands. There was just enough room for a person to fold their legs into a crouch and fit inside.

Eliza took a deep, wavering breath and folded herself into the cubby, her burgeoning belly poking between her knees. She had no idea what she was going into, or who might be at the bottom of that shaft. Malcolm could be setting a trap for her. But if he was, she would be ready.

Her heart pounded like the surf as she threaded the pulley rope between her hands and pulled. The dumbwaiter jumped. She said a silent prayer and tugged on the rope again. The pulleys creaked and groaned, but she began moving slowly downward, the floor of Ada's room closing like a camera shutter as she plunged into darkness. She kept going, feeding the rope through the squeaking pulley.

As she descended, the air around her grew colder. Finally, a sliver of yellow light showed at the bottom of the dumbwaiter. She pulled one last time and the rope went lax in her hands. She crashed to the bottom of the shaft. What she saw next took her breath away.

"I was wondering when you were going to show up."

CHAPTER 45

Eliza stared at the man who looked just like Malcolm. He was tied to a chair, his lean face gaunt, his left eye blackened and bruised. Still, he managed a smile. And in that moment, she knew.

"Gabriel?"

"The very same. And how good it is to finally hear my *real* name on your lips, mo chridhe."

She tumbled out of the dumbwaiter, her mouth agape. "You . . . I . . ."

"I wooed you, I courted you, I loved you, and I married you."

Eliza tilted her head, incredulous. "But . . . you're supposed to be dead. I saw you, in your coffin."

"It was a ruse. We've been pretending to be the same person for years. Ever since the fire. Get me out of these ropes and I'll explain everything. The other half of me is still sleeping, but we have to make haste."

Eliza didn't know if she wanted to slap him, kiss him, or kill him. Instead, she cried.

"Darling, I love you for loving me enough to cry. But we do have to hurry. Malcolm's gone barking mad."

Eliza rushed to Gabriel's side. Her fingers fervently worked at the knots binding his hands to the chair's laddered back. The hands that had loved her, pleasured her, cherished her. It all made sense now—the differences in mood and temperament. But why had Malcolm imprisoned his own brother? Why the duplicity and the lies?

The room they were in was fully furnished, lit with warm lamplight. This had once been Beatrice's room, she imagined. A sturdy bed stood in the middle of the chamber, a pair of leather riding boots propped against the footboard. On the opposite side of the room was a red door, its arched top ventilated by a small grate. She'd nearly gotten the first knot worked loose when there came the rattling of a key in the lock.

"Dammit, he's heard us," Gabriel whispered. "Get back in the dumbwaiter and hide."

Eliza soared back to the cubby, pulling the door shut with a sliding sigh, leaving the top cracked just enough that she could see out. She watched as the door swung open and Malcolm strode in, dressed in his pajamas. It was bizarre, seeing them together in the same room. Like a trick from a carnival sideshow. They were a mirror image. Two sides of the same coin.

"I heard noise," Malcolm said. He ran a hand over his hair and fixed Gabriel with a sullen look. "You know I don't like my sleep interrupted."

Eliza rolled her eyes. It took everything she had not to launch herself out of the cubby.

Gabriel laughed. "Probably just those pipes you're always on about, brother. Say, are you ever going to feed me? I'm feeling rather peckish. And how long, exactly, do you plan on keeping me locked up?"

"Shut up!" Malcolm said. "We had a plan. You ruined it."

Gabriel sighed. "We've been over this. Many, many times. I kept up my end of things, didn't I? She's with child. I've given you something you wouldn't have without me."

"And yet, you'd leave me!" Malcolm roared. "For her! You were the only person I could trust. She didn't suspect a thing until you started breaking the rules!"

"She deserves to know the truth. You aren't thinking clearly because you're not well. And I'm sorry, but it won't get better, your illness. We'll make sure we see the game through until the end of your days, but not unless Eliza is a willing party to it."

"I am not bloody dying!"

"You are, brother," Gabriel said, his voice gentle. "Things are going more quickly now. It's why you've changed. Why you've turned into this. Your mercury treatments are only poisoning your mind and prolonging the inevitable. You're dying."

Eliza gasped. The box she was in amplified the sound. Gabriel winced and swore beneath his breath. Malcolm had heard her. He stalked toward the dumbwaiter, his eyes gleaming maniacally. Eliza rested her fingers on the hatpin in readiness.

He flung open the door. "You clever little cunt." He hauled her out of the cubby, lifting her by the elbow. "Neatly done. Well, what now? Our game is up."

"We'll tell Eliza everything and carry on. Or you can let us go. We'll ride to Scotland and disappear." Gabriel's voice was steady, calm.

Malcolm sneered. "I don't think so. Have you forgotten everything you've done?"

Gabriel gave a smoldering look. "Don't."

"Malcolm, please. You're hurting me," Eliza said. His fingers were digging like daggers into the flesh of her arm as he held her tightly. "We can work this out. I understand why you've done what you've had to do."

"You don't understand. You can't," Malcolm said, spittle flying from his lips. "You were going to take my only brother away from me!"

"No! I didn't know anything, I swear it." Eliza's free hand hovered over the hatpin's pearl. *Not. Yet.* She gathered her wits. If she'd learned anything about Malcolm, it was that flattery dissolved his rancor. He craved the sort of approval his father had never given him. She sought the frightened little boy behind the bitter man, reaching for the right words to disarm him. "You're so clever to come up with such a ruse. To hide Gabriel in plain sight! I never suspected a thing."

Malcolm's grip on her arm eased slightly. "You didn't?"

"No! I'm ever impressed by your brilliant mind. And even though you're angry with me right now, we can work through this together, because you love me. I felt it that day by the pond. That *was* you, wasn't it? And it was real, Malcolm. It was honest and true!"

"But *you* don't love me. You love *him*."

"I love you too, Malcolm," Eliza lied. "I do. I love you both."

Gabriel met her eyes and gave a small nod.

Encouraged, Eliza pushed onward. "I'll take care of you in your sickness, I promise. Things can be as they were—as you and Gabriel planned. I'll keep your secrets. No one will ever know."

"None of this is Eliza's fault," Gabriel said.

"Aren't you worried what she'll do? Who she'll tell?" Malcolm spat. "Have you forgotten? As an officer, you'd be looked upon as a deserter from the Royal Navy during a time of war. If they discover you've neglected your duties to play dead all this time, they'll court-martial you. You'll likely hang for treason. I'd reckon she knows about your killing Eastleigh now, too. You can't trust her. *We* can't trust her."

Eliza drew in a steadying breath. "You killed Eastleigh?"

Gabriel sighed. "Yes. I followed you to Southampton when you left me. I was in the room next to yours at the hotel the entire time. I followed Eastleigh to the station after I saw you together on the street. The eleven o'clock was reliably on schedule. I only did it to keep you safe. It was a bloody business, darling, but necessary. I'm sorry."

"Oh my God." He'd killed to keep her from a man she'd nearly given herself to in desperation. A man who had forced Ada into concubinage. "You really killed him?"

"If you only knew the extent of what Eastleigh's done . . . what he was capable of . . ."

Malcolm laughed. "See? She's horrified by you. You're only a murderer to her now." He forced Eliza against the stone wall, one of his hands curling around her throat, a feral madness glinting in his eyes. The scald mark on his face reddened beneath its oozing blisters. "She'll ruin you, brother. Ruin us! Do you really want to swing for her duplicitous cunt? Better for her to die, I say."

Malcolm lifted her by the throat and a thousand pounds of lead dropped in her stomach as her legs went numb beneath her. No. No, she wasn't going to die this way. Not here. He wasn't going to kill her. He wasn't going to kill her baby. *Gabriel's* baby.

"Malcolm, no!" Gabriel roared. "Let her go!" He bucked in the chair, futilely trying to get to her despite his fetters. It toppled over, and he lay there helpless, panting and wincing in pain.

Eliza kicked, her feet finding no purchase as Malcolm's long fingers closed around her throat, squeezing painfully. Her heartbeat surged as her fingers found the hatpin. She drew it out. The room grew black around the edges, her consciousness flickering like a flame starved of air. She grasped the hatpin in her fist, blindly stabbing, again and again, until she felt his flesh give way.

Malcolm howled in surprise as she pushed the pin to the hilt. He released her and stumbled against the wall. She'd gotten him in the gut, the red stain of his blood blooming through the fabric of his pajamas as he clutched his side.

She scrambled over to Gabriel, her throat throbbing with pain. Her clumsy, shaking fingers worked at the knots. His eyes met hers. "No, my darling," he said sadly. "You need to go."

"I've almost got it . . . I . . . ," she rasped.

"You goddamn whore!" Malcolm screeched, fixing his wild gaze on Eliza. He hurtled forward, blood seeping between his fingers as he pulled the hatpin free and threw it to the floor.

"Eliza! Run!"

Eliza looked at Gabriel and thought of their baby in her womb—the child they'd made from their passion for one another. A child whose heart would cease beating if hers did. She thought of Lydia, and Albert, and Mimi Lisette. She thought of the pale, lifeless girl at the bottom of a pond made of glass, unloved and drowning in her guilt and grief. And she ran.

CHAPTER 46

Eliza flew through the red door, not knowing where it led, all of her instincts screaming for survival. Malcolm was roaring like an angry lion behind her. His wound had only inflamed his madness and rage.

She took a deep breath, her throat still stinging where Malcolm's thumb had nearly crushed her windpipe. She'd almost died in that room. But she couldn't think about that right now. She had to think about her baby. Herself.

After a few moments of blind stumbling in the dark, Eliza realized she was in the basement passageway she'd explored days before. The smell of damp earth surrounded her, and up ahead, lit by the open trapdoor, was the spiral staircase that led to the south wing.

She hurtled forward and heaved herself onto the first step, using the metal railing to propel herself upward.

"Eliza!" Malcolm's voice was a ragged screech as it echoed off the stone walls of the basement. "Come back! I won't hurt you—I promise. I'm so sorry."

She wanted to scream curses at him. Instead, she remained silent, trying to get a sense of how far he was from her. A plan was beginning to form—a way she could save Gabriel. Her real husband. The man who loved her. A memory of their wedding flashed across the back of her eyes—a memory of promises made in another man's name, but no less true. No. She wouldn't lose him. She would fight.

In an instant, prey became predator.

Eliza hoisted herself through the open trapdoor. *Quickly, Liza. Move!*

She ran to the window and tore the ragged drapes free, dust and soot flying into her face. She layered them over the chair she'd fallen over the night she'd discovered the room, then took up her post, crouching behind the pile of detritus.

It wasn't long before she heard Malcolm's labored breathing at the bottom of the stairs. He was muttering to himself, his words indiscernible. Eliza reached into the pocket of her dungarees and slid open the lid to the tin of matches. She took three out. And waited.

And then there he was, the top of his head emerging through the open hatch. He chuckled as he saw her. "Ah, there you are, my pretty little wife. My angel in the house."

"Please don't hurt me, Malcolm." The wheedling tone in her voice was pure artifice. Inside, she felt only rage.

"I'm afraid I have to, darling." His mouth wrenched into a pained rictus. "I only have one regret."

"What is it?"

"That I didn't take you that day in my study when you opened your pretty quim for me."

"It could still happen, Malcolm. We could truly be as man and wife. I could fetch a doctor to treat you with new medicines. We'd be happy, the three of us. True libertines. Think about it." She was moving now, sidestepping, leading him toward her. "No one would ever have to know our secrets."

"You're ever the temptress, aren't you?"

"I have your heir, Malcolm. Here." Eliza rested her hand on her belly. "Don't you want to see him?" She took another step. He mirrored it. "Don't you want to have more?"

"I'm dying, remember? I have nothing to lose. Nothing to gain."

"Then why kill *me*? Why kill our baby?"

"*His* baby."

"No one has to know." Eliza strove for the right words. "I'm so sorry your father hurt you. He turned you toward wickedness with his hateful words and his cruelty. But I see you—I see your goodness beneath all that anger. I won't desert you. You can trust me, I swear it."

"I can't trust you, darling. You've proven that." He strode closer, so close she could see the runnels of sweat trickling from his temples. His lips widened into a vulpine grin. "But if I'm to be honest, that's not the reason I'm going to kill you. No. I merely want the pleasure of watching you die. And I am more my father than you know." He lunged toward her, his hands grazing her throat.

Now! Eliza roared and torqued her leg upward, her knee solidly connecting with his groin. He toppled backward, falling to the floor as he clutched himself and howled. She jumped over the chair and crouched, striking all three matches against the floor. The scent of sulfur blossomed as fire flared in her hands. Eliza threw the matches onto the chair, where the threadbare drapes and horsehair stuffing kindled immediately.

Malcolm's eyes widened in panic at the sight of the flames. He gave an infuriated howl as he struggled to stand. The hem of his pajamas caught a tongue of flame, and fire raced up his leg. He thrashed and rolled on the floor, trying to put it out. To her horror, a shadow slowly emerged from the wall behind Malcolm. For a moment, she thought it was only smoke, until it took on the form of a man, looming and dark with anger. Her stomach turned, just as it had at the séance. Old Havenwood.

Eliza bounded toward the trapdoor, her knees quaking with fear. She jumped through, pulling it closed and buckling the hasp. Malcolm screamed over and over, his cries harrowing. She was a murderer. But she couldn't dwell on that now. She had to save Gabriel. If she was lucky, she had perhaps ten minutes before the fire consumed the south wing and crossed into the north. Once the fire made it to the north wing, the gas lines would ignite. If that happened . . .

Panic hurtled her onward, as she relied on memory and adrenaline to guide her steps through the dark corridor. Finally, she saw the slender cone of light leaking from Gabriel's room. Eliza rushed through. He opened his eyes, shock flashing across his face. He'd been crying.

"Eliza! What are you doing?"

"We have to go. I've set the house on fire."

"Oh my God."

She worked at the rope, her fingers brittle and sharp as daggers. Still, the knots held fast. "Do you have anything? A knife, scissors?"

"Yes, there's a hunting knife in my bureau, in the top drawer."

Eliza rushed to the chest of drawers and flung the top one open. A bowie knife lay neatly on a stack of handkerchiefs. She knelt at Gabriel's side and started sawing at the wiry hemp. The acrid smell of smoke curled through the door. They didn't have much time.

Finally, she had one hand free, and then the other. Gabriel took the knife from her and sawed through the rope at his feet. Overhead, there was an earsplitting crash.

"Likely the floor to the room you set fire to," Gabriel said, panting.

The room Malcolm had died in. She couldn't . . . no. No guilt. Not now.

Gabriel got shakily to his feet, swaying. "We can't go back through the south wing. There's another way out."

"Save your breath and show me," Eliza said. She grabbed the handkerchiefs from the drawer. "Put these over your nose and mouth."

Eliza propped Gabriel's arm over her shoulders, supporting his weight, and they went out. The passageway snarled with bouncing, hellish orange light. Above her head, black smoke choked the air like a funeral pall. Panic flared again in Eliza's gut, momentarily paralyzing her and numbing her legs. She shook her head and covered her mouth and nose, taking shallow, spare breaths.

"We have to go to the right. There's a service stair by the . . . coal chute," Gabriel said weakly.

They trudged forward. Gabriel's height made the going even more difficult as the passageway narrowed, and he was growing heavier by the moment. Eliza's eyes stung as the heat from the fire channeled down the corridor. Finally, a dim square of moonlight appeared through the tumbling smoke. It was the opening to the coal chute. Eliza moved toward it, and Gabriel pulled her to the left.

"No. The door . . . is there."

As they pushed forward, Eliza tripped, falling against the edge of a stone step. She pulled Gabriel up with her, his breath rattling in his chest. She put her hand out to feel in front of her. After five steps, there it was—dry wood splintering beneath her fingertips. The door.

"I'll have to let go of you for a moment to find the latch," Eliza said.

Gabriel didn't answer. Instead, he went completely lax, his weight pulling Eliza down as he collapsed, his head hitting the stone step beneath them. No, no, no. Not now. Not when they were so close! Eliza found the latch and the door sprung free, snow blowing over the threshold. She grasped Gabriel beneath the arms and pulled. His great length dragged forward, one agonizing inch at a time.

There was another crash, then a low rumble vibrated through her feet. A sound as if a thousand cannons were being fired all at once blasted from above. The gas lines had ruptured. The house was going to collapse, and they were going to die here, buried beneath flaming rubble. The conflagration above roared in her ears, shaking the foundation of the house like an earthquake. Suddenly, a light as bright as a thousand suns careened down the basement corridor toward them with a deadly, searing heat.

Eliza saw her death coming and denied it.

She gave a Valkyrie's scream and pulled with everything left in her.

They were free then, alive, tumbling onto the snow-covered ground. The cold air woke Gabriel from his stupor. He rolled onto his knees and coughed raggedly. Eliza helped him to his feet, and together they hurtled to the safety of the gravel service drive as another explosion rocked the ground. She eased Gabriel gently down, then turned to witness the hellish inferno that was now consuming Havenwood Manor. The hell *she'd* wrought.

All three stories were fully engulfed, orange light bouncing off the skeletal trees, vivid against the indigo night. Smoke billowed heavenward, sparks flickering like fireworks as flames licked at the windowsills and roofline. It was a terrible kind of beauty.

A cacophony of ringing bells and clattering hooves broke through the low roar of the fire. The fire brigade burst through the main gates and rattled up the drive. A hodgepodge of volunteers made up of young men from the village hopped off the wagon and began priming the water pump.

"Man the line, men! Hurry, now. Aim for the roof and the foundation!" the fire chief barked. Lengths of hose uncoiled like serpents and water spurted forth, but it was far too late. With an agonizing groan, the house Eliza had once loved collapsed as if it were falling onto its knees in surrender, its new slate roof flinging smoldering embers through the air as its weight forced the brittle wooden frame to the earth.

The tower had fallen. And it had fallen by her hand.

Eliza covered Gabriel's body with her own and wept.

⟨❋⟩

Clarence drew back the bed curtain with a squeaking rasp. Gabriel lay sallow and drawn on the white mattress, his eyes flickering beneath purple-veined lids. She reached out to stroke his stubbled cheek, tears coursing down her face.

"He's sustained a severe concussion and formidable damage to his lungs, I'm afraid. He may not survive. The heart often tires in situations like this. The next few hours will tell it."

Eliza sank into the chair next to the hospital bed, cupping her forehead in her hands. "He has to live. He has to."

"He was in a state of near starvation and dehydration, Eliza. Do you happen to know why?" Clarence was studying her with a mixture of empathy and curiosity as he blinked behind his owlish spectacles.

"He'd been under the weather for some time. Not eating much. I thought it was the flu. We'd just returned from London after Lord Eastleigh's funeral when he fell ill."

"Right. Could be influenza, certainly. I'd like to keep you overnight as well. You've been under immense strain. I'm concerned about a miscarriage. I'll bring a cot and a fresh gown."

Eliza cradled her belly. She couldn't miscarry. Not after all she'd come through. A rush of unexpected sympathy went through her, thinking of her own mother. How many times had Maman worried over her own babies, hoping that each would be born healthy and alive, just as she was doing right now? Eliza felt forgiveness grow within her. Hadn't her mother loved her like this, once? Perhaps she'd just not known how to show it. Perhaps . . . she'd done the best she could. "You're going to come through this, little one. And so is your papa. We both love you, so much." The baby fluttered in response.

Clarence wheeled in a folded army cot and handed her a clean cotton robe. "I'll be in to check on you and his lordship every hour. I can give you a mild sedative if you'd like."

Eliza cast a furtive glance toward Gabriel's sleeping form. "No thank you, Doctor. I think I only want to rest my eyes."

Clarence turned with a crisp nod, closing the door to the ward with a gentle click.

As there were no other patients in the room, Eliza stripped down to her camisole and drawers. She pulled on the clean dressing gown and closed it over her aching breasts, then crawled beneath the cool sheets. Every muscle and joint in her body felt like a lead weight had been tied round it. She turned in the narrow cot and watched the shallow rise and fall of her husband's chest until morning broke.

Gabriel. Ada's warrior. Honest and true.

⁕

Two days later, he still slept.

Eliza had only broken her vigil to go to the washroom or take the air for a few moments away from the sterile confinement of the hospital ward. Sarah had visited the morning after the fire, dressed in cheerful scarlet wool. She'd brought Eliza a change of clothing and a tin of her favorite tea biscuits, as well as news of Polly's elopement, which had brightened Eliza's mood.

After she dressed in Sarah's borrowed gown and washed the soot from her face and hands, they went out to the sun-filled hospital court-yard. Sarah took Eliza's hair down and gently began combing through it with her fingers. "What happened, darling?" she asked. "How did the fire start?"

Eliza flinched. "I'm not sure. I smelled smoke, and it roused me from my bed. I went to wake Malcolm, but he was locked in his rooms. I had to kick down the door."

Sarah dropped the hank of hair she was untangling. She came around and knelt at Eliza's knee, fixing her with meltingly soft eyes. "Look. You don't have to lie to me, Eliza. I know more than you think. Malcolm's dead, isn't he? It's Gabriel in that bed. I'd stake my life on it."

Eliza's stomach flip-flopped.

Sarah reached for Eliza's hand. "I've known something was amiss ever since my party last summer, right after you'd wed. Remember how he mentioned the girl with the flaxen hair at the ball in Somerset when we were sixteen? Malcolm wasn't there. But Gabriel was."

336

"Why didn't you tell me?" Eliza asked.

Sarah gave a mournful smile. "I was angry at him, at first. I wanted to broach the subject with you—I just didn't know how. And then, after the séance, I felt you probably knew, and were party to it, and I couldn't quite reconcile how I felt about that. Still, as your friend, I should have come to you sooner. I'm so sorry, love. Can you forgive me?"

Eliza stroked her thumb over the roundness of Sarah's cheek. "It wasn't your fault. You were caught out, just like I was. I'm still working through my feelings as well. I don't have all the answers yet. I'm not sure I ever will."

Sarah shook her head. "They wouldn't have pulled it off for so long for any frivolous reason. There had to be some rationale behind it. Gabriel didn't—doesn't—like lying. Not as a rule."

"I wonder if it was because Malcolm had syphilis."

Concern widened Sarah's eyes. "Oh no. You're not infected, I hope?"

"No. I don't think so. Malcolm and I never lay together. I thought it was him, but it was always Gabriel in my bed." Eliza searched Sarah's round, honest eyes. "Do you think he loves me, Sarah? Can I trust him not to lie again, even after all this?"

Sarah's smile spread across her entire face. "Oh, darling, he adores you. Our Gabriel has a true heart. Believe that."

Eliza wanted to believe it. She wanted to try to understand the story behind their deception. All of it. She wanted to try to forgive and move forward. To trust again. Perhaps they could come to some sort of accord, at least for the sake of their child.

If only he would live.

⁂

Later that day, as the afternoon sun blazed through the thick green glass of the hospital windows and the unsteady whoosh of Gabriel's sleeping breath whispered next to her, she began a letter to Lydia. She would tell her the full truth, someday. But for now, all Lydia needed to know was that her sister and her sister's husband were alive.

Clarence swung through the door and lifted Gabriel's wrist to check his pulse, then gently began to palpate his abdomen.

"Lydia told me to ask after you in her last letter," Eliza said, lifting her pen from the paper. "I'm writing to her now. What should I say?"

Clarence smiled, brightening at the mention of Lydia's name. "Tell her my heart is steadfast, and that I look forward to the day when she rejoins me in our work. Tell her she's the brightest and most beautiful woman I've ever seen, and the finest nurse I have ever worked with. There's more I could say, but I don't suppose you'll have room for it in your letter."

"She'll be glad to hear all of it." Eliza smiled. "She's studying at Charity in New Orleans. They have a well-regarded surgical program. One of the best in the world, in fact. Lydia is just as anxious to return as you are to have her, I believe. And I am anxious to gain a new brother."

"Yes. Very good, very good." Clarence coughed roughly into his sleeve, but not before Eliza saw the faint glimmer in his eyes. She turned back to her writing to spare Clarence the embarrassment of having seen his tears. She wrote, *Clarence misses you. I miss you. On your return, we'll redecorate an entire wing of Sherbourne House for the two of you. You'll want your peace and quiet . . . because you're going to be an aunt, Lyddie! Malcolm and I are expecting. The house might be smaller, with all of us in it, but things are turning out just how you wanted, all the same.*

⁂

Eliza was walking back from mailing Lydia's letter when she saw a man in a derby hat go through the doors of the hospital. There was something familiar about his face, as if she'd seen him somewhere before. Could it be? She picked up her step.

When she pushed through the doors to the recovery ward, the man was standing over Gabriel, his hat in hand. He took Gabriel's hand in his own and kissed it, silent tears rolling down his cheeks. Eliza cleared her throat.

The man turned, hastily wiping his eyes.

"Oh, sorry. Hello. You must be Eliza."

"I am."

"You don't know who I am, do you?" He offered a tentative smile— one tinged with the kind of sadness she'd once seen in a portrait.

Ada's portrait.

Eliza drew in a sharp breath. Her heart gave a kick. "No . . . I think I do."

CHAPTER 47

"I know—it's rather a lot to take in, isn't it?"

Eliza gave a nervous laugh. "I'm at a loss for words, my la . . ."

"It's Matthew, m'lady. Just Matthew."

Eliza laughed again and ran her hands over the slippery borrowed taffeta covering her arms, not sure where to look. "Ah. The mysterious Matthew."

"So you've heard of me, then." He peered at her through dark lashes, fringing a pair of violently green eyes. "I'm sure you'll have lots of questions, darling, so we'll get on with it. Do you mind if I smoke?"

"Of course not."

He sat next to Gabriel's cot and took a pipe out of his striped waistcoat, packed it with tobacco, and lit it with a match, drawing air into the bowl through his lips. There were a few lines around the edges of his otherwise youthful face, and his dark hair was streaked with shimmering lines of gray, but he was so much like Malcolm and Gabriel in manner it was uncanny. He even crossed his legs in the same way Malcolm had, placing right over left as he slouched in the chair by Gabriel's bed.

Eliza drew up another chair. "I can ask you anything? Even the tricky things?"

"Don't be bashful." He gestured toward the window. "I'm used to questions and I've heard all their rumors already, I assure you."

"I'll start with the worst, then. People implied incest—that you became Malcolm's lover."

Matthew smiled wistfully. "*People* being Una?"

"Yes."

"Ah, that girl is a fair piece of work. I promise you, my lady, I never took carnal liberties with my own sons. The very thought disgusts me."

"I didn't think you would. But why would she say such a thing?"

"She was always jealous of how close we were. One evening when old Havenwood was away, I meant to dress up in Malcolm's clothes to meet my lover in Winchester. It was a pleasant game for me to play at being the average, middle-class bloke out at the pubs with my lady paramour. Such reckless freedom for a lesbian, you can only imagine. At first it was a way to avoid salacious talk, but then it became more natural. I felt more and more myself as Matthew, eventually. At any rate, on that particular day, when Una saw us, I had taken my overdress off and Malcolm was helping me tighten my binding corset over my shift. He was only doing up the laces at the back. Una walked by the door and thought she'd caught us in the middle of a tryst."

"I see. Was it Beatrice your secret letters were meant for, then? I decoded them."

"Clever thing, aren't you? I may well blush."

"They were beautiful. I'm so sorry I read them, but I've become rather obsessed with you. I found your journal as well. Duncan said Beatrice went back to Guernsey, but I knew she was lying."

"Yes, that's the story, isn't it? So many of them, one loses track." Matthew bit his lip and turned to the window. "Beatrice and I were merely companions at first—until I realized my feelings for her ran much deeper than friendship. I kissed her in the gardens one afternoon. When she returned my ardor, I knew I'd found my truest love. Our housekeeper orchestrated our downfall when she discovered our affair."

He gave a distasteful snarl. "Galbraith. How I hated that woman. She thought *she* deserved to be Lady Havenwood. She was incredibly cruel to me, from the first moment I set foot in that house, a scared and pregnant girl of sixteen."

"She also found out about Beatrice's spying, correct? From the dumbwaiter."

The color flared in Matthew's cheeks. "Oh, my. You really do know everything about us, don't you? Yes. Bea and I had planned to run away together. Galbraith found out our game and confiscated our letters and Bea's journal. Bea threatened old Lord H with going to the papers. She would have ruined Thomas and Eastleigh for my sake, so they murdered her."

"I'm so sorry."

"It's all right, love. You weren't meant to know all our secrets. It was imperative you didn't, in fact."

"Why?"

"Because my son's life depended on it. He was the only witness. Malcolm was away, taking his final term at Eton, and I was in Winchester, waiting for Bea at the hotel where we had our trysts. Gabriel had come home early from the pub and heard strange sounds from belowstairs. He went to investigate and caught them in the act of dismembering her body." Matthew's eyes hardened. "They made him help with their gruesome business, then had Gabriel bury her body in the birch grove, so that he would be culpable. An accessory to murder. Eastleigh stalked him mercilessly afterward. It became too much. It's the main reason they pretended to be the same person after the fire. Had nothing at all to do with fighting over who would claim the title or any of that nonsense. Gabriel couldn't have cared less about being a country lord. It was always going to be Malcolm."

"How did you convince everyone he was dead?"

"Malcolm gave him a heavy sleeping draught before the wake. It slowed his heartbeat so he would appear dead, even to a coroner."

"Like *Romeo and Juliet?*"

"The very same. Belladonna. It was so effective it was terrifying. We went to the crypt that night to revive him, then I left. I've lived as Matthew MacCulloch ever since."

"I knew Mal . . . I mean, Gabriel, was keeping something from me—something to do with Bea—but I was looking at the wrong things. And all this time I've been searching for you, you've been right here."

"Not exactly. I live in Oban now—where I'm from. I'd only come back to Hampshire or London to see my sons, then go home to Blanche. That's my lady companion. My wife." His voice fell into the lilting, northern cadence she'd often imagined while reading Ada's journal. "My boys made a pact, after we started the fire. They swore to protect one another, and me, at all costs. Malcolm took it too far. He's always been a wee bit rigid. Gabriel wrote to me—he was upset over the way Malcolm had been treating you. He intended to bring you to Scotland over the holidays and have you meet me. Together, we were going to tell you everything. Malcolm got wind of it, and in his state of illness, well. Logic was no longer his ally."

Eliza remembered the day on the train when Malcolm had gone into his demented fit after Eastleigh's funeral. She'd unwittingly given the game away when she'd asked about their Scottish holiday. It's likely he'd imprisoned Gabriel upon their return. Eliza looked over to her sleeping husband. His once strong arms were so pale and thin, and his hollow cheeks skeletal. "Malcolm was envious of Gabriel, wasn't he?"

Matthew's lips curved in a sad smile, and he took a pull on his pipe. "Aye. But Gabriel was envious of him as well. They were so different for looking just the same. My Colm was a bit awkward round the edges. Easier for his father to break. Gabe is more like me, you ken? That's why I was harder on him. Always getting into scrapes and falling out of trees." He paused, worrying with his cuff links. "He didn't deal well with the duality of my nature, I'm afraid—how one body could contain two spirits and shift between them."

"I'm only relieved he took his temperament from you, and not his father."

Matthew gave the wide grin Eliza knew so well. "As am I, but since we're at the business of laying secrets out on tables, I must make a confession—old Havenwood wasn't their true father. He'd been sterile since he was a boy. Mumps and fevers."

"I'd wondered," Eliza said. "The dates in your journal didn't line up with your confinement."

"You should go to work for Scotland Yard, you know." Matthew took a drag off his pipe, the red glow illuminating his face. "I didn't know myself when I was young—wasn't ready to know myself. I'd dressed up as a page for our ghillies ball—Cherubino—which should've been a hint. It was such fun. A beautiful lad I'd never seen before turned me round and round in the reels, then took me out for a little walk around Brynmoor. He spread his jacket on a stone slab and proceeded to show me, definitively, that I didn't enjoy sexual congress with men. You could say he gave me three gifts that night—one of them the relief of my naïveté."

"Did you ever see him again?"

"Never. He was ethereal. Tall and slender, with the queerest eyes— like whisky held up to the sun. Perhaps not even of this world. I suppose I like to imagine it, at least. We Scots are superstitious, and my boys *were* rather uncommon.

"As soon as my condition was discovered, instead of being angry, old Havenwood was overjoyed, and we married within the month. He got part and parcel—an heir and a spare and a young wife who didn't mind his sterility. You'll know the rest about our marriage from my journal—how it ended too, I'd imagine, canny as you are." He leaned forward and tapped the spent embers from his pipe into the narrow grate. "When Gabriel finally told me what they'd done to Beatrice, I crept into Galbraith's quarters and smothered her in her sleep. Then I shot Thomas in his bed with Gabriel's service pistol. The twins and I started the fire to cover things up."

Eliza's mouth went dry, remembering the séance and how old Havenwood's spirit had spelled out the word *shot*. She searched for the right words and found none.

"It was ghastly and terrible. But I don't regret it. Every time I saw that bastard beat my bairns or felt the stinging slap of his hand across my face, I murdered him in my mind. That night was simply the following through."

"I can't say I blame you." She'd done the same, after all. Eliza's head spun, remembering the manic look in Malcolm's eyes, the sharpness of his fingers closing on her throat. There was no doubt that Thomas's spirit had somehow influenced Malcolm in his weakness of mind.

"Was his ghost still knocking around the house?" Matthew asked. "Old Havenwood? The twins saw him, several times."

"Yes, unfortunately. I've had my encounters. He was violent. He pulled one of our workers off a scaffold."

"I daresay. That sounds just like him. And my Beatrice? Did she ever visit you? She certainly visited me. Only—I didn't know it was her at the time. She would sit on the edge of my bed and stroke my hair, smelling of birch leaves."

Eliza smiled, remembering the tapping in her room, the wavery writing on the fog of the window, and the apparition she'd seen in the south wing, pointing her to the truth. "Yes, she did the very same with me. I rather thought she was my friend."

"Well, she would have liked you. I hope she's found peace at last." Matthew's voice cracked. "That's what she deserves, my sweet Bea."

"I'm not sure how you survived everything you've endured."

"We're often stronger than we think we can be, aren't we? Especially for our children. My angels were the reason I fought to carry on through a wretched marriage. Otherwise, I'd have weighted my apron with stones and wandered into the Avon." Matthew closed his eyes. "My sons protected me. I've a free life because of them. I'll never be sure we went about things the right way. It was an awful burden on them both, keeping all of these secrets. And now, my Malcolm is dead."

"I'm so sorry." Once more, Eliza pushed back against the sharpness of her guilt. She'd killed Malcolm, as surely as Matthew had killed Thomas. Yet how could she confess it to the very person who had brought him life? No. This was one secret she'd have to keep. "I suppose none of us can know what twists and turns life will bring us through, can we? Or what we'll do for the ones we love?"

"Indeed. But doesn't it make for a queer tale, after all?"

❧❦❧

Matthew and Eliza stood on the train platform in Winchester, their breath curling into the cold air.

"Will you tell Gabriel I was here when he wakes?"

"Of course. Perhaps when he's recovered and my confinement is passed, we'll pay you a visit with the baby. He promised me Scotland, after all."

"I'd like that." Matthew smiled, the corners of his eyes crinkling. "The two of you have a right to be happy, you know. We do no service to our dead when we linger too long in our misery." He pulled on his gloves and lifted the brim of his hat. "Write to me often, darling, and do take care of yourself and my naughty son."

"I will, I promise. Godspeed, Matthew."

"Godspeed, Lady Havenwood."

❧❦❧

Gabriel woke on Christmas morning.

The chapel chimes had just rung the hour of eight when Eliza heard a dry whisper of sound. She leapt up from her chair by the grate, the book she was reading falling to the floor and her heartbeat quickening as she rushed to her husband's side.

He blinked, wincing at the sterile brightness of the ward. She touched his hand and he turned toward her. A weak smile tilted the corners of his mouth. "Am I really alive?"

Eliza's tears rolled fast and hot down her cheeks. "You are."

"I need water," he rasped.

"I'll fetch Dr. Fawcett straightaway!"

Eliza flew from the room, tearing down the hallway to Clarence's office. She flung open the door. He looked up from his paperwork, startled at her sudden intrusion.

"Doctor, come quickly! My husband is awake!"

❦

They moved into Sherbourne House on the first day of the new century—a morning so bright and full of sunshine it chased every shadow from the empty house as soon as Eliza pulled the drapes.

Lydia had left things immaculate, the furniture neatly covered with sailcloth, the dust on the trimwork barely perceptible. Gabriel sat warming by the fireplace in the parlor as she flurried around, fluffing pillows and tidying up the kitchen. Finally, she sat next to him, her face heated by her exertions. He pulled her close and kissed her temple. "My darling, you've done enough. There will be time for more adjustments once Turner and Duncan come home."

Eliza thought of the ruins of Havenwood Manor, smoldering as the last of the fire spent itself on the cold ground. "They'll be devastated, won't they? It all seems like a nightmare. Did they know anything about your ruse? I have a feeling they did."

"Yes, they were party to it. Malcolm and our mother had to tell them everything in order to keep me hidden away. It meant we couldn't hire on more staff, and as Malcolm's paranoia grew, he began to trust even their loyalty less." Gabriel closed his eyes. "I wish you could have known him in the years before his illness took away what was left of his gentleness. He was troubled, tortured and shaped by our father's cruelty. But he wasn't evil."

"I saw glimpses of his true nature, from time to time." She pulled away from Gabriel and moved to the hearth. A log cracked, sending a flurry of sparks from the grate. She quickly stomped them out with her shoe. "I started the fire that destroyed your home and killed your only brother. How can you forgive me for that? And then there's the matter of Eastleigh. What if someone finds out what you've done? I'm still not sure how we're meant to move forward from all of this. How can I trust that you won't go down the same path as Malcolm? That you won't turn to murder and thievery ever again? I don't even know who you are."

"Eliza, look at me. *Really* look at me."

She turned to study him. His cheeks were less gaunt than they'd been days before, the fiery spark in his viridian eyes returning. But for the first time, she noticed the subtle differences—the pale scar that marked his forehead like a shooting star, the mole beneath his left ear. How could she not have known?

"I love you," he murmured. "*I* love you. There will be no more lies, at least between these walls. I'm sorry for the horrible things I've done. And as for Malcolm and the fire . . . you had no choice." Gabriel stood and drew her to his chest, the subtle rattle of his breath rumbling between them. "Every moment from this day forward will be spent regaining your trust and love. We'll raise our family, we'll carry on, and we *will* be happy again, my darling. I can promise you that."

EPILOGUE

June 1905

Eliza watched Lucy and Miriam frolicking beneath the branches of the great oak tree in front of Sherbourne House, their dark curls braided into pigtails, both girls dressed in white lawn tied with violet sashes. They were playing hide-and-seek with Lydia's daughter, Rosaline, and Lucy had cheated. She scrambled over the fence, rowdy as a boy, startling Miriam from her hiding place like a scared rabbit. Rosaline shrieked at her cousins and gave chase, her honey-blond curls streaming behind her.

"Mummy, Daddy!" Miriam called. "Lucy doesn't play fair! She peeked!"

"Lucy, no cheating!" Gabriel scolded.

Lucy scowled and crossed her arms, stalking off with Rosaline toward the rose garden Eliza had planted in Beatrice's memory. Miriam flailed on the ground as if the world were ending, tears spilling from her blue eyes. "You're spoiling Miriam," Eliza teased. "She's got to learn to manage Lucy on her own, without your interfering."

Gabriel pulled Eliza close from behind, nuzzling the curve of her cheek with his nose. "I suppose you're right. They *are* a handful, aren't they?"

"How will I ever manage another?"

"You will, because you're a wonderful mother, mo chridhe," Gabriel said, cupping Eliza's rounded belly.

"Am I, Lord H?"

"The best."

The soft whickering of a horse came over the moors where Havenwood Manor once stood. Eliza gazed with pride at the white paddocks rimming the hillside. Grazing Thoroughbreds and Friesians dotted the pastures, their flanks gleaming. "Our best mare will be foaling after the new year. And two of our broodmares will be ready to breed soon after. We'll have to expand the stables to make room."

"All sorts of babies being born. I couldn't be happier about it, could you?" Gabriel swung her around for a kiss, his lips igniting the same flare of passion they had on their wedding night. Eliza melted into her husband's arms, her joy bubbling up like the finest champagne.

It hadn't always been easy, their love. In the months after the fire, when Gabriel strove to rebuild her trust, she'd flinched away each time he touched her, remembering Malcolm's madness. He was patient, shouldering the burden of the betrayal he had helped to sow. When Lydia brought their babies into the world—healthy, fat, and warm—the last remnants of Eliza's fear fell away in her labor bed. Gabriel held her hand through every push and cry, brushed her hair from her fevered brow, and walked the floors with the twins so she might sleep. With every word and action, he told Eliza she was safe. He showed her she was loved.

Her life had certainly taken her through a strange dance. Some of it had been more painful than she thought she might bear. The old sorrows would always remain, but they were tucked well away now and only brought out as memento mori. During those brief storms of grief, when the dead brushed up against the living, a dark veil fell over Eliza's mood and she wept.

But mostly when Eliza's tears fell, they fell because she was happy.

AUTHOR'S NOTE

When an author goes through the strange alchemy that occurs between the first draft and a final, published work of fiction, several facets of inspiration come into play—some of them unusual and unexpected. The idea for *Parting the Veil* first manifested over two years ago, after I woke from a surreal dream of a fire-gutted Beaux Arts mansion. From there, it evolved into the gothic romantic thriller you have just read. But it all started with a house.

Havenwood Manor is the conduit for Eliza's psyche, a symbol of grief, and a character in its own right. It was inspired by myriad grand Second Empire houses—some of them no longer in existence, like the Earl Wheeler mansion in Sharon, Pennsylvania, which is unfortunately now a parking lot. My amateur appreciation for the architecture of Richard Morris Hunt, the decadent artwork of Alphonse Mucha, Paul Berthon, and Georges Privat-Livemont, and the textiles of William Morris all helped enrich the atmosphere of the fin de siècle world Eliza lives in.

While Eliza herself is purely fictional, several real-life American heiresses who married into British and Continental aristocracy informed her characterization—chiefly Clara Ward, Consuelo Yznaga, and Jennie Jerome, Winston Churchill's mother. Like Eliza, these wealthy young women crossed the Atlantic with trunks full of Worth gowns and the naïve hope of an adventurous new life. Unfortunately, their mothers' ambitions were often greater than the desire for their daughters' happiness, and these whirlwind marriages between strangers—little more than financial contracts—often culminated in lives spent in genteel poverty, unhappy marital relations, and societal ostracism. *The Husband Hunters: American Heiresses Who Married into the British Aristocracy* by Anne de Courcy, as well as Smithsonian Channel's documentary series *Million Dollar American Princesses*, helped inform the experiences Eliza and Lydia would have likely had in England among the landed gentry. Anne Sebba's *American Jennie: The Remarkable Life of Lady Randolph Churchill* was also indispensable during my research. Savvy readers will notice my homage to Jennie in Ada's diary entries, where she is mentioned by name.

Though the titles and peerages mentioned within are mostly fictitious, Malcolm was very loosely based on Lord Randolph Churchill, who was charming but mercurial and high-strung, according to several accounts by his peers. Malcolm's decline into paranoia and violence are completely my invention, although many sufferers of syphilis, who were often treated with strong doses of mercury and potassium iodide, descended into severe psychosis as their illness progressed. The cure was often as horrible as the disease. During my writing, I referred to *Pox: Genius, Madness, and the Mysteries of Syphilis* by Deborah Hayden as well as *History, Sex and Syphilis* by Tomasz F. Mroczkowski, MD.

Cheltenbridge, while fictional, could be any number of idyllic small towns along the River Avon, nestled within Hampshire's wild and beautiful New Forest. I took artistic license with my descriptions of historical Southampton (I'm not sure if there was ever a carousel on the pier, or a hotel across from the Grand Theatre, for example). My descriptions of the long-demolished Grand are also conjecture based on limited images I gleaned from online sources. Sarah Bernhardt did indeed appear at the Grand for one night only, but I have taken liberty with the exact date of her performance. Furthermore, Rameau's *Castor et Pollux* was not performed in the UK until 1930. Artistic license was also taken with weather and travel time/distances and train routes.

I consulted several books to inform my research on the rise of Victorian Spiritualism, mourning and funerary practices, and day-to-day life in the late nineteenth century, as well as the political and LGBTQ+ culture of the time. Among them: *Between Women: Friendship, Desire, and Marriage in Victorian England* by Sharon Marcus; Byron Farwell's *The Great Boer War*; *How to Be a Victorian* by Ruth Goodman; Barbara Weisberg's *Talking to the Dead: Kate and Maggie Fox and the Rise of Spiritualism*; and the very excellent *Dirty Old London: The Victorian Fight against Filth* by Lee Jackson. For Lydia's knowledge of herbal medicine, hoodoo, and voodoo, I consulted Tayannah Lee McQuillar's definitive guide, *Rootwork: Using the Folk Magick of Black America for Love, Money, and Success*, as well as *Old Style Conjure: Hoodoo, Rootwork, and Folk Magic* by Starr Casas. Romey Petite and Veronica V. were also very helpful in guiding me with Lydia's multiracial heritage and characterization as well as the Louisiana Creole society in which she and Eliza lived.

In writing Eliza's story, I wanted her arc to honestly convey the oft-conflicting emotions of grief, PTSD, and depression. As she does the hard psychological work of confronting the past—as symbolized by Havenwood Manor—she moves through guilt, denial, anger, melancholy, bargaining, and eventually . . . acceptance and self-love. The scientific advances of Carl Jung and his extraordinary grasp of human psychology and the cognitive/behavioral therapies that eventually resulted from his work are in no small way an influence on this novel and upon my own life, as well.

This novel includes subject matter such as domestic abuse, addiction, suicidal ideation, pregnancy/child loss, murder, mental illness, and implied incest and sexual abuse. If anything written within these pages creates a traumatic response, please reach out to someone who will listen without judgment. Just like Eliza, you are worthy of love and happiness. If you or someone you know is suffering from thoughts of self-harm, please call 1-800-273-TALK (8255) to speak to someone who will listen and help. You are not alone.

ACKNOWLEDGMENTS

When I first began working on *Parting the Veil*, I had no idea it would become my debut novel. Writing this book has introduced me to some wonderful people, and I am grateful to them all.

A huge, heartfelt thank-you to the team at SDLA and my agent, Jill Marr, who has been a phenomenal advocate for Eliza's story and a dedicated career partner. An equally enthusiastic thank-you to my editor, Jodi Warshaw, whose expertise and encouragement during the editorial process has been limitless. Special thanks to the Lake Union production team: Nicole Burns-Ascue, Amanda Gibson, and Nicole Brugger-Dethmers, who helped me polish this book to a shine. Thank you especially to Gabe Dumpit, who answered my questions with patience and positivity. Everyone at Lake Union has been a joy to work with, and I am so thankful to be involved with such a supportive and innovative publisher.

A five-star, emphatic thank-you to Amanda Hudson at Faceout Studio for designing the most beautiful cover ever. I simply cannot stop staring at it. I only hope my words do it justice.

There are several people who helped with earlier versions of this novel, but none deserves my appreciation more than freelance developmental editor and fellow writer Maria Tureaud, who discovered my manuscript in the Revise and Resub (#RevPit) slush pile and convinced me not to shelve it. Without her guidance and belief in this story, it would not exist today. Thank you for everything you've done for me.

A multitude of thanks to Thuy Nguyen—my DM confidant and critique partner, who has been a fountain of positive energy tempered with honesty. She helped me tear down, rewrite, and hone this manuscript to near perfection before sending it out into the world. I cannot thank you enough for your help and kindness, my friend.

Several peers and mentors gave of their time during my writing process—from manuscript and query critiques to offers to write endorsements . . . or they simply gave an abundance of moral support while I was querying and on submission. Much appreciation to Elizabeth Blackwell, Jenna (JM) Jinks, Nicole Eigener, Justine Manzano, Olesya Salnikova Gilmore, Sam Thomas, Jo Kaplan, Elle Marr, Megan Chance, Barbara Davis, Kim Taylor Blakemore, Stacie Murphy, Shyla Shank, Jolie Christine, Harlequin and Astrid Grim, S. Kaeth, Laura McHugh, Jessica Lewis, HM Braverman, Romey Petite, Belinda Grant, Alex Gotay, Hester Fox, Lydia Kang, Sasa Hawk, Stephanie Whitaker, Megan Van Dyke, Sierra Pung, and Sheri MacIntyre.

A multitude of thanks to my bookish friends who volunteered to read the earliest draft of this work, including Amber, Dana, Courtney, Rosalinda, Janet, Paula, Caroline, and Brittany, who also helps me with my taxes. Although the novel has changed significantly since its first iteration, your thoughtful insights helped to shape my characters and this story into their current form.

The writing community on Twitter has been a continuous source of inspiration, especially the Writer in Motion group chat. Every writer needs to feel like they have people rooting for them, and I'm lucky to have found my people. Special thanks to Jeni Chappelle for everything you do to help writers.

Thank you to Brenda Drake and the #PitMad Pitch Wars team for creating a platform for new authors to pitch their work and get noticed.

I never expected *Parting the Veil* to receive the response it did during my very first PitMad. I'm thankful to have had the experience.

I would be remiss not to mention the two standout teachers who always believed in my writing: my third-grade teacher, Mrs. Kathy Jolovich of Springfield Public Schools, and Dr. William J. Burling of (Southwest) Missouri State University, a great writer and professor of English who is sadly no longer with us. Teachers do make a difference. And I'm grateful to have had two of the best.

I'm thankful to my family, especially my mom, to whom this book is dedicated. She taught me to read and always made sure I had a steady supply of books, even if I preferred to read her romance novels on the sly. My dad was an amazing songwriter and storyteller, and I think he'd be super proud of me for chasing my dreams. Thanks to Lula, my sister and first friend, who still lovingly teases me about all the characters I created when we were children. I'm also grateful to the Hughes and Roberts families, who have been so enthusiastic about reading this book. I hope you enjoy it!

I also want to extend a thank-you to my Missouri friends, Sa'dia and Betsy, who listened patiently while I explained the ins and outs of publishing and who have always had my back. You're the best. When I come home, you make me feel like I never left.

And finally, to Ryan and Avery—every bit of this was done for you. Thank you for your patience. I'm so sorry for all the takeout. I love you.

ABOUT THE AUTHOR

Photo © 2021 Paulette Kennedy

Originally from the Ozarks, Paulette Kennedy now lives with her family and their menagerie of pets in a quiet suburb of Los Angeles. When she's not writing, you'll find her tending her garden and trying to catch up with the looming stack of unread books next to her bed. You can connect with her on Twitter, Facebook, and Instagram.